It started with a terrific hook - who can resist a talking cat sent to deliver a message? It starts off strong and just continues that way.

READER COMMENTS—

I enjoyed the suspense of thinking the imperial constables might catch him at any minute! —Denver, Colorado

Even the cat and the dog were instantly real....—Albany, New York

... a milieu of uneasy distrust and ominous foreboding. (Ah, but the barmaid offers hope!) I was completely intrigued.... — Virginia

This brilliant story....We like this lonely kid with a decent heart, a distracted brain, just a few coins, and a battered old boat.... — Santa Fe, New Mexico

Move over your treasured copies of Tolkien and C. S. Lewis and make room for Wolkomir.—Waitsfield, Vermont

Richard Wolkomir is a long-time contributor of award-winning articles and essays to such magazines as Reader's Digest, Smithsonian, and National Geographic. Now he is writing speculative novels and short fiction, with science fiction and fantasy stories appearing in a variety of literary journals.

Visit the author at www.richardjoycewolkomir.net.

Also by Richard Wolkomir

Sinnabar
(A New Jersey BMX biker vs. a dystopian wizardarchy, with two
worlds at stake—a fantasy novel)

Dog Dance of Snikia
(A comic novella about a pear farmer's feckless son, and his
incompatible animal partner, a genius dog.)

Junkyard Bandicoots & Other Tales of the World's Endangered
Species
(with Joyce Rogers Wolkomir)

WIL DEFT

Richard Wolkomir

Cover Design by Stephanie Tkach
    pageweavingcoverdesigns@yahoo.com

As always—

For Joyce Rogers Wolkomir,
Writing Partner, Life Partner

But ask now the beasts, and they shall teach thee....

—Job 12:7

WIL DEFT

CHAPTER ONE

"Come," said the cat.

She licked a paw.

He didn't know what to say to a cat, so he slouched in his chair, scowling at her.

"It's time," the cat told him.

She yawned, unpleasantly, showing tiny, pointed teeth.

He said nothing.

She wasn't a village cat. He knew them all, and all the dogs, and all the other village beasts, tame or wild. She'd come from the forest. He knew that. She'd come through the open window into his hut, and now she sat on his table, beside the apple he'd been eating for supper. She looked at him with faintly malevolent blue eyes, a black cat with white whiskers.

She licked a different paw.

"They summon you," she said. "Come."

"No," he said.

Anyone looking through the hut's window, seeing the two sitting in the lamplight, would've seen nothing peculiar, not a conversation between a young man and an animal. No lips moved, only minds.

He'd never heard an animal speak like this. Since childhood, in his mind, he'd heard their whisperings. And as he grew, their whispered voices grew louder and clearer. But mostly they spoke of seeds, rich in good oils, or of sunshine on fur, making you sleepy. Some, ascending the village's oaks, expressed joy in high-branch leaping. They spoke of such simple pleasures, and of fear, anger, hunger, satiation, contentment, desire. But this cat spoke as a person might speak, almost.

"It's time," she said.

He felt her interest dwindle.

She'd done as bade. This lanky young man meant nothing to her, with his long hay-colored hair, so needful of licking, and his ragged mustache. Her tail thrashed irritably across the table. He glimpsed her thought, of peering into the darkness under forest trees, for squeakers—a paw flashes out, snatches.

She was gone.

Out the window. Back into the forest.

"They summon you," she'd said.

Who those summoners might be, he guessed.

And he'd said, "No."

After the cat left, Wil Deft slumped in his chair, frowning, yellow mustache curled down. Abruptly, he shuddered. He grabbed his leather jacket, where it lay on the floor, and hurried out, shaking his head as if to erase what was in it.

He found his way through Fishtown's dark streets by slivers of lantern light shining through shutter chinks. But mostly he remembered how the cobblestones felt underfoot, worn here, broken there, and then two missing, marking where he must turn down stone steps to the wharf. There he untied his battered skiff. Long ago he'd spotted it floating down the river, probably loosed by some upstream storm, and he'd swum out to claim it. It was all he owned, besides his hut, inherited from his fisherman foster father and washerwoman foster mother, and his ragged clothes, and two fishlines and five hooks. Sometimes, when he needed a few easy coins, he rowed the skiff out to catch mudfish to sell to the smokehouses, but he mostly used the skiff as he used it tonight, to get to Horse Skull Island.

Only starlight's silver glimmer on the water showed him the river. But he needed little light. He could navigate with his nose. Here by the docks, the river smelled of decaying wood pilings and waterweed and the shoreline smokehouses, where fish lay drying on pole racks. But as Wil oared the skiff out into the current, the river's aroma freshened, deep water mixing with cool night air, touched with Fishtown's hearth-fire smoke. Here the great river ran deep, and stretched nearly a mile across. Horse Skull Island lay midway, and already he smelled ale. He rowed toward the island's southern tip.

Beyond the island, the far shore's black hillside seemed sprinkled with yellow stars. It was lantern light, squeezing through cracks in the shuttered windows of Breming, a village a bit larger than Fishtown. As he rowed, Wil recited to himself a rhyme every Fishtown child could chant: "Breming men dig in bogs. Breming men smell like hogs." Breming's men did mostly dig peat, to ship downriver to the imperial city. Wil had been to Breming just once, as a child. To travel between villages, except on imperial business, was forbidden. But other children had dared him and his friend, Kobar, to go to Breming. And so they'd rowed over in the night and walked along the wharves and a little up the central street, but quickly fled, because the town's strangeness unnerved them, although they had difficulty explaining to the others, when they returned, exactly how Breming differed much from their own Fishtown.

Wil stopped rowing, to stare.

Breming's lights, on its southern edge, winked out. More lights darkened. Now all Breming stood black.

And then he saw why.

A dark mass floated before him. Its bulk hid Breming and the far shore. After a while, in the starlight, he made it out: a great ship. It lay silent in the water, its lanterns cloaked. Every so often, its banked oars swept, steadying the ship against the current.

High above him, on the ship's stern, iron struck flint. Tinder flared—a man firing his pipe.

In that flash Wil saw the ship's flag: it depicted the imperial fist, clenching a sword, pointed up. Above the sword's tip floated a disk, glowing white. All knew that emblem: the Starstone.

And the man lighting his pipe wore the yellow cape and red jerkin—an imperial constable.

Now the tinder flickered out. Darkness returned. And in that darkness, Wil sat as if stone.

Imperial galleys rarely oared upriver to these nether regions, a week's journey north from the great city. But last summer one did come—a slaver. Red jerkins and yellow capes appeared in Fishtown. They took three. One was Wil's friend, Kobar.

He dipped his oars, making no splash. Silently he rowed around the galley's high stern. On the far side, he saw a davit extended, its ropes dangling in the water. A lowered boat had left the galley.

Did that boat lurk in the darkness?

But whether the galley's tender rowed toward Breming or Fishtown, he didn't know, so he rowed ahead, softly dipping his oars.

He rounded Horse Skull Island's downstream tip, into a cove. Ahead, familiar windows glowed yellow. He bumped his boat against a dock and tied it to a cleat, tethering it among other boats bobbing here. Two he didn't recognize, which was odd.

He knew most of the Horse Skull Tavern's patrons. They were Fishtowners and Bremingmen. Farmers, too, sometimes rowed here, from upstream or downstream, briefly escaping the isolation of their riverbank tracts, carved from the great forest. Such mingling was proscribed. But constables rarely patrolled this far north. In any event, the tavern hid in its cove.

Wil climbed the stone steps up from the wharf, unsettled by the forest cat's summons: "Come," she bade him. But where?

Ever since that childhood escapade with Kobar, sneaking to Breming, he never rowed out onto the river without wondering: what lay beyond? To the north stretched endless forest, dark and weird. So it was said. Southward, where the river flowed into the ocean, lay the imperial city, its harbors filled with sail ships, fragrant with spices and precious woods, and its palaces like dreams. Was the city truly roofed in gold?

Kobar now labored in that city, a slave.

Wil's mustache curled down. Bad thoughts bedeviled him tonight. He needed ale.

He pushed open the tavern's oaken door and stood half blinded by the light from lanterns hung under the blackened ceiling beams. He relished the heat from the great hearth's driftwood blaze, shooting up crackling spark bursts, and the hubbub of slurred voices, and the smell of ale and the stench of Breming peat diggers and Fishtown mudfish smokers. Already his head pleasantly buzzed. He sidled past tables, waving to familiar patrons, making his way to the bar.

"Nabob or pauper?"

It was the usual question posed by the proprietor, Blossom. He towered above Wil, even leaning over, resting massive forearms upon the bar. He gazed bleakly out his good gray eye. A black patch covered his other eye. Out from under the patch, a white scar ran down his face's tanned hide to his vast chin. In his long-ago youth, Blossom had been a river pirate. So it was said.

Now, the huge old man implacably awaited his question's answer: "Nabob or pauper?" It was a reasonable question, because Wil did sometimes show up at the Horse Skull Tavern lacking even one bronze coin, hoping someone inebriated into altruism would treat him to an ale, or two, or a generous three. Tonight, though, he felt smug.

"I've come into my inheritance," Wil said.

From his trouser pocket he pulled a leather pouch. He held it upside down over the bar, and out tinkled coins. Blossom eyed the little heap—seven bronzes, four coppers, one silver.

"Smokerie work?" he rumbled.

"Three days shouldering fish crates to the wharf, for when the freighter rows in," Wil said. "And a day up on cottage roofs, helping the thatcher."

"Good boy," Blossom said. "Lazy hands earn no ale."

He extended his enormous paw, and between forefinger and thumb, almost daintily, plucked up a bronze. He clinked it into the coin pail behind the bar. Then he reached up to an overhead shelf for one of the carved-elm tankards. Wil watched as if it were a solemn rite: Blossom held the tankard beneath a keg's tap, twisted the handle, and a stream the color of moonlight gurgled convivially into the mug. Blossom twisted the tap handle closed with a professional flourish and thumped the brimming tankard down on the bar in front of Wil, sloshing ale.

Wil yearned to gulp it down in one continuous, cat-forgetting swig. But he fought the urge. He meant to savor his ale.

Blossom remained before him, leaning those enormous forearms on the bar, staring at him one eyed, which was unusual. Never had Blossom said much more to him than "Nabob or pauper?"

Closing his eyes, Wil drank a draught. Then he wiped his mustache with the back of his hand. When he opened his eyes, Blossom's giant head still loomed a few inches from his own.

"Strangers tonight," Blossom said, his good eye surveying the room, then returning to stare intently at Wil.

Wil yearned to swallow his ale and order another. But he felt compelled by Blossom's unprecedented conversational gambit to look around the room, too. And it was true. There were strangers.

At a table in a shadowy far corner sat two tall men wrapped in cloaks, despite the room's heat. They both wore shiny boots, in a place where boots were mostly battered and begrimed. And their dark hair seemed too slicked back, their mustaches and beards too neatly trimmed. They did not sip from their tankards. They sat silently in the shadows, watching. Their eyes glittered.

Wil thought of weasels.

"Who are they?" he asked Blossom.

And the tavern keeper regarded him balefully.

"They hunt," he said.

Wil pushed his tankard forward.

"Another," he said.

Blossom studied Wil, considering.

"They watch Pim over there," the tavern keeper said, pointing his chin toward the hearth.

Wil followed Blossom's glance. He saw yet another stranger. This man, round-headed and clean shaven, dark hair standing up as if lightning just struck him, sat in the big chair beside the hearth. His legs were so short that his pointed-toe shoes dangled above the floor. He looked like an owl, all the more because he wore round iron-rimmed spectacles, askew on his nose. He frequently reached up a forefinger to adjust them.

"Those two strangers hunt that man?" Wil asked.

Blossom regarded him.

"They hunt you," he said.

Wil stared at the huge man behind the bar. But now Blossom moved away, to serve another patron. Wil thought: he teases me.

In his chair by the hearth, the owlish man—Pim—sat looking benignly around the room. His pale-blue gaze met Wil's. It sharpened to a point. Then he looked away.

Will quickly drank another draught.

Now he saw Blossom handing tankards of ale to a serving girl. And she, too, he didn't know, which surprised him, because he knew all the barmaids, and kept company with many of them, until they realized he wasn't husbandish. But this one he'd never seen. He watched her place tankards upon her tray, balanced upon one hand. It tipped. She put up her other hand to steady it. Now it tipped in the other direction.

She wore her red hair cropped short, this new barmaid with no experience. He thought her hazel eyes didn't match her hair. As she moved among the patrons, she frowned, peering worriedly around the room, not watching where she walked. She repeatedly bumped tables and chairs.

Blossom returned, again leaning against the bar before him. Blossom, too, watched the barmaid.

"Breming woman?" Wil asked.

Blossom shook his head.

"Mita Sooth, her name is," he said. "From away."

It further unsettled Wil. A woman from elsewhere? How could that be? So many strangers in the tavern tonight, all looking.

Tonight was askew, starting with the cat from the forest. Only a wood-cutting trail led from Fishtown into the forest, and it quickly ended. No villager ever walked far into that gloom, where you'd hear distant laughter, sometimes, or bells tinkling, or roars. Strange things lived in the forest, like conversational cats.

Wil saw Blossom still scrutinized him.

"I'll have another, Blossom, for I'm a nabob tonight," Wil said, pushing forward his tankard. He turned on his stool to watch Mita Sooth.

She looked young, hardly more than a girl. Abruptly, a wave of pity for her washed through him, although he didn't know why. It must be the ale, he thought. She clumsily banged down tankards on tables, extending her palm for coins, offering patrons no grin or wink to soften their pain in relinquishing a brass or copper. Instead, waiting palm outstretched, she frowned worriedly around the room. Mostly she peered toward the two svelte strangers at the shadowed corner table. But sometimes Wil saw her exchange a look with Pim, the owlish man sitting in the big chair by the hearth. Blossom, too, now caught her eye, and Wil saw the old pirate nod in his direction, as if pointing him out. She looked at Wil, and their eyes met.

The air rippled.

Faint, this rippling. But it stunned him, his tankard stopped halfway to his mouth. He felt the world shifting, as if a new road now opened before him. "It's time," the cat had said. What she meant, he didn't know, or where this road led, or why it was time.

He had felt, since the cat bade him "Come," like a snail pulled from its shell, naked under the sky. Now this rippling. It went deep into his core. It terrified him. Because down there— since childhood he'd sensed it—a stranger slept. And now that stranger stirred.

He abruptly stood, eyes wild. He meant to flee the tavern.

Heavy hands pushed him back down. A large man gripped Wil's shoulders. He smelled of Breming's peat pits.

"That's the one, eh?" the man said. "Who they foisted?"

He spoke to an old man Wil knew, Tunkle, of the peg leg and stained beard. Tunkle ran errands for food. Here at the Horse Skull Tavern he cadged drinks. Wil suddenly saw himself, some distant day, just such an old man. And that horrified him.

"Doesn't look magical, does he?"

Saying that, to Tunkle and to a second peat digger, who stood beside him, grinning, the Bremingman pressed down harder on Wil's shoulders. Wil wished he hadn't drunk so much ale, because the room seemed slanted.

"Wil's a good fellow," Tunkle said weakly.

"Never saw a Forester before, up close," the peat digger said. And to Wil: "Your kind sneaks through towns at night, don't you? Cursing people's kids and chickens?"

"I'm a Fishtowner," Wil said.

"That's not what Tunkle here told us," said the man.

"Now, now," Tunkle said, making placating motions with his grimy fingers.

"Tunkle says Foresters foisted you here," the peat digger said, pressing down harder. Wil felt rising anger. Once again, because Tunkle hoped to trade gossip for ale, he must answer to this thing, not of his doing. He knew no more of Foresters than did other Fishtowners.

"Wil got raised by Fishtown folks," Tunkle said. "At night, a woman passing through the village, she gave them Wil."

So they said, that fisherman and washerwoman who fostered him. Maybe, they said, that woman came from Breming. Or maybe from another town, upstream or down. Maybe she fled a cruel husband. Or perhaps she fled because there was no husband. And they, childless, took her baby as a kindness. So they said.

They didn't fish or launder much, after Wil came. Yet, they had coppers and silvers to spend. Fishtown whispered about that. But they raised him kindly.

One spring day, in Wil's fourteenth year, his foster father and foster mother rowed out in their skiff to catch greenfins, up from the ocean to spawn. No fish tastes better than a springtime greenfin. But a wind gusted down off the escarpment beyond the great forest. Rivermen call such gusts "wavemakers." Wil's foster parents' skiff swamped. And they were like most fisher folk— they couldn't swim. When they pulled them from the river, that good man and good woman, they lay on the shore gray faced.

"You're a filthy Forester," the peat digger said.

Wil shook his head. What did he know of Foresters? But, once again, he felt shamed.

"They foisted you here," the peat digger said, yelling in Wil's ear.

Fishtown whispered: Foresters paid the fisherman and washerwoman to raise the baby, silvers and golds. Wil, as he grew, heard those whispers: Forester spawn.

Weren't Foresters, by imperial edict, declared realm enemies? Hadn't their ancestors, the ancient Forest Kings, worked dark sorcery? And couldn't Foresters, ragtag descendants of those ancient sorcerous Forest Kings, curse you into a mouse or housefly? And they thieved. And if your baby got colic, or your cow died, who could say it wasn't by Forester curses? And they conversed with beasts.

"What do the squirrels and rats tell you?" the Bremingman holding him whispered in Wil's ear.

Abruptly, the man lifted him from his stool and held him up, his feet barely touching the floor. Wil twisted and thrashed, but found no leverage to strike back. And he had drunk so much ale he no longer could make his legs or arms do as he wished. As he flailed, a voice suddenly spoke inside his head, a voice he knew.

"Little flutterbird," it said. "Eats too many berries, gets woozy—easy to snatch."

He saw her now. She sat beneath the owlish man's hearthside chair. She stared at him, eyes blue, fur black, whiskers white. And beside her sat a dog. Honey-colored and white, this dog. His legs improbably short. His eyes preternaturally bright.

Now the dog, too, spoke in his head, as the Bremingman shook him.

"Pim says we're all going back to High City, so we can be friends, Wil, and I'll show you the best places to lie in the sun— do you like getting sleepy?"

11

Wil groaned.

"It's you Foresters who cursed our peat fields," the Bremingman said.

He dropped Wil back onto his feet and spun him around, to glare into his face.

"You took our peat with your filthy magic," he said, and Wil felt his spit on his face.

Suddenly, his attacker shouted: "Show us your magic, Forester boy!"

His shout filled the room. He meant it to. He wanted all in the tavern to witness.

In their shadowed corner, the two glittery-eyed strangers jerked to their feet, staring. Exultant, they ran toward him.

Wil saw Blossom grab a cudgel from its hiding place under the bar. He saw owlish Pim jump up from his hearthside chair and run toward him, weaving between tables, knocking benches aside. Across the room, Mita Sooth dropped her tray of tankards onto a table, spilling ale over startled patrons. She waved her arms, hands clenched, but with each little finger extended. Brow furrowed, eyes closed, she muttered to herself.

Wil felt himself thrown onto the floor. He saw the Breming peat digger looming over him, his boot drawn back to kick his stomach.

Everything froze.

Now the kicker stood transfixed, one foot in the air. Wil, too, couldn't move, and he saw everyone in the tavern frozen, a living statue. Only Mita Sooth still moved.

Slowly, she stopped gesturing. She stared about the room, looking horrified. Slowly, her expression changed, to something like pride.

She pointed her index finger at Pim. He had frozen vaulting over a bench, both legs in the air. Wil saw Mita mutter.

Abruptly, the owlish little man collapsed to the floor. But he instantly got to his feet and surveyed the room.

"I did it," Mita exulted.

Even the fire had frozen in the hearth, its crackling stopped. There was no sound in the room.

"Undo the others, quickly," Pim said.

Mita pointed her index finger at Blossom, who stood frozen in the act of raising his cudgel. She muttered, and Blossom took away his hand from his cudgel. But the cudgel remained suspended in the air.

"Don't forget the Taker," Blossom said.

Now Mita pointed her finger at Wil, frozen on the floor. He found he could sit up.

He thought: "The Taker? Why am I the Taker?"

"What about them?" Blossom said, pointing to the two glittery eyed strangers petrified in the act of running toward Wil, their faces triumphant.

"They're imperial constables," Pim said. "Kill them."

Mita looked stricken.

"They'll carry word," Pim said. "Do a death spell on them."

Mita stared at him, eyes wide. Blossom now shook his head.

"No," he told Pim. " "If these two don't return to their galley and report, we'll have more than one imperial patrol on us—we'll have an armada coming up the river, full of red jerkins and yellow capes. Think about it, Pim."

Not responding, the short-legged man with a face like an owl adjusted his spectacles, which had gone askew. He looked petulant.

From the floor, Wil asked: "Why am I the Taker?"

They ignored him, so he sat watching the dog and cat emerge from beneath their chair. They stood beside Pim. The dog gazed brightly at Wil. And the cat, too, stared at him, but her blue eyes looked cold.

"Well, if we don't kill them, what?" Pim asked. "This spell isn't going to last that much longer...."

"I'll do a spell of forgetting," Mita said.

Blossom and Pim considered.

"That's harder than a spell of immobility," Pim said.

"I can do it" Mita said. "I'm ready."

"Good," Blossom said. "That's what to do, then."

Now they looked at Wil, as if considering a new problem.

"He has to be gotten out of here," Pim said.

They stood pondering. Wil still felt the floor slanting under him, because he drank so much ale. And the room spun a little. He remembered, with great affection, the apple he'd left half-eaten on his table. He wished he were eating it now. It deeply upset him, this talk of imperial galleys and patrols, and of killing, and this room full of frozen people. He looked up and saw the thug who'd assaulted him still standing immobile in his meanness, like a troll caught by sunlight, his boot still drawn back to kick.

"Let the animals guide him to the skiff," Blossom said. "While we finish in here..."

"Yes," Pim said, thinking out loud. "We'll row him upstream to where the creek comes in, and we'll hide the skiff there, and slip him into the forest." He adjusted his spectacles again. He looked satisfied.

"Take him to the boat, Lal," he told the cat. "You and Tobi."

Blossom helped Wil up from the floor and gently pushed him toward the door. Under his feet, the floor still felt tipped, making it hard to walk. But outside, in starlight, the cool air cleared his head a little, as he followed the dog and cat to the dock.

"Here," the cat said, leaping into a skiff, her words forming in his mind. After her, the short-legged dog clambered in . He sat in back, staring at Wil, those bright eyes shining in the starlight. And, in Wil's mind, the dog spoke.

"We'll be friends, won't we Wil?"

"No!" Wil yelled.

No talking cats.

No talking dogs.

No spell-casting barmaids.

Right now, he thought, with an inward shudder, in the tavern, Mita mumbled incantations. Blossom and Pim watched. And everyone else in the room, each a statue, would be losing his memory of all that had just happened.

No, he thought. No magic.

He lurched away. He stumbled along the dark dock to his own skiff. He untied it.

He felt the cat's irritation. And from the dog, he felt disappointment.

"We could be friends," the dog's voice called to him, in his mind.

But already he rowed toward the cove's mouth. He rounded the point. Digging in his oars, he glided the skiff out onto the open river. Water gurgled in the skiff's wake. He rowed far upstream, avoiding the imperial galley, with its cloaked lanterns.

Finally, he tied his boat to the Fishtown wharf. In the dark, feeling safer with each step, he hurried along cobblestoned streets to his hut. He struck flint and lit his lantern. He closed his door. He sat at his table. Soon he would sleep.

But first he ate his apple.

CHAPTER TWO

Wil awoke sprawled on his cot, still in yesterday's clothes.

He moaned, pressing his fingers to his forehead. He opened his eyes, but dawn light knifed in. So he shut his eyes again.

Abruptly, he sat up, alarmed. Ale fogged last night. Even so, what happened in the Horse Skull Tavern he remembered well enough: two constables hunted him, merciless as weasels. Did they mean to enslave him, like his childhood friend, Kobar? Or worse?

But no.

Mita, the magical barmaid! The spell of forgetting!

Wil flopped back down on his cot, grinning at the rafters. Now in good humor, despite his throbbing head, he composed an imaginary Edict of Celebration.

"By declaration of his Imperial Majesty, today will be known, throughout the realm, as the Day of No Rude Cats, and it pleases his Majesty to require all peoples of the Great Land to today venerate Normal Life, excluding all thought of Foresters and Constables, but to appreciate laundry spread on bushes to dry, red shirts and white bedsheets, and to savor the aroma, from cottage kitchens, of baking oat bread. So commandeth His Magnificence, Torpan the Twenty-Ninth."

Wil found his edict cheering. So he climbed out of bed to obey.

He walked out his hut's door. He would savor the morning.

But he stopped on the stoop, gawking.

Normally at dawn Fishtown's cobble streets and gray stone cottages seemed awaiting a curtain's lifting, to start the daily entertainment. From backyard pens you heard bleats and moos. A rooster would cockadoodle-doo, and then from the village's far side would come an answering cockadoodle. But only the watchman would be about, wrapped in his woolen cloak against the nighttime chill, hurrying home to his bed. From inside cottages you heard crockery set down on board tables, and you saw smoke wisp from chimneys, as wives still in nightgowns built up their hearth fires to cook morning porridge, the march of groggy workers down to the riverfront smokeries still an hour away. This was Wil's favorite time to walk the streets.

He liked to hear orioles high in the village elms sing their claims to aerial acreage. Dogs curled up on stoops wagged a greeting. And they might complain to him about the dog next door stealing their buried bone.

All this lifted Wil's heart.

But today the street buzzed—villagers still in nightclothes stood in knots outside their cottages, animatedly talking. Arms flew up. Fists emphatically pounded palms. Hands reached out to earnestly grip another's shoulder.

Now old Bamba Moke stomped by in her widow's black dress, which she'd worn all of Wil's life. Her cane, an old stick of oak, thumped the cobblestones. She was on her way to her cottage, across from Wil's hut, where she lived alone.

"Bamba," Wil said. "What has happened?"

Normally, the old woman snubbed Wil. She claimed he cast Forester spells on the daffodils she tried to grow by her stoop, so they failed to flower. She called him "Wastrel." And "Idler." Lately she had taken to hissing "Besotted Lazyboy!" Then she'd stomp into her cottage and slam the door. But this morning, when he spoke, she came to a stick-thumping halt. She fixed him with a stare and spoke.

"Kobar's back," she said, eyes narrowed. "Yes, he came in an imperial galley, which is now docked at the wharf, for I just walked down and saw if for myself, a huge thing with its sails furled up and its oars—two-hundred, at least—drawn in. Inside the slaves must still sleep. But on the deck you see imperial agents in their yellow capes and red jerkins and…."

"But you saw Kobar?" Wil said. "He's one of the oarsmen?"

She stared at him sharply, eyes narrowed even more. For a long time she studied him, saying nothing. Finally she spoke.

"Kobar's no longer a slave."

Wil stared at her.

No villager, enslaved, had ever again walked free. And slaves, once taken, never came back.

"Not a slave?" Wil said, perplexed.

"Oh, no. Not a slave!" Bamba said.

Again she stared, silent, eyes narrowed. When she finally spoke, it sounded like a snarl.

"Kobar now wears the imperial jerkin and cape!"

Wil stood astonished.

"Yes," said Bamba. "He found such favor with the great ones that they freed him from slavery, and they took him into the imperial service!"

Bamba peered at him, a calculating look, as if gauging his mettle. Maybe she thought he'd envy his old friend's joining the imperial staff.

"Do you grasp it, Forester foundling?" she hissed. "Through your ale fog?"

Wil whooped for joy.

Who could have imagined? He'd given up his childhood friend for lost. But now—somehow—Kobar was back. And one of the emperor's own men.

"I must see him," Wil said. "He's in his father's home?"

18

In mid-nod, Bamba's expression changed.

"Besotted Lazyboy," she hissed. "Off to grovel before imperials, and offer your neck."

Then she thumped off to her cottage. Wil heard her door slam. But he was already hurrying down the street, eager to see his friend and offer his congratulations on such stunning luck.

Kobar's father answered Wil's knock. Not since years ago, when his wife died of the pox, had the village's gentle teacher looked so worn.

He gazed at Wil speechless. His watery eyes behind his spectacles blinked wearily.

"My boy's home," he finally said.

"Kobar!" Wil called into the house. "It's me!"

Kobar's father seemed about to speak. Instead, he sighed. He stepped aside, so Wil might go in.

This room he knew by heart. Those shelves of ancient books. So patiently had Kobar's father taught him to read them. And on the table, those slates. How many sentences had they chalked on those, and how many sums? And as Wil's eyes adjusted to the room's dim light, he picked out the hearthside armchair where Kobar always sat when they did their lessons.

Wil laughed, for joy.

In that hearthside armchair, once again, sat Kobar.

"Look at you!" Wil exclaimed.

Kobar studied his hands. Finally, he stood. Wil extended his hand. But Kobar seemed not to see it.

"You've become magnificent!" Wil said.

Kobar had always been handsomer. But now he wore his brown hair slicked back. And he had grown a small, precisely trimmed mustache and a pointed beard. He wore polished black boots, with creased gray trousers tucked in, and a shirt of soft fabric the color of pearl, with a flowing collar. And over that shirt

19

he wore a red leather jerkin. And down his back, suspended from his neck by a silver chain, hung a yellow cape.

"Kobar!" Wil cried, grasping his friend's shoulders. "What have you become? Look!"

Kobar looked away. His lips curled up in a smile, but it became a grimace.

"How was it, being a slave?" Wil asked. "And how'd you get freed? Now an Emperor's man!"

Kobar's gray eyes slid around the room. Finally they rested on his father. Wil saw the two men exchange a look. Kobar looked away, but the teacher continued to gaze at his newly resplendent son. Then he walked to the window. With his hands clasped behind his back, he stood looking out.

Wil took a seat, resting his elbows on his knees and his chin in his hands. He looked at Kobar expectantly.

At first, Kobar studied his boots. Finally, he jerked up his head and stared at Wil.

"Remember when we played we were scouts in the Rebellion, fighting the Forest Kings?" he said.

Wil grinned.

"We sneaked into the Forest Kings' enchanted city," Wil said. "We captured the Starstone—actually, it was just that chunk of quartz we found…."

Kobar looked away.

"You cannot understand how it is, in that palace," Kobar finally said, as if speaking to the door. He suddenly fixed his gaze on Wil. "We're mice here, in this…." He extended a hand to indicate Fishtown outside the door. "Wealth. You can't believe it. And so much power. It blinds you! They pull strings, the mice dance…."

"And now you're one of those great ones," Wil said, shaking his head. "But how did you…."

Kobar looked away.

"Something they needed, I could give," he said finally, to his gleaming boots. "You'd have done the same."

"No," Wil said. "If they'd taken me a slave, I'd be a slave still. I never had your ambition. You thought to become even the village's assessor of levies...."

"Child's prattling," Kobar said, disgusted. "Those are mice things."

Someone knocked hesitantly on the door.

Kobar strode across the room, irritably booting a chair aside. He flung the door open.

Outside cringed a ratlike man in rags. Wil saw lash marks across his face.

"If it please you, Sir, at the galley, they ask if you're ready to lead them to..."

"Tell them I'm coming," Kobar interrupted. "Hurry, or I'll have your ears cut off."

Bobbing his head, the slave backed away, then scurried toward the docks. Kobar turned down his mouth, watching the slave hurry off, a look of contempt.

"You have to treat them with authority," he said. "Give them a finger's span and...."

"But you, just recently, were one..."

Kobar gave him a pained look.

"I have to go," he said.

Kobar turned and walked out the door. Wil stood in the doorway, troubled, watching him stride down the hill toward the docks until just the yellow dot of his cape remained visible, and his jerkin's red. And then Kobar was gone.

Kobar's father turned from the window. He walked to Wil. Reaching up, he put his hands on Wil's shoulders and gazed up at him.

"You were like another son to me," he said.

Wil hugged the old man around his shoulders. He did not know what to say, and so he hugged him harder.

A moment later, he released Kobar's father and started out the door.

"Wil," said the teacher behind him. "Do you remember how much you enjoyed reading the old books of realm history?"

Half turning, Wil nodded.

"Don't believe all those books proclaimed," Kobar's father told him. "Remember who wrote the books—remember."

Now the old teacher grimaced. He seemed to struggle for words. Finally, with an almost imperceptible shudder, he did speak.

"Where you came from, go there," he said.

Wil didn't understand.

"Hurry," Kobar's father urged. "Run!"

It unsettled Wil. It frightened him.

But already Kobar's father was closing the door.

With a gesture of farewell, Wil turned and walked away.

Head down, he trudged up the hill toward his hut. He stopped once and stood befogged. He turned, looking back down the street toward the docks, and his mouth opened as if to say something. But he walked on, eyes on his feet, frowning. He wandered past his own hut, and Bamba Moke's cottage, to the fringe of tall grass marking the village's edge, where the great forest began. Hardly noticing, he started down one of the wood-cutting trails winding into the trees.

He reached the path's end, surprised. Had he walked so far, looking at his feet? He looked up.

"You!" he said.

Before him stood the white-whiskered black cat. Lal, he remembered. She stood where the trail ended in a final patch of sunlight, before the great branches arched far overhead, creating a green gloom. She looked tiny under those huge chestnuts and oaks, staring at him blue eyed. Her tail swished. Words came into his mind.

"I will take you to them!"

She padded into the forest. As she walked, she turned, to make sure Wil followed. But he stood rigid. Lal stopped, staring back at him. He felt her exasperation. Now her words seemed to scratch.

"Squeaker—they come to eat you!"

But sayings he'd heard all his life shot through his mind, like poisoned arrows.

"Forester words, all twisted."

"No more honorable than a Forester."

Of a thief villagers would say, "He earns Forester wages." If your cow sickened, or if your hen laid spoiled eggs, or if your child misbehaved, or if your husband died of the coughing disease, "smokerie lung," that was Foresters working wicked spells. Who could say it wasn't? "Forester bargaining" meant cheating. If you smelled a nighttime stench, it must be Foresters passing you in the dark. They consorted with bears, and with wolves. Foresters plotted against the realm. In their malice, they sought disorder. Long ago, when they were the Forest Kings, the Rebellion snatched away their Starstone, snuffing out their sorcery. Then the golden Empire began. But deep in the great forest, they lived on as a sorry remnant, the ragtag Foresters. And they conspired still. They yearned to again infect the world with their sorcery. For that reason, all official speeches ended: "And may the Emperor foil Forester perfidy."

Wil thought: "I hear beasts speak!"

It shamed him, this secret. He knew its meaning.

"I'm a Fishtowner," he told himself.

He knew nothing of Foresters. He knew only what his neighbors knew. He was a Fishtowner.

Yet, he heard beasts speak.

Foresters now summoned him. He didn't know why. "It is time," the cat had told him, as she sat on his table. Now, at the great forest's start, she glared at him. Her tail swished. Wil opened his mouth, as if to speak, but made no sound. Fishtown sayings shot through his mind.....

"Foresters crave babies' blood."

"Asp, spider, Forester—which venom kills faster?"

"Children who sneak out at night, Foresters snatch."

"Tell a lie, summon the evil ones."

"If a Forester whistles past your cottage...."

Wil spun around, ran toward home.

When he reached the trail's beginning, just to one side of Bamba Moke's cottage, he stopped. Breathing hard, he peered through a screen of head-high grass.

Men in red jerkins and yellow capes milled around his hut. All wore swords in scabbards. Some methodically jabbed spears into the shrubbery, surely thinking he hid there.

To be hunted so fiercely! In his stomach, he felt snakes slithering. And why did they hunt him? A mere villager. He craved a hole to crawl into, where he could crouch and cower.

Through his hut's window he saw yellow-caped men upending his cot. Others circled the hut's perimeter, peering at the ground, seeking footprints. On his stoop two men stood, watching the others search. They turned, showing Wil their faces, and he gasped. One man wore neither cape nor jerkin. But his boots and cloak were finer than any Wil could have imagined. Silver streaked his black hair, and the dark eyes in his swarthy face flicked everywhere, observing, evaluating, as he listened to the younger man beside him.

That younger man was Kobar.

Kobar spoke animatedly to the great one. He nervously gestured. Finally, he pointed toward the path where Wil now hid behind tall grass, as if suggesting a likely place to hunt him.

Kobar?

Lightning flashed in Wil's mind.

"To buy his freedom, he…."

Surely the great ones questioned all new slaves. He now saw it as clearly as if it were written in fire across the sky: the imperials hunted a particular Forester foundling. They hunted Wil Deft. Those two disguised constables at the Horse Skull Tavern—it was Kobar who told them Fishtown's suspicions about Wil, and where to seek him. But why did they hunt him so fiercely? Surely not for his childhood venture across the river to Breming, or for patronizing the Horse Skull Tavern in defiance of the mingling prohibition. So many defied that law.

But Kobar….

On the stoop, the dark man raised an arm, summoning a squad of swordsmen. He pointed a brown-gloved hand toward the trail. Unknowing, he pointed just where Wil hid in the grass, and Wil's heart pounded. Five constables started toward the trail at a trot, swords clanking rhythmically in their scabbards.

Wil dropped to his knees, cringing.

They'd pass within a sword's thrust of where he knelt, and this grass wouldn't hide him. He watched the five constables trot toward him, their swords' rhythmic clanking like march music. It mesmerized him, weakened him. He felt himself a rabbit, huddled trembling in the grass, listening to the howls of oncoming hounds. His thoughts skittered, and he remembered a foolish childhood game—"Pilfer."

He'd excelled at Pilfer.

Beside a "Starstone" sat a "guardian," watching for pilferers out to steal it. If he spotted one, he pointed and yelled: "Burglar, robber, thief—I bring you grief!" That pilferer must freeze in place until all were frozen, or one grabbed the stone. Wil always sneaked by the guardian. He always snatched the Starstone.

"Why do I think of this now?"

Still he knelt frozen, watching the constables trot toward him. And still Pilfer played in his mind.

He played many Pilfer tricks. One was flattening himself against the ground, so that the guardian's eyes passed over him, not seeing.

He lay flat now.

And he would wriggle through tall grass like this, silently, using just his elbows and stomach muscles and knees to propel himself forward, so that he stayed flattened against the ground.

He wriggled now.

Fear welled up, and despair, and a need to yell. He stifled it, biting his hand. Then he forced himself to wriggle on through the grass, away from the path. But not too fast. Another of his tricks: barely move. Don't let the grass overhead wave, because that gives you away.

Dirt got into his nose. He squeezed shut his eyes and grimaced, to avert a sneeze.

Behind him, where he'd knelt in the grass just a moment ago, swords rattled in scabbards. He heard a boot toe stub against a stone, a man's curse. Wil lay motionless, flattened against the ground, eyes squeezed shut. He held his breath, expecting a sword through his back.

They passed. He heard their swords clank down the path, into the forest. He nearly wept. But relief turned again to fear. They'd quickly reach the trail's end. Then the constables would come clanking back. This time they'd peer into the brush and grass on all sides, parting it with their swords. Where they couldn't see, they'd jab their spears.

Wil raised his head, just enough to see his hut through the grass. Constables still searched inside. On the stoop outside, the dark noble swept his eyes along the street, up to rooftops, along fences and hedges....

All the while Kobar talked to the man. As he spoke, he nervously gestured, repeatedly glancing at the great one, to make sure his words were well received.

Kobar....

Wil felt knifed.

He crawled again, exquisitely slowly, careful to move no grass. For the great one would see. What did those sharp dark eyes not see? He wriggled—each motion precise—until finally Bamba Moke's cottage stood between him and his own hut, hiding him from the imperials.

But he was safe only for a moment. Soon the dark man would send his constables tramping everywhere. He'd order them to sweep the grass with their swords. Spears would jab.

Wil eyed Bamba's cottage, numb. If he crossed the river to Breming, they'd report him, a stranger. That would be so in any river town. But the great forest—he couldn't flee there. Evil hid in that gloom. Everyone knew. And in the forest he'd starve. Unless, somehow, he found the Foresters.

His people.

Thinking it, he shuddered. Practitioners of filthy magic, suckers of babies' blood—they hunted him, too, with their talkative cat and tailless dog. Wil Deft, foster child. Thatcher of roofs. Lugger of mudfish crates. Drinker of ale. Connoisseur of barmaids. Hunted by both, Foresters and imperials. He cringed before the empire. That dark aristocrat with the sharp eyes would stomp him, like a mouse. Yet, he shrank from the Foresters, too, living secretly deep in the murky forest. Nobody knew what mayhem they schemed. Casters of malice. Skulkers and sneaks. Sickeners of chickens. All his life he'd heard such things.

"No mire so filthy as Forester magic!"

No, never the Foresters.

So it would be the river. His hope lay there, with the water.

He must last until tonight. Then, in the dark, he'd sneak out in his skiff. Upstream would be safest. To the south, toward the river's mouth, there lay the great city. Constables surely swarmed there. So he'd row northwards, toward the Empire's edge. He'd seek refuge at isolated farmsteads, offering to work. He'd stay just so long, then disappear in his skiff to seek another farm even farther north. He'd play that game as long as he could. And all the while they'd hunt him.

Kobar called villagers like him "mice." It was true, he thought, prone in the dirt. I'm a squeaker, and they mean to eat me.

Wil found himself staring at a pair of black shoes.

They stood level with his eyes, inches from his nose. Dirt flecked the leather toes. Beside the shoes the point of a gnarled stick dug into the ground. Looking up, Wil found himself staring into the crazed eyes of Bamba Moke.

He thought about leaping to his feet, clasping his hand over her mouth. That would stop her from hollering to the constables across the street. But then what? He knew he couldn't bring himself to hurt her.

"Bamba…"

He meant to offer her his hut in payment, if she let him go.

"Shhh!"

She pressed her forefinger angrily against her lips. He heard her hiss to herself, "Stupid boy."

Beckoning with a finger, Bamba turned and marched toward her back door, stick thumping into the ground with each step. After a moment, Wil gathered his wits. He got to his feet and followed her. She walked inside, leaving her door open, and Wil followed her into her cottage.

Never before had he come inside. And it astonished him.

Instead of the usual plank table, Bamba ate her meals at a crafted piece with carved legs and fluted edges, its top a single round of maple, cut from some great tree, smooth as glass, varnished to reflect your face. Carved and inlaid cedar chests rested everywhere on the floor. One chest's lid stood raised, and inside Wil saw brocaded fabrics. Here and there stood ceramic urns and ewers. Bamba dismissed it all with a gesture.

"My husband was a river trader, with his brother," she said. "What remains are these things."

Through the cottage's window, Wil saw the constables still milling around his hut. Bamba mystified him. Had she invited him inside on some crazed whim? When constables walked by, would she suddenly fling open her door and turn him over? Reward might prompt her, or malice. But if the constables were to leave without Bamba noticing….

"Your husband, a great one, I didn't know!" Wil said.

To distract her was his sole hope. Maybe the constables would go.

"An imperial license!" Wil enthused. "To travel the river, to buy goods and sell them, in all the villages and in the great city, that's no small thing, and…."

"Don't prattle," Bamba said. "My husband and his brother had no imperial license, and they sailed at night."

Through the window Wil now saw Kobar and the swarthy noble surveying the street. With his gloved hand, the great one began pointing out the cottages along the street, one by one.

"At night, only?" Wil said. "But…"

"Smugglers," Bamba snapped.

She, too, now looked out the window. On the street in front of Wil's hut, constables were gathering.

Wil blurted: "Do you mean to turn me in?"

Bamba didn't respond. Instead she opened a chest. She fished inside, then extracted a dagger in a sheath. In the bone hilt and in the sheath's leather gleamed inlaid cords of gold and silver.

"It's a Forester weapon, old," she said. "It was with Foresters my husband and his brother traded, meeting at wild places along the river...."

Wil looked at her blankly. Outside boots shuffled, and someone shouted orders.

"A galley stumbled upon them one night," Bamba said. "My husband and his brother were strapping men, and many imperials died."

She said this with satisfaction.

"They slew my husband. But my husband's brother swam ashore, wounded," Bamba said, now oblivious in her reverie to the sounds from outside, coming nearer. "He came here, and I hid him and nursed him, and...."

"Bamba, I think they're coming," Wil said, terrified.

She looked at him, as from far away.

"My husband's brother sold some of the goods they stored here, for money to open a public house...."

"Bamba," he said. "I hear them coming."

She handed him the dagger she'd fished from the trunk. He held it, staring at it.

"I'm not a fighter," he said.

"Idiot," Bamba spat out. "They've chosen fighting for you."

"I don't even know why they hunt me," he said.

"They hunt you for a Forester-born fool, who should've done more with himself," Bamba snarled. "Or because you're a

30

besotted lazyboy, and a wastrel, and an idler, who doesn't even know whom he is, and what he must do."

A fist pounded the door. Wil stood paralyzed. Bamba pushed him toward the cottage's back door.

"Crawl into the cote, in the back, where I once kept sheep," she hissed.

Wil started out the door. But he paused.

"Bamba," he said. "Who was your husband's brother?"

Another angry rap on the door.

"Blossom," she hissed. "That was his name—now hide!"

Just as the front door burst open Wil dashed outside. He saw the old sheep cote, against the back of the house, and he crawled through the small opening. It smelled of animal inside, but faintly, no sheep having lived here in many years. Wil pulled the dagger from its sheath and looked at it in the dim light. Then he grimaced and slid it back into its sheath and thrust the knife and sheath into his pocket.

From inside the house, he heard an angry voice. "Why didn't you open the door?"

"Because old women move slowly."

That was Bamba's voice.

He heard Kobar speak. "Bamba, where's Wil Deft?"

"Why chase that wastrel?" Bamba asked. "Wasn't he your good friend?"

Another voice, low pitched and even: "He's an enemy of the realm, old woman, and he means to work great evil."

"Then look for him along the wood-cutting trails, where he walks instead of working," Bamba said. "Or maybe he's on the river, fishing for mudfish to sell for coppers."

"What are these rich things in your cottage, old woman?"

Wil guessed that low voice belonged to the great one, to whom Kobar deferred.

"I've lived many years, accumulated many things," Bamba said.

"Not such things as this. Kobar, what of this woman?"

"A widow, for as long as I can remember." Wil imagined Kobar shrugging. "Her husband died before my birth, but it was said he came and went, nobody knew where...."

"I see." That low voice.

There was silence a moment. Then the voice spoke again.

"It's like this, old woman—I suspect you know where your neighbor hides. And if you tell, I'll forget all this contraband, for which the laws decree execution."

Silence again.

"You won't tell?"

More silence.

"You, corporal—perform the execution."

Wil heard a clank. He heard the trod of a heavy boot.

"Will you tell?" Again, the noble's voice. "That fierce stare won't save you."

For a moment all was silent. Then he heard the voice again, still low and even. "And spitting will particularly not save you—corporal!"

Wil heard a scream. It trailed off to a gurgle. Then he heard a thud.

Silence, but for just a moment.

"Take this to the village center."

It was that low voice again, the tone unchanged, still even.

"Hang it up, and on its dress pin a notice saying, 'For Protecting the Realm's Enemies.'"

Wil heard the house's back door burst open. And through his cote's low opening he saw Kobar's boots and Kobar's knees. He saw that Kobar stood bent over. And then he heard retching.

"Make that notice's letters large and black and clear," said the voice inside the house.

After that he heard a sound of something being dragged. And then that even voice was nearer, at the back door.

"When you finish, Kobar, search the cottage."

Wil fought his own need to retch.

He saw Kobar's legs straighten. He saw him walk toward the door. He waited a few moments. From inside he heard thumps and the sound of crockery breaking. He peeked out the cote's door. No one was in the yard. They'd closed the cottage's back door, and he saw nobody at the window. But from inside he heard furniture overturned and muffled orders barked out. Soon they'd search outside.

Wil squeezed through the cote's opening and scuttled, bent over, across the yard to where the tall grass grew, at the great forest's edge. He lay in the grass and looked back at the cottage. He expected to see constables running towards him, but none came. They hadn't seen him.

He lay on his stomach in the grass, smelling the earth.

They'd soon search the yard. He heard more constables, farther away, sweeping through the grass and bushes along the forest's edge. And these sounds of swords swooshing through grass, and whacking into bushes, and men cursing, moved toward him.

He began crawling through the grass, toward the river. He thought of his skiff, bobbing at the dock. He loved his skiff. He remembered rowing out on the great river, under the sun, casting a line for mudfish. His skiff would gently pitch in the waves, and yaw, and he would watch gulls glide overhead. And he would lie in the skiff holding the line and think of things, and grow sleepy.

But that now seemed a different life.

Hours later, Wil huddled in an old shed across from the docks. Here fishermen stacked their nets and lines and oars. All afternoon he'd hidden in this shed, awaiting darkness. Now it had come.

From some street up the hill, he faintly heard Fishtown's watchman call. "Midnight, and all's well."

He peeked out the door. He could see the black shape of the great imperial galley, roped to the smokerie pier, where fish-hauling freighters usually tied. Lanterns made yellow pools on the big boat's deck. Voices sometimes reached him, men on watch. But tonight was moonless. In that, he was lucky.

He needed to cross the dark street, to the wharf, then make his way across the planks to where his skiff bobbed. No great distance, but all evening he'd put off leaving this hiding place. When it's darker, he told himself. And then it was black as ink. When I'm sure they're all asleep, he thought then, but now he saw that the emperor's men watched all night, in shifts. And he knew an hour would soon come when the darkness lightened.

"Now, then," Wil told himself.

He stepped from the shed. He paused, peering up and down the street, ears straining. But there was nothing.

Darkness. He could not see the cobblestoned street running along the river. But he remembered how it went. So many times he'd crossed it, at all hours. He stepped lightly, setting down his feet with no sound, a talent he had. Here and there, glimmers of lamplight from the docked imperial galley glinted on a windowpane or paving stone. Wil avoided such glimmers, moving from dark pool to dark pool.

Across the street, he made for the broken-wheeled cart that had long stood beside the docks. He crawled underneath to listen—now he heard voices approaching.

In the darkness, two men strolled toward him along the dark street.

"What's this?"

It was the low, even voice of the great one.

"It's just an old cart, which broke a wheel here before I was born and never moved again."

Kobar.

Now the two men stopped. Wil felt the cart shift above him, as they rested their backs against it. Crouched underneath, he could just make out their two pairs of shiny boots.

Wil heard the dark aristocrat's low voice: "If the Foresters find him first, that brings great danger."

He heard Kobar speak then: "He must be hiding in Fishtown—he's good at that."

Wil fingered the hilt of Bamba's sheathed dagger, sticking from his pocket. "They've chosen fighting for you," she'd said. Inside him, something stirred, something new. It felt like cold fire. He saw himself pulling the dagger from its sheath and stabbing it into Kobar's chest.

"I suppose," Kobar said offhandedly, "I should see my father once before we go."

Wil clenched the dagger's hilt, but didn't draw it from its sheath. He felt the wagon shift as the two men leaning against it stood straight. And then he heard their boots, walking toward the galley.

"I let thoughts of Kobar's father stop me," he thought.

He no longer felt so afraid. He climbed out from beneath the cart and stood a moment, listening in the darkness. When he heard nothing, except distant voices on the galley, he walked across the cobblestones until he felt the dock's planking. He made his way to his skiff and untied it. He climbed in, shoving off from the dock with one foot. He smelled the rotting piles and the smokeries. He eased his oars in the water, soundlessly, and sent the skiff out of the dock's little cove. Two more silent pulls on the oars and he was in the current. He knew because the air smelt fresher.

Something splashed, just ahead.

In the darkness, a voice: "Hey, what's this?"

A deeper blackness loomed before him, against the night's dark. Lantern light from the galley glinted on something— the white of a man's eye. A clicking of flints. A lantern flaring, and he saw: a short jump beyond his skiff's prow floated a patrol boat. Two men in red jerkins and yellow capes stood in it, staring at him, one holding up the lantern.

"Look—it's that Forester they call the Taker!"

Wil stared at them, stunned, as the constable holding the lantern thumped it down on the boat's seat and drew his sword. Now the other drew.

Wil thought: "To have gotten so far...."

"Come around here or we'll kill you on the spot!"

Their skiff floated broadside to his own, blocking his way. One man bent and reached out, to grab the prow of Wil's skiff.

Cold fire flared up inside him, and somebody roared. Him! He heaved on his oars, heaved again—his skiff thudded against the patrol boat's gunwale, rocking it back.

Now the two constables danced, arms flailing, their swords flying into the darkness beyond the tipped-over lantern's light. Both men toppled, legs kicking in air, then splashed into the river. In a moment they surfaced, coughing and cursing.

Wil roared a second time, exultant.

He backed off from the still rocking patrol boat and rowed around it. Then he turned his skiff upstream and rowed north.

"Now they'll know I took to the river," he thought. "And which way I went."

But that seemed a worry for tomorrow. He rowed until he no longer heard the curses of the swimming constables. He rested on his oars, breathing hard, feeling spent. Now all seemed quiet.

A rising tide flowed in, up from the ocean. And a wind blew from the south. So instead of the current taking his skiff down toward the great city, as it otherwise would, tide and wind wafted him northward. He didn't even need to row.

Wil sat motionless, watching the imperial galley tied to the smokerie wharf slowly slide astern. Here and there in Fishtown, through window chinks, a few lanterns shone, looking like fireflies. And then the last cottages of Fishtown slid behind him. Black forest extended down to the river's banks.

After a while, he lay down and looked up. Stars shone. At some point he drifted asleep.

CHAPTER THREE

Oatcakes danced in his mind.

Hot pudding.

Wedges of sharp-tasting cheese.

His last meal was two nights ago, an apple. He no longer brooded over Bamba Moke. Or listened to the white gulls mewling overhead. Or noticed the sudden swirls where some great fish momentarily surfaced.

Corn soup filled his thoughts.

Raspberry pie.

And the ache in his arms.

He'd rowed beyond the world he knew.

Here tall pines and hemlocks crowded to the river. Spruces. Cedars. Pointed firs. The sinking orange sun sent their shadows across the water.

Long ago he'd passed the last farm. Ever since he'd seen only an occasional ramshackle dock, with a rowboat tied to it, and gray hearth smoke twisting above the trees. Who lived in these places he didn't know, but now he sought such a spot, meaning to beg supper, and hide.

Because he'd tipped the patrol boat, the constables would know he rowed north, seeking sanctuary in these fringe lands, where the empire petered out. Probably they already chased him, but he felt too weary to row farther. Even his fingers hurt, from clenching the oars. So he eyed the riverbank ahead, and saw a cleft where a creek swirled into the darker river.

He remembered a snatch of conversation: "We'll row him upstream to where the creek comes in, and we'll hide the skiff there, and slip him into the forest."

Who said it?

Wil rested on his oars. Immediately the river pulled his skiff southward. Pim said it. The short-legged Forester. He said it in the tavern when they meant to spirit Wil away.

Wil had run from them.

And now Bamba Moke was murdered.

Ever faster, the skiff slid backwards down the river. With a groan, Wil dug in his oars, pulled, then again, until the boat inched forward against the current. He turned into the creek.

Hemlock branches arched overhead, a tunnel. With each oar's stroke away from the river, he felt safer He rounded a bend, and saw ahead a makeshift dock, with three rowboats tied to it. Nearby a rotted hulk lay half sunk, its prow up on the muddy bank.

He had no food. No flints to make fire. He must land here, or starve.

He tied his skiff to a post and climbed onto the dock, barely able to walk, and leaned against a piling, head down. He looked up to see a plump boy staring at him, open-mouthed.

For a while, they both stared. Wil finally spoke.

"Are you a Forester?"

A shift in the breeze brought an aroma. Roasting chicken.

The boy brushed unkempt brown hair from his eyes, the better to see this apparition that had appeared on his dock. Wil sniffed, hypnotized by the aroma of spitted chicken turning over a fire. Abruptly the boy shoved his hands into the pockets of his crudely sewn leather trousers, pursed his lips, and produced an astonished whistle.

Wil swallowed.

"Supper," he said. "If you're a Forester, I'm wondering…."

But the boy ran away up a path through the trees.

Moments later, from beyond the screen of hemlocks, Wil heard a yell: "Papa! Grandmama! On the dock! Just what they said! And he thinks we're Foresters!"

Wil followed the boy. A few paces up the path, he stepped from the hemlocks into an old field, growing up to brush.

Before him sprawled a ruined manor house. Tiles from its caved-in roof lay in the rubble. Pines grew up through what remained of the rafters. Vines snaked up the brick walls. Attached to the ruin, like barnacles, clung a ramshackle array of thatched huts and sheds and pens and barns, all weathered and rickety. Everywhere dark-red hens and roosters pecked at the ground. Somewhere a sheep bleated.

On the manor's brick veranda, its fluted columns no longer supporting a roof, stood side-by-side wicker chairs. In one sat a huge man. His girth was immense. But for all his height and fat, he sat lightly in his frail chair, one leg over the other, relaxed. Beside him, in a matching wicker chair, sat what seemed a rag doll. Wil made out an ancient woman. She was so tiny and shriveled she looked mummified. But her eyes peered at him like a kestrel's, dark and crazily sharp. On the veranda steps stood the plump boy, excitedly pointing at Wil.

"Why just you look, Grandmama," exclaimed the man sitting on the veranda. "Here's a visitor!"

Beside him, the rag doll's desiccated wrinkles slightly shifted. Wil felt the kestrel gaze.

"Skinny creature, shabbily dressed. A peasant."

A squeak of a voice from the rag doll.

"Now, Grandmama," said the fat man, giving Wil a conspiratorial wink.

Wil walked up to the veranda. But then he noticed smoke rising from one of the huts, and again smelled roasting chicken. He froze, staring at the hut, his tongue's tip wetting his

40

lips. He imagined a heaped plate, steaming slices of breast, succulent drumsticks, crackly browned skin….

Benevolently, the man on the veranda smiled, blue eyes twinkling. He slapped his knee.

"Why, wasn't I just saying, Grandmama, how fine it would be to have a visitor join us for dinner? Didn't I just say we needed to be learning new things and hearing about that grand world out there? Now, you tell the truth, Grandmama. Didn't I say that?"

Again the old woman spoke.

"We had candles that produced the scent of roses or mint, and linens the whiteness of snow, threaded with gold, and…."

"Grandmama, you do go on about those old days," said the fat man. "You know that was long before you ever walked this earth."

He regarded his tiny grandmother with twinkling blue eyes. Then, for Wil's benefit, he elaborately shrugged, and turned up his gaze, amused, in mock embarrassment.

Wil started to speak. But the man, smiling, held up a hand.

"Now, don't you say a word," he said. "You'll be wanting a good supper—and I mean a substantial supper—and then we'll make you tell us all sorts of things, and pay us in absorbing conservation for any everyday roasted chicken and baked yams and green beans and corn dripping butter we might put on your plate!"

Wil started to speak again. But the man laughed heartily, as if at a fine joke, and held up his hand once more.

"We'll be wanting to hear all about your adventures, Wil Deft, but I do believe it's time for dinner!"

With his hands on the chair's arms he pushed his immense weight upwards, until he stood. Then he cupped his hands around his mouth and called.

"Gather all! Evening repast! A guest!"

From inside the hut with the smoking hearth walked a tall, thin woman carrying a heaped platter. She peered toward Wil, to view the stranger. But, without speaking, she set down her platter on a long trestle table set up in front of the hut. After her, three girls carried trays of crockery out of the hut, one after another, the first plump, the next two thin, each a few inches shorter than the one before. Each peered at Wil before setting out her plates and cups. They all filed back into the hut, tittering. They quickly reemerged, carrying more heaped platters. From behind the ruined manor, where Wil guessed a garden grew, shambled a white-bearded man, followed by his twin. After them came a younger man carrying a hoe.

Because he was so ravenous, Wil could think only of chicken. He followed his huge host to the table, entranced by the sight of so many platters of meat, and steaming vegetables, and dishes of yellow butter, and pitchers of apple cider.

Had he introduced himself to his host? For the man had called him by name, "Wil Deft." He didn't remember giving his name. But he must have told them his name, then forgotten telling it. It must be so. In any event, his thoughts were on chicken.

An hour later, Wil still ate. His host watched approvingly as Wil finished off yet another plateful.

"Now, look here, Wil, you have more of those yams, and more of that chicken, too, or all these wonderful ladies will fret that you disapprove of their culinary skills, and I know you do approve."

So said the host, with a wink at Wil. He took in another huge forkful of yam himself, and rolled up his eyes blissfully.

"Corn," he said. "Pass that corn, and that butter, because Wil wants some more—I know he does!—and I do, too."

With unabashed zest, the corpulent man slathered butter on the corn. Then he took a bite from the middle of the cob and looked enchanted. He put his right hand's forefinger and middle finger to his lips, and kissed them, to express how succulent he found the corn, and how perfectly prepared.

Wil continued to eat, thinking he might never reach his fill. Meanwhile, he learned his host's name, Marston Ker Veermander. Marston, while continuing to enthusiastically extol the food, managed to introduce each person around the table, and tell a little story about that person. For instance, Marston's wife, the tall, thin woman, had recently chased a forest lion from the barnyard, all by herself, with a broom. Wil now officially met the plump boy, Marston's son. Also, he met Marston's two daughters, and his cousin's daughter, and his two old uncles, and his cousin, the younger man who arrived carrying a hoe, whose wife had drowned just three years ago rowing upriver to visit her sister, a terrible tragedy, teaching us that life is unsure, all the more to be treasured, and would Wil please, if only as a favor to Marston, have more chicken? For the dark meat was particularly savory tonight, although there was plenty of white, too, if Wil preferred.

Afterwards, in a satiated trance, Wil sat on the veranda with Marston and his grandmother. It was dark now, but Marston had, with a flourish, lit two pine-pitch torches, which flickered and flared, so that Wil saw Marston's and his grandmother's faces alternately dimmed, then brightly lit.

"…and we journeyed on the great river in a vessel painted cobalt, trimmed with gold, the sails also cobalt, and…"

"Long ago, Grandmama, long ago," Marston said, with a sigh. "Grandmama lives a thousand years ago."

A torch's sudden flare revealed Marston gazing sadly at his knees, and shaking his head.

"This manor was ancient even then, even a thousand years ago," Marston said. "Our ancestors weren't Forest Kings, not of their sorcerer stock, but they were great barons and earls, raised up from among the peasants and huntsmen who lived here because the Forest Kings discerned their ability! And in those days all these brushy fields were sowed and tilled, with boats of all sorts docking, and emissaries arriving from the Forest Kings, who worked wizardry to encourage the corn. Do you know, Wil, that lions would come out of that forest, for visits of state? Delegations of bears or foxes would arrive to share their thoughts, for they could do that in those days, and ask for this or that. Oh, we were quite the grandees."

Wil only half listened. Marston must wonder why he came up the river. Should he tell? What if they sent the boy to fetch constables?

"I myself, I'm only a villager," Wil said. "I rowed up the river to explore, and...."

"Explore!" Marston said, as if delighted with the concept. "Do you hear that, Grandmama? Wil said he rowed up that big river to 'explore.' Discretion! Now there's your marker of true gentility. Didn't you teach me that, Grandmama?"

"Lord Gormic Ker Veermander once took a commission from the Forest Kings to explore in the northeast, beyond their magic's sway, to see what might...."

"Now, we mustn't weary our guest with stories one-thousand-six-hundred-and-seven years old, Grandmama," Marston said. "I'm sure he knows all about the Forest Kings."

Marston took the opportunity of a torch's flaring to give Wil a knowing wink.

"You must be eager to rejoin our friends in the forest," Marston said, patting Wil's knee. "Momentous times!"

"I'm just a villager," Wil said, confused. "I decided to row up   the   river…."

"Ah." Another wink from Marston. "Discretion it is, then. You know, don't you, that I'm actually a count? Count Marston Ker Veermander. Oh, yes, right down the line, father to son, son to grandson, and so on. And when it comes to discretion, Wil, you can count on a count!"

That provoked Marston to guffaw, and slap his knee. Wil smiled weakly, increasingly confused.

"All gone," Marston's grandmother squeaked. "Those brutes marched up from the south, so many, and twisted the common people's minds, and fomented the Rebellion. Wicked! Wicked!"

Wil realized that, in the darkness, the old woman wept.

"…they stole the Starstone…."

"Grandmama, don't you go upsetting Wil with that sorry tale, you hear?"

"Losing that talisman…."

"You take my handkerchief, Grandmama." And to Wil he whispered: "She's upset herself, like she always does, talking about those old days, poor thing."

"…weakened the Forest Kings, from sorcerers into mere magicians…."

Now the torches barely flickered, their pitch consumed. Wil could hardly see. But he imagined the old woman's kestrel eyes, sharp and crazed, focused on sights inside her own mind.

"Descendants of those great Forest Kings, now called Foresters, hiding among the trees, vilified…."

"Now you stop that weeping, Grandmama, because our Forester friends don't weep about what they lost, those thousand years ago," Marston said. "You know they're gathering strength,

Grandmama, to take back that Starstone, and they'll be Forest Kings again!"

Wil felt increasingly confused. His childhood history books said the Forest Kings worked evil. Noble people marched up from the south, to undo the realm's bewitchment. They stole the Starstone and broke the Forest Kings' power, scattered them into the forest. There they still plotted, or their descendants did, the wicked Foresters. So said the books.

What did Kobar's father admonish him?

"Remember who wrote the books—remember."

"Poof!" the old lady said in the darkness.

"Poof, Grandmama? Whatever do you mean, 'Poof?'"

"'A thousand years to gather strength, to martial a stroke,'" intoned the old woman, quoting.

"Now do you hear that, Wil? How she memorized the *Codex Mysterium?* Every single word?" Marston whispered. "Her so old. Doesn't it just touch you how she does that?"

"One thousand years. Done!" exclaimed the old woman. "Now for the strike!"

Not even Marston spoke after that. For several minutes they sat silently in the dark. Suddenly, in her squeaking voice, the old woman giggled. She spoke one word.

"Poof!"

When he awoke the next morning, in one of the thatched huts attached to the ruined manor, Wil knew what he must do.

But how to do it?

He didn't even know which way to go. North? East? Westward?

And could he trust Marston?

From conversations last night at the dinner table, he gleaned that others also lived at this ruined manor. Two young nephews had gone off. Wil didn't know why. And a niece,

Marston told Wil, with a flurry of winks and knowing looks, had "made a wee junket out into the trees." What were they doing, those three? Summoning imperial constables?

Did they plot, Marston and his grandmother, to beguile Wil into staying? Did they mean to hold him until constables came?

Wil didn't believe it. They seemed so antipathetic to the empire. Marston's grandmother seemed genuinely mad. And last night, talking about the thousand-years-ago overthrow of the Forest Kings, she wept real tears.

Another point was Marston knowing his name. Wil Deft, he'd called him. Wil had searched his memory. He never told them his name. He now was certain. Yet, these manor people knew him. And they expected him to come.

Who told them? Wil believed he knew.

He could hide here, eating chicken and yams. But the imperial galley would arrive. It would anchor in the river. Constables would row a boat up the creek, seeking him. That would be soon. Could he ask these people to hide him?

Bamba Moke hid him.

He could row farther up the river. But his two oars couldn't outrow the imperial galley's two-hundred oars. Wil guessed that swarthy aristocrat would require Kobar to do the killing. His old friend would draw the sword slowly, his soft features convulsed, confusion in his eyes. Then that face would harden, the mouth turn cruelly down. Even in childhood ambition ruled him. Kobar would do anything to ascend. He would do as bidden.

Why the empire hunted him mystified Wil. But they surely hunted him.

What he must do now, he found frightening.

"Marston, the real reason I rowed up the river…."

47

But the obese man raised a hand and smiled.

"Running from constables, Wil? Say no more. To hear you say that delights me. Yes, it does. Do you know why?"

Wil shook his head.

"All that discretion last night! It did trouble me. I confess. It suggested not trusting. Am I right?"

Wil spread his hands and nodded.

"You can trust us, Wil. You can!"

Amidst the remains of breakfast, Wil sat alone with Marston at the outdoor table. They sipped spearmint tea.

After a silent moment, Marston's face suddenly reddened.

"Burn this empire!" he cried.

He banged his fist onto the table.

"Arrogance."

Another bang of the fist.

"Cruelty."

Bang!

"Oh, believe us, who lost so much—we do crave it crushed!"

Wil gasped.

To openly defy the emperor!

Marston pulled a handkerchief from his pocket to wipe his forehead. As an afterthought, he blew his nose. His breathing gradually grew regular. He shook his head, as if to throw off his anger's ashes.

It eased Wil, those words, that pounding fist. All his life he'd felt separate, a Fishtowner, yet not a Fishtowner. For the first time, he felt less alone.

"Where you came from," Kobar's father told him, that last day in Fishtown, "there you must go."

That good man, Wil thought.

This morning, awakening, he'd remembered those words, and knew what he must do.

"I have to go to the Foresters," he said.

Marston wrinkled his brow, puzzled.

"Well, of course," he said. "Pim told us what happened in that village—Fishtown, is it called?—them killing that old woman, and Pim losing you there, and that we should look out for you...."

"You know Pim?" Wil said.

"Certainly," Marston said. "A man of such importance. And when they came through here, on their way into the forest, I met Mita, too, that charming girl, and Blossom....no, not himself Forester, but with them! And so are we, Wil. So are we."

"Which way do I go, Marston?" Wil asked. "Which direction in the forest?"

Marston looked appalled.

He shook his head.

"Not into the forest, Wil, not by yourself!" he said. "You weren't Forester raised, we know that, and the forest...."

Marston again shook his head.

"We're sending word, Wil," he said. "They'll come. Wait with us a while."

Wil offered to work, to earn his keep. Marston made shooing motions with his hands, dismissing the thought. What his host wanted, Wil realized, was to talk. And so talk they did, all that day.

In these northern parts, Wil learned, a scattering of ruined old manors like this one hid along the river. They remained from the Forest Kings' regime. And they traded still with the ancient sorcerers' descendants, the Foresters. They exchanged their farms' produce for the Foresters' crafted goods, and charms and potions.

It was, of course, illegal.

Marston shrugged.

"No nasties patrol so far north," he said. "It's not worth their rowing." He smiled sadly. "Our season is short, Wil. And these soils are good for pines, not corn. But long ago....Bounty! We had the sorcerers' enchantments, Wil. What a blooming! Now we just eke."

Down the river, crops grew better. Wil remembered watching boats from nearby farms unload their milk and cheese at Fishtown's wharf, and their oat flour, potatoes, onions, carrots, corn. Freighters transported most of it down the river to the emperor, along with Fishtown's smoked mudfish and Breming's peat. It was payment. Did not the emperor permit the little people to live? Also, his patrols warded off mischief-making Foresters, and other evils that might creep from that ancient forest. So of every ten parts a farmer or villager grew or netted or dug, eight parts went to the emperor. It recompensed him for his benevolence and protection.

Thus it had been in all memory.

"Here, we never learned to be slaves," Marston said.

At midday, a young woman emerged from the forest. She turned out to be Marston's niece, back from her mission.

"I visited the hermit," she told Wil.

"You kept to our way?" Marston asked.

Because she was young, and full of life, her uncle's concern made her laugh. She spread her arms and pirouetted, to display herself returned, unharmed.

"Here by the river the enchantments dissipated long ago," Marston told Wil. "But in the forest...."

Wil learned that Foresters showed the manor people the way to the hermit's cave. No manor dweller ever saw the hermit. He hid in his cave. They addressed him from the cave's mouth, giving him messages for the Foresters. In response, they would hear only a groan, or cough, or some such sound. It meant he heard. How he conveyed their messages to the Foresters, they didn't know.

"I told the hermit you were here, and they should come for you," the niece told Wil. "And he made a sound like clearing his throat."

So the Foresters would come for him. It gave Wil hope. And it unsettled him.

All afternoon some part of his mind worried about it, as he sat on the veranda with Marston, talking. Wil told of growing up in Fishtown, of his loneliness and his happiness, and the decency of his foster parents, and the kindness of his teacher, Kobar's father. He told of the murder of Bamba Moke. He talked of his bewilderment. Why did the empire hunt him so fiercely?

"I do know we've come to a dire time," Marston told him. "Oh, yes. Since the stealing of the Starstone—one thousand years! Things stir. Because the Forest Kings, when they were ruined, foretold it would take that long for marshalling their depleted magic for a counterstroke. And from what the Foresters said….Wil, everything depends on you!"

"Me?" Wil said.

"Indeed, it does," Marston said. "Grandmama recites to me the *Codex Mysterium* she learned so long ago, and still remembers every single word. Isn't that wonderful, Wil, so old, to have a memory so strong? Well, it's all in there, although I haven't read it myself. And I wouldn't understand if I did. But don't think the emperor's men don't know about you, because they surely do. And you terrify them. Yes you do, Wil. You give them weak knees!"

Preposterous. Wil began to say so. But he kept silent.

It occurred to him that every morning Count Marston Ker Veermander awoke yearning for the ancient realm's return. Let Marston dream, Wil thought.

That evening, at supper, up from the creek, hooves thudded. Out from the hemlocks galloped a pair of plow horses, ridden by two young men.

"The galley!" cried one youth, jumping down. "It's just starting around the bend!"

"They're on the deck, looking at the shore," said the other.

Marston received the news with merely a headshake.

"So soon," Wil heard him mutter. Aloud, he asked the youths: "How long?"

From their lookout spot, they'd galloped all the way, the youths said. One hour, they guessed. No more. Then the galley would reach the creek.

Marston rose up. He looked down upon all their faces, each one. In his expression, Wil saw immense fondness.

"Do what we planned," Marston said. "All to the boats!"

Wil sat not knowing what to do.

"They'll disperse up the river, to our friends and relatives, until the galley goes," Marston told him.

As he spoke, the women cleared the table of crockery, for the plates revealed how many had dined. The men ran to the huts, emerging with bundles of clothing and other possessions, to carry down to the boats.

"Wil, into the forest," Marston said.

He told Wil to row his skiff farther up the creek, and he explained where to hide it, in the place the Foresters hid their boats. He described the safe route through the trees to the hermit's cave.

"It's not so far, Wil," Marston assured him.

But they both knew night was coming on.

Marston's wife passed, on her way to the boats. She presented Wil with an old knapsack.

"Food," she said.

Marston and his wife then embraced. Wil saw tears on her cheeks. And, in Marston's eyes, gazing down at her, he saw love.

In a moment, the last of them disappeared down the path to the dock. Wil stood alone in front of the manor, with Marston and Marston's grandmother.

"Hurry," Marston told him.

"Where will you go?" Wil asked.

Marston laughed. It was as if Wil had uttered a fine joke.

"Why, we'll go sit in our wicker chairs on that veranda, just like every night," Marston said.

Wil stared at him.

"Obfuscation!" Marston said. "That will be our little task. Isn't that right, Grandmama?"

He gave Wil a sly wink.

"Bamba Moke...." Wil said.

Marston held up a hand. He waggled it from side to side.

"We'll be telling those constables we live here all alone, won't we, Grandmama?"

Marston stood silent a moment, lips pursed, as if composing in his mind exactly what he would tell the constables.

"And we'll be telling them we surely did see you," he said. "And that we wanted nothing to do with anyone defying the mingling rules, so we gave you a chicken leg and sent you on your way, and that we saw you cross the river to the other side, because we wanted to make sure you went, and—looking way over to that eastern shore—we saw you turn south, just a speck, and that you looked to be rowing hard. And it relieved us, seeing you go. How does that sound?"

Wil groaned, in anguish.

"Marston, get into one of those boats!" he cried. "You and your grandmother! Row for your life!"

Marston laughed.

"Why, you do see what I am, Wil," he said with a wink. "Wouldn't I just sink one of those puny rowboats? And then what about all the others? And you know Grandmama is too old for nautical adventures, and that she would never leave this old manor, so don't you worry, and you hurry along, Wil."

"Come into the forest with me," Wil urged. "Hide!"

"Hide?" Marston said.

It seemed to Wil that his host's mild gray eyes now had iron in them.

"I am Count Marston Ker Veermander," he said. "Grandmama is the Countess Dola Ker Veermander. This is our ancestral home. We are host here, and hostess, and we do not run and hide."

"Please!" Wil said.

Marston shook his head. He and his grandmother walked to the veranda. They sat side by side in their wicker chairs.

Wil followed them. He held out his hands, begging.

"No, we do need to make those constables welcome, and engage their attention," Marston said, chuckling. "What stories we'll tell! Grandmama and me! And all that time our people will be rowing away up the river. And you, Wil! You'll be vanishing into those trees. So much depends on that."

Wil looked at him. He started to speak.

Marston held up a hand.

"Everything depends on you, my good friend," he said. "Do your important work. And remember the count and countess! Remember—they served with honor!"

Wil lifted the knapsack Marston's wife had given him. Walking backwards, he watched Marston and his grandmother sitting on their veranda. For all his bulk, Marston sat lightly in his wicker chair, one leg crossed easily over the other. And his grandmother sat beside him like a tiny rag doll, with fierce eyes.

Wil pushed his skiff into the creek. With a savage dig of one oar, he turned it upstream. He rowed, splashing his oars as if he struck an enemy. Behind, in the stream tunneling under overarching hemlocks, the skiff left a churned wake, leading back to the manor's dock. But the dock dwindled, grew dim. And then he no longer saw it.

He rowed less angrily now. He sank the oars' blades into the water steadily. A not caring came over him. A numbness.

He stopped rowing, to listen. But he heard no sounds from the manor. It seemed far away.

So he rowed on.

Gradually, the creek slimmed. Marston had said it would. He came to a spot where cattails grew out into the water. Here he turned toward the shore. As he'd been told, behind the cattail marsh, hidden from the creek, a small stream flowed into the creek. He rowed up this stream until his skiff became engulfed in a willow swamp. He couldn't see ahead. However, following instructions, he pushed through and found himself in a tiny, watery clearing. He saw a rowboat drawn up on shore.

He recognized it. He'd seen it docked that night at Horse Skull Island, the Foresters' boat. He ran his skiff onto the bank beside it. Climbing ashore, he pulled the skiff farther up. He removed his knapsack from the boat and flopped it onto the ground, then sank down beside it, under the willows, and held his head in his hands.

He huddled that way a while. Finally, he sat up. He looked eastward, toward the manor.

"Goodby, my good friend," he said.

Then he stood, slung his knapsack over his shoulder, and looked about. All around rose the great forest. Night gathered. High over his head, the entangled branches held only faint violet light.

"From where you put in your boat, walk west," Marston had said. "Every time you come to one of those giant pines, you stay to its right. And every time you come to a giant fir, you stay to its left. And you'll see a birch, a giant white thing amidst all those gloomy evergreens. Then you'll be close."

So he'd been told.

He started westward. Trunks rose around him, each thicker than his Fishtown hut. He seemed to walk among great columns, as in a temple. Because of the brown needles under his feet, layered deep, the walking was soft. His shoes made no sound.

But the forest wasn't silent.

He heard whisperings.

In Fishtown, whenever he stood at the great forest's edge, he heard such whispers, but here they seemed clearer. They spoke all around him, high and low.

"What moves below?"

"Two legger."

"Darkness comes."

"To the nest."

Off in the darkness, something stretched after a long day's sleep. He felt its hunger. He felt its readiness to prowl.

In another place, he felt a tininess, scurrying across brown needles, drawn from a hiding place into danger by a scent of seed.

After he walked a while, he had another sensation. Something feline moved. He felt its interest in him, to itself thinking, "What is this?"

He felt it following.

"Too large a one?" it thought.

Wil reached into his trouser pocket. He withdrew the dagger Bamba Moke had given him. Holding it, he walked on, his nape's hair standing up.

56

"It holds a fang. It walks resolute. Not this one."

And the threat faded away into the forest.

Before long Wil could barely see where he put down his feet, for it was the nether side of twilight. He found himself relegating the voices he heard to the back of his thoughts. Sometimes, he again sensed some large creature taking an unfriendly interest in him, and he instantly became alert, but most of the voices issuing from the darkness among the trees concerned themselves with other things, and he learned to let them whisper without listening. He concentrated on finding his way. Right of pines. Left of firs. But now it was too dark to distinguish pine from fir.

Off in the darkness under the trees, something laughed. It sounded wicked.

He stopped, heart beating.

Again he heard the laughter. But it dwindled away.

Enchantments from long ago lingered in the forest. That he knew.

He walked on, listening for the laughter to resume. Instead, behind him, he felt menace.

He heard nothing. Saw nothing. Yet, it crept slowly toward him through the trees. He felt it. It seemed like a shriek, yet he heard no sound.

He sank against a tree's trunk and pulled out his little dagger, clenching it, staring into the darkness, feeling the invisible menace about to engulf him. Then it vanished. He sat breathing hard, his back against the great tree's trunk.

Should he stumble on in the dark? Should he sit here, holding his dagger, waiting for dawn? He felt weary. Terrified as he was, an uneasy sleep might come upon him. What might happen then?

Somewhere over his left shoulder, how far into the trees he could not discern, he heard sighing. It sounded like bereavement, or like wind in pines. He thought he heard a voice chanting, but couldn't make out any words.

"Who are you?" he called. "Can you help me?"

Abruptly, the chanting stopped. Then, to his right, farther off, it resumed. A different sound now, like a choir singing in a language he didn't know, voices ethereal and high.

Wil jumped to his feet.

Instantly the singing stopped.

Off among the trees, a yellow flickering. It bobbed up and down, gliding towards him. Two tree trunks away, it winked out.

Something snickered, full of malice. On his nape, the hairs stood up.

He ran. He heard that wicked laughter, chasing him. He tripped over a root, sprawled, struggled back to his feet, ran on. Something whipped his face. Something grasped him around the belly. With a cry, he reached down to pull it off him. Branches. He wrenched them away, to run on. But he felt the bush reach out and grab his ankle. He toppled onto his face. He lay, gasping. After a while he reached down and pulled the branch from his ankle.

Wicked laughter again.

He reached into his knapsack. He pulled out a piece of roasted chicken, put there for him by Marston's wife.

Staring fiercely in the direction of the laughter, he bit into the chicken. He ate it, defiantly, throwing down the bone. Then he grabbed a slab of buttered bread from the knapsack. He ripped off a chunk and stuffed it into his mouth. He chewed it and swallowed. Then he ate more.

He still heard laughter. But it sounded changed. Maniacal. Crazed. He realized the laughter he now heard was his own.

His laughter stopped, with a sob.

Silence.

He sat beside his knapsack in the darkness. He tried to fill his mind with the kindness of Marston's wife. At such a time, she'd thought to give him a knapsack of food. It almost calmed him.

But then he felt a tickle at his nape. He sat, frozen, as something—oh, so lightly—entwined around his neck. A cold entwining, and slimy. Almost imperceptibly, it tightened.

Wil yelled.

He yanked the thing off, and then he ran, blind in the dark.

Something smacked him onto his back. He got to his feet, ran again. He tripped, continued running on his knees, regained his feet, ran on, and then—suddenly—he could run no more.

Warm wetness gripped his feet, like oatmeal. He tried to lift his legs, but the ooze rose to his knees. He felt himself sinking.

It reached his chest. He flailed his arms. He yelled for help, but who could hear?

In the darkness, a thud, as of ponderous feet on the forest floor, and a sound like a cough—he tried to yell again, but the warm thickness gripping him rose above his mouth.

CHAPTER FOUR

He lay on his back.

Above him rose an immense white birch. Through its leaves, spread high overhead, he saw specks of blue sky.

He felt like lying here forever, peacefully listening to the small voices all about...

"That branch, a long leap—I can do it! I did!"

"Raspberries!"

"This hole's dark, among the roots, and what's inside? Hmm? Shall I see?"

He sat up.

He remembered stumbling through darkness, into a morass that sucked him down, closed over his head.

A dream?

No. Dried mud covered his shoes and trousers, his shirt, too, and his hands. Probably dried mud made his face gray.

Somehow, he'd fetched up under this great birch. It rose in a small clearing, its white bark bright amidst the surrounding evergreens. How did he escape the morass? He didn't remember. And how did his knapsack come to lie beside him?

He got up and searched among the trees for the morass, but found only a small pool, where rainwater collected in a hollow under a spruce. He drank. Then he removed his clothes and bathed. Finally he washed his clothes, too, and spread them on low-growing bushes to dry.

In his knapsack he found yet another piece of chicken, and more buttered bread. He ate it all. It made him think of Marston, and his kestrel-eyed grandmother, and Marston's wife, who'd thought to give him food at such a moment, and of all the manor people. He thought, too, of Bamba Moke, who hid him. But he shook the thoughts away.

"Do your important work," Marston had told him.

He didn't know what that important work might be. He didn't even know what to do next, lost in the great forest.

As he sat by the little pool, he noticed a patch of fallen pine needles, the color of old rust, slightly indented, as if something heavy stepped here. Farther on, he saw a similar patch, and another. He followed until he came to a swath of moist earth, under a cedar, left from a recent rain, and there he saw a full print, the size of a dinner plate.

It was the pawprint of an enormous bear.

It didn't alarm him. Why he didn't know, except that it felt so peaceful under these trees.

By now his clothes had nearly dried. So he dressed again.

It occurred to him that the huge birch might be the tree to which Marston had directed him—"And you'll see a birch, a giant white thing amidst all those gloomy evergreens. Then you'll be close."

Just beyond the birch, a shale ridge thrust up from the forest floor, forming a wall twice Wil's own height, and near its center he saw an opening, large enough for even an enormous bear to enter.

It's the hermit's home, he thought. And the hermit is a huge bear.

He stood at the cave's mouth, peering into the blackness. He wondered how to address a hermit bear. Finally he simply spoke.

"Hello, Bear," he said.

Silence from the cave.

"I'm Wil Deft," he said. "Can you help me find the Foresters?"

From deep in the cave, he heard a sound like a cough.

Wil waited. But no further sounds issued from the cave. He remembered conversing with the black cat, forming the words in his mind.

"Will you help me find the Foresters?" he said, speaking that way. "I think they seek me."

This time he did hear a voice from the cave, although not with his ears. It was low, the words slow.

"From the slough," the voice rumbled. "Heard fear. Pulled you."

"Thank you, Bear," Wil said.

Both were silent.

Wil finally spoke again.

"I'm lost and alone," he found himself saying. "I can't go back to where I'm from, but I don't know the way to the Foresters. Would you tell me the way?"

"No."

So said the rumbling voice from underground.

"But what shall I do?" Wil said.

"Wait," said the voice.

"Why won't you tell me?" Wil asked.

No response.

Wil waited. He thought he heard that voice from the cave speak again. But not to him. Its message seemed directed far off into the forest. And he could not decipher the bear's low rumble. So he continued to sit by the cave's mouth, waiting.

An hour passed. Wil sat, exasperated with the bear.

"Why won't you tell me?" he asked again.

This time he heard an answering rumble from beneath the ground.

"Twisting journey. Dangers! Wait."

Nothing happened. Wil sat with his chin on his hands, looking gloomy.

From the light shining through the branches high above, he judged the sun had moved across the sky, and now started down. He sighed. He lay on his back. He dozed. But an approaching sound made him sit up.

Something black flapped toward him, weaving its way among the great trunks. A raven. It perched on a branch of a nearby fir, a low-growing sapling. Fussily, the raven adjusted its weight, fanning out its tail feathers. Then it preened its breast feathers with its beak, head turning from side to side. It seemed to ignore Wil, sitting just below. But, after a while, he noticed the bird studying him as it turned its head, first with one sharp eye, then the other.

A high-pitched voice spoke, but not to him.

"So that's the one, the skinny one, the yellow-headed one, hah!"

A low rumble from the cave.

"Lal, Tobi. To be fetched."

Still eyeing Wil, the raven poked its bill into the feathers under one wing. It seemed preoccupied.

"Go now!" Again the rumble from the cave.

Instead, the bird poked its beak into the feathers under its other wing.

Wil sensed, from the raven, mischief. And from the cave he detected rising irritation.

"Go. They seek this one!"

"Hmm," the raven said, staring up toward the intertwining branches high overhead. "A bite! Time for a bite! Shall I forage among the trees? What might I find?"

"Orphan. They fed you. Reared you. Asked now, do for them! Always!"

Wil thought he saw the raven eye the cave mouth with amusement.

"And you, fat lumberer, whose stupid mother lost him among the trees—they reared you, too! And what now? Hide in your hole! Hide in your hole!"

"Nights for roaming," rumbled the bear. Wil sensed mounting anger from the bear, which seemed to make the raven's sharp eye twinkle.

"Ooh, that hole in the ground smells, ooh, ooh, like spoiling meat down there!"

From the ground, a snarl: "Mine."

Now the raven stood on its branch, staring at the cave mouth, as if thinking. Abruptly, it drooped, tail down, wings slack, neck bent.

"Failing," whined the high voice. "So hungry. Fly for Lal and Tobi? Too weak. Starving. Goodbye, Bear. Now I go into the darkness...."

From the cave, rage radiated. Wil heard a roar. And then the cave's mouth filled with the head and shoulders of an enormous black bear, its little eyes red with fury. One of its huge paws clenched a chunk of meat, which it hurled at the raven.

"Eat!" the low voice rumbled as the great bear retreated back into the earth. "Eat, then fly."

Instantly the failing raven recovered its vigor. It gave Wil a glance that seemed amused, and fluttered down to the meat.

"Generous bear," the raven said. It pecked thoughtfully at the meat. It pecked again and again, until just a bite remained.

"Stupid bear. Lal and Tobi—already summoned. By you! For the manor people. Not far. You could have called them yourself. Good meat!"

From the cave a roar. Teeth snapping, the bear erupted from the earth, running at the raven in a rage, its great paws thudding on the ground. Wil, terrified, ran to the trees. But the raven looked unconcerned. As the bear charged, it continued to peck at the meat. At the last moment, it fastened its beak on the final chunk and carried it up into the sapling, where it perched jauntily, eating.

Angry now beyond thought, the bear swiped at the sapling with one huge paw, ripping it from the ground by its roots. Startled, the raven flapped upwards, hovering, wings beating.

"Peace be with you, my friend," the raven said blandly.

The bear jumped at the bird. But the raven fluttered higher.

"Go!" roared the bear, jumping again.

From his hiding place behind a spruce, Wil felt the ground tremble as the huge bear fell back onto its hind paws.

"Goodbye, fat one," said the raven, as it set out through the trees, southwesterly. "Goodbye, lazy hole-dweller," it said, its high-pitched voice fading as it flew away. "Goodbye, rump of lard…."

Glaring toward the disappearing raven, the bear roared in frustration and anger, making Wil cower behind the tree. Dropping back to all fours, it thudded toward its cave, grumbling. Wil watched it disappear back underground. Only then did he come out from behind his spruce.

He considered saying something to the bear, a mollifying word. But he thought better of it. Gingerly, he sat down with his back against a tree, farther from the cave than he'd sat before. It grew dimmer now. Wil gave the cave mouth frequent glances, fearful the enraged beast would emerge. But he heard nothing from the cave. After a while, when darkness came, he lay on his back. His eyes closed.

Off in the forest he heard snickerings, and that wicked laughter he'd heard last night. Once, faintly, he heard a flute. But the sounds didn't frighten him here, although he hoped the bear wouldn't blame him for its irritation with the raven.

After a while he closed his eyes.

"He's sleeping, Lal."

"So?"

"He should rest for our journey."

"Foolish, this one. Runs from help."

"It's good for him to nap, Lal. I want to nap."

"Of course you do—Tobi naps, eats, plays with a stick, naps, eats...."

"Hah! What about you? Lal chases mice, eats tiny bites, naps, stalks bugs, naps again...."

Hearing the voices in his sleep, Wil awoke.

Dawn light dimly illuminated the forest. But it was enough for Wil to see.

To his left sat the black cat with white whiskers, Lal, who'd appeared at his Fishtown hut. To his right sat a small dog. He'd seen this dog only in silhouette at night, in the Foresters' boat at the Horse Skull Tavern. Now he saw it to be honey-colored, with white face markings and white socks, and perked-up ears. It had no tail. Its legs were preposterously short. It sat glaring across Wil's supine body at the cat. The cat, irritably twitching her tail, blue-eyed, glared back at the dog.

Wil sat up.

"Hello," said the dog, seeming to smile.

"Now we'll go," the cat said. "The way is long."

She stood, stretched, licked a paw.

"I'm Tobi," the dog said, ignoring the cat.

"Hello," Wil said, feeling odd, talking this way to a dog.

"Bear might have food for us," Tobi said. "Do you think he does, Wil?"

Wil thought of the half-rotted chunk of meat the bear threw at the raven. Involuntarily, he grimaced.

"I don't think so," he said.

Palpable disappointment emanated from Tobi. Lal looked at the dog with disgust.

"Walking stomach," she muttered. "Eats, naps, eats, naps...."

Tobi ignored the cat. He brightened now, smiling at Wil.

"We'll be friends," he said.

"Are you taking me to the Foresters?" Wil asked.

"Unless you run away again," Lal said dryly.

Wil stood. After thinking a moment, he walked to the mouth of the cave.

"Thank you, Bear," he said.

From below, he heard only a low rumble, "hmmm." But the bear no longer sounded enraged.

Wil tried to think of something else to say to the bear. But he couldn't. So he simply expressed a wordless sense of gratitude. Then he slipped into the straps of his now empty knapsack. He turned and followed the cat and dog into the forest.

They walked southwestward.

For a long stretch they plodded in murky shadow, under evergreens. Pitch and spruce gum scented the air. Later, they walked among ancient maples and hickories and ashes. Here the light brightened, faintly green. Their feet scuffled leaves fallen in former years, sending up a dry aroma. It reminded Wil of Fishtown's late-autumn Day of the Catch. Then children ran through the streets flying fish-shaped kites—Wil, too, once—and villagers roasted river fish and yams over leaf fires, for the smoky flavor. Remembering the smell of those smoldering leaves, Wil felt his stomach ache a little. It ached from hunger, but also because he could never return to that village life. It made him anxious.

Mostly the dog and cat bickered.

"We should go the mountain way," he heard Tobi say.

67

"Why?" Lal sneered. "Truffles?"

"It's shorter," Tobi said. "Up and over."

"Truffles, truffles, truffles—Tobi thinks in his belly."

Tobi plodded sullenly behind the cat. Abruptly he surged ahead, shouldering the much smaller Lal aside. Now he sauntered in the lead, visibly pleased with himself.

For a while Lal padded behind silently, radiating malice.

"What if they eat him?" she said finally. "Those foul night things? Back at the High City, what will you say? For truffles?"

"Up and over, shorter," the dog insisted, smugly.

After a few paces, Wil heard Tobi mutter to himself: "Truffles, truffles, mountain truffles, yum."

Lal: "Hah!"

As they trekked deeper into the ancient forest, Wil noticed the great trunks thickening, the branches spreading higher. Lal and Tobi continually bickered, but he no longer listened. Ever more clearly he discerned the thoughts of forest animals creeping about them, or leaping high above, or flying. And below those intertwining voices he sensed a resonant hum. It seemed eons old. It was about cold moisture, drawn from deep in the soil, and about sunlit crowns, and the turning of days, and seasons, and he knew it was the trees humming, inside their bark.

When the light dimmed, now slanting from the west, Lal and Tobi stopped at the end of a small glen. Wil had never noticed any particular trail they followed. They zigzagged. Aromas lured Tobi aside. A rustle under a bush would draw Lal. But generally they moved southwesterly. All day Tobi and Wil ate nothing. Lal snagged a mouse, but refused to share it with Tobi. She climbed to the top of a sapling hemlock to eat it. After that, Tobi looked increasingly sullen. Wil, too, felt famished and a little cranky.

Now the dog and cat sat facing each other. Wil flopped onto the ground. He rested the back of his head against a knob of root projecting up from the forest floor. But it was uncomfortable, so he made a pillow of the knapsack Marston's wife had given him. He'd emptied it of food, but he carried it anyway, now his only possession.

"We'll go the mountain way," he heard Tobi say brightly.

Lal, radiating disgust, licked the fur on her chest.

"That's a good way to go," Tobi said.

He gave Wil an engaging smile.

"Shouldn't we, Wil? Go the mountain way? Up and over?" Tobi asked. With his pink tongue, he licked his own nose.

"I don't know," Wil told him. "I don't know the paths."

"It's good, the mountain way," Tobi said. "You'll like it, Wil. And I know where truffles grow, so we can have a snack."

Lal turned pointedly away from the dog. She stared at Wil.

"In the mountains foul things lurk," she said, words dripping malice. "Maybe they'll eat you."

Tobi snorted, derisive.

"She just wants her own way, Wil," he said. "Don't listen to her."

"Safer, the valley way," Lal told Wil. "We'll pass a Forester village—food."

"Too far, far, far," Tobi said, glaring at the cat.

"Truffles!" Lal said. "Tobi eats truffles. Then a mountain night thing eats Tobi. 'Ah,' it says. 'Doesn't this taste just like a little truffle?'"

Tobi, aloud, barked at the cat. Then he turned away from her. He sat staring stubbornly into the forest.

Lal spoke to Wil, emphasizing each word.

"He's-not-capable-of-making-his-own-decisions."

Wil turned up his eyes. All day they'd bickered. It put him out of sorts. So did his hunger. Why should he decide? He didn't know the forest. He didn't know the routes. Why did the Foresters send these squabbling animals?

"Well, how much longer is the valley way," he asked wearily.

"Days longer, Wil," Tobi said earnestly. "Days and days." Sullenly, to himself, the dog muttered: "Nothing to eat."

"But on the mountain there are dangers?" Wil asked.

"Don't be scared, Wil, because I'll be there," Tobi said.

"Hah!" Lal said.

Wil put his head in his hands and sighed. Finally he looked up.

"This valley way," he said to Lal. "No dangers there?"

"Bad things, that way, Wil," Tobi immediately interjected. "Mires and trees that whip at you and forest lions and great flowers that suck you in and…."

"That way's dangers we can avoid," Lal said. "Go around, sneak by, not so hard."

"No food, the valley way, Wil," Tobi said. "Not for a long, long, long time…let's go the mountain way, up and over."

"Both fools," he heard Lal mutter to herself.

Never a kind word, Wil thought bitterly. Not one. His stomach ached from hunger. He knew it muddled his mind. Even so, a rude cat. A bossy cat. It irked him, a cat who regarded herself superior. Tobi, on the other hand, respected him. Tobi liked him. He could tell. And something to eat soon! That thought he found irresistible.

"Then we'll go the mountain way," Wil blurted out, surprising himself.

Tobi immediately barked for joy and victory.

Lal hissed.

Upon her two companions she turned ice-blue eyes.

"Then go alone, worm brains," she said.

With a switch of her tail, she walked off among the trees. She   was   gone.

Wil had now followed Tobi for two hours. Because aromas frequently drew the dog aside, they trod an erratic path. But mostly they walked westward. In late evening, the ground beneath their feet began slanting up. Walking grew harder. Now darkness was almost upon them. Wil barely saw Tobi ambling ahead, but he heard his prattling.

"...truffles, truffles, not long, Wil, because I remember, you go up....Lal thinks she knows everything. It's better just us. Do you like truffles, Wil? Do you like the mountain way? Up and over. Smell that badger over there. Let's let him be...."

Wil caught Tobi's memory of a previous badger encounter. Teeth. Razor claws. A torn leg. A painful limp home.

"...so we don't like badgers, do we, Wil? Let's go this way, around these rocks.   Do you think it's a good way? We're friends now. I like you, Wil. When we get back to High City we'll have the same room. I like to be with you. Now we're hungry, aren't we? Truffles, truffles, mountain truffles, yum...."

In fact, Wil felt famished. He wondered when those promised truffles would appear. Not tonight, he suspected. They now climbed the slope in the dark. He repeatedly stumbled over rocks.

"Tobi, let's stop until morning," he said.

"Truffles," Tobi said. "Up ahead."

"How far?" Wil asked.

From the dog came only a desolate feeling of hunger and not knowing.

"Let's stop," Wil said, with a mental sigh. "We'll go on when it's light."

"All right, Wil."

71

Later that night Wil sat up, heart pounding.

He'd dreamed of Fishtown, the Day of the Catch, a feast table lined with platters of leaf-roasted fish and yams, and just-baked oat bread, bowls of honey, plates of raspberries....

What awoke him?

Off in the trees, a blue glow.

It bobbed near the ground, a globe. It rose, sank again. Watching it waft among the trees, Wil felt his nape's hair rise up. It searched. He was sure. And he knew, somehow, it hunted Tobi and him.

"What's that?"

Tobi had awakened. He sat up, peering groggily at the blue glow moving in the forest.

"Shh," Wil said. "It'll find us."

"But, Wil...."

"Shh!"

Off among the trees, the blue thing stopped, floated upwards, almost as if it heard. It turned, this way, that way. Tentatively, it moved toward them, weaving among the trees, closer. Wil unconsciously reached out and pulled Tobi to him, feeling the dog's warmth and his breathing. He tried to empty his mind of thoughts. He hoped Tobi would be content to be held, and wouldn't prattle.

Closer.

Wil now saw the blue globe more clearly: a disembodied eyeball. Its iris seemed smoky, as if almost blind.

"I don't like it, Wil!"

Instantly the glowing blue eye's smokiness considerably cleared. It stared toward them. But it didn't yet see them. Wil was sure.

He sat in the dark, holding the dog, staring in horror at the floating eyeball. He imagined himself an ancient ash. He tried to hum the tree song, about cold moisture and sunlit crowns. Trees all around hummed. He tried to intertwine his own chant with theirs. It was a way to hide. For he believed the eyeball tracked them by their thoughts.

Smoke again occluded the blue eye. It moved to their left, searching. Abruptly, it shot high up. Wil saw it among the treetops, then above the forest. It flashed away toward the west, up the mountain.

It left Wil shaken. He thought about the morning, when they'd start again up the mountainside. He felt dread. Yet, they'd come too far to go back. If they didn't find food soon, they'd starve.

"Tobi," he said, as they sat in the dark, too frightened to resume sleeping, "where are the truffles?"

"Up," Tobi said. "I remember we climbed up, Wil. And the trees got small and far apart, and I found truffles."

"How often have you come this way?" Wil asked.

"Just once," Tobi said brightly.

"And what was at the top of the mountain?" Wil asked, because he had a terrible feeling about the blue eyeball.

"I don't know," Tobi said. "Isn't it nice being together like this?"

Wil now questioned the dog. He learned that Tobi had never actually climbed over the mountain. He and Lal, on one of their Forester missions, sought a shortcut home. Instead of going around the mountain range, they tried crossing it. By evening they reached the patch of truffles Tobi remembered with such relish, but Lal sensed danger ahead. Then she saw creatures moving in the night. They stood her fur up. At dawn, she led Tobi, protesting, away from the truffles, back down the mountain to their regular route.

"I wanted more truffles," Tobi complained now. "Too bossy. Do you like her when she does that, Wil?"

Lal had called them "worm brains."

Worm brains we are, Wil thought. Both of us.

For the rest of the night they sat side by side, Tobi leaning against Wil's leg, Wil's arm over the dog. Tobi eventually dozed. Wil, however, kept watch. He feared what might next come down the mountain.

With dawn came fog. All around the trees seemed dimmed. A wind gusted, cold and damp. Wil nudged Tobi awake. The dog stretched, yawned, then sat looking blankly at the fog, which writhed in the gusts.

"Let's find truffles," Wil said.

Once more they started upwards. Beneath their feet the slope steepened. Wil felt weak, chilled. Hunger dulled him. Tobi no longer prattled. They climbed silently, both breathing heavily. Gradually, the forest thinned. The trees shrank. Boulders frequently blocked their way, forcing them to go around.

Wil saw no blue eyeballs. Only a raven flapped up from below. It alit upon the tip of one of the slope's small firs. Maybe it was the raven that tormented Bear. Wil didn't know. From its treetop perch the black bird watched them struggle upward. After they passed, Wil heard it croak overhead. He saw it glide up the mountainside. It faded away in the fog.

At some point, the ground leveled. As if awakening from a doze, Wil saw they'd reached a broad shelf on the mountainside, protected from the wind. Here oaks grew. Squirrels chattered in the branches. Tobi sat, looking dully about. Then he barked.

"Truffles!" Wil heard him say. "Here, here, here!"

He watched Tobi zigzag through the grove, nose to the ground. Abruptly, the dog stopped, dug. Looking triumphantly back at Wil, he pulled a tan blob from the earth with his teeth, and ate it.

Later, they lay under the oaks, truffle filled and sleepy. By now the fog had lifted a bit. Overhead, the grayness seemed brighter.

"Should we go back down the mountain and try to find Lal?" Wil asked.

"I think I'll want to eat more truffles," Tobi said. "They're good, aren't they, Wil?"

"Yes, good," Wil said.

He felt stronger. But he hadn't slept last night, and his legs ached from climbing. He guessed the ridge remained far above them. To continue upwards frightened him. What lurked up there? Better, he decided, to descend. They'd go the valley way after all. Maybe they'd find Lal. But for now they'd rest. Later they'd eat more truffles, and grow stronger. He'd pack truffles into his knapsack, to eat as they trekked through the forest.

"Isn't it nice, lying together here like this?" Tobi asked, almost asleep.

"Yes, it is," Wil said.

He slept.

He awoke in darkness. He couldn't move, numb, all but his eyes.

"Tobi?" he called, in his mind.

No answer.

Water gurgled. Dripped.

After a while the numbness ebbed to his neck, then his shoulders. He could move his mouth, and his tongue.

"Help!" he yelled.

His cry reverberated. He lay, he thought, in a cavern.

"Supper?"

Time had passed. How long he didn't know. He couldn't see the speaker. His mind heard the rasping voice.

No numbness now. Even so, he couldn't move, lying on his back, on rock. Something wrapped him, pinioning his arms and legs. His body ached.

"Tobi?" he called.

No answer.

"Spit them?"

Another rasping voice.

"Sting's worn off, on the big one."

"I like an arm."

"Leg."

"Who gets the little morsel?"

Many voices, all rasping.

"Raw, ripped apart?"

"No, spit roasted."

He heard a scuffling, as of many feet. Flints struck. Flames licked up, then roared. In the orange light, one of them scuttled by.

Eight-legged.

Twice his size.

It toted sticks to the fire. Its forelegs ended in hairy hands, clawed.

Body black, yellow-striped.

Another loomed over him, looking down. A head like a human skull. White hair. Fangs.

Ruby eyes studied him.

"Not much meat."

Wil realized his body lay shrouded in gray. Beside him lay a smaller gray bundle. Tobi.

He thought: "We're wrapped in cobweb."

One eight-legger approached carrying an iron shaft.

"You grab him, I'll spit him."

Clawed hands dug into his shoulders, hoisting him. Other hands aimed the spit down his open mouth—he screamed. He shut his eyes, still screaming. He waited for the iron to plunge through his living body. Would he know, when they put him over the flames?

A clattering on the cave's stone floor. The spit?

He felt himself dropped onto the stone. He opened his eyes.

Beside him, crumpled, lay the spit wielder. Dead.

Above floated the blue eyeball.

No smoke occluded the iris. Its gaze felt like winter.

Wil lay where the eight-legger dropped him, on his side. From this position he saw they all now knelt before the blue eyeball, heads down. One spoke.

"Master…a long patrol, hunger…we forgot, please…."

"Ah, you forgot…."

This new voice was like wind hissing across a basalt crag. Ice was in it, and no mercy.

"Bring them, you were ordered…and you forgot…."

"Yes, Master, never again…hunger…."

Its eight legs abruptly collapsed. It sprawled on the cavern's rock floor, its eyes' red gleam dulled. Each broken joint oozed green.

"Alas, we require yet another sergeant—you, Zelt."

"Yes, Master."

"Your memory, Zelt, is it robust?"

"Master, please…."

"Let us hope. Let us hope. Bring them. Both. Can you remember, Zelt?"

"Yes, Master."

Wil saw the blue eyeball flash away.

Straps now held him atop one creature's back. Behind, another bore the little bundle that was Tobi. They scuttled through the unlit tunnel. Wil saw only red glints from the eight-leggers' eyes. But he heard feet scuffle on stone, and water dripping. He sensed they carried him upward.

"Wil?"

Tobi's voice in his mind.

"I'm here," he said.

"I slept, Wil. Now I can't move."

"I know."

"Did the night things get us?"

"Yes," Wil said. "But I'll think of something."

"I'm glad you're here, Wil."

"I'm here, Tobi."

He tried, as they carried him, to notice their route. But lying immobile on his back, strapped atop an eight-legger's carapace, he saw little. He guessed, from the air's thinness, they had climbed high above the truffle field. Now torches lined the stone tunnel. But they didn't blaze with fire. They emitted a blue light, heatless, undisturbed by air currents.

After a while, the tunnel's raw stone smoothed into black-shot gray marble. They passed a statue, a leather-winged creature, its open beak showing teeth. Farther along, in a wall niche, stood a carved turtle, but with a woman's head, tusked.

Old as the mountain, this place seemed. Or older still.

Now the tunnel leveled. They passed through an arch of carved garnet blocks, each a grinning skull. Beyond, they entered a vast chamber. Unflickering torches lit it blue. Wil guessed they stood in the mountain's hollowed-out crest.

Clawed fingers undid the straps holding him atop the eight-legger. He tumbled onto the slate floor. He heard a thump behind him and, in his mind, Tobi's voice. "Ow."

Silence.

Then he heard again that disembodied icy sibilance.

"Aaaah, our intriguing guest, at last. And his pet. Uneaten. Commendable, Zelt. Release them."

"Yes, Master."

Wil felt claws snip the cobweb shroud binding him. He sat up on the slate floor. Tobi sat beside him. Ahead, against the chamber's marble wall, on an immense stone throne, sat...nothing.

Yet, a Presence occupied that throne. Wil felt its power.

"And what brings a Forester to our mountains, hmmm?"

Wil cringed. It felt ancient, that Presence. And powerful beyond comprehending.

"We lost our way," Wil said. "I'm not a Forester, not really..."

"Yet, you have that charming Forester fragrance, hmmm? That faint scent of petty magic?"

"I know no magic," Wil said.

"No? In that truffle patch, you clouded your thoughts, a clever feat...."

Wil remembered. The Presence had projected itself as the blue eyeball, to hunt them. He hid by mimicking the trees' humming. Was that magic?

"And you have the thought-hearing knack...."

"I was Forester born, they tell me," Wil said. "But I grew up in a river village. A fisherman raised me, and his wife, a washerwoman."

"Fascinating," said the voice. "And the Foresters? They parceled you out for being a naughty boy?"

"I was an infant, and I don't know," Wil said. "Now the emperor's men hunt me. I seek haven with the Foresters—can you tell me the way?"

79

He sensed unkindly amusement. Then, a sudden change in mood.

"They hunt you, do they? The emperor's men...."

Wil felt the Presence before him recede, as if into thought. Abruptly, it flared up, energized. For a moment, he dimly perceived a towering blue shape on the throne. Something thrust into his mind, probing. So powerful was the intrusion that it dropped him to his knees.

Laughter.

Icy glee.

"How pleasing, this visit, Wil Deft," the voice hissed.

He felt himself a game piece, upon a board. He didn't know the game's rules, nor its object, nor the players. How long had the game been underway? He didn't know. Nor how far the play extended. But moves would be made. He'd be moved. And who would move him?

Wil stood.

Beside him, he heard growling. He looked down. Tobi, teeth bared, glared at the Presence on the throne, snarling. Tobi barked.

"Gallant little fellow," said the Presence, but with irritation.

In mid bark, Tobi toppled.

"You've killed him!" Wil shouted.

"No, your pet merely naps. Your little friend needs discipline. Surely you agree?"

Wil felt himself tested. Would threats to Tobi compel him to obey the Presence's power?

"I suppose," Wil shrugged. "I've had no time to train him."

Now the Presence regarded him.

"What do you know about a thousand years?" it demanded.

"It's been a thousand years since the stealing of the Starstone," Wil said. "So somebody told me recently." He shrugged, holding up his palms, to show the information meant little to him.

"Stolen!"

Suddenly the Presence flared again, so that he almost saw it.

"Yes. Stolen from the Forest Kings. But, long before that, the Forest Kings stole it! From its makers! Do you approve?"

"I'm against stealing," Wil said.

"Upstanding! Principled! What a noble young man," said the Presence.

Wil felt mocked. He sensed amused malice. Then, triumph. The voice lowered to a hiss.

"Tell me about the Taker."

That night, at the Horse Skull Tavern, the Foresters used that name. Had they referred to him?

"I know nothing," Wil said.

Again he felt a probe deep into his thoughts. Again it felled him. Then it withdrew. He felt the Presence laughing, exultant.

"What an honest fellow. What shall we do with you?"

"Let us go," Wil said. "We mean no harm. We don't even know who you are. We seek the Foresters. We just lost our way."

"Ah, yet Zelt and his troopers, hungry after their long patrol—shouldn't you be their snack?"

Wil didn't plead. Something in him forbade it.

He sensed the Presence silently laughing.

"Or might you run a little errand?"

Again, something inside forbade Wil to speak. He stood looking toward the huge throne, where he imagined the Presence to be, wondering what moves might be afoot in this game he didn't understand.

"Hmmm, merely a trifling errand. Yet, in its way, delicate. Would you serve? Or would you do better as supper? A decision to be mused upon. Hmmm?"

Wil felt the Presence laugh at him. But he sensed underlying excitement. His coming, he felt, presented the Presence with a possibility, unanticipated. What errand? He didn't know. But his usefulness might keep him alive.

"Zelt, take our Forester friend to that guest room where our last Forester visitor enjoyed our hospitality—how long ago was that social occasion?"

"I don't know, Master. Before my time."

"Yes, it was centuries ago. I believe our current visitor's predecessor still occupies the chamber. It will be convivial. And find some nearby hole where the sleeping pet might lie, awaiting discipline."

Clawed hands carried Wil and Tobi from the chamber, through an arch carved with runes. Beyond the arch, they marched down a tunnel, rounded a bend, then a second turning. Here the eight-leggers tossed the unconscious dog into a tiny stone cage. They carried Wil around a third bend. He could see little in the near darkness, but he heard an iron door clank open. They shoved him, and he tumbled to his knees on stone, hearing the door clank shut behind him.

From down the tunnel came a faint blue glow. One of the torches, Wil supposed. He sat on the stone floor, waiting for his eyes to adjust. Gradually he made out a cell carved from the mountain's rock. It contained no furniture. But in one corner, on the floor, lay something white.

A skeleton.

The previous Forester prisoner, Wil guessed. Dead for centuries.

After sitting despondent a while, Wil got to his feet and looked about his cell. Was there a way out? He tried the door, made of iron bars, and couldn't even shake it. No window. This cell lay deep inside the mountain, Wil guessed.

Dig his way out? It seemed unlikely, but he had no other plan. So he circled the cell's walls, feeling for a loose stone. No stone budged.

The floor?

On his knees, he shuffled across the floor, trying each paving stone in turn, until he reached the reached the skeleton and stopped.

"Pardon me," Wil found himself saying to the dead man. "I have to move you."

Gingerly, he pulled on an arm bone. The skeleton instantly fell apart, clattering on the stones, making Wil gasp.

For a minute he sat gathering nerve. Then he gripped a bone and moved it aside. One by one, he moved them all, to lie atop paving slates he'd already tried. He arranged the skeleton as closely as he could to its original form, which seemed respectful.

Then he tried the stones beneath where the skeleton had lain.

One moved slightly. Wil fingered one side up, but too little to give him purchase. He kept trying, fruitlessly, until an idea came to him.

He removed his belt. Using its buckle as a pry, he managed to lift the stone a bit higher, enough for a grip. It was a large stone, and heavy. But he managed, finally, to wiggle it out of its place in the floor and slide it off to a side. Then he reached eagerly into the cavity that had held it, hoping it might lead to a way out.

He felt solid rock.

But his fingers did touch some small thing in the cavity, like a smooth stone. He pulled it out, peering at it in the dim blue light.

He saw merely a gem, some ornament. It looked milky. An opal, he decided. Yet, inside, he saw faint colors swirl. Reds. Yellows. Where it lay in his palm, his skin tingled, so slightly he decided he imagined it. Otherwise, he seemed to hold an ordinary gem.

And that was all.

Wil sighed.

He guessed his predecessor in this cell hid the little talisman under the floor stone. Then he died.

There was no way out.

For a moment, as Wil stared at the opal, it faintly glowed. At least, so it seemed. Then it dimmed again.

He dropped the gem into his knapsack. Why not die rich?

Then he replaced the stone he had pulled from the floor. He felt it best to keep whatever he did secret.

He shrugged the knapsack off and set it against a wall— the wall farthest from the skeleton. He lay on his back on the stones, using the knapsack as a pillow. He stared at the stone ceiling. He'd do the one thing he could do—he'd wait.

CHAPTER FIVE

He waited.

Somewhere, water dripped onto stone. Occasionally, in his mind, he heard eight-leggers' voices rasp, as they scuttled along distant passageways. He listened, but all he gleaned was a sense of tunnels intertwining far out into the mountain range.

He daydreamed of Fishtown.

He remembered river water slapping skiff hulls. At the Horse Skull Tavern, a blue-eyed barmaid serves golden ale. "Midnight," the watchman cries. "Sleep in peace!"

Mostly he sat vacant eyed.

Why did this cell's former prisoner hide the opal?

That thought awakened him.

He pulled the gem from his knapsack. It seemed an insignificant ornament. It had value. But did that long-dead Forester sneak into these tunnels—swarming with eight-leggers—merely to snitch one small gem?

Perhaps so.

Here he'd lain. Under a death spell, perhaps. Or starving. Or wounded. With his last strength he'd hidden the opal. Surely it was because the Presence must not have it.

Wil decided to return the gem to its hiding place, but before he could again pry up the stone, he heard feet scuffle toward him. Eight-leggers clanged open his cell door. He dropped the opal back into his knapsack. They reached for him, as he shrugged into the knapsack's straps. They carried him off.

"What shall be done with you, hmmm?"

He was back in the blue-lit chamber, before the great throne occupied by nothing visible. He sensed a change in the Presence's mood.

Invisible hands hurled him upward.

He hung, spread-eagled, just beneath the chamber's marble ceiling, slowly turning. He stared down three stories to the stone floor. Let go, he'd plummet, smash.

"Do you understand?"

Wil understood.

His life lay in the Presence's hands. This was a demonstration. He was a flea. At will, the Presence could crush him.

"Ah, so you grasp it. Such a bright young Forester."

He plummeted.

Just above the marble-tiled floor, his fall slowed. He landed lightly on his feet, but his fear-weakened knees buckled, and he sprawled before the throne.

"You shall perform an errand," the Presence said.

"What errand?" Wil asked.

Laughter.

"What does it matter?" the voice hissed in his head. "You will perform it. All the pieces and perturbations and moves and countermoves are in place, beyond your understanding. Only one small adjustment remains."

Wil sat upon the marble slabs. He stared at the empty throne in terror. Yet, deep inside, he felt a thin thread of resolve.

He gasped.

Something unseen, like a white-hot poker, stabbed into his chest.

It seared him inside.

It withdrew.

He sat on the marble floor. All was as before. But he felt changed.

He knew he'd never again be as he was.

"You begin your service, Forester," hissed the voice.

He felt the Presence contemplate him with satisfaction.

Images flickered in his mind. Shadows, he guessed, of the Presence's memories, millennia old. He saw beings so powerful they needed no bodies. He saw them gather starlight. He saw them weave that purest of lights into a talisman. With their own incalculable power they invested it.

Then, perfidy.

The talisman lost.

"You will seek it," the voice hissed. "For that you were bred and born. You will think the seeking is for your own people. Perhaps you will die. But if you finally put your hand on it, what remains of it, this mountain will know. You shall be summoned. You will try to bring it to your kin, but you cannot resist the summons. You are marked. You will bring it here. And then the world, as it was of old, will begin anew."

In all those words, Wil grasped just one thing: the Presence found him useful. And that meant he'd be let go.

"Here is good advice, errand runner—do not tell your Forester friends of your marking. They will slay you!"

Eight-leggers bustled him through tunnels. He tried to remember their route, but they scuttled in darkness. He sensed their way slanted down, and knew each downward step took him farther from the Presence he feared and loathed.

Ahead, dim light. Brightening. The tunnel's mouth. They passed from the subterranean darkness into the sunlit world. Trees towered over them. Thrushes sang. Wil judged they were at the mountain range's base.

Now the eight-leggers slowed. It seemed to Wil they weakened.

At a certain point, the slope's ever lessening slant flattened. Exactly there, the eight-leggers stopped. The claws holding him let go, dropping him to the forest floor. He lay inhaling the aroma of fallen pine needles, sun-warmed and brown.

"Here the Presence's power ends," he thought. "Its creatures can't go farther."

He looked up to see the platoon of eight-leggers climbing back up the hill, at first slowly, but faster as they scuttled higher, until they disappeared among the trees.

Wil lay on the pine needles on his back, looking up through branches to specks of blue sky showing through. Sunshine filtered by the needles overhead warmed his face.

Eventually, he sat up, knowing the stone tunnels lay behind him. The Presence, too, and the blue eyeball, floating over the truffle field.

Wil's features sagged.

"No!"

He clambered to his feet, staring back toward the mountain.

"I can't!"

He turned. He ran through the trees, away from the mountain. As he ran, his knapsack slapped his back. It seemed an admonishment.

He stopped.

Bamba Moke appeared in his thoughts, glaring. Marston Ker Veermander smiled encouragement. He imagined Marston's grandmother, fierce in her madness. Marston's wife offered the knapsack, filled with food.

Wil sat on the pine needles. Resting his elbows on his knees, he put down his head into his hands. Eventually, he sat up, looking bleak, then stood.

"I'm coming, Tobi," he thought.

He thought it dully. Without hope, he trudged back toward the mountain.

Finding the tunnel mouth proved easy. When the eight-leggers carried him down, they'd walked a straight line. So he walked a straight path back up. Soon he came to a black cleft among boulders.

His legs froze.

"You must," he told himself.

He thought of Bamba Moke's sharp rebukes. He remembered Marston Ker Veermander's kindly drawl, too, that intonation of an ancient aristocracy, bound by honor.

He walked—once again—into the darkness.

Far ahead, he saw faint blue light. He'd been stumbling up the dark tunnel for perhaps three hours. Only now had he reached this point, where the unflickering blue torches lit the way. But something followed him.

He sensed it. Once, he thought he heard a dislodged pebble roll a few inches. Once he seemed to hear pattering, like feet in soft shoes. But mostly he simply felt it, something following him up the tunnel.

This was new, this sensing of things unseen and unheard. He wondered if it came from the Presence's marking him. Then he thought, no, it's the opal.

He stopped walking, to pull it from his knapsack. Within its milkiness, faintly, he saw what looked like swirling fire, and he felt a minute movement, as if the gem breathed. Impulsively, he put it into his shirt pocket, near his heart.

He felt alone, and the opal seemed a kind of companion.

Behind him, down the tunnel, he again sensed something silent, moving toward him. He bit his hand to keep from crying out. He had his knapsack. The opal. Anything more?

Patting his trouser pockets, he discovered the Forester dagger Bamba Moke had given him. Long ago, it now seemed.

Against the Presence it would be useless. Against an eight-legger, it would be puny. But he pulled it from its sheath and clenched it.

Should he run?

He'd be running toward the Presence. And his shoes would clop.

He backed against the tunnel's side. He could barely see in the faint light from the far-off torches. Maybe his stalker would pass him by in the dark. He waited, pressing his back harder against the rock, clenching his knife.

"You go the wrong way."

A familiar voice.

He mustered only a mental whisper.

"Lal?"

"I came," she said.

He could just make her out, sitting near his feet, on the tunnel floor, looking up at him. In the faint blue light, her blue eyes glinted. She blinked.

"Lal!" he said.

Abruptly, he sat down hard. He fought the urge to laugh, to clench the cat, hug her to him. She'd dislike that, he guessed.

"Raven saw eight-leggers take you," she said. "Raven fetched me. I came."

And he heard her mutter, as if under her breath: "Worm brains."

"I got free, but Tobi...." Wil said. "I'm going back for him."

"No," Lal said. "Bring you safe. They told us."

He needn't go on! They wanted him safe!

90

He could go with Lal. Back down the tunnel. Out of the mountain. He had no place in the world, except with the Foresters. What they wished, surely he must do.

He sighed.

"I can't leave him," he said.

"Worm brain," Lal said.

But when he started again up the tunnel, she padded beside him.

It came to Wil why the Foresters sent Lal and Tobi on missions. They could hurry through the trees, quietly, sensing dangers. At least, Lal could. She hunted her own food, too. And in villages, a cat or dog would go unnoticed.

Now, as they moved into the tunnel's torchlit section, Wil wondered if eight-leggers would ignore a cat. After all, forest animals must wander into these tunnels. Perhaps even the Presence would disregard a mere cat.

They reached the point where the tunnel's raw stone became gray marble, streaked with black. Here they stopped, listening.

Wil detected far-off voices of patrolling eight-leggers. He sensed no nearby thoughts, not even Lal's.

He studied her, sitting at his feet. Tobi habitually prattled. But most animals, he realized, thought only when they needed to. Otherwise, they maintained a watchful mental stillness.

"Be like Lal!" he admonished himself. "Watch! Be still!"

They walked on. Now they passed wall niches, displaying statues. Wil remembered them. Here stood the leathery winged creature, its open beak showing teeth. Then the carved turtle, its head a woman's, with tusks.

Wil stopped beside a niche displaying a stone chair, lizard legged, its arms fanged snakes. Which way?

91

Tobi's cell lay in a tunnel branching off from the throne room. So to that vast chamber they must go.

Wil shuddered.

"Silence," he told himself.

And he was silent.

In his silence, he heard feet scuttling along marble floors. Not far. Approaching.

Voices rasped.

"Master's gone again. Hey, Zelt? Why patrol?"

"Shut up. Master always returns."

Wil fingered the dagger in its sheath in his pocket. Then he let it go. He could not fight eight-leggers. He stood indecisive. Lal, too, stood frozen on the stone floor, fur up, staring up the passageway.

Wil scooped her up.

He climbed into the wall niche. He sat upon the lizard-legged chair. Holding the cat in his lap, he froze in a pose. He grimaced to show his teeth. Lal seemed to understand. She, too, sat as if carved from stone.

"Check the prisoner?"

They stopped, four of them, before the niche where Wil and Lal pretended to be carvings. Wil fought to keep his thoughts still.

"That stump-legged tidbit?"

Tobi.

"It sleeps still. It's nothing. It's only that yellow-haired one Master wants alive."

"Then let's eat that little one."

"Shut up! Do what we're told."

One eight-legger glanced directly at the stone chair. Wil stayed motionless. His mind, too, kept still. Lal sat frozen, in his lap.

Blankly, the red eyes passed over him. They shifted away.

"Master didn't say where to patrol."

"Storehouse, Zelt. Let's patrol there. Killed grouse in there to munch."

Another eight-legger looked directly at Wil, seated on the lizard-legged chair. Again, the red eyes shifted away, unseeing.

A grunt from Zelt. The platoon scuttled off down the tunnel.

Wil breathed again. Weak-kneed, he climbed down from the wall niche. He put Lal on her feet on the tunnel floor.

How could the eight-leggers look at them, but not see?

"Pilfer!" Wil thought.

It was the Fishtown children's game at which he excelled. "Pilferers" tried to sneak past a "guardian," to steal a stone. If the guardian spotted them, he cried: "Burglar, robber, thief—I bring you grief!" Caught pilferers must freeze. The game ended when all pilferers stood frozen, or one stole the stone. Wil always snatched the stone.

Now he remembered a particular game. Kobar played guardian. He sat beside the stone, resting his back against an apple tree. Wil lay in brush, watching. He saw Kobar scanning the ground for crawling pilferers. Finally, he pointed at one, shouting "Burglar, robber, thief…." At that moment, when Kobar's attention was fixed, Wil quietly climbed the tree against which Kobar leaned. He stood directly above Kobar, in plain sight. Kobar, however, resumed scanning the grass, looking low, not high. Once he did glance up. But his gaze slid past Wil. He sought crawling foes. So he didn't notice Wil in the tree, until Wil jumped down and snatched away the stone.

Now they reached the arch of garnet blocks, each carved into a grinning skull. Wil crouched behind the arch. From that low position, he slid just his left eye past the arch's edge to peer into the throne room.

He didn't sense the Presence. Blue torches still lit the vast chamber. Yet, it felt empty.

Lal, standing beside him, also seemed to sense no immediate danger. She gazed quietly about the room.

Wil remembered the eight-leggers saying the Presence had gone. He silenced his mind, sending his awareness out through the mountain, and the opal—faintly pulsing in his shirt's pocket—seemed to help. He detected nothing. It was as if the Presence had left the world.

Wil stepped into the throne room, then stopped. A trap? He cringed, expecting cold laughter, but heard nothing.

"Go left, I think," he told Lal.

He led her along the great chamber's marble wall, then stopped at an arch, each garnet block carved into a snake's head. He studied it, then walked on. The next arch, carved with eyes, he passed by. At a third arch he stopped. Here each block displayed a rune. Wil couldn't read the ancient writing, but was sure the eight-leggers had carried him and Tobi through this arch to cells in the tunnel beyond.

They rounded a bend in the tunnel, then a second bend. Yes, two bends, he remembered, and there the eight-leggers caged the dog.

He motioned Lal to stop.

Low along the stone wall stood a small recess, shut with an iron-bar door. A lock secured the door. Tobi lay inside. Lit by blue torchlight, the sleeping dog looked blue.

Wil studied the lock. It required a key.

Eight-leggers held the keys.

He sat on the marble floor, wrapped in cobwebs of fear.

An hour later, he still gazed through the cage door at sleeping Tobi. Lal had long ago padded off down the tunnel to

94

scout, but he sat slumped, wrapped in fear-induced lethargy. His mind gnawed at the question: how to steal the key?

It was a Pilfer problem.

Lal returned.

She stared at him, silent. That was good. Eight-leggers might hear. But she conveyed wordless images. Lal turning a tunnel corner. Eight-leggers standing before her. One grabbing for her. Missing. She darts out of reach. They ignore her. Just another forest animal, wandering the tunnels. Good to eat, if caught. Otherwise, unimportant.

Then she showed him Zelt. From the eight-legger sergeant's neck hung a chain. And from the chain jangled keys.

Wil groaned.

On leaden legs, he followed Lal down the tunnel. He had no plan.

At an opening, Lal turned. She led him down stone steps to a new tunnel, cut through raw rock. Lal padded ahead in the blue torchlight to a bend in the passageway. Here she stopped, looking back at him, and he froze. From around the bend, he heard rasping voices.

"Shut up!"

"Master won't know. Let's go out, kill deer."

"We're supposed to patrol inside."

"Fresh meat's better than storeroom meat."

A long pause followed. Wil imagined Zelt thinking, his thoughts like fumes. Fresh meat. Good. Angry Master. Bad. Meat with blood in it...."

"You go."

Zelt's voice sounded sly. Let them take the risk.

"You five go—if Master returns, I'll say we heard something."

Grunts. A sound of many feet moving.

"What you kill, you bring!"

More grunts. Footsteps receding. A sense of all now gone. Except Zelt.

"A game of Pilfer," Wil thought. "Zelt plays guardian."

He peeked around the bend, seeing a chamber opened off the tunnel, entered through a narrow arch of rough-hewn blocks. Silently, he climbed up the arch's blocks, chinks between the stones his toeholds, fingerholds. Near the top, he eased just his left eye around the blocks to peer into the room, a Pilfer trick, spying from an unexpected spot.

Zelt sprawled on a cot, jointed legs splayed. He looked asleep.

Wil climbed down.

He feared words might be overheard, even words in his mind. So he showed Lal images of what she must do. Lal hurrying down the tunnel. Lal watching for the other guards' return.

How long would it take the eight-leggers to hunt down and kill a deer?

Lal padded away. Wil now stood alone, unable to breathe.

"Just a game of Pilfer," he assured himself.

With a sudden inhalation, he stepped into the chamber.

Cots crowded the room, a barracks. Scattered across the floor lay gnawed bones.

Wil dropped to hands and knees, and crawled across the littered floor, careful not to send a discarded bone rolling and rattling. Nearing the eight-legger's cot, he crawled ever slower. Finally, he snaked on his belly. If the creature awoke, he'd be below its line of sight. So he hoped.

He drew close enough to touch the skull-like face. Zelt slept open mouthed, showing pointed fangs. From each fang's tip, a greenish venom oozed. The sleeping eight-legger's breath smelt like congealed blood.

Zelt lay prone. His neck chain dangled over the cot's edge, its iron links ending in a loop of rawhide, holding the keys. Rawhide and keys rested on the floor.

Wil lay still, gazing at the keys. Finally, his mustache curled down in decision and he reached into his trouser pocket for his dagger, wiggling it from its sheath. Clenching the knife, he crawled under Zelt's cot.

Now the keys rested on the floor before his nose. Seven keys.

His dagger's blade must be sharp.

He reached for the rawhide. But his hand shook. He stared at it. "Pilfer," he told himself. It calmed him, this idea of merely playing a game, but he couldn't shake at all. If he inadvertently pulled downward on the leather loop, the iron chain to which it was knotted might clink. Or the pull might awaken Zelt. If he pulled upwards, the keys would rattle against the stone floor.

He stared at the rawhide thong, thinking how to cut it. Finally, with his forefinger, he pressed the leather against the floor. Farther down the strip's length, he pressed his thumb against another bit of the leather, leaving a short strip between his forefinger and thumb, taut against the floor.

He sawed.

His blade made only a faint mark. He spread his fingers, pulling the strip tighter.

Zelt stirred.

Wil froze, dagger blade poised over the rawhide.

No further movement.

Wil sawed.

With each pull of the blade, the cut deepened. Another slice. Now only a thread held the rawhide loop together.

He severed it.

A clink, the chain against the cot.

But the eight-legger lay still.

With his free hand, Wil picked up a key. He moved slowly, fearful of clinking one key against another. He slid it into his trouser pocket. He picked up another. He slid it into his pocket. And another. Seven keys finally rested in his pocket.

It was over.

Now he need only crawl from beneath the cot. Crawl across the floor. Crawl out the arch. Free.

Just a game of Pilfer.

Lal reappeared.

She stood in the archway, staring at him. He received an image. Eight-leggers. Carrying a dead buck. Scuttling toward this barracks room.

Wil crawled from under the cot. Holding his left hand against his pocket to quiet the keys, he crawled on his knees and his right elbow, still clenching the dagger in his right hand.

Lal spat in alarm. She stared toward him, back arched, hair up.

Something dug into his shoulders, lifted him, thudded him onto his back. Zelt loomed over him, ruby eyes smoldering with rage. But they exulted, too. Joy of the kill.

In that head like a skull, the mouth opened. Needle fangs, oozing green.

Wil yelled.

"Master wants me alive!"

But the ruby eyes never flickered, stupidity deflecting the argument, because the eight-legger stood over prey. It must kill.

Wil watched the skull-head, mouth wide, descend towards his neck. He smelled the fetid breath.

A roar, Zelt recoiling, staggering backwards.

Sticking from one ruby eye, a dagger's hilt.

"Did I do that?" Wil thought.

Insanely, he felt guilt.

Zelt crumpled to the floor. His jointed legs writhed, seemingly forever. Finally the writhing stopped. The ruby eyes dulled.

Wil felt sick.

But he forced himself to extend a shaking hand to grasp the dagger's hilt. Its blade slid easily from the eye.

Wil ran, slipping on gnawed bones. He followed Lal from the barracks room into the tunnel, around the bend, his shoes slapping against the stone floor. Unconsciously, he adjusted his gait, running lightly, like Lal.

Up the stone stairway.

Behind them, uproar. The returning hunters had found Zelt dead.

There would be confusion. No leader. So a little time.

But he sensed other eight-legger patrols moving through the tunnels. Some nearby, others far off. Soon, he guessed, the passageways would teem.

Lal stopped, looking back at him. They'd reached the small cage.

Behind the bars, Tobi slept on his side, blue in the torchlight.

Wil pulled the keys from his pockets. He laid them— seven keys—on the stone floor. They all looked alike.

He tried one. It didn't fit. Neither did the next. Nor the next.

He fitted the fourth key into the keyhole, turned it. The lock opened.

Wil clanged open the barred door. Reaching into the cage, he pulled Tobi to him, limp in his sleep.

He lifted the dog in his arms. Wil felt his warmth, and his breathing.

How far could he carry Tobi before his arms wearied?

He shrugged off his knapsack. Gently, he lowered the sleeping dog inside. Tobi just fit. Wil then sat with his back to the knapsack, pulling the straps over his shoulders. To stand, he had to struggle a little against Tobi's weight.

Now they ran back toward the throne chamber. The cat led.

"Faster," Wil admonished himself. "Eight-leggers...."

He followed Lal through the arch with blocks displaying runes. They turned right, ran along the blue-lit chamber's wall. They passed the arch carved with eyes. Then, the arch showing snakes' heads. Just ahead, the arch carved with grinning skulls.

That arch opened into the tunnels slanting down the mountain, out into the sun. If they could just stay ahead....

He hit an invisible wall.

He froze, one foot up for his next step.

A voice hissed, like an icy gust.

It mocked him.

"Burglar, robber, thief—I bring you grief!"

Were he not frozen, he'd crumple to his knees. He'd beg mercy. He'd wail in terror.

But he could only stand as he was, feeling the Presence's cold fury.

"So, Forester—you return to our mountain."

He found no reply.

"Defiance—what might be the penalty?"

From the Presence, he received an image of an inexorable force ripping his left arm from his body. His right arm. His left leg....

"Murder, of a loyal guard—what penalty for that?"

Another image. His body engulfed in blue flames, seared. Eight-leggers eating the cooked carcass.

Wil yearned to fall to his knees. To plead.

But he stood frozen in place.

He felt the Presence study him.

"Gone so briefly, yet you return a little changed."

He saw Lal huddled in the arch of skulls, staring at the empty throne. Run, he thought. For your life.

"Why have you changed?"

"I didn't know I'd changed," Wil said.

He couldn't move his body. But now he could speak with his mind.

"You're odd, Forester boy," the voice hissed. "Why dare return?"

"To free the dog," Wil said.

"Ah."

He instantly regretted speaking the truth. It increased the Presence's power over him. Threaten Tobi, control Wil. Yet he must tell the truth. If he lied, the Presence would look inside him and see.

"This dog helps me," Wil said. "I'm told I must retrieve something, bring it here. I don't know where it is. I do not know what to do. But this dog helps me find my way in the world."

Silence.

In that silence, he sensed a tiny spasm. It was as if he crossed swords with a master fencer, yet managed a nick.

Suddenly, the Presence's wrath struck him, like ice. It froze his eyes.

A vision, imposed upon him, shoved aside his own thoughts. He saw his world. Powerful currents swirled unseen through the world, shaping and reshaping beasts, villagers, imperials, Foresters, landscapes, events. He saw one obscure grass blade. On the grass blade huddled a gnat. He was the gnat.

Then he saw another world, much like his own, yet different. And then another. And another....

101

He lay on the marble floor, sobbing. He could move again, but he felt puny, lost, alone.

Peace.

He sprawled before the throne. And the Presence showed him peace.

Why make his way alone amidst those powerful currents? Why be pushed, pulled, twisted by forces he could never discern?

He need only submit.

He need only obey.

"You will now think," the Presence told him.

Wil found himself refrozen. So he sat as he was, sprawled before the throne. And he thought.

He thought about Tobi. He felt the sleeping dog's weight in his knapsack. And that weight, in that knapsack, seemed meaningful.

Why he didn't know.

To submit to the Presence, to accept its direction. That would be peace. A kind of peace.

But it repulsed him.

Still....

He thought about anger.

In his mind, Fishtowners pointed fingers at him, for being Forester born. It wasn't his doing. And what, really, had Foresters done to Fishtown?

People told of spells, curses, but who'd actually seen such things? They just believed their own stories. And he'd been lonely, a Forester foundling, held apart.

Or had he held himself a little apart? He didn't know. Both, perhaps.

He thought about fear. For in these blue-lit tunnels he felt fear always.

Changed, the Presence said.

How had he changed? The opal?

Maybe possessing the gem, whatever it might be, made him seem different to the Presence. He did believe the opal helped him sense what he couldn't see, but that seemed a small skill, really. Animals did that.

He didn't see how he'd changed. He'd merely came back for Tobi.

Something disturbed his reverie and he looked up. Lal stood against the great chamber's far wall, a tiny mite. She wanted to tell him something, and he heard.

"It eats your fear," she said.

Then the cat scampered away, through the arch of grinning skulls.

Again he could move. Sprawled on the floor, he looked up at the empty throne.

"You shall die slowly," the voice hissed. "How shall you die?"

Once again he felt the probing of his mind.

"So, little one, we fear snakes."

Once, as a boy, walking along the village's woodcutting trail into the forest, Wil had thought to sit upon a fallen tree trunk. But he heard a hissing. Where he would have sat, a forest adder lay coiled, the gray of the trunk's bark. Its black eyes stared into his own. He saw the long, legless body expand and contract as the creature breathed. Suddenly, it lashed toward him.

Wil jumped backwards, just avoiding the white fangs. Then he ran toward Fishtown.

Ever since, snakes terrified him. He would stand at the edge of a brook and see a brown-and-tan water snake. He knew it to be a bad-tempered biter, but without venom. Even so, its body seemed repulsively thick, coiling and uncoiling under the water. And fear like lightning would crackle up his spine.

"Look at this, Wil Deft."

Wil looked.

Through the arch carved with serpents' heads slithered a huge snake. Black eyes in its triangular head, held six feet above the floor, stared into his own. A blue forked tongue flicked in and out.

Slowly, the snake slithered toward him, its great body moving in sinuous waves. Its scales scraped on the chamber's stone floor.

Wil's insides felt liquid.

"Its fangs inject deadly venom, Wil," the Presence hissed. "But it will not kill you immediately. First comes searing pain."

Wil's knees gave out from fear, and he sat down on the stones. Inexorably, the snake writhed toward him, its black eyes glinting.

He knew it to be a projected snake, fashioned by the Presence.

"It eats your fear," Lal had said.

This snake was made of Wil's dread. It inhaled his terror. In its black eyes gleamed his own fright.

He knew it to be so. Yet, he had no doubt the approaching apparition of a snake could kill him with a bite.

But would the Presence slay its own marked errand runner?

He grasped for hope.

Because, just as he had loneliness inside, so did the Presence. He sensed it, but a loneliness of eons passing, of vast distances traversed. Perhaps he helped the Presence assuage loneliness, the way an island castaway might divert himself with a cricket.

Maybe for that the Presence would save him.

Now the serpent reared over him, its head held high above his own. Its black eyes stared down into his.

If he died now, what then? He didn't wish to die so young, to cease being. He'd done little. He'd labored only intermittently. And the few coins he earned went for ale and pursuing barmaids. He tried to think of one good, important act he'd ever done, to hold in his mind as his consciousness faded away.

"I came back for Tobi," he thought.

That was all.

And the snake didn't strike. He felt some alteration, beneath perception, as if the room's air had minutely thinned.

"Yet, you are an amusing little Forester boy."

So said the voice.

It seemed to him that hissing voice sounded less sharp. By some nearly imperceptible fraction of a degree, it didn't cut through him quite so much.

He opened his eyes.

Wil sat sprawled on the marble floor. He stared up at the snake looming over him, and its eyes seemed dimmer.

This truly was a game of Pilfer, but too complicated to understand, too strange. Still, he excelled at Pilfer.

"It eats your fear," Lal had said of the Presence.

Yes, he thought. My fear strengthens it. My loneliness, too. My anger. My resentment. On all such things, it feeds. He sprawled on the marble floor, thinking, I'm not lying here because of the Presence's power. It's because I came back for Tobi.

I decided.

He sensed the Presence studying him.

Abruptly, the great snake turned. It slithered from him. It disappeared through the arch carved with serpents' heads.

"What shall be done with you, Forester? What next?"

"Have you ever been loved?" Wil asked.

He felt a slight recoil.

It was as if, again, fencing with a master swordsman, he scored a nick.

"Such an inquisitive Forester."

He didn't understand this game he played with the Presence. Yet, he'd advanced one square. He sensed it.

"Consider."

Now the Presence filled Wil's mind with visions. He understood each to be a possible future. He saw Tobi slain by eight-leggers, eaten as he helplessly watched. He saw himself broken, hobbling through the world, all turning from him in revulsion. He saw Fishtowners, faces contorted by hatred, beating him to death with sticks, yelling "Forester! Forester!"

"You've puffed yourself up, Wil Deft," the voice hissed. "You serve this mountain. You are marked. But it may be you grow too impudent to live. This must be weighed."

Scoring points, Wil saw, he lost ground. He'd revealed to the Presence that he might learn to play this game too well.

Now the Presence truly considered crushing him.

"Go ponder your nothingness."

Invisible hands lifted him. Propelled by the Presence's anger, he flew across the chamber, through the rune-carved arch, down the tunnel beyond.

Once again he sat on the stone floor of his cell.

An eight-legger guard slammed shut the door. Ruby eyes leered. It turned the key in the lock. Then it pulled the key and hung it from a spike nailed into the passageway's rock walls.

Wil could reach his arm through the bars. But he could never reach the key.

Did the eight-legger's fumy brain allow humor? It seemed amused, staring at him, red eyed, evaluating.

"I'll have the haunch," it rasped.

Then it scuttled down the corridor. Wil sat alone.

He thought of Fishtown. He thought of the workers marching at dawn down the stone streets to the smokeries. He could have joined them. Only his own decision kept him apart. And he remembered kindnesses. His foster parents. Kobar's father. And murdered Bamba Moke. She seemed to despise him, but she despised only his unwillingness to become whatever it was she saw in him.

If he could reach the key....

He considered removing his clothes, tying shirt and trousers together, casting the garments out through the bars. He might then flick the key from its spike, draw it to him across the floor. But he saw that, no matter how many pieces of clothing he tied together, and his shoelaces, too, their length would be insufficient to reach the key.

He sat on the floor of his cell, chin in hands, staring at the key. He sat alone, knowing he could do nothing.

Lal appeared.

She'd padded down the tunnel and now sat outside his cell, staring at him through the bars.

"It's gone, the thing on the throne," she said.

"Gone from this world," Wil said. "But only for a time."

No reply from the cat. She didn't know of such things.

"Lal, can you jump as high as that key?" Wil asked.

She looked at the key.

"It's not so high," she said.

Lal crouched, eyeing the key. She jumped.

Her feet hit the wall above the key.

She sat again, studying the distance.

She leapt. This time her front paws jangled the key, left it swaying on its spike.

Once more she sat on the tunnel floor, looking blue-eyed at the key. She licked a front paw. Then she licked the other paw. Her tail switched.

Again she leapt.

This time, her front paws hit the wall above the key. With her hind paws, she kicked, slipping the key from its spike. Lal and the key hit the floor together.

"Can you bring me the key?" Wil asked.

Lal batted the key with her front paw. It moved a few inches toward Wil. She studied it. Carefully, she clenched it between her needle teeth. She carried it to Wil's cell door and laid it on the tunnel floor. She regarded it, head cocked to one side. With a front paw, she abruptly batted it through the bars into Wil's cell.

"Thank you, Lal," he said.

Holding the key, he reached through the bars. He slid the key into the lock. He turned it until it clicked. He pushed open his cell's door.

"Is the Presence truly gone?" he asked Lal.

"Yes," she said, stretching.

"Then we'll go through the throne room and out the arch with the skulls," Wil said. "That tunnel leads down the mountain and out into the world."

"All right," Lal said.

When they reached the throne room, they felt its emptiness. In the blue torchlight, Lal leading, they made their way along the wall to the arch carved with skulls. Here they paused.

Wil sensed eight-leggers moving through the maze of tunnels under the mountain. But he sensed no urgency in their movements. And the tunnel ahead felt empty.

He felt Tobi's weight in his knapsack. Still the dog slept.

They walked through the arch into the tunnel.

When they passed the last blue torch, they stopped. Again, there seemed no alarm in the mountain, nothing to suggest the eight-leggers had discovered Wil's escape.

They walked on down the tunnel, into darkness.

Wil could see nothing. But somehow Lal could find her way. So he removed his shirt and tied one sleeve gently around Lal's middle and held the other sleeve. In this way, she led him down the tunnel.

They walked steadily for hours.

At branches in the tunnel, Lal seemed to know which to choose.

Up ahead, at last, Wil saw faint light. It elated him.

They rounded a corner. Ahead glowed light. But the light was blue.

He faced the blue eyeball. Its glow made the light he saw.

It floated in the tunnel, blocking the way.

This time no smokiness dulled its iris.

"Now what, Forester?"

At the sound of that hissing voice, Wil felt his insides shrivel. He stood looking into the blue eyeball.

"Did you think you might leave this mountain so easily?"

He heard mockery in the voice.

Dully, he realized that his escape was not entirely of his own making. For its own reasons, the Presence had arranged his opportunity. He played against a foe of immense power. And what power did Wil Deft wield?

"So resourceful a lad," the Presence said. "If you live, you might actually find that for which you are sent."

Wil said nothing.

"Yes, you are of use."

For a long time, he stared at the floating blue eye. And the eye stared back.

"When summoned, you will come," the voice said.

Slowly, the eyeball floated higher. It floated over them.

Wil thought he heard laughter.

It turned, looking back at him. It floated up the tunnel, into the darkness, always looking back. It was gone.

Wil followed Lal down the tunnel until it brightened. Then he untied his shirt from her body and put it back on.

They walked out of the tunnel onto the mountainside.

Sun shone. Thrushes sang.

"Wil?"

A voice in his mind, coming from the knapsack. Yes, he thought. We pass beyond the Presence's power. It cannot induce sleep here.

It can only, when the time comes, summon me back.

"Wil? Are you hungry? I am. Where do you think there's food?"

He took off his knapsack and opened it. He lifted Tobi out, and set him on his feet, and they walked on.

CHAPTER SIX

Lal led them southward through the forest.

They rested in clearings, where Wil and Tobi found raspberries to eat. Lal hunted in the undergrowth. Then they resumed their march along the mountain range's flank.

As they moved steadily southward, Wil heard Tobi composing tuneless ditties about himself.

"Into the mountain went Tobi,
And all the spiders fled!"

"Who growled at the bad thing
You could not see?
Tobi! Tobi! Tobi!"

Lal once abruptly halted, as if listening.
"We'll go around," she said.

And so they arced away from their route, then back again. Lal explained, tersely, "Eat-you flowers."

Wil sometimes spotted a pair of black wings flapping among the trees ahead, or heard a raucous call. He guessed Raven scouted their path.

Nights they lay beneath some thick pine or hemlock, upon fallen needles still warm from day. Off in the forest, things snorted. Yellow lights flickered. Lal and Tobi seemed unworried. Nor did the nearby thud of heavy paws bother them. Once, in moonlight, when he heard the thudding, Wil saw an enormous black shape pass. And so he knew Bear guarded them.

"Bear goes as far as Pinewich," Lal said.

"Everyone in Pinewich likes me," Tobi assured Wil. "And we're hungry, aren't we?"

As an afterthought, he added:

"Her comes Tobi!
Get out the bowls!"

When they reached Pinewich, a Forester hamlet at the mountain range's southern terminus, villagers in brown tunics and leggings greeted them with solemn applause. Stepping forward from the crowd, the headwoman said, "Welcome, Wil Deft." Wil heard whispers. "The Taker!" "He's come!"

They rested a night in one of the hamlet's octagonal wooden cottages, tucked under the trees. Wil apologized for having no coins to pay for the baskets of food the villagers brought, but the headwoman hushed him with a hand wave. Children, and adults, too, peeked in the open door to see Wil. It embarrassed him.

As it grew dark, the headwoman appeared. She pointed an extended finger and the cottage's dark interior glowed pale golden.

"We're not supposed to work spells, because of the strength-gathering for the war," the headwoman said, apologetically. "But for you...."

In the morning, after a breakfast of hazelnut-flour buns, with blueberries and honey, and mint tea, and with food packed inside Wil's knapsack for their journey, they set out again. Villagers followed them. They passed through the hamlet's garden plots, in sunny patches beneath the trees. Where the unsettled forest began, Wil waved goodbye and Tobi barked. Two girls rushed forward. Each handed Wil a long-stemmed red trillium, then scampered away.

Wil put the flowers into his shirt's buttonholes. He wore them as they left Pinewich behind, but he felt uneasy. What these people—his people—expected of him, he might be unable to do. And even if he did retrieve their lost talisman, what then?

He'd be summoned to the mountain.

For a while, Wil followed Lal and Tobi with his head down. Then he thought, "Let the future be what it must."

And so he walked through the forest feeling lighter. Fishtown seemed long ago, and what lay ahead, who could know?

Eventually, beyond the trees, he saw the mountains ending. Lal now turned right, westward, leading them around the range's southern terminus.

To pass the time, Wil asked the animals their stories.

Lal, he learned, was forest born, wild. Once a great owl took her in its talons, flapping high, only to lose its grip on her. She plummeted through branches and lay broken on the ground, where a Forester found her. He took her to High City, and a healer's magic restored her. Since then, she'd made herself available to the Foresters, doing what she could for them, even though she disliked High City. Its tame cats irritated her. Its dogs bored her. It was a place of "bad hunting." So when the Foresters had no need of her, she returned to the forest to prowl.

"She comes back smelled up," Tobi told Wil earnestly.

Tobi, on the other hand, had been born in High City. And that, he made clear, marked him as superior to forest creatures, particularly Lal. He resented the Foresters' continually sending him on errands with so barbaric an animal.

"She thinks she knows everything about the forest, Wil. But we don't care about that, do we?"

Tobi informed Wil he knew all of High City's nooks and turnings, and where to show up for tasty handouts, and when, and where sunlight pooled at different times of day, for dozing and basking. "You'll like High City," Tobi assured him. Still, not all was perfect. For instance, High City's other dogs were to be ignored. Wil found it difficult to understand why, except that they were a dreary lot.

"You'll be my friend, Wil, and we'll be together, and we won't pay attention to them, will we?"

Now they turned right again, for their final trek, northwards up the mountain range's far side. Here the trees grew even taller, their trunks thicker. Their branches spread so high overhead that Wil had to lean his head far back to glimpse the canopy of green needles and leaves. He guessed it would require stacking fifty of his Fishtown huts, one atop the other, to reach the treetops. And he estimated each huge trunk's breadth equal to three of his Fishtown huts.

As they made their way north, Tobi grew increasingly eager. Wil gauged the dog's excitement by his prattling, which now consisted entirely of ditties about himself.

"Here comes Tobi!
Home! Home! Home!"

"Closer and closer,
And closer and closer!"

"Tobi's back! Tobi's back!
Everyone cries—
Hurrah for Tobi!"

After intoning that message, Tobi sat on the forest floor and stared at Wil with shining eyes. He barked aloud, excitedly. Lal, too, sat. She licked a paw.

"Why are we stopping?" Wil asked.

"High City," Lal said, uninterested.

"Home!" Tobi cried. And again he barked aloud.

Wil saw nothing except the great tree trunks rising all around. But, after a while, in the branches above him, he heard creaking. Looking up, he saw a wooden-plank platform descending. As it dropped lower, he saw ropes stretching from the platform's corners up into the branches, higher than he could see. A man stood upon the contraption, and Wil knew him.

When the platform touched the ground beneath the tree, by way of greeting, the man posed a question to Wil.

"Nabob or pauper?"

"Nabob," Wil said.

He grinned. But he really wanted to sob, and even hug the huge old man with the eye patch and the scar running down his face.

"Nabob, is it?" Blossom said. "So, you've made your fortune?"

"No," Wil said. "But we're alive, we three."

"Raven told us you were taken, on the mountain...."

Blossom peered at him with his one eye, brow furrowed.

"Wil, you should...."

"Yes?" Wil said.

He thought the former tavern keeper looked troubled.

"Well, up with us then, lots to do," Blossom said.

Wil and the two animals climbed aboard. Blossom tugged on one of the ropes. And then the platform slowly ascended.

"Used to be, they'd magic you up," Blossom said. "But they're saving their powers for the war, so we've got this winched thing."

After a long ascent up the bare trunk, the platform rose into the branches. Wil no longer saw ground below. Now they moved upward through out-stretching limbs and green clouds of leaves and needles.

Near the treetops, when Wil glanced upward, he saw a sort of ceiling overhead, stretching through the trees in all directions. But then the platform on which they rode rose up through an opening. What had seemed a ceiling proved to be the base of a town built among the treetops.

They stood in a wood-floored square, amidst two-story and three-story wood-sided buildings, with wooden streets stretching away from the square out among the tree limbs. A throng of Foresters lined the square's edges, gazing solemnly at Wil. Four men worked the winch that hoisted the platform. Beside the winch mechanism stood three official greeters. Wil recognized two of them, from the Horse Skull Tavern.

Pim, the short-legged Forester, stood with his arms folded, studying Wil through askew iron-rimmed spectacles. He resembled an irritable owl. Beside him stood Mita, the red-haired barmaid. She leaned forward awkwardly, hazel eyes squinting. She seemed even more worried than in the tavern. Wil didn't know the third greeter, a small and slender woman, white hair swirling around her fine-boned face. She regarded him with an intense blue gaze.

"What happened on the mountain?" Pim demanded.

Mita cringed.

"Pim—not now," said the white-haired woman.

All the while she gazed at Wil. She seemed kindly, yet shrewd, and somehow otherworldly.

"You'll be weary," she said. "And confused, I think, for no doubt the animals have told you little, yes?"

"I have many questions," Wil said.

"We'll go to a quiet place," she said, smiling at him. "My name is Zadni Druen."

At his feet, Tobi barked sharply. He looked down to see the dog sitting close to his legs, glaring at the greeters, barking at each in turn.

Zadni Druen laughed.

She sank gracefully to her knees and took Tobi's head in her hands.

"How could we forget you, dear boy?" she said, gazing into his dark eyes. "You, too, have journeyed a long way. Welcome. Welcome home."

Tobi abruptly licked her face. Then he prattled.

"In the forest, there were flowers that eat you, but I was there to protect Wil, and we got lost on the mountain, so I had to fight giant spiders, and also...."

"Without Lal, none of us would be here," Wil told the greeters.

He feared they would forget the cat.

Lal sat off to the side, not looking at anyone. She licked her chest.

After a silence, in which all regarded the cat, Pim spoke.

"Lal knows how we value her," he said. "But she wishes to return to the forest."

Now he switched to mind speaking, which the animals used.

"Stay with us a bit, Lal," he asked. "We have things yet to learn from you."

Wil sensed Lal's grudging assent.

In a meeting hall along the square, they sat at a round table, cut from a single great tree trunk. High City's headman arrived, with other dignitaries, to meet the Taker. Ordinary people also filed in to extend their greetings to Wil, and to see him. They brought baskets heaped with loaves of hazelnut-flour bread. They brought apples, pears, cherries, raspberries. Boiled eggs. Roasted carrots, squash, and eggplants, in sauces. Round cheeses.

After a while, Pim shooed all away, except Mita and Zadni and Blossom. As they began their meal, he rocked back in his chair, staring through his spectacles at Wil, as if weighing his every move and fleeting expression.

Lal, sitting atop the table, received a bowl filled with small baked fishes. Tobi ate some of everything, and finished off the fish that Lal left. Now he lay curled on the floor, leaning against Wil's ankle, half asleep, half listening.

"For the welcome, thank you," Wil said. "I'm...."

"What happened on the mountain?" Pim demanded.

His abruptness rendered Wil mute.

Zadni Druen broke the silence.

"Of course, we'll want to hear about Wil's journey, all the details," she said. "But we should answer Wil's own questions first. Do you agree, Pim?"

Pim's face reddened. Wil could not tell if the man was angry or impatient or something else. In any event, instead of answering, Pim pointedly turned his chair. Slouching, arms across his chest, he glared out the window at the square.

Zadni eyed Pim, faintly smiling.

"What can we tell you?" she asked Wil.

Even as she invited him to speak, the white-haired woman's eyes, as otherworldly blue as the zenith, studied him. Mita, too, stared at him, but not in scrutiny. Her hazel eyes seemed widened in dismay. Blossom, grimly, looked from Pim to Zadni.

What the Presence had said burned in Wil's mind—

"Here is good advice, errand runner—do not tell your Forester friends of your marking. They will slay you!"

So the Presence had warned.

Wil thought: my every word has dire weight.

What should he tell them about his imprisonment inside the mountain? He didn't know. And so he stalled.

118

"Why was I sent as an infant to Fishtown?" he asked.

Pim turned his chair back to the table.

"My idea," he said.

"Pim is Lord of the War," Zadni told Wil. "Strategy, he oversees, and marshalling our forces...."

Pim waved an impatient hand.

"Your parents," Pim said. "They went to the imperial city, wanted to scout for the Starstone, insisted on it..."

"They meant to ease your task, when your time came," Zadni said.

"But they were caught, just as I warned them," Pim said, obviously still upset, decades later. "Executed...."

"They died bravely, Wil," Zadni told him. "Meanwhile, here was their infant son, bred to be the Taker...."

Now, for the first time, Mita spoke up.

"As Taker, you must go by stealth among the empire people," she said. She spoke earnestly, and a little mechanically, as if reciting a lesson. "I'm the Wielder, so I must wait for you to find the Starstone, and steal it, and bring it. And then I....but you must move among them, of them, in a way...."

Her voice trailed off.

"Yes, so we sent you to be a village boy," Pim said. "And there were ancient prophesies...."

"And what if, in that village, I truly did become one of them?" Wil asked. "What did I know of Foresters?"

In truth, it made him bitter, deep down. They had toyed with his life, fashioned him into an instrument for their own use.

"We watched over you," Pim said. "Our scouts visited your foster parents, at night. We placed guardians...."

Blossom interrupted.

"I was your guardian," the old man rumbled. "But it was my brother's widow who watched over you, day by day."

"Bamba despised me!" Wil said.

119

Blossom laughed.

"She feared you grew too harum-scarum for your great mission," he said.

Pim flicked his hand again, impatient.

"We had no fear of losing you to them," he said. "You are Forester born—you have the magic in you."

Wil shook his head.

"I work no charms," he said.

Zadni now laid a hand on his arm.

"There are many kinds of magic," she said.

These were his own people, Wil thought. But if he told them what happened inside the mountain, they'd slay him. He looked at Zadni—blue eyes and fine bones, swirling white hair—and sensed her power. She could probe inside him, for the truth. Somehow, he knew it. Even now, with her hand upon his arm, she'd begun her search of him.

"And you?" he asked Mita. "What has your life been?"

"I've studied spells, incantations…here in High City…words of bidding," she said. "Making myself ready…."

Lessons, he thought. And seclusion, all she knew. So much responsibility. It suffocates her. She feels dread.

He thought: I pity this girl, this Wielder.

"Enough!"

Pim had risen. Hands on the table, he leaned toward Wil.

"What happened on that mountain?"

Under the table, Tobi now awoke.

"Giant spiders!" he told everyone. "I fought and fought, but there were too many, and they took us up inside the mountain where it was dark, and nothing to eat, and a blue room with a throne, with something on it I couldn't see, and I hated it, and I growled…."

Tobi faltered at this point, because he'd slept through all that happened after that.

120

"Tell us about that!" Pim said, staring fiercely at Wil through his spectacles. "That unseen thing on the throne."

"I called it the Presence," Wil said. "Its real name I don't…"

"It was a Nameless One," Zadni told him.

"I don't know what Nameless Ones might be…" Wil said.

Pim thumped his fist on the table.

"Read the *Codex Mysterium* tonight," he said through clenched teeth. "But now, tell us what happened."

"Wil, when you were in the Caverns of the Nameless Ones, what befell you?" Zadni now asked him. "It matters more than you can know."

She kept her hand on his forearm.

All right, Wil thought. Slay me then. But I will play this game.

"It frightened me, that Presence on the throne," he said. "It tossed me up to the ceiling…it produced a huge snake…but Lal told me, 'It eats your fear.' And I saw that was true, and I thought maybe I could starve it a little…."

He yearned to tell them all. Were these not his people?

"It locked me in a cell," Wil said. "With a dead man's bones…."

Pim and Zadni exchanged a look.

"Lyntor Deft," she said. "It must be."

And to Wil, she said: "Your ancestor, three centuries ago—he made his way into those caverns, to hunt for the Opal of Living and Dying, lost so long, and he never returned…."

Wil thought: it rests in my pocket.

What is this Opal of Living and Dying?

A man died for it, he thought. Should I keep it? Might it help me? Or should I give it to them? Will they then let me live? Is it enough?

No, it was not enough. They wanted the Starstone.

But he knew they also feared his finding the Starstone.

Would he deliver it to them? Or to the Presence?

Pim abruptly pushed back his chair. He strode to the window and stared into the square, his back to them. Then he whirled. Wil saw stress in his face, and perhaps longing. He thought Pim might collapse. But, instead, the little man pointed his finger at Wil.

"How did you get out?" he demanded.

Wil met his gaze. He yearned to tell the truth to these people. His people. He craved their help.

Zadni's hand still clenched his forearm.

"It seemed to leave the mountain," he said. "It seemed to leave this world…"

"Nameless Ones move among many worlds," Pim said.

He stared at Wil.

"Then?"

"Lal helped me get my cell's key," Wil said. "No eight-leggers patrolled nearby. We followed a tunnel down the mountain, and out."

Pim looked at Lal, who sat atop the table, apparently bored.

"Was it like that, Lal?" Pim said. "So easy?"

Lal looked at Pim and at the others.

Now I'll die, Wil thought.

Lal had seen that floating eyeball. She saw it confront him at the tunnel's end. She heard it mock him.

For a long time Lal didn't speak, as if she thought.

"Yes," she said finally.

And she said: "We walked out of the cavern, into the forest."

Pim collapsed into his chair.

He rested his face in his palms, covering his eyes. Wil heard his voice, muffled by his hands.

"If it were so…."

Lal had saved him.

Wil didn't know why. But surely now they'd let him live.

Lal was looking away. He sensed she wearied of these things, wished to return to the forest, but he felt great gratitude. They'd suspected the Presence had marked him, but now surely their fears were allayed.

Their instrument had become an instrument against them, but they didn't know.

Wil felt Zadni's hand tighten on his forearm.

She gazed at him, eyes half closed. He thought: She doesn't see my face. She sees inside me, and more than that.

"What do you see?" Pim asked.

She didn't respond. She sat silently looking where others' eyes couldn't go. Her hand on Wil's forearm continually tightened its grip. Eventually her eyes shut completely. Still she didn't speak.

"Zadni is High Enchantress," Mita whispered, awed. "And Diviner…my teacher…."

Still the white-haired woman did not speak.

And then she did.

"A terrible struggle," she said.

Her voice sounded hollow, and far away.

"He is good, this young man, our Taker. In his goodness, he is strong. Mightier than he knows. But there is great evil, intertwined. The threads—will, deed, counter-deed—they tangle, swirl. The outcome, undecided."

For a moment all were silent. Then, as if in pain, Pim cried out—

"Will he bring it? Will he bring us the Starstone?"

Zadni, eyes clenched shut, seemed to go far away, although her slight body remained in the room, hand clenching Wil's forearm. A minute passed. And then she breathed deeply.

"He will struggle to bring it," she said. "He will battle to bring it. He will risk all to bring it. Beyond that, the threads remain unbraided. There is no telling. Ahead lies murk. But one strand shines golden—he will strive, our Taker. He will strive to do right."

And then she opened her eyes. She unclenched her hand from Wil's forearm and sat back in her chair. She looked wearied, but serene.

Pim slouched in his chair. He sat awhile with his short legs stretched out, his head thrown back. He stared at the ceiling.

Finally he sat up. He removed his spectacles, and his eyes abruptly looked blurred.

"Strategy…" he mumbled, speaking to nobody in particular. "Tactics…."

He frowned, then shook his head. He replaced his spectacles. Behind the lenses, his eyes sharpened. He stared at each person around the table in turn. And then he spoke, grimly.

"Adjustments must be made."

After that, the meeting ended. Blossom led Wil along one of High City's wooden streets to a building near the square, where Pim and Zadni had arranged an apartment for him. It proved open and airy, the floors and walls and ceilings of clean white wood, with a good bed and a woolen rug on the floor beside it.

"I'll sleep here," Tobi told Wil, curling up on the rug. "We're friends now, aren't we, Wil? And we'll do everything together, won't we?"

Lal had followed them to the apartment. Blossom left, promising to return later to answer questions. When he was gone, Wil spoke to Lal.

"Thank you for not telling them all that happened at the cave," he said.

She didn't answer him. She sat on the wooden table, gazing out the window.

"Why did you help me?" he asked.

She looked at him. Not for the first time, he felt odd, conversing with a blue-eyed black cat.

"It smelt best," Lal said.

That was all she said.

Now she stretched. She jumped lightly from the table and walked out the open door. Wil followed her down the street, sensing that High City's doings faded for her now, and the great forest drew her.

In the central square she walked onto the platform and sat. As if they had served the cat in this way many times before, the winch operators rose from the table where they sat, outside a café along the square, and worked the winch's cranks.

"Goodbye, Lal," Wil said, as the platform began its descent.

But she sat with her back to him and didn't look around.

As the platform lowered, he saw her lick a paw. And then the platform descended among branches, where he couldn't see, and Lal was gone.

...and in those times they ruled this world and other worlds. No material bodies needed they, so mighty were these Nameless Ones, these ancient beings. Rivers ran where they willed, and they bade mountains fall, and new mountains rise. Not the Nameless Ones of Light, these, but Nameless Ones of Darkness. For the Nameless Ones of Light did not rule here. And all living things walked as the Dark Ones directed, and ate one

another, and menaced one another, for upon fears and miseries and all dark thoughts did the Nameless Ones of Darkness nourish their power. But they were few...

In his apartment, Wil sat in a circle of lamplight, reading an old text, which Zadni had given him. It was the evening of his first day in High City. Blossom had brought blankets, and carved oak plates, and spoons and forks.

"Whatever you need, send Tobi to us, and we'll bring it, Wil," Blossom told him, on his way out. "For you're truly a nabob now—you carry our hopes."

They felt heavy, those hopes.

Not long after, Wil answered a soft knock on the door. Mita stood there, holding a heavy tome.

"Tomorrow we start training together," she said. "I thought you might like to read a little, in the *Codex Mysterium*..."

Awkwardly, she handed him the book, and he took it.

"Would you come in?" he asked. "We should know each other better."

She looked confused.

"No, I.... Thank you," she said, already turning away. "I hope...."

But she hurried off before she could say what she hoped.

Now, in his apartment, in the lamplight, with Tobi asleep at his feet, Wil read the ancient book of the Foresters.

...and so, because they were few, the Nameless Ones could not reside simultaneously in all their many worlds, but most go forth, from world to world, harvesting their crops they planted there, of misery and fear and malice. And so they must sometimes leave their throne in one world or another vacant a time. And that irked them. For without their sorcery directing even the flap of a moth into the mouth of a brown bat, benevolence

might momentarily flare, or peacefulness, or brief amity between creatures, and that would weaken them.

Now of the many worlds these Nameless Ones ruled, some resembled this world, different only a bit, and others had strangeness. But of those many worlds only the Nameless Ones know.

On this world, in those ancient times, tribes dwelt scattered in the great forest. And among these tribes, certain men and women found they had some small ability for magic. It marked them off from their fellows, and troubled them. So, over time, these scattered demi-magicians found one another, and recognized one another as kin, and joined together by ones and twos and threes, and over the centuries they became a new people. And, thus joined, their powers grew stronger.

Foresters, they named themselves.

Now the Nameless Ones looked upon this new people, these Foresters, and thought upon them….

"Wil?"

Tobi had awakened from his doze, and lay looking up at Wil.

It seemed to Wil the dog must have dreamed something that troubled him. For his brown eyes looked anxious.

"Wil? Other dogs here live with a person, and that's their person, Wil. Or a family…."

Because the dog looked up at him with such a frowning brow, Wil put aside the *Codex Mysterium* and gave Tobi his attention.

"Don't you have a family?" he asked.

"Sometimes I'm with Pim, and sometimes Zadni, and with Mita, and sometimes with other people, Wil," Tobi said earnestly. "And everyone loves me."

"That's good, isn't it?" Wil asked.

"But I want one friend, and we'll do everything together, and I won't have to go off with Lal anymore," Tobi said.

"I see," Wil said.

"You're my friend now, aren't you, Wil?"

"Yes, I'm your friend," Wil said.

"That's good," Tobi said, and the relief in the dog's face made Wil wince.

How much of others' hopes he could carry, he did not know.

"Tomorrow we'll go to the side of the square where the sun shines in the morning, and we'll enjoy that, won't we, Wil?"

Even as Tobi said that, he subsided back into sleep. Wil saw his eyes close, and his brow unfurrow. And soon the dog lay at his feet, breathing regularly, and at peace.

...Why not slay these demi-magicians? For they might grow in their magic, and oppose us.

So said some in the councils of the Nameless Ones.

But others said no. We are few, they said. And we cannot always be on our throne here. Why not raise up these Foresters, and make them ours, and teach them, so that in our absences they might rule for us, and carry out our will in this world? And we would make them our satraps, and our agents.

So it was decided, in those councils of the Nameless Ones.

And this was all long ago, in the world's youth.

But for such responsibilities the new satraps were too puny in their magic.

So the Nameless Ones gathered starshine. For sunlight would be too powerful, and even moonlight. But starshine is cool and distant, and glitters like a gem. And the Nameless Ones fashioned the starshine they gathered into the Starstone. And with their own immense power they invested the Starstone. And they kept the Starstone safe in their mountain, amidst great spells of protection. And yet, they made those spells such that the Foresters could draw some potency from the Starstone, enough to strengthen them from mere magicians into sorcerers.

But they kept the Starstone apart from the Foresters, in its net of spells, lest these people receive the stone's full power, and attain almost the might of their masters.

Now the Foresters became second only to the Nameless Ones. And they wielded power over landscapes and peoples and creatures and events and all things.

But the Foresters drew no nourishment, as the Nameless Ones did, from pain and misery and fear and enmity and such. And they chafed, ruling in the Nameless Ones' stead, for what their masters' bade them create.

They brooded upon this. And plotted.

They learned to husband their magic, to store it up and strengthen it. This they did, keeping it secret from their masters. And there came one of those days when no Nameless Ones were in this world, which they left to their satraps to rule, the Foresters. And by husbanding their magic, the Foresters had become more powerful than the Nameless Ones knew.

Inside a mountain lay the stronghold of the Nameless Ones, for they preferred darkness always to light, and night to day. And inside this mountain they kept the Starstone, girt around by spells. But the Foresters, now strengthened by their husbanding, did battle with the spells, and broke them, although many perished in the battle against the spells. But one part of the Starstone, its centerpiece, the Opal of Living and Dying, that broke off in the battle. And it lay hidden in a crack in the floor, and they could not find it. So they took the Starstone for their own, even without its centerpiece, and went away from the mountain.

Now they wielded great power, these Foresters. And they used that power to weave mighty spells of keeping around the Nameless Ones' mountain. And when the Nameless Ones returned to this world, they cried: "Perfidy!"

For the Nameless Ones could not break the spells, and no longer wielded their power over the world, although what they had wrought of malice and darkness did linger in the world, unto this day. But the Nameless Ones now must stay within their mountain. And at their mountain's edges, there does their power end.

129

But ever since that taking of their Starstone, they have returned, now and again, to their mountain on this world. And the Nameless Ones sulk inside, and plot to regain the Starstone, and so regain their sway over this world. And they can wait, and nurse their grievance, for they live forever...."

A rap on the door awakened Wil. He found himself sprawled in his chair, the ancient tome in his lap. Morning sunlight slanted through the window.

When he opened the door, Blossom stood outside.

"Off we go, Wil—back to school!" the huge old man announced.

"I remember," Wil said. "Mita said we'd start training together."

Blossom frowned, as if wanting to say something. Instead, he shook his head.

"Change of plans," he said. "Pim called Zadni and Mita to some sort of parley, and I'm delegated to start you on the one thing I know anything about, besides smuggling, which is how to fight."

"I'm not a fighter," Wil said.

"You will be," Blossom said. "Might be the saving of you."

Later, after a quick breakfast at one of the square's café's—"No charge to you," the proprietor insisted—Wil and Tobi met Blossom in a kind of gymnasium.

"Kids play their sports in here," Blossom said.

He upended a leather case he carried, and swords and daggers clattered onto the floor.

"Take this," Blossom said, thrusting a broadsword's hilt into Wil's hand. "How's that feel?"

"Awkward," Wil said.

130

"Well, you're standing square towards me, making a big target," Blossom said, eyeing Wil critically. "Turn sideways—give me just your skinny flank to slice into."

At first, as the two men clanged various swords together, Tobi raced around them barking. However, after an hour of watching Wil learn thrusts and feints and parries and counter-thrusts, the dog grew visibly bored. Tobi finally walked toward the door, giving Wil a sense that he meant to present himself at various handout sites around town, and maybe to visit Pim and Zadni. Wil, engrossed in warding off Blossom's thrusts and slashes, hardly noticed Tobi leaving, for he was discovering a rhythm in swordplay, and how to unexpectedly break that rhythm to score a hit.

"What is Pim's plan?" Wil asked, as he practiced using his upraised leg and foot to push off a foe who came menacingly close.

"Higher with that knee!" Blossom said. "His plan, last I heard, was for you to sneak into the imperial city and snitch the Starstone, then fetch it back to Mita."

"That frightens me," Wil said, warding off Blossom's downward stroke with his own blade—a clang, sparks—then crying "Ooooph," as Blossom abruptly reversed his swing and caught Wil a mighty whack on the side. It would have been death, except that he wore a padded fencer's vest. Even so, it knocked him from his feet.

"Of course it frightens you," Blossom said, regarding his fallen pupil. "Now, reverses, that's a thing to keep in mind—easy way to die."

They went at it for hours—broadswords and rapiers, and also just fists and feet, and elbows in stomachs and fingers in eyes. Wil felt so fatigued he ached. It amazed him that his huge teacher, so much older, fought on and on, with relish. Finally, however, Blossom declared a break and headed to the square for "a little something moist." Wil declined to go along. Instead, he lay on the floor on his back, exhausted.

While he lay that way, Tobi raced back into the gymnasium.

"Wil!" the dog cried, radiating misery.

Tobi jumped onto Wil's supine body and stood on his chest. The dog peered into Wil's face from inches away, his own eyes full of alarm and unhappiness.

"Wil, they said you're going away!"

"Who?" Wil asked.

"Pim, and Zadni, and Mita," Tobi said. "Wil, you said you'd be my friend, and we'd be in High City together!"

"Let me sit up, Tobi," Wil said.

"They said Blossom would go, and Mita would go—and you would go! Wil! What about Tobi?"

Wil felt struck.

He'd expected to sneak alone into Imperia, the emperor's city. Alone, he'd hunt the Starstone. Bad enough. But now Mita was to go? This cloistered girl? She'd burden him, and she knew nothing of empire life. They'd see her for a Forester.

He thought, I must talk to Pim.

"What else did they say?" he asked Tobi.

"I don't know!" Tobi said, in a wail. "Going away, they said. That star thing. Bringing that. Or maybe not bringing. I don't know. Maybe back to the mountain, they said. And then a death spell thing, and I don't know. Wil...."

Now the dog climbed into Wil's lap and stood with his front paws on Wil's shoulders so that he could look into Wil's eyes.

"You promised!"

Wil hardly heard him. His mind raced over what Tobi told him. He tried to see things as Pim might.

He did see.

It made perfect sense. And it felt as if a sword swinging down upon his head unexpectedly reversed its swing, and sliced into his side.

If I retrieve the Starstone, good, he thought. And if I bring it back, good. But what if I show I'll deliver it to the mountain instead? Then the Nameless Ones would regain this world. And so Mita must speak a death spell. She must slay me. Then she and Blossom must bring the Starstone back to High City. Or perhaps even wield it in Imperia, to bring the empire down.

What else could Pim do?

I'm marked, Wil thought bitterly.

If I grasp the Starstone, I'll be drawn back to the mountain.

He yearned to run from High City, disappear into the forest, but he wasn't Lal. He'd die in the forest.

He left the gymnasium, feeling heavy as granite, to wander the wooden streets, and the dog trudged behind him, in misery.

CHAPTER SEVEN

Wil walked looking at his feet. Tobi plodded behind, and he, too, walked downcast.

They walked a lane ending at High City's edge, where branches stretched out into a green landscape of leaves and needles. Dragonflies swooped in sunshine, flashing cobalt and copper.

Wil stood gazing.

"I know all of High City's sunny places," Tobi assured him. "We could lie in sunshine every day, Wil—it makes you sleepy."

Wil's thoughts jumbled.

So he returned to his apartment, Tobi trudging after him. Again he opened the Codex Mysterium.

In those ancient pages, he sought some answer.

...and for a thousand years, then another, did the Foresters rule, called now Forester Kings, or Forest Kings.

They learned the tongues of beasts, to speak and listen. And so the furred ones partook of the realm, and the scaly ones, and feathered ones.

They levied no tariffs. Instead, they traded in magic. They made skimpy crops bountiful, in exchange for only a small portion, and eased the digging of ores, and made water flow for the turning of mill wheels.

Upon the people lay only this stricture: raise no hand against neighbors, nor swindle.

So the world increased in enchantment.

Yet, the Forest Kings faltered in their greatest work, that of undoing the dark magic laid down at time's dawn by the Nameless Ones. For the ancient sorcery lingered, and could not be entirely dispelled, and those cruel spells stained the realm....

A knock on the door—Blossom.

"You abandoned me at the gymnasium," he said.

"I feel unwell," Wil told him.

He spoke truthfully. He felt sick in his heart.

"You rest, then," Blossom said. "Tomorrow you're to start sessions with Mita. But we'll get back to it, you and I. We have dagger work to do!"

"All right," Wil said.

Blossom, he saw, searched for words. Finally the old man spoke.

"At night, on the river...smuggling," he said. "Up ahead, constables. Too many to fight. What then, Wil? Well, you find a way around."

"Yes," Wil said. "In the forest, too—flowers that eat you grew along our path, so Lal led us around."

Blossom nodded.

"Think on that," he said.

He looked at Wil with his one good eye. Again, he seemed struggling for words.

"Whatever fix you're in...."

Blossom knows, Wil thought. He wants to help me, but he's loyal to the Foresters. So he cannot.

For many moments the old man looked down at him. Abruptly, he spoke again, haltingly.

"Pim, Zadni, every one of us....We're hoping...."

He stopped, gazing down at Wil. His hand went up to rub the scar running down his face from beneath his eye patch.

So they stood a moment, the giant old fighting man, and the rangy youth, with the yellow mustache.

Blossom abruptly clapped a huge hand onto Wil's shoulder. It felt like a basket of lead.

"We're hoping the Taker finds a way."

Blossom left.

Wil sank again into his chair.

Tobi lay at his feet. Resting his muzzle upon his paws, the dog gazed steadily at Wil with unhappy eyes, brow furrowed. Wil knew that Tobi, too, grappled with a dilemma. Through all of High City, he roamed freely, welcome everywhere. Even so, Tobi felt alone.

"We are something alike, Tobi and I," Wil thought.

Tobi yearned for a family, and a home. He'd set his heart on Wil. But now Wil would leave, and so Tobi, in his own fashion, pondered what to do.

Wil sat silently.

After a while, he once again opened the ancient book.

...and because in the beginning the Nameless Ones stained the world, so they might sow cruelty and discord, and reap it, and feast upon it, some in the realm of the Forest Kings did raise hands against neighbors, or swindled. Some thereby felt ill-used. They asked: Why does it go ill for me and not for my neighbor, who assaulted me, and cheated me? They lamented: these Forest Kings must make league with my neighbor, for his enrichment and for their own, and for my impoverishment, and my woe.

And in those early days, the Forest Kings did err. For the Nameless Ones had ruled the whole world, and laid dark spells everywhere. But the Foresters chose to rule just those parts from which they sprang, the Great Forest, and the River Valley, and that part of the Shore adjacent. And they were content.

Southward lay other lands. There a new people arose, much poisoned by the ancient dark spells. A people of the sword, these. By conquest, they lived, and raiding and seizing. And this people looked northward. For the Forester realm prospered. And they saw the Forest Kings had no armies. For these southerners sent spies into the Forester lands, who learned what was to be learned. And they learned the Forest Kings ruled by sorcery, too strong for this people's swords and soldiers. But a crafty people, it was.

In their councils, they asked, why not poison minds against these Forest Kings, and foment a great uprising? For these Foresters abhor conflict, and forbear to kill, not even beasts. And so, to strike against their own, would they not be loath?

And they did raise rebellion. For these invaders from the south sowed in people's minds the thought that whatever went ill, be it a blighted crop or a sickened child, that must be the doing of the Forest Kings.

But the Forest Kings wielded sorcery so potent they repelled the invaders, and also weakened the rebellion. These invaders then fell back, hurt. But it had been the realm's law that miscreants, unrepentant, be exiled. And from such cast outs the invaders took counsel.

Those exiles said: seize the Starstone. Then the Forest Kings will be brought low.

So the invaders sent agents into the very stronghold of the Foresters, disguised as emissaries from dwellers in the great manors, northward along the River, who remained staunchly loyal to the Forest Kings. And these pretenders did steal the Starstone, using certain ruses and stratagems, and did spirit it away to their own masters.

Now the Starstone could not be wielded by these invaders from the south, for they had no magic. But its loss weakened the Forest Kings. Their sorcery lessened, over time, into ordinary magic. Also, while the invaders could not wield the Starstone, its possession strengthened them, making them ever mightier in their arms and in their ability to fuddle minds with lies. And so the invaders stoked their power, and forged an empire and built a city, Imperia, and ruled iron handed. Now the people truly did live under a heavy yoke, and their lot ever worsened. But lies fuddled them. And after a while they remembered only those lies and forgot the truth.

And the Forest Kings, again mere Foresters, lived hidden from the empire in the Great Forest. And the people reviled these Foresters, although they did not know why.

Wil put down the book onto his lap. He remembered Fishtown's adages and imprecations. Foresters caused stillbirths, those sayings charged. Or stole chickens, or coins. Or sent sicknesses.

He knew he was Forester born. Fishtown never let him forget that. And those sayings stung. He felt apart.

"Yet, here I am at last, among the Foresters, my own kind, and how do I feel now?" he thought, with bitterness.

...but the Foresters decided once more to husband their magic, as they had in the beginning against the Nameless Ones, building its strength. Some among them showed vigor in spell wielding, more than most. These the Foresters asked to wed among themselves, and their offspring to wed, so to create a line of ever-more powerful spellcasters, the tribe of Sooth. And they set a thousand years for this raising up of their strength, generation by generation, stronger and stronger, until from the line of Sooth would come the Wielder, born and bred to grasp the Starstone and invoke it.

They sought, too, those adept at the magic of ferreting out, and hiding, and perceiving others' thoughts and intent, thus to preserve the self in adversity. And these, too, they asked to wed and breed, for the good of all. So began the line of the Defts. And for this, too, the raising up of a Taker, they set a thousand years.

And in that thousandth year—when the Wielder would be among them, of the tribe of Sooth, and the Taker, of the tribe of Deft—then they would husband their magic the most, making ready for their great counterstroke against the empire.

For they wished with a powerful wish to take back the Starstone. And they wished to bring down the empire, to restore the world.

So they planned....

Wil laid down the text beside his chair, and brooded, elbows on knees, chin in palms. Tobi, however, stood on his four stumpy legs, gazing dark eyed at Wil, and barked. Afternoon sunlight slanted through the window, catching Tobi in the yellow shaft. It made his fur, honey-colored and white, seem golden.

"We'll go out," Tobi said. "We'll see things."

It amused Wil, in his despair, to see a crafty look on Tobi's handsome face. He realized the dog, lying on the floor, had been thinking. Tobi had concocted a plan to convince Wil to stay in High City. Wil saw that Tobi believed his plan could not fail.

And maybe it won't fail, Wil told himself.

He thought: "My only real friend is a dog."

He feared to go to Imperia to hunt for the Starstone. He feared even more finding the Starstone, knowing he'd be drawn back to the mountain, forced to hand the Starstone to the Presence. He shuddered.

Besides, if he did retrieve the Starstone, it would be Mita's task to watch him. When the mountain drew him, she'd see. Then she'd cast the death spell.

She must.

"It's right," Wil told himself.

Even so, he felt an urge to hunt for the Starstone, find it, take it. At least, to try. Otherwise, it would be a thing undone. And what else of importance did he have in his life? It drew him—even as it frightened him—his mission to steal the Starstone.

It would be the greatest of all games of Pilfer.

Yet, he was marked....

At first, after Tobi persuaded him to go out, Wil thought the dog led him aimlessly through High City.

139

"Now, here, we can sit before the sun comes up, and smell the dawn," Tobi told him earnestly, as they stood at the eastward ending of a wooden lane. "Isn't that good, Wil?"

Next, the dog led him to a café along the square, and introduced him to the proprietor, who seemed faintly amused. As they walked away, Tobi told Wil, with the air of imparting an important secret, that after lunch the proprietor often had leftovers to give, and after supper, too.

They visited aerial platforms among the treetops where peppers, corn, squashes, beans, and other vegetables grew. They spoke with the gardeners, and Wil learned that magic helped the growing. Because of the coming war, the Foresters husbanded their magic, but used just enough for their sustenance.

"These gardeners work away from town a little, where it's lonely, Wil, so when we come, they'll always be glad to see us, and that feels good," Tobi explained.

Sometimes, as they walked High City's wooden streets, another dog would hurry out a door and greet Tobi and grin at Wil, exuding friendliness. Tobi, however, turned stiffly from these overtures. He quickly led Wil away.

"We don't care for them, do we, Wil?" Tobi said. "We don't even notice them, do we?"

Wil understood. Tobi feared he would befriend other dogs, and that Tobi would then mean less to him. So he took care, with other dogs, to be merely civil. For he did not wish to distress his friend.

As Tobi led him to his favorite places along the wooden streets, he saw High City as Tobi saw it. Here were bakers and carpenters and café waiters, and makers of potions to secretly trade with citizens of the empire, despite the emperor's decrees against concourse with Foresters. He met importers of vegetables and grains, too, and fish, from that same illicit trade. He saw finely carved willow bowls arrive from Forester hamlets among the trees. From those same hamlets, High City's jewelers received gemstones, to set in swirls of silver or gold, each charmed to avert illness or induce peace, or to bring about whatever quality the buyer ordered. Wil saw what Tobi wished him to see: all these workers would gladly pause in their labor to exchange a friendly word.

"They save food for me there, Wil," Tobi said, pointing out a wooden house along a wooden street. "I'm always welcome to sleep the night."

Walking these streets, Wil glimpsed contentment. He imagined himself living here in the treetops, among fluttering butterflies. He would be a carpenter, perhaps. Surely someone would teach him the craft. Or he might keep a shop, selling finely wrought pewter tableware from the Forester hamlets, each mug and bowl lightly charmed to enhance the flavor of ale or cider or soup poured into it. Tobi would keep him company, in his shop. Evenings, they would dine with friends. Every day they would stroll these wooden streets. They would walk among the treetops, in sunshine.

Tobi's message was clear: "Stay here in High City and be happy—stay here with me."

If he did, Wil thought, he would face no danger in Imperia. There would be no summoning to the mountain. No death spell.

He pondered: What if I refuse this mission? What if I stay here instead?

Would that not be a way around?

That night he slept peacefully.

He would not go.

In the morning, when a messenger summoned him to a session with Zadni and Pim and Mita, he strode off whistling an old Fishtown ditty.

141

"I won't tell them right away," he told himself, as he strolled along the street. "I'll see how things lie. And I'll tell them a bit at a time, so they'll see it's best."

So when he reached the room where Pim, and Zadni, and Mita sat at a table, awaiting him, he merely greeted them cheerfully, and took a seat. It was as if an illness had lifted. Now he felt energetic, and buoyant. He imagined his pewter-ware shop.

"This is what we seek," Pim said.

He opened an old scroll. It showed a crystal disc, the size of a plum. Wil guessed magic imprinted the image, for the crystal appeared graspable, floating above the parchment. Within, it shimmered, its light clear, but touched with cold blue.

"Starstone," Pim announced.

Pim fell silent, staring at the image on the parchment. As he gazed, it seemed to Wil that the owlish little man drifted away.

Wil imagined the Lord of the War, alone in his quarters, unrolling this scroll. Day after day. Year after year. Wil shuddered. He suspected the lost Starstone—even its mere image—might slowly seize a mind.

Zadni spoke, gently, as if to break Pim's trance.

"At the Starstone's center, you see an indentation."

Wil saw a faint concavity.

"That is where the Opal of Living and Dying originally fitted," Zadni said.

Under his shirt, suspended from a cord tied around his neck, Wil wore a leather pouch. Inside the pouch, he carried the gem he had found inside the mountain.

"Tell me about the Opal of Living and Dying," he said.

Zadni spoke.

"When our forebears took the Starstone from the Nameless Ones, and battled the guardian spells, we lost the

Opal," she said. "Lyntor Deft—your ancestor, Wil—sneaked into the mountain to find it, but never returned…."

Should I tell them, Wil wondered?

If he gave them the Opal, would they be satisfied? Would it be enough? Would they then accept his decision not to go?

"What were the Opal's powers?" he asked.

"It intensifies you," Zadni said. "If you grasp the Starstone itself—if the magic is in you—you enter into its immense power, and you can direct that power, but…."

Pim, as if suddenly awakening, thudded his fist onto the table.

"That's all we need," he said, glaring about the table. "That power."

"Of course," Zadni told Pim soothingly. "Wil, when you retrieve the Starstone, and give it to Mita, she will perceive the currents invisibly holding up the empire…

"Currents?" Wil asked.

"Events create currents, or alter existing currents—even events yet to unfold," Zadni said. "Beliefs form currents, too, and feelings, thoughts, all flowing together….Some currents the Wielder will dry up. Others she will redirect. One by one. Until the Empire sags…."

"And we reign once more," Pim said, barely audible.

"Sorcerers again," Zadni said.

Wil saw her give Pim a troubled glance.

Her words seemed a subtle rebuke. Did it disturb her, the notion of rule?

Wil thought: here, too, currents invisibly intertwine. But I cannot make them out.

"And the Opal?" he asked.

"Before the Nameless Ones ever came, even then, it lay in the mountain," Zadni told him. "They merely found it, so old—it makes you who you rightly are."

Abruptly, she looked at him sharply. She suspects, he thought.

Still eyeing Wil with narrowed eyes, Zadni spoke again.

"Let us say, Wil, that when you were inside the mountain, you found the Opal—if you are good, deeply, the Opal will intensify that goodness. It will, more and more, rule your living, and shape your dying. If you are evil, the same. And if you have a knack—let us say to understand others, to sense what they think and feel, Wil—that knack strengthens in you."

"That's true of a people, too," Mita suddenly said. "If a people possesses the Opal, they become ever more what they truly are…."

"What if you possessed it, Mita?" he asked.

"It would strengthen my talent for casting spells, so that I would wield the Starstone more powerfully, and in wielding the Starstone I would be directed more by my innermost self…."

As always, it seemed to Wil that Mita recited lessons inculcated in childhood. Her hazel eyes glanced from face to face.

Wil thought: she is afraid.

"So, when I wield the Starstone…."

Mita seemed to lose her words.

"What will happen to you?" Wil asked.

Mita gasped.

Pim made a sound like a snarl. In the owlish man's jaw, a knot pulsed.

Zadni exchanged a look with Pim. Then she gazed at Mita, sadly.

"I will be changed," Mita whispered.

Pim rose, scraping his chair backwards.

"Enough!" he said.

He glared at Wil.

"I show you this image of the Starstone so you will know what you seek," Pim said, through clenched teeth. "It is your destiny to seek it. It is Mita's destiny to wield it. Do you understand?"

"Is that the only way?" Wil said.

He met Pim's glare.

Pim braced his hands on the table, leaned toward Wil.

"Yes," he said. "That is the only way."

Behind his spectacles, his eyes—inches from Wil's own—seemed to bulge.

Wil looked thoughtfully at the Lord of the War.

"And yet," Wil said, "as I stroll with Tobi through High City, butterflies flutter around me, crimson, saffron, turquoise, violet. At night, clouds of fireflies light my way…is that not enough?"

Pim snorted. He stalked to the window. His back to them, he stared out at the square. Wil could see his neck stiffening with controlled rage.

"It's not so simple," Zadni told Wil. "We live in peace here, yes, for now…."

"They grow ever stronger," Mita said. "They have the Starstone…."

"They fear only us," Zadni said. "When they feel ready— Soon!—they will come for us, to kill us all."

Wil had not expected this.

"Yet, it could be even worse…."

He said it to himself.

What if he retrieved the Starstone? He might elude Mita's death spell. Surely he would try. And then he would bring the Starstone back to the mountain.

Will, too, turned silent.

They sat, looking at one another. No one spoke.

In the silence, from outside, they heard voices murmuring, excited. Approaching.

Abruptly, the door flung open.

145

Blossom rushed in, Tobi at his heels, barking. Behind them, a crowd followed, but Blossom closed the door. His face seemed turned to rock, his one eye hard.

"It's begun," he said.

They all looked at him.

"Raven just flew here…News…."

Still they all sat mute.

Blossom put a hand to his forehead and held it a moment. They he took away his hand and glared fiercely from face to face.

"Marston Ker Veermander—murdered."

Wil felt his breathing stop.

"A sword through his skull," Blossom said. "And his grandmother. On their verandah. Everything torched."

"But his wife, and children, and the others," Wil said. "Safe, up the river?"

"Murdered," Blossom said. "Every one. And all their kin. And all the old manors burned. Gone."

Nobody spoke. Wil saw Blossom's huge right hand clench, as if the old man gripped the hilt of a sword.

"All up and down the river, their galleys—rooting out those they suspect of trade with us, or of insufficient loyalty, mostly innocents….lashings, hangings, executions…."

"Fishtown?" Wil said.

Blossom looked at him, his eye like a stone.

"Fishtown received special attention," he said. "After all, there the Taker grew up. Houses burned, deaths."

"Who?" Wil said.

"The schoolteacher, for one," Blossom said.

"Kobar's father!" Wil cried.

"Yes, for partiality to Foresters, for anti-imperial teachings, for…."

"How?" Wil asked, almost a whisper.

146

"They execute by placing a sword tip under the jaw," Blossom said. "Then they thrust it up into the skull."

Wil felt as if his tongue swelled to filled his mouth.

"Lord Domallon," Blossom said. And then, as if spitting the words: "Justice Minister."

Wil felt as if he listened from far away.

"Stood with that faint smile, watched the sword going into the schoolteacher...."

Wil thought: that dark aristocrat who ordered the killing of Bamba Moke? Mentor of....

"Kobar!" Wil said. "Wasn't he there? Couldn't he stop it?"

"Your old friend was there," Blossom said.

"And they made him watch?" Wil said.

"Watch?" Blossom said.

He stared at Wil. And the look in his one eye seemed to pity Wil, and challenge him.

"Kobar thrust the sword."

Wil stared at Blossom, wide eyed. Abruptly, he stood, his chair falling over backward behind him. Even as it crashed to the floor he pushed past Blossom, out the door.

Tobi ran behind him, barking.

A throng still lingered in the square, murmuring over the news from Raven. Wil pushed through. He hurried along the wooden streets, head down, too stricken to notice the dog at his heels. He came to the lane that ended at High City's edge. Once again he stood at the rail, looking out upon the foliage landscape, where dragonflies swooped in sunlight.

Kobar....

He remembered Kobar's father watching them chalk lessons on their slates, those gentle eyes.

Kobar enslaved.

Kobar returned, changed.

147

And yet not changed.

To elude slavery, and to rise, Kobar had turned on his childhood friend. Now, in his ascent, he sacrificed even his father.

Seeds of these things were in him, Wil thought. And these seeds the empire nurtured, magnified.

Kobar became his worst self.

"Like the Opal of Living and Dying," Wil thought.

But the Opal magnified whatever was in you, good or bad. The empire nourished only the bad.

Wil thought: the Nameless Ones still rule. Even confined in their mountain, they rule, because their ancient spells still stain the world. And that stain gives this empire its strength.

Now galleys patrolled the river. Burning. Lashing. Killing.

Wil suddenly drew in his breath.

Because of me!

That the Taker lived among them, they suspected. From rumors? Spies? From what Kobar told them when he bargained to be freed? And they knew this to be the thousandth year. So they hunted him. And others paid the price.

Bamba Moke. Dead. Because of him.

Kobar's father.

Marston. All the manor people.

How many more?

To himself, he protested: I never asked to be the Taker!

Did that matter?

Tobi barked. From far away, it seemed.

However, the dog sat at his feet, staring up at him.

"Stay here in High City," Tobi said. "Stay with me."

"I don't know what to do," Wil said.

"Stay here," Tobi said. "There's sunshine to lie in, and food, friendliness, all nice things, Wil, and we'd do everything together."

Wil thought, "Yes, to stay here would feel good...."

But would it feel right?

"Tobi, what if we live together in a house," Wil asked. "And one night, while I sleep, evil enemies break in to knife me where I lie?"

"Bark," Tobi said. "Jump. Bite. Bite. Bite."

"But, Tobi, those robbers might kill you instead of me."

"Bite!" Tobi said.

In the little dog's dark eyes, he saw fierceness. And he saw a kind of wild joy.

"Why would you do that?" Wil asked.

"It would feel best," Tobi said.

Abruptly, the dog's eyes filled with puzzlement.

"Do we have evil enemies?" he asked.

"Yes," Wil said.

He made his way back to the meeting room, on the square.

Pim had spread a map on the table, his finger running up the line of the great river.

"So they've withdrawn from the upper reaches..." Pim was saying.

"Why not?" Blossom said. "They've killed every manor dweller."

"And their patrols?"

"Galleys on the river, up to Fishtown. On the roads, constables. And they guard Imperia's three gates like hornets buzzing around their nest."

"The ports?" Pim asked.

"They search every incoming scow and skiff," Blossom said.

"What about our people?" Pim asked.

"None arrested...yet," Blossom said.

"Is the plan unchanged?" Zadni asked.

"I see no reason to change," Pim said, not looking up from the map.

Not for the first time, Wil felt himself a piece in a game.

"What is the plan?" he asked.

Pim glanced at Wil. His eyes, behind his spectacles, seemed focused far away. He made a dismissive motion of his hand.

"You'll be told your part," he said.

Wil looked irritably at the owlish little man, who had resumed studying the map.

"Who'll go into Imperia?" Wil asked, an edge to his voice.

"You, Mita, Blossom," Pim said, not looking up. "Our agents there will assist...."

"So you, personally, won't go into Imperia?" Wil asked.

Pim's head snapped up. Wil saw anger working in his face.

"I'm Lord of the War," he said. "I plan. I stage the attack. I oversee our forces."

"Our forces?" Wil asked. "How many battalions?"

Pim's face muddied with rage.

Zadni rested her hand on Wil's shoulder.

"It's true, just three of you will go into Imperia," she told him. "But we'll all be waiting—here in High City, and in the forest villages. And when Mita grasps the Starstone, we'll know, and we'll enter into the magic, to help her work the undoing of the empire. Do you understand, Wil? Our part is here. But if you fail, if Mita fails, they'll hunt us down. We'll all die."

"You think I fear to go...." Pim said, his face contorted.

"Wil, there's agents to coordinate," Blossom interjected. "Houses where we'll hide, all that planning, and without Pim...."

Wil and Pim stood glaring at each other.

"I will do this thing," Wil said.

A wail. Mournful beyond bearing.

Tobi stood by the door, looking at Wil in misery. Again he wailed. And then he padded through the door, head down, and was gone.

Pim involuntarily shivered, as if shaking off the dog's unhappiness, a distraction.

"To take back the Starstone…you were born to do it," he told Wil.

Wil thought: was I born to make my friend unhappy?

Another thought occurred to him: there is no Mrs. Pim.

No little Pims. No friends of Pim.

Pim's only life—this struggle against the empire.

How did that come to be?

"I was not born for it," Wil said.

"Bred for it," Pim insisted. "Born for it."

"No," Wil said. "What I do, I choose to do."

Pim shrugged.

"Tell yourself what you want," he muttered. "Just do what's expected of you…."

"No," Wil said. "Do what's right."

Pim stared at him a moment, then waved his hand.

"What matters is what's at stake…."

"Many things are at stake," Wil said.

He glanced at Mita, slumped in her chair, eyes downcast. She looked pale.

"Yes, that is true," Zadni said. "Many things."

She peered at Wil, frowning. Suddenly, she reached out and gripped his arm. It seemed to Wil that she began to fade. Some part of her seemed to leave this room, this time. Slowly, her eyes shut.

Her grip on his arm tightened.

Tighter.

Tighter still.

And then, slowly, her hand relaxed.

Zadni's eyes fluttered, opened.

"So it may be," she said.

She seemed returned from far away.

"What did you see?" Pim asked.

She shook her head, brow furrowed.

"I saw what is at stake," she said.

She sounded grim.

"So many things."

In the gymnasium, with Blossom, swords and daggers. Elbows and fists.

And in the room on the square, days spent memorizing. Palace protocol. Passwords to use with Forester agents among the citizens. Imperians' customs, and manners, and ways of speaking. Maps—the great city's streets, its three gates, its river docks, its harbor wharves, entrances into the Great Palace, and within that vast edifice, hallways, chambers….

They would, the three of them, Pim announced one afternoon, make their way to Imperia's North Gate, in disguise. Blossom would be a farmer, pushing a barrow loaded with melons. Beside him would walk his daughter, Mita.

To the North Gate's guards, Blossom would say: "We're going to the market on the Street of the Heroes of the Starstone." And he and Mita would produce travel papers and market papers, all stamped.

Unseen in the wheelbarrow, hidden under mounded melons, would ride the Taker, sought by every soldier and constable in Imperia, and up and down the river.

"So you'll get into the city that way," Pim said, looking satisfied.

"No, I won't," Wil said.

As often happened now, Pim and Wil glared at each other. Pim then stalked off to stare out the window at the square.

Over his shoulder, he snarled: "You're not Lord of the War."

"I'm the Taker," Wil told him.

Pim walked out into the square. He did not look back.

So it went, day by day.

In the evenings, Wil returned unsettled to his apartment, to find Tobi lying in a corner. And the dog refused to look at him.

One evening, Wil said: "I have to go. Don't you see, Tobi?"

No response.

Wil muttered to himself.

"Even a wife would understand, but not this dog!"

No response from Tobi.

So it went every evening, Wil unhappy for his friend, the dog refusing to respond. After a while, Wil would sigh and stand looking out the window at the fireflies winking. He'd make a supper for himself and put out a bowl for Tobi. And the dog wouldn't eat.

Four days passed like this. And now Wil sat again in the room at the square, for another strategy session. He slouched in his chair, arms crossing his chest.

Pim spoke, ignoring Wil's glare.

"So, inside the city, you'll proceed to the market. Our agents will have a stall for you, Blossom. You and Mita will sell melons. When nobody is looking, you will whisper to the Taker, and he will make his way out from beneath the melons...."

"This isn't a Forester village!"

They all looked at Wil.

"Soldiers everywhere, hunting me," Wil said. "And you think they'll let a melon cart through? Swords, Pim! Thrust into

153

those melons! I'll be dead. Mita and Blossom, tortured, executed!"

"This is the plan!" Pim retorted. "A cart full of melons! There's no other way."

"Yes there is," Wil said. "Nobody under the melons."

Pim put his head into his hands. For moments he sat that way, visibly calming himself. Finally he looked up.

"And where will our Taker be?" he asked.

"It'll be night," Wil said. "I'll be coming down the river in a skiff."

They argued.

Wil spread out maps of the realm, and of Imperia, and plans the Foresters' agents had prepared of the palace, and government buildings, and other structures. He jabbed his finger at the point where the river flowed into the ocean harbor. There the docks made a right-angle turn. At that point, he argued, he'd squeeze a skiff through the pilings. And on the right angle's joint, there must be a small opening in the dock, against the shore, where he'd climb out in the dark, and disappear into the streets.

"This is dangerous!" Pim exploded. "Do you know for sure there's an opening, big enough to squeeze up through? Do you know for sure you won't be seen?"

"Do you know for sure I won't get a sword through my neck, lying under those melons?" Wil said.

Nobody announced it, but a time came when it was understood the plan had changed.

That evening, Wil returned to his apartment eager to tell Tobi. He'd finally persuaded Pim.

He found the apartment empty.

Every evening when Wil came home, Tobi lay miserably in his corner. Wil told the dog the day's events. Tobi pretended not to hear. And, later, when Wil made supper, Tobi refused to eat.

154

Wil worried the dog would starve. But he noticed that Tobi grew no thinner. Finally, he understood: while he worked on fighting skills in the gym with Blossom, or attended strategy sessions, Tobi visited his friends throughout High City. At every stop, they offered him food, which he gobbled.

Wil laughed aloud.

So the hunger strike was a sham.

Yet, the dog's unhappiness was no ploy. Every dog in High City had a home, a family. Only Tobi did not. And he wanted Wil to be his family.

"I, too, feel lonely," Wil thought. "But it's not so simple for me."

Wil left the apartment to look for Tobi in all the places where the dog had friends. Finally, in the square, he saw Tobi leaving a tailor's shop. Instead of slouching, disconsolate, as he always did now, Tobi walked with his head up. He strutted.

"Wil!" Tobi said. "Everything will be good."

"What do you mean?" Wil asked, pleased to see the dog looking so happy.

"You'll see!" Tobi said.

And he strutted ahead of Wil toward the apartment.

Looking back over his shoulder, Tobi said: "We'll have supper now—won't we, Wil?"

Dawn.

A chill wind out of the north, foretelling autumn.

In the square, most of High City waited, gazing solemnly at four people standing beside the elevator platform.

Wil, pensive, shrugged to adjust his knapsack, heavy with food. From beneath the knapsack's flap projected a sword's hilt. He'd shaved away his mustache, scissored his yellow hair short.

Blossom rested one huge hand on Wil's shoulder, speaking to him.

155

"...so Mita and I, we'll start in a week, give you time to get to your skiff, start down the river...."

Pim stared at Wil, evaluating.

"They'll be in Imperia before you," he said. "They'll occupy the house, meet our agents....This is insane. You should go together. Watch over each other. Blossom...."

"I'm trained," Wil said, giving Blossom a wan smile.

His eyes searched the square. Why wasn't Tobi here? When he awoke this morning, Tobi had already gone.

He wished to bid his friend goodbye.

"I'll go now," he said.

Pim nodded at the two winch operators, who stood aside, waiting. They stepped forward to work the levers.

Zadni moved closer to Wil, staring up into his face.

"We'd like to send you down with a spell," she said, white hair swirling around her face. "But we're saving our strength, even that little bit..."

Wil turned up his palms, to show he didn't care.

"But there is one small expenditure of magic we must make," Zadni said.

She moved her hand across his face, index finger raised. His hair turned black. She pointed her finger at his left eye. It changed from blue to brown. Then she changed his right eye.

"You're best friend from Fishtown would not recognize you now," Zadni said.

Wil smiled grimly at her. Then he looked at Mita, who stood beside Zadni, pale.

"How do I look?" he asked.

Mita tried to respond, but she only whispered, and he couldn't hear.

"In Imperia," he told her.

He stepped toward the elevator. Then stopped, hearing a sharp bark.

Tobi ran into the square, jubilant. He sat at Wil's feet, panting from his run, dark eyes glinting. Strapped on his back, a knapsack.

That tailor, Wil thought. Tobi got him to make this knapsack.

Wil thought he might weep.

"I'm ready," Tobi said. "My knapsack's full of food, so we won't have to worry about that, will we?"

"Tobi...." Wil said.

"I'll help," Tobi said. "We'll do everything together."

"No," Wil said.

Tobi's jaw dropped.

"I have to go alone," Wil said. "I can't look after both of us."

Wil watched the jubilance fade from the dog's eyes.

"I'll go if I want to," Tobi said, suddenly sullen.

He looked stubborn.

Wil sighed, spread his hands.

Then he stepped onto the platform and closed the gate.

Tobi stared at him, stricken.

Wil motioned to the winch workers. They began moving the levers. Slowly, the platform began its long descent.

Wil saw Zadni hurry to Tobi, kneel. She put her hands on the dog's head.

Just before the platform sank below High City, Wil saw Zadni's eyes closing. Her hands holding Tobi seemed to tighten.

CHAPTER EIGHT

Wil watched the platform ascend to High City, dwindling upwards until it vanished among the branches.

A gust, cold, blew his collar up. He buttoned his jacket and readjusted his knapsack's straps. Then he stared at the trees, bleakly.

Finally, he started his journey, but after a few steps he stopped and turned, hearing a sound behind him, like tiny bells— just above the forest floor floated a silvery cloud. Within the tinkling cloud stood a figure, insubstantial, translucent. Abruptly the cloud evanesced, and Tobi stood looking up him, wearing a knapsack.

Tobi looked jubilant.

"What happened?" Wil asked, although he guessed.

"Zadni sent me down," Tobi said.

And he pointedly added: "She's my good friend."

Tobi's occasional petulant barbs normally amused Wil. But now he felt irked.

Sneaking into Imperia, hard enough. But encumbered with a dog?

Zadni had put her hands on Tobi, closed her eyes. What she saw persuaded her to expend precious husbanded magic, to send Tobi down. But what did she see?

Nobody told Wil.

"Born for it," he sneered aloud, echoing Pim's words. "Bred for it."

He thought: bred to be a game piece, moved by others.

He glared at Tobi.

"I'll travel alone."

158

Turning, he strode southward, under the great trees. After a while, he looked back.

Tobi plodded defiantly after him.

"I've got my own knapsack," the dog muttered.

"Don't expect help from me," Wil said.

He walked faster, knowing the short-legged dog couldn't keep up. By noon, when he looked back, Tobi plodded far behind him. Too upset to trade thoughts with the dog, Wil cupped his hands around his mouth and shouted: "Go home, Tobi. Go back to High City."

But the dog pretended not to hear him, and continued plodding forward.

"Suit yourself," Wil said.

Now he nearly ran.

At one point he stopped to look back, and couldn't see the dog. Head down, he stared at his shoes. Finally, straightened and strode on, southward.

Near dusk, he realized Tobi carried food, but couldn't open his knapsack, having only paws.

"Go home, Tobi," he thought. "Everything ahead is dark."

Night.

He stared into his campfire. Had the dog turned back to High City? In darkness, the forest's ancient enchantments stirred.

He envisioned Tobi plodding through the night. Hungry. Alone. Lost.

He threw another stick on the fire, so savagely sparks crackled up.

What awaited him in Imperia? Constables? A torture chamber? And if he found the Starstone, grasped it....

Summoned.

But, before he reached the mountain....

159

Death spell.

Mita, too, he thought. Also a mere token in this game.

If she wielded the Starstone, she'd be changed. But into what? Fear of it made her pale, widened her hazel eyes.

Off in the forest, something gibbered.

He hurled another stick on the fire.

A sword held beneath your jaw. How did it feel? Then rammed upward into your skull....

Somehow he slept.

He opened his eyes.

Silence. His campfire down to embers. And in the darkness, movement.

"Tobi?" he called.

A yellow glint, to his left.

Something moved toward him, heavy.

"Tobi?" he called again.

From the forest, silence.

He groped in the dark for his knapsack, to draw his sword.

"It smells my fear," he thought.

Probably it had followed him all day. Smelling his fear for himself, and for Tobi, it grew ever hungrier. Now it stood just beyond the embers' dim light.

Fumbling in the darkness, he found his sword's hilt, sticking up from his knapsack, but the blade stuck inside. He struggled to undo the knapsack's flap.

A blow threw him onto his back. Fiery drops fell onto his face, venomous drool, while above him a snakelike neck swayed, silhouetted against faint starshine filtering through foliage. Its yellow eyes glowed.

He crawled back to his knapsack, fumbled again with the flap imprisoning his sword.

Another blow. On his back again. Breath gone, he struggled, but couldn't move because heaviness pressed his chest, and he felt claws. From above, a huge head descended and he shut his eyes.

Sharp barks.

Over him a small body hurtled, then clung by its teeth to that snakelike neck. Roaring, the huge beast tossed its head, to fling away its attacker.

Wil rolled to his knapsack, fumbled with the flap's button, got it open, slid out his sword. Above him, the small assailant still clung to the thrashing neck, so Wil thrust his sword lower, straight ahead, feeling the blade sink into muscle. He withdrew it. Thrust again. Again.

Silence, then a thud, shaking the ground.

"Tobi?" Wil cried.

He scooped up sticks, flung them onto the campfire's embers, blew on them. A flame flickered, caught. Fire now lit the campsite.

Wil saw his sword stuck in the ground. To the sword's left lay a small body, its fur honey-colored and white.

"Tobi!"

He lifted the dog up, but it lay inert in his arms. His hands felt no broken bones, and he saw no blood.

A small sigh: he felt the limp body stiffen, move. Tobi's eyes opened, looking blankly into his own, but then they sharpened, gleamed.

"Bark!" Tobi cried. "Jump! Bite! Bite! Bite!"

Wil put Tobi onto his feet. He sank beside him, and buried his head in his hands.

"I followed your smell, Wil," Tobi said. "Then I smelled that thing, and I ran, and I jumped."

"Thank you," Wil said.

"I bit it," Tobi said. "Bit it and bit it."

161

For a moment, they sat silently. Then the dog spoke.

"Wil, I'm hungry now."

At dawn they began their hike, at first in silence. Tobi spoke first.

"Where did that monster go, after I killed it?"

"Magic made it, long ago—we killed it, and it was no more."

"I killed it, Wil. Bite!"

"Yes, Tobi, but what actually killed it was my sword going into it."

Silence for a while.

"I killed it, Wil. I jumped."

"Not being afraid of it killed it."

They hiked on. And then Wil heard Tobi's voice again.

"Here comes Tobi,
Brave and bold.
He bit the beast.
Now it's cold."

"That's good, Tobi. You're not going to spend this entire journey making up ditties about yourself, are you?"

Silence.

Because he wanted to know, but partly to ward off further rhymes, Wil asked Tobi a question.

"Why did Zadni send you down?"

"Because she's my good friend, Wil."

"But she put her hands on you and looked into the future—what did she say? That she sent you to help me fight that beast?"

"No, about that Starstone thing, Wil. I don't know what."

They walked on, each deep in thought.

Abruptly, the dog burst into another recitation.

"Wil said,
'Tobi, you go home,
Because I want to walk alone.'
But Tobi followed, all the way,
And that dark night he
Saved Wil's day!"

By the time they started northward, up the mountain range's eastern flank, and he had heard Tobi's hundredth ditty about himself, Wil thought: why did that forest monster not eat me? Finally they reached Pinewich, to rest a night and restock their knapsacks.

Wil walked out that evening for a stroll. He found Tobi in the village square, surrounded by open-mouthed children, listening to the dog declaim—

"Wil cries, 'Tobi!
Save me, please!
This monster has me
On my knees.'
Tobi leaps!
He bites that beast!
Roast it, Wil—
We'll have a feast!"

Wil stalked back to the cottage the hamlet provided them. He got into bed. When Tobi returned later, he pretended to be asleep.

At dawn, when they resumed their journey northward, Wil told Tobi: "No more ditties about yourself."

Tobi looked sullen. But they walked on in silence.

At a certain point Wil glanced up and saw black wings flapping through the branches above them.

"Raven?" he called.

"Looking ahead, far ahead, seeing what's to see," came the response. And the black bird disappeared before them.

That night, Wil heard heavy footsteps in the darkness beyond their campfire. He tensed, but Tobi merely yawned. And so he knew they were guarded.

"Hello, Bear," Wil said into the night.

No answer came, except a sound like a cough.

They trekked ever northward. They passed Bear's cave. Wil hailed him, but received no answer.

"Off in the trees—smell him?" Tobi said. "He's chasing away bad forest things, because Pim told him to. But he won't visit us. Bear's always grumpy."

They came at last to the swamp where Wil hid his skiff, fleeing Marston's manor, ahead of the imperial constables. It rested where he left it.

He carried a pouchful of coins, silvers and golds, ample to purchase a boat. But in any river town, a boat-buying stranger would alert constables. So would a boat thief. Besides, he didn't wish to steal some poor fisherman's skiff. So they'd detoured far upriver, to retrieve Wil's own skiff. And now, with Tobi sitting in the bow, Wil pushed off.

He let the little stream's current carry them eastward, toward the great river. He dipped the oars only to steer.

Maples and oaks along the banks showed touches of gold, scarlet. Wil barely noticed. Around a bend, Marston's rickety dock thrust into the river. Wil bowed his head, hid his face in his hands.

"Are you upset, Wil?" the dog asked. "I haven't made up more rhymes."

Wil shook his head.

"There's a manor behind those trees," he said. "People there helped me, then died for me—it makes me feel guilty, and sad, and angry."

"Do you want to bark, Wil? And jump? And bite, bite, bite?"

"Yes."

Wil pulled into Marston's dock, and began to tie up. But he stopped, one hand on the dock, the other holding his skiff's rope. He knew what lay behind the screen of trees. All those wooden shacks attached like barnacles to the ruined manor— torched, strewn. And would there be bones?

He threw the rope back into the boat, pushed off from the dock.

"When your friends' died, did you feel lonely, Wil?"

"Yes."

They floated downstream. In the prow, Tobi gazed silently at Wil.

After a while, the dog spoke, but to himself, the words barely registering in Wil's mind.

"Each dog in High City has a home.
Only Tobi lived alone.
We journey now, so far we roam,
But Tobi and Wil—now at home."

When they reached the stream's mouth, at the great river, they found Raven awaiting them, perched on an overhanging branch. Wil stopped the skiff beside the tree.

"What do you see, Raven?" he asked.

"No galleys until the town stinking of fish."

"Fishtown," Wil said.

"A delicious stink," Raven said.

"And in Fishtown?"

"A galley docked, marchers in the streets."

"Red jerkins, yellow capes?"

"Many, and south of there, ever more galleys, ever more marchers."

"Thank you, Raven."

Abruptly the black bird flapped its wings and lifted from its perch, hovering above the skiff.

"Back to my forest," Raven cried. "Go well! Go well. Bear needs teasing."

Raven flew westward, growing smaller. But after the bird disappeared over the trees, Wil heard its voice in his mind, faint.

"Go well! Go well!"

Wil sat thinking. Tobi, meanwhile, looked bored. After a while, the dog's brow furrowed in concentration. Several minutes later, he began reciting a new ditty, about jumping and biting and having no fear. Wil glared. Tobi hushed. He sat in the skiff's prow, looking out at the river moodily.

"Here's how it is," Wil finally told the dog. "Between here and Fishtown, no galleys. Raven said so. Why not go down now in the daylight, make good time, no patrols to catch us. Get to Fishtown—after that, we'll sneak. What do you think, Tobi?"

Tobi looked solemnly at Wil, as if considering. Finally he spoke.

"I'd like to eat now, Wil."

An autumnal wind blew them downstream. They rode the current, too. And then the cresting tide turned seaward, speeding them on. Wil rowed only to steer the skiff tight to the western bank.

No other boat moved on the river. Occasionally a collapsing dock marked a farmstead, hidden behind the trees. Wil thought: torched.

Dusk.

Ahead, low and dark, Horse Skull Island. Eastward, lanterns glinted behind Breming's shutters. On the western bank, stone cottages climbed the hill to the great forest's edge—Fishtown. Here, too, just-lit lanterns shone through shutter chinks. Wil caught the first whiffs of racked mudfish from the smokeries.

He rowed crosscurrent to the island, then down its western flank. In light so dim, Fishtowners wouldn't see him. He rounded the island's southern tip and slid the skiff into the Horse Skull Tavern's cove. At the wharf, no boats bobbed, and now the stone stairway led only to blackened beams, ashes.

After a while, it grew too dark to see.

"Night comes early in this season," Wil told Tobi.

They sat silently. Water slapped the skiff's hull. Wil finally spoke.

"I'll go to Fishtown."

He sounded defiant.

"I'll be only a few moments, just to see."

Silence from Tobi.

"Well, what do you think?" Wil demanded.

"All right," Tobi said.

Another silence.

Wil blurted: "Why do you let me do this insane thing?"

"You want to, Wil."

In darkness, Wil steered the skiff silently downstream past Fishtown's wharf. No moon shone tonight, and clouds hid the stars. But he knew this shore, and in his mind, as the skiff glided by, he saw the long-abandoned boatyard. Here, on the rotting hull of an uncompleted galley, he and Kobar, in their childhood, played river pirates.

He passed the three-story brick home of the imperial assessor of levies. Every window glowed yellow. From the mansion emanated faint fiddling. Beyond the assessor's house, he rowed into a swampy bay.

From memory, he followed a familiar channel through cattails and willows to the muddy banks. Once, nightly here, under shoreline oaks, he met the assessor's third daughter, until she outgrew so unpromising a boy.

"Stay in the skiff, Tobi," he said.

From the dog's knapsack, stashed under the aft seat, beside his own, he extracted biscuits, prepared for Tobi by his friends in High City. He laid them on the boat's forward seat.

"I want to go with you," Tobi said.

"I need to sneak," Wil told him.

"I can sneak, Wil."

"No you can't, Tobi. Eat your biscuits."

Tobi looked from Wil to the biscuits.

"All right," he said.

Wil left Tobi sitting in the boat's prow, looking at the biscuits. Through the oaks, yellow glints shone from the mansion's windows. He groped toward them, stepping carefully. Wavelets slapped the river's banks. Behind him, he heard loud crunching.

"Tobi!" he thought. "Chew your biscuits more softly!"

He hoped no sharp-eared constables patrolled here.

"This is insane," he told himself.

But to walk in Fishtown, one last time....

And he wished—he didn't know why—to see his enemies' faces, to hear their voices.

He reached the last line of oaks, along the mansion's lawn. Beyond, enough light shone from the windows to faintly see. He lay down among the oaks, watching. After a while, he heard footsteps, swords clinking in scabbards, and seven men marched around from the front of the house. A pool of lantern light spilling from a window revealed their red jerkins and yellow capes. As they passed the spot where Wil huddled under an oak, hidden in shadow, he heard a man grumble.

"Won't see nothing in this dark anyway."

A second voice, the patrol's leader: "Shut up and do your duty."

Now Wil heard a third speaker.

"Domallon's not out here in the dark, marching in circles—he's in the fancy house eating dainties, and dancing, and we're…."

But the patrol passed around the house, along the riverfront. Wil heard only faint fiddle music, from inside. Three minutes later, the patrol reappeared, continuing its circling of the mansion. Wil heard the same voices.

"…must be one powerful swordsman, this Taker fellow, if he's got Domallon so scared…."

"Lord Domallon's not scared, idiot—he wants the Forester outlaw caught and gutted."

"Well, that young jackanapes, what Domallon hauls around in his pocket these days, he's supposed to know how the Taker looks, so why don't they…."

Again the patrol disappeared around the house.

"Kobar won't know me now," Wil told himself, for he'd shaved his mustache and cropped his long, blond hair, and Zadni's magic had turned his hair black, and his blue eyes brown.

He chewed his lip. After a while, he told himself: "Everything else I've done this night is insane, so why not this?"

He waited for the grumbling constables to pass a third time, on yet another circuit. As soon they disappeared around the house toward the river, he sprinted across the lawn, avoiding the pools of window light. Below one of the great windows—it opened from the mansion's parlor, he knew—he stood with his cheek pressed against the building's bricks, listening. He heard only fiddling from inside. Reassured, he reached high, gripping with his fingertips a crevice between the bricks, and pulled himself up. He braced the toes of his shoes in crevices, reached up again, and pulled himself higher still. He could now peep through the window, just his left eye, concealing the rest of his head behind the window's frame.

A fiddler stood on a platform to one side, bowing his instrument. Constabulary officers uniformed in red, with yellow collars and epaulets and belts, danced with finely gowned women. He recognized only the assessor of levies' wife among the women, and his three daughters. Kobar danced with the third daughter. As they swirled about the floor, Kobar spoke, and she smiled.

"Yes, he's more promising than I am," Wil thought.

Kobar now looked even more resplendent than when he first returned from Imperia. He no longer wore the constable's red jerkin and yellow cape. He wore soft gray boots and black velvet trousers, with a shirt of gold thread. He wore a black velvet jacket brocaded in gold.

Wil thought: "To wear velvet, you murdered your father?"

Off to the side, talking with the assessor of levies, stood the swarthy noble Wil had seen before. Lord Domallon. Wil saw that the fat assessor spoke eagerly to him, looking up, hands fluttering. Domallon listened, but his eyes followed Kobar on the dance floor.

"Do we three dance?" Wil thought.

He clung to the bricks like a squirrel, peering in at this great lord, and at his childhood friend. Those two dined and chatted, warm inside, in convivial light. He hid in darkness outside, in danger.

"Yet, I endanger them, too," he thought.

He thought again: "They must fear me."

A gust from the north chilled him. But beneath his shirt he felt warmth from the Opal of Living and Dying, in its leather pouch, hung from his neck by a cord.

Domallon glanced toward the window. Wil pulled back his head, but the movement cost him his grip. He thudded to the ground.

"What's that?"

He'd forgotten the patrolling guards, to count the passing three minutes of their circuit.

"Heard a thump, over that way."

Wil lay on his back, unable to breathe, momentarily paralyzed.

"Over here?"

Feet tramping towards him.

"Wait."

The feet stopped.

"What?"

"Oh, it's just a dog."

"Probably the pet of them that's inside."

"Their dogs live higher than we do."

"Quiet—you don't know who might hear."

And the patrol moved on around the house, toward the riverfront.

Wil sat up and found himself looking at Tobi.

"I ate my biscuits," Tobi said. "Then I sat a while, smelling the night, and then it was lonesome, so I followed your smell through the trees and here I am."

"Tobi...."

"Yes, Wil?"

"We're in terrible danger here—go back to the boat."

But the dog turned away and sat looking out toward the river.

"You hear me, Tobi."

No response.

From the front of the house, a sound of marching feet, swords clinking. Three minutes had passed. The patrol approached on its circuit.

Tobi growled.

"Hush," Wil said.

"I don't like their smell," Tobi said.

Wil sighed in exasperation.

"Then come with me—but sneak, Tobi! Quiet!"

"All right, Wil."

Keeping to the gloom between pools of window light, Wil led Tobi to the yard's edge, then hunched down. Close to the house, the patrol marched its circuit, toward the river. As the constables passed, Wil ran after them in the dark, silently, following them around the house. Tobi padded alongside him.

To his right, Wil heard the river lap at the embankment. It smelled of fish and mud and water. If it came to it, he thought, he'd grab Tobi and leap over the embankment, swim downstream to the skiff.

But they'd catch him, so many constables.

"This is insane," he thought.

Silently in the dark, he followed the patrol around the house. Ahead, torches lit the mansion's entrance. Constables guarded the portico, and stood along the drive.

Wil hid behind an oak, in shadow. Tobi sat beside him.

"What now?" Wil asked, although not aloud.

"I don't know," Tobi said. "What do you want to do, Wil?"

"I want to see our enemies," Wil said.

"To bark?" Tobi asked. "And jump? And bite, bite, bite?"

"Yes, I'd like to do that," Wil said. "But there are hundreds of them, and I left my sword in my knapsack in the skiff, lying next to your knapsack, so I've only got the dagger in my pocket."

"When you want to bite, you should do it," Tobi said.

"That's not good advice," Wil said, and they sat in silence.

After a while Tobi lay down, resting his muzzle on his paws. Soon, from his breathing, Wil knew the dog slept.

He waited, although he didn't know what he waited for. On the portico, the guards occasionally stamped their feet, against the autumn cold seeping through their boots.

A half-hour passed. Abruptly, the mansion door swung open, letting out light and fiddle music from inside. Lord Domallon appeared in the doorway, still pulling on his coat. Beside him walked Kobar, a sheathed sword slapping against his velvet trouser leg. After them came the assessor of levies and his wife and his three daughters, none wearing cloaks.

Daughter number three, Wil noticed irritably, managed to position herself beside Kobar, who stood with his hands clasped behind his back looking upwards at nothing in particular. With hands fluttering, the assessor of levies executed a series of small bows, directing them towards Domallon while not excluding Kobar. Domallon exchanged a few words with the man, looking bored, as he pulled on gloves. Finally, with a languid wave, Domallon walked off the portico, Kobar at his side. They started down the drive. Without looking back, Domallon raised his gloved left hand, crooking his index finger. Immediately three of the portico guards picked up lanterns from the porch and fell in behind him, at a respectful distance. They followed Domallon and Kobar down the drive.

On the portico, their hosts gazed at the retreating pair, the assessor still executing small bows, unseen. Abruptly, with a shiver, the oldest daughter hugged herself, clasping her hands on her bare shoulders, chilled. Their mother then ushered them inside, with backward glances down the drive. But the third daughter lingered on the portico, gazing wistfully after the retreating guests. Then, with a sigh, she too went into the house and shut the door.

"Do you know what Kobar has become?" Wil thought angrily.

He touched Tobi's head. When the dog awoke, looking up, Wil spoke.

"More sneaking and hiding—can you do that, Tobi?"

"Yes, Wil."

"If you bark or growl, they'll kill me."

"I won't bark or growl, even if I want to," Tobi said.

To himself, however, the dog muttered: "Bite, bite, bite!"

"Tobi, will you do this for me?"

"I'm your friend, Wil. I'll do anything for you."

"Fifteen minutes from now, will you remember?"

Wil said it to himself. But Tobi answered.

"I'll remember, Wil."

He led Tobi through the trees, parallel to the torchlit drive. They ran silently in the dark. When they drew abreast of Domallon and Kobar, they slowed to a walk, keeping pace with the two. Fearful of the guards, Wil dared not creep too close, but he heard snatches of their conversation.

"...dreary provincial affair..."

"Yes, your Lordship."

"And yet, Kobar, you found the youngest daughter of interest."

Kobar snorted.

"She once threw herself at Wil Deft, and now it amuses me to show her...."

Weariness washed over Wil.

Moments ago, this girl's fancying Kobar stung. Long ago, it seemed, Kobar felt a similar sting. In those days, Kobar aspired to become imperial assessor of levies, succeeding the girl's father, living in that riverside mansion. To marry the daughter....

Dust, such things now seemed.

In its pouch next to his chest, he felt the Opal of Living and Dying grow warmer. It almost seemed to breathe. In his mind he saw tendrils—cause and effect—entwining him with the two men he followed. With every act, every decision, the tendrils grew denser, tightened.

There would be a death tonight.

Wil shuddered.

"It's better not to foresee," he thought.

Now they'd reached the drive's end. Wil hid behind a tree with Tobi, watching. Domallon and Kobar walked out of the torchlit drive into dark River Street, followed by the three constables. After a few moments, Wil walked after them, still in the shadows, Tobi at his side. He sensed the dog's excitement. But his own belly felt sick with fear.

Someone would die tonight.

This gem he wore around his neck changed him. Now he glimpsed the future.

I'm a Forester, he thought. And the Opal of Living and Dying brings out the magic in me.

Ahead, a lantern flared. In its glow, Wil saw a constable pocketing the flints he'd used to light it. Then a second lantern flared, and a third. Now the constables walked closer to Domallon and Kobar, holding up their lanterns to give them light. Wil saw them strolling toward the town's center, talking, but he could no longer hear them.

"Stay close to me, Tobi," he said.

He followed them along the stone street, moving between pools of shadow, from doorway to alley. They came to Kobar's father's cottage. Torches blazed, lighting it front and back. Constables carried equipment out of the house, heaping it in the dooryard. Wil made out folded tents, swords, crossbows, knapsacks. Through the cottage's lighted windows, he saw more constables working inside. In the front dooryard stood a table, with two chairs. Domallon sat in one, Kobar in the other. An orderly set out before each a stemmed glass. Another brought from the house a bottle of wine, and poured. Wil watched the two men talking, as they eyed the bustling constables. He yearned to hear what they said. But he hid beyond the circle of torchlight, across the street in a lane between two cottages, too far to hear.

"Tobi," he said. "Do you see that big maple tree at the edge of the dooryard?"

"Yes, I see it, Wil."

"I am going to sneak there, and hide behind that tree, and I must ask you to do something for me."

"All right, Wil."

"I ask you to stay here in the shadows, and don't make noise, and if I call you and ask for help, to come."

"All right, Wil."

"Tobi? Will you fall asleep?"

"I won't nap, Wil."

"Good."

Wil started out from the lane, keeping his eyes on the constables heaping gear in the dooryard, and on Kobar and Domallon at their table. If they looked his way, he'd freeze. Behind him, Tobi spoke, and he heard the dog's words in his mind.

"I don't like them, Wil."

"Don't growl."

"I won't, Wil."

But, to himself, the dog whispered, "Bite!"

Beyond the torchlit circle, Wil made his way in darkness, pausing in doorways, behind a fence, beside a chicken coop. Once, he stopped, overcome by a thought.

176

Who'll die tonight?

Tobi?

If they attacked Tobi, he'd pull his dagger from his pocket, assail them. He knew it, deep inside. They'd kill him. They'd keep the Starstone. Their strength would grow. They'd overwhelm the Foresters and rule forever.

Yet, he'd fight for Tobi.

That he knew.

Bent over, hands brushing the ground, he glided through darkness to the maple tree at the torchlit circle's edge. He stood six steps from Domallon and Kobar, talking at their table as they watched the constables heap gear, and he listened.

"...and it's not too late to cancel it, Kobar."

"No, your lordship. It's for the empire."

"And perhaps also to garner glory, and rise?"

"I would show myself worthy of your patronage, Lordship. And if I do find their High City...even root them out...."

"With one-hundred constables I doubt you'll do much rooting out."

"They have no army."

"They have magic."

"But I grew up with a Forester, and Wil Dent never produced one magic spark."

"Kobar, would you necessarily recognize magic? It might be subtler than you imagine. And in that great forest, it's said, lurk enchantments, dangers...."

"I'm not afraid."

Lapsing into silence, the two men sat musing over their wineglasses. Wil had been crouching behind the tree. Now, to ease the strain in his knees, he carefully stood. As he rose, from the darkness behind him, he heard a gasp.

Dimly he made out the form of a man. Darkness had concealed him. Yet, all along, he lay sleeping on the ground beside a fence. Now he awoke. Wil's movement startled him. He sat up.

Wil considered.

Run?

With a hundred constables at his heels?

Despite the torchlight, this side of the tree remained in shadow. Wil doubted the man saw him clearly. Yet, the man's form in the darkness, and his movements, seemed familiar. With his own long, yellow hair now short and black, and his blue eyes brown, no Fishtowner would recognize him. But precisely because this awakening Fishtowner couldn't see those changes in the dark, might he recognize Wil's form, and movements?

Wil slid his dagger from his pocket.

Someone will die tonight.

Before him, the sleeper lurched to his feet, peering at Wil in the dark. Wil suddenly knew the man, for his right leg ended in a wooden peg.

Tunkle.

He couldn't see him in the dark, but Wil knew that stained gray beard, those watery blue eyes. Old Tunkle, who lived in a riverside hut of flotsam. Errand runner for food. Cadger of ales at the Horse Skull Tavern.

Wil had last seen him that night at the tavern. Tunkle wanted to curry favor and wheedle a free tankard of ale from those two Breming bullies, so he'd pointed out Wil as a Forester foundling. That night when his life changed.

Wil thought now: Tunkle, do you remember I bought you ales, sharing my few coppers? Do you remember I helped you repair your hut's thatching? Will you turn me in?

That night in the tavern, Wil feared he might become Tunkle, old and poor, a cadger of drinks. Must he now slay Tunkle?

Six paces away, at the table, Domallon spoke.

"I had a son, Kobar...."

"I didn't know, your Lordship. Is he...."

"Defying me, he joined the constabulary, a lieutenant, ambitious to make a name for himself—he would've been your age now."

"He died, your Lordship?"

"His patrol galley, night on the river, overran smugglers—they slew many constables, including my boy."

"I'm sorry."

"One got away, a huge hulk, one-eyed. If I catch him...."

"I'm sorry, Lordship."

"Just your age...."

Wil slid his dagger back into his pocket. He started toward Tunkle. He meant to clasp his hand over the old man's mouth, silence him, carry him away. But what then? If he left him alive, Tunkle would tell—the Taker had been here. They'd know he made his way down the river, toward Imperia. Peering at him in the dark, the old man spoke.

Wil?"

Just then, something rolled under Wil's foot and he toppled at Tunkle's feet. Lying there, he knew he'd stepped on an emptied ale jug Tunkle left lying before dozing off.

"What's that?"

Domallon's voice.

Kobar: "Something in the dark, over behind that tree."

Domallon: "Get constables!"

As he lay on the ground, Wil saw Tunkle suddenly arouse himself, step over Wil's fallen body with that wooden peg, stride into the circle of torchlight. Just then the old man began to lurch and mumble and stagger.

Wil thought: You awoke sober, but now you pretend drunkenness.

As the old man reeled toward them, Kobar and Domallon stood. Kobar drew his sword, but then laughed.

"It's only an old drunk from the town, your Lordship. May I introduce to you Tunkle, the ragged and aromatic?"

"What were you doing there, old man?" Domallon demanded.

"Ah, good ale I had this evening, a gift from a dear friend, for whom I plucked a chicken, and then I felt dozy, and lay a moment by that fence…."

He helps me escape, Wil thought.

While the old man distracts them, I can make my way in the dark across the street to Tobi, and then to the boat. And I can spend the rest of my life thinking this old man had more parts to him than I knew.

"This shambles was a friend of Wil Deft's, a fellow ale sucker," Kobar sneered.

"Yes, and I watched the two of you growing up," Tunkle said, real anger in his voice. "One boy kind, and one lusting to rise, possessed you were, and you slew that good teacher your father, in every way your better…."

"Shut up, flatulence!" Kobar said.

"Yes, never worth Wil Deft's toenail, you were, and now you serve these oppressors, who grip all our throats, and…."

Kobar suddenly gripped the old man by his hair, and pulled back his head, and put the point of his sword to his throat.

"Yes, you serve these oppressors…."

Tunkle's words ended in a scream, for Kobar thrust up the sword.

He withdrew the blade, red now. He released Tunkle's hair. And the old man fell to the ground and lay still.

Wil thought: Tunkle! I had no time!

"Better get some men and search over there," Domallon said, gazing down with cold eyes at the dead body.

Kobar started toward the constables. But he took only a step before Domallon reached out a hand and grabbed his arm and stopped him.

"You see what's happening?" he said

"Just an old fool...."

"No, it's begun," Domallon said. "He's loose, their Taker, and their Wielder's ready, and the Foresters stir now...."

"But just an old man," Kobar said, looking down at Tunkle's body.

"An old man who spoke out against the empire, to imperial officers, Kobar. I said the magic is subtle. Already it's working on the people, stroking their defiance—get constables, search over there."

Sitting on the ground where he'd fallen, Wil saw Kobar hurry to three constables, just carrying tents from within the house. He pointed toward where Wil lay in the darkness, spoke. Dropping their tents, the constables drew swords, marched toward him, scanning the darkness as they walked.

If I run, they'll see me, Wil thought.

In his mind, he called.

"Tobi!"

He heard no response.

Asleep.

"Tobi!" he called again.

"Yes, Wil?"

Groggy.

"Tobi, run toward these men, and bark for my life."

In the darkness, Wil heard scampering from across the road. A moment later, he saw Tobi running toward the maple tree, pass him, stand at the torchlit circle's edge, glaring at the approaching constables.

Tobi barked.

"What is it?"

"Just some village dog."

"Well, shut it up, then."

Wil saw a constable unsheathe his sword. He pulled his own dagger.

"Now run, Tobi," he cried. "Meet me at the skiff."

"Bite!" Tobi said, standing his ground, as the constable approached, sword raised.

"No!" Wil said. "Run!"

With a final fusillade of barks, the dog turned and sped off into the night.

As the constables ran half-heartedly after the dog, Wil slunk away from the maple tree, crossed the street in shadows, and then melted into a dark alleyway.

CHAPTER NINE

They traveled nights.

In coves, imperial cutters lurked. To get by, Wil hid with Tobi below the gunwales, letting the skiff float past like driftwood.

He eluded galleys by rowing in their wakes, close under their sterns. No watchmen looked there. When the galley stopped some scow to search, he let the current waft the skiff away in the boarding's uproar—oath-shouting constables flinging aside tarps, stabbing broadswords into heaped potatoes or onions.

"Got a youth on board? Lanky? Blue-eyed? Yellow mustache?"

In moonlight, Wil kept to shadows cast by islands or shoreline forests.

Days, he hid the skiff among marsh reeds. He and Tobi took turns, sleeping and watching. But usually Wil awoke to find the dog sprawled in the bow, napping.

"It's boring," Tobi explained.

Northern forests gave way to southern farmlands. Towns grew more frequent, and each succeeding swath of lantern-lit windows stretched farther along the river's flanks. It grew warmer, too. Wil no longer buttoned his jacket.

Days, hidden in reedy marshes, he watched sailing freighters wallow toward the imperial city, laden with peat or lumber or apples or cheese rounds. Fishing skiffs dotted the river.

One afternoon a galley rowed downstream towing an imperial barge. Under the barge's canopy, striped crimson and gold, dignitaries in ornate chairs dined at a carved table. Wil recognized Lord Domallon, by his muddied complexion, as if from an excess of blood. And he made a gesture Wil remembered—pointing a thick forefinger at the person he addressed.

So now Domallon returned to Imperia. Did he suspect the Taker had slipped by? Then the capital would be guarded fiercely.

Wil didn't see Kobar aboard the barge. He guessed his one-time friend now led his hundred-constable battalion into the great forest, to torch any Forester hamlets he found, and to hunt for High City.

One afternoon, on Wil's watch, unfamiliar white birds glided over the river. He heard them, in his mind, speak of the schooling fish they followed upstream, and of the sea—so close—to which they'd soon fly back.

So he neared Imperia.

No moon shone that night, but galleys crisscrossed in the darkness. Wil heard their splashing. He dipped his own oars silently, and with exquisite care, because a galley's watchmen might see even an oar blade's starlit swirl.

Along both shores, buildings more massive than Wil thought possible now loomed. Warehouses, he guessed. Factories. Here and there, rows of lit windows marked workers' tenements.

Just after midnight, the great river bent rightward. Now the air changed, a new scent.

"Ocean," Wil told himself.

It smelled of brine and iodine, mixed with peat fumes from the capital's chimneys. Buildings now stood on either side like cliffs. Wharves lined both banks, and Wil made out docked ships larger than any he knew, their masts thrust up into the city night's dim yellow glow.

He knew this spot. All those afternoons in High City, studying Pim's maps—he knew every street in Imperia, each avenue, lane, alley, bridge, every dock and ferry landing.

"Don't bark or growl, Tobi," he said. "If you make noise, we're dead."

"It smells strange here," the dog said.

"Yes," Wil said. "In this strange place, do what I say, or we're dead."

"All right, Wil."

He glided the skiff in among the great docked ships, and then farther, into the darkness beneath the wharves. It smelled here of rotting wood, and muck. He steered through the maze of supporting struts.

In the beams overhead, tiny feet scuttered. Wil heard squeaking voices, and knew they spoke of grains fallen between planks, bits of meat, and of animosities over territories transgressed, and over mates tempted.

Tobi, in the bow, stared upwards. Wil saw the dog's eyes glint, his chest swelling.

"Tobi, don't bark!" he said.

"Rats up there," Tobi said.

"Don't bark," Wil said.

"All right, Wil."

They squeezed ahead through the pilings. Wil braced an oar against a rotting post and pushed. The skiff inched forward, then stopped with a shudder.

"Its nose is stuck," Tobi reported, from the bow. "Between two of those wooden things."

Overhead, boots clomped. Then, voices.

"You hear a bump down there?"

"Nah—you're spooked, all this Taker talk."

"Something bumped."

Wil sat frozen, looking up.

185

Silence from above. He knew they stood listening.

On a beam overhead, a sudden squeaking. A faint thump. A tiny scuffle.

"Oh, damned rats."

The boots clomped away.

Wil silently made his way to the bow, braced an oar blade against one of the imprisoning pilings, pushed. He pushed again, harder. With a jerk, the skiff freed itself, floated backwards.

Now, with subtle motions of the oars, Wil inched the skiff ahead, peering over his shoulder to see a way through the pilings rising all around.

Ahead, a ladder rose to an opening. He slipped past it. Surely, up there, a constable watched.

Now the wharf angled sharp right. Wil sensed the water broadening, for here the river emptied into the ocean harbor. It was this turning of the docks he sought.

"Tobi," he said. "Do you see that spot overhead in the planks, at the corner toward the shore, where a little light comes in?"

"Yes, Wil. Yellow light."

"I want to go there, but I have to row and push—I want you to look ahead at all those posts sticking up, and all the struts, and tell me whether to push the boat straight or toward the shore or toward the water."

"All right, Wil."

With exquisite care, for he didn't know if guards listened above, Wil now oared the skiff ahead.

"Straight," Tobi said, from the prow.

Then: "Turn a little, Wil—toward the water."

Slowly, they inched a zigzag course, Tobi reporting pilings in their path, Wil veering left or right. All the while Wil listened for sounds from above, but heard only rats scuttling.

Nearing the opening overhead in the planks, he braced the oar against a post, then pushed. Looking over his shoulder, toward the bow, he gauged the boat's forward glide. Just as it slid under the opening, he lowered his oar blades into the water, braking. Then he sat looking up.

It was as he'd imagined, from the maps. Where the wharves turned sharp right, on the inside corner, the planks didn't quite meet, creating a triangular opening, just wide enough for a dog and a rangy man to squeeze through. But one point he'd missed: the opening looked to be twice his height above him. He'd planned to jump upwards, grip the opening's edges, pull himself up and through, but he couldn't jump so high.

He slumped in his seat and sat, chin on his chest. After several minutes like that, he looked at his knapsack lying at his feet. He fished a hand inside and pulled out the end of a rope, eyeing the knot he'd tied there, to keep the rope's tip from unraveling.

"Tobi?" he said. "Please come here and bring your knapsack—I need your help."

Tobi crawled backwards toward Wil over the skiff's seats, gripping his knapsack with his teeth and towing it after him. Wil looked into the dog's knapsack. It still contained sufficient food to last Tobi several days.

Would a knapsack-wearing dog provoke suspicion?

From his own knapsack, he pulled the long rope. Then he stuffed Tobi's smaller knapsack inside, recoiled the rope, and put that inside, too.

"I'm going to put you into my knapsack," Wil told the dog. "Then I'm going to hoist up the knapsack with an oar, to the opening, so you can crawl out on top—can you do that for me, Tobi?"

Wil saw the dog frowning up at the opening, far overhead. Tobi then looked unhappily at Wil's knapsack.

"I don't like that, Wil, because I'll be squeezed in your knapsack so I can't move my legs, and also I don't like being up high like that," Tobi said.

"It's important, what I'm asking," Wil said. "If you don't do this for me, I don't know what will happen to us."

"It's high, Wil," the dog said.

"Yes, it's scary," Wil told him. "But when I lift you up, I'll hold the oar with all my might, and your head will be outside the knapsack, and also your front legs, so you'll be able to see and to scrabble out when you get to the top."

"I don't like it, Wil."

"Will you do it for me, Tobi?"

"Yes."

He lifted Tobi and gently slid him into the knapsack, with just his head and forelegs outside. Then he entwined the knapsack's straps tightly around an oar's blade, and tested the heft to make sure the straps held.

"All right, Tobi," he said.

"I don't like it, Wil."

"You'll be up in a moment," he said.

He gripped the oar at the blade's base, then lifted.

Now the knapsack, with Tobi inside, hung suspended just above the skiff's floorboards. It felt heavy. But he heaved upwards, resting the oar's nether end on the skiff's floor planks, braced against his foot, and levered it nearly vertical. Tobi, suspended inside the knapsack, looked into his eyes.

"It'll be all right," Wil said.

He heaved again. Now the oar, its base resting on the skiff's bottom, pointed straight up. Tobi hung a half-foot above his forehead. For a moment, he rested. Then he knelt, sliding his hands down the oar. He got a grip, far down, right hand below, left hand above, steadying the oar. Slowly, he stood, balancing the upright oar, raising Tobi toward the opening.

He groaned.

"I'm swaying, Wil!" Tobi cried. "I don't like it at all!"

Wil—grimacing with the strain—stopped the oar's teetering. He looked up. Tobi hovered below the opening.

"A little more," Wil said.

Grimacing again, he raised the oar an inch. Another. Then a few inches more.

He groaned, his neck's tendons taut. He dared not look up.

"Are you high enough?" he asked. "Can you get out?"

Wil felt movement at the top of the oar.

"I need to go a little higher, Wil."

He stood a moment, gathering strength. He heaved the oar up, and held it.

He felt the oar's blade move. Abruptly, the oar lightened in his hands.

"I'm out on top," Tobi said.

"Are people there?" he asked.

"I don't see anyone," Tobi said. "I smell people off in the dark."

"How far?"

"I don't know—not so far."

"All right, Tobi—I'm going to lift the oar a little higher and let the knapsack rest on the planks."

"It's resting, Wil."

"Good—can you loosen the straps with your teeth and get the knapsack off the oar?"

From above, he heard a faint scratching.

"It's stuck, Wil. I smell rats."

"Don't think about the rats, Tobi. Work on the knapsack."

More scratching. Finally the sound stopped.

"It's off, Wil."

With a sigh, Wil lowered the oar. He shook the ache from his arms.

"Tobi," he said. "Put your head into the knapsack and find the rope and pull it out with your teeth."

Silence. Wil sat down in the skiff.

"I pulled out the rope, Wil. I smell rats everywhere."

"Please ignore the rats, Tobi—and don't bark!"

"I want to bark."

"Don't."

"All right, but it would be good to do."

"Tobi, I want you to look for something you can wrap the rope around—like a post sticking up, or even a nail."

Moments passed, then minutes.

What if the dog could find no place to fasten the rope?

Then he'd have to tell him how to find the house where Mita and Blossom hid. For a long way, because he'd memorized the maps, he could direct Tobi through Imperia's streets, speaking to him in his mind. But eventually Tobi would be too far off for talking. If he told him the remaining streets, would the dog remember them? Probably he'd forget. He'd become lost in Imperia. Even if he did remember the way, and fetched Blossom, surely Blossom would be caught, and Wil, too.

"I found a place at the edge where the boards are a little apart, Wil, and I can make the rope go between them."

"Good, Tobi, good."

He sat in the boat, thinking.

"At one end of the rope, there's a knot—can you find it?"

He waited.

"I found it, Wil."

"All right, Tobi—wedge the rope between those two planks you found, so that the knot is underneath and holds the rope if you pull on it."

190

"Wil?"

"Yes, Tobi?"

"I really want to bark at the rats and chase them."

Wil sighed.

"Please do this for me," he said. "And don't bark!"

Minutes passed.

"I did it, Wil."

"Good!" he said. "Now take the free end of the rope in your teeth and drop it down through the opening, so I can get it."

A moment passed. Then the rope slid down toward him. He reached up, grasped the end.

"That's good, Tobi—now I'll pull it down and you'll sit up there quietly and make sure nobody comes."

"All right." Grudgingly.

Wil pulled the rope and it fell towards him, one length, then another. Finally the rope tightened.

"I'm coming up," he said.

He climbed the rope, hand over hand, clamping the rope between his feet to steady it, and to hold himself in place when he rested. He climbed again. His head poked out the opening.

Tobi sat on the wharf, head swiveling, eyes gleaming. Wil knew he smelled rats.

"Don't bark!" Wil said.

He loosened one hand, relying on his feet clamped against the rope to hold him up, and gripped the wharf's planks. Then, feet still braced against the rope, he let go his other hand from the rope and gripped the planks with that hand, too.

For a moment, he rested like that, head down.

"Just a bit more," he told himself. "I can do this."

He heaved upward, all his strength. Now he half lay on the planks, his legs still below. He rested again. Stifling a groan, he lifted his legs out of the opening and lay stomach-down on the planking. He rolled onto his back. He looked up at the city sky's dim yellow glow.

So he'd come to Imperia.

After a few moments, he sat up, listening in the dark. He heard no voices, no boots.

"What do you smell, Tobi?" he asked.

"Rats!"

"Besides that."

"People off that way, Wil," the dog said, looking back up the river.

"And that way, too."

This time Tobi looked in the other direction, where the wharves extended along the ocean harbor.

Wil guessed guards watched all hatches in the wharf, where the Taker might climb up a ladder. They'd not thought of this accidental crevice, at the wharf's turning, where the planks didn't quite meet. But guards must stand all along, on either side in the dark, listening.

"Tobi, we're going to leave here now, without making one sound," he said.

"But the rats...."

"When we were still in the forest, you promised me you could sneak, Tobi—do you remember that?"

"No."

"Can you sneak?"

"Yes."

"We're going to sneak, Tobi. If anyone hears us, we're dead."

"All right, Wil."

He coiled the rope and stowed it in his knapsack. His knife stayed in his pocket. He remembered his sword, stuffed inside the knapsack. To be caught armed would mean arrest. He considered throwing the sword into the water. But it would splash. He could leave it on the dock, but they'd surely find it. And it would tell tales, for it was Forester forged. Besides, if caught, with no way to escape, he might as well fight.

"I believe Blossom taught me well," he thought.

He strapped on his knapsack.

For a moment, he stood, peering into the dark. To his right, up the dock, a spark. A guard, he guessed, striking flints to light his pipe. Not far off.

"Stay beside my feet, Tobi," he said. "And sneak!"

They set off, Wil picturing the maps he'd studied. Ahead of them, he knew, beyond the wharf, lay the palace. If they turned left now, and continued walking along the wharf toward the ocean harbor, they'd come to Emperor's Dock, where the royal boats and ships and barges tied up. That way lay a gate. Lights. Guards. To their right, not far up the river, a guard stood puffing his pipe. So they must now leave the wharves, and get onto the palace grounds.

"This way," Wil said. "Stay close, Tobi."

They walked to the wharf's inland edge. There it butted against a high stone wall, which blocked them.

Wil peered at the wall in the darkness. He knew from studying the maps in High City that a wall ran here. But he had experience climbing walls. He felt its stones with his hands.

Again, he pulled the rope from his knapsack.

"I'm going to tie this around you, Tobi, like a harness," he said.

"I don't like being tied," Tobi said, as Wil wrapped the rope around the dog's body.

"It's just for a few moments," Wil said. "I'm going to climb this wall, holding the rope, and when I get to the top I'm going to lift you up with me."

"Wil, all this lifting up makes me want to growl."

"It'll be over soon," he said.

193

He felt along the wall. At the height of his knee, he found a crevice between two blocks and inserted his shoe's toe. Then, above, he found a fingerhold. He raised himself, found more chinks for toes and fingers, and continued his ascent. Just below the wall's top he stopped, like a bat clinging to a cliff, listening. Then he raised his head to peer over.

Below, the city's dim glow revealed manicured lawn and trimmed bushes, and groves, with walks intertwining. Beyond loomed the palace's immense flank, most of the windows lit yellow. Against the sky's glow, he made out battlements and turrets, high up. He saw no guards, but knew they must stand everywhere. After listening awhile, and looking to catch a shadow moving, or a pipe's glow, he pulled gently on the rope trailing behind him down the wall.

"I'm going to pull you up now, Tobi," he said.

"All right, Wil," Tobi said. "Then we'll sneak."

"Yes," he said. "Then we'll sneak."

He pulled the dog up, as gently as he could, hearing Tobi's claws sometimes scrabble against the wall's stones. And then they both lay atop the wall, looking over.

"What do you smell?" Wil asked.

He heard Tobi sniff.

"People out there, Wil, this way, that way…."

But to return to the wharf would be pointless. They could only go forward.

"We'll go down now, Tobi," Wil said. "Remember, sneak!"

"We'll sneak," Tobi said. "Sneak, sneak, sneak…."

"That's right," Wil said. "No barking. No growling."

"Sneak!" Tobi said.

Wil lowered the dog, inch by inch. Then he swung his own legs over the wall's edge, found a niche with his toes, and began his painstaking climb down. When he finally sat on the ground at the wall's base, he unwound the rope from Tobi and stowed it back in his knapsack.

"Now it becomes difficult," he told himself.

They had to make their way around the palace. But everywhere in the dark stood guards.

Should they wait until dawn, when ringing bells announced the curfew's lifting? Then visitors and strollers would appear in the palace park. Might they blend with them? But those strollers in the park would be aristocrats, or wealthy merchants, or officials summoned to the palace on imperial business. His clothes and unkempt hair marked him as a poor man. Constables wouldn't recognize him as the Taker, now that Forester magic had blackened his blond hair, and turned his blue eyes brown, and he'd shaved his mustache. But for a poor man to trespass here—that alone could mean death.

Should he pretend to be a thatcher, hired to renew a stable roof? But the forged papers he carried identified him merely as a gatherer of rags and other discarded items. Such scavengers filled the city, and so Pim had chosen it for him as the most plausible identity. In any event, if anyone stopped him, he could produce no authorizing summons to the palace.

"I'm tired now," Tobi said. "Should we lie down and sleep a little?"

"Not yet—we have to sneak, and night is our friend."

Tobi remained silent, thinking. After a few moments, he began a recitation:

"Who tiptoes in the night?
Sneak! Sneak! Sneak!
Who gives rats a fright?
Sneak! Sneak! Sneak!
Who sniffs out paths for Wil?
Sneak! Sneak! Sneak!

Who...."

"Tobi, stop!" Wil said. "You promised, no more ditties about yourself."

"I don't remember," the dog said, sounding cross.

"Well, you did," Wil said. "When we're safe in the apartment, you can make up all the ditties you want."

"This is a good one."

"You insisted on coming with me," Wil said. "Remember?"

Tobi remained sullenly silent.

"Look for enemies in the dark, Tobi. Listen for them. Sniff for them. And sneak!"

"Sneak," Tobi said, miffed.

But as Wil started off, the dog padded close by his ankle. In the darkness, he heard Tobi snuffling, and he felt reassured. Guards hid in the nighttime dimness, but they couldn't hide their scent.

Wil led them away from the wall, for he guessed sentries guarded it. He also eschewed the park's paths, also surely watched. Sky glow and light from palace windows cast shadows, though, so they zigzagged from bench's shadow to shrub's to grove's. Wil peered into the murk, looking for glints from bronze buttons or sword hilts. And he listened for a boot's shuffle or a cough or a scabbard's clank. Mostly, he relied on Tobi's nose.

"People coming, Wil!"

They stood hidden under a willow's drooping branches.

"Stay here," Wil said, placing a hand on Tobi's head. "No sounds!"

Shoes crunched a path's gravel. Two men's voices.

"...and so she's out again, Dapik..."

"Guarded?"

"Five men..."

"Then let it be—here's a bench."

They sat just outside the veil of branches where Wil and Tobi crouched. Darkness hid their faces. But the man named Dapik—that voice Wil knew.

Lord Domallon.

"How goes the hunt, Dapik?"

"He eludes us," Domallon said, a shrug in his voice. "We've plugged every slither hole into Imperia. Still, their magic…."

"But we have the stone, Dapik!"

"Hmm."

"Without it, they are worms. No?"

"Hmm."

"Do not worry, Dapik—does not His Magnificence, Torpan the Twenty-Ninth, guard the Starstone himself? And so resolute!"

"True, every night, reassuringly, he strokes it…in his magnificence."

Neither man laughed. Yet, in this dry exchange, Wil sensed a private jest between them.

Domallon then spoke.

"And in the palace, Garrent, while I was up the river, how do things go?"

"Our effort with war machines continues apace."

"Ah, " Domallon said. "His Magnificence fails to flag in his pursuit of these wondrous new weapons...."

"Unwavering in that pursuit, Dapik, unwavering! And, as always, there is the daughter...."

"Yes, night adventures…."

Both men sat silently. Finally the other man spoke.

"A thinning of the line…."

"In the best of families," Domallon said.

"We were warriors, Dapik—steaming horses, spears bloodied, battlefields heaped with enemy dead...."

Silence again.

"My aide now leads a battalion through the great forest," Domallon said.

"What's the lad's name again?"

"Kobar," Domallon said.

"Yes. Still promising?"

"He's not my son."

Silence.

Domallon again: "Ambition drives him. Ambition can serve as spurs...and reins, too. He's tested—I bade him execute his father, a dreary little teacher."

"Yet, this lad's a villager...."

"No, he's not of our line, Garrent."

Silence. Both men thinking. Domallon finally spoke.

"At the Foresters' defeat, so long ago, we were few enough, and since then...marrying among ourselves...."

"To keep the warrior line pure, Dapik, no? And the villagers—sheep."

"Yes, sheep—but so many, Garrent. Perhaps some wolf blood there, a few drops. An elixir, hmm? But these Foresters...."

Again the men sat silently. Domallon finally spoke.

"This evening, when they carried my chair along the Imperial Way, I parted the curtains to look out the window, and I saw...."

He fell silent. Remembering.

"Yes?" his companion prompted. "A woman, perhaps?"

"Beside that shop selling crystal chessmen, or you can get them in gold, onyx.... Do you know it?"

"I bought a set there, fine ivory, shipped from some southern land, I believe...."

"In front of that shop, from my chair, I saw a constable shove a churl from his path."

"Taught the wretch manners," Garrent said.

"No," Domallon said. "I saw the man glare at the constable's back, and then his face twisted in rage—No effort to hide it!—and he shouted some insult...."

"Skewered, surely!"

"Well, the constable spun around, drew his blade, but the man slipped into the crowd."

"That is troubling," Garrent said. "Tougher training, then, for the constabulary?"

Domallon sat silently.

"It was that the churl dared," he finally said. "To curse an emperor's man...."

"A lunatic, probably," Garrent said.

"Perhaps," Domallon said. "But on that crowded street, nobody grabbed the man, turned him over, lest they be punished for standing by...."

"Hmm," Garrent said.

"I even thought I saw approving smiles."

"But surely, Dapik...."

Both men fell silent, thinking.

Domallon finally spoke again.

"Where is the Taker? Maybe his task terrified him. He fled into the forest. He hides from us there, but from them, too, and maybe Kobar will catch him, " he said. "But here's a question—where's their Wielder?"

"Ah, the Wielder—I'd forgotten that one."

"Here, Garrent? Hiding in Imperia? And if the Wielder is so close to the Starstone, half the city away, perhaps, what then?"

"Surely, Dapik...."

"Proximity—what effect?"

Again the two men fell silent.

Finally the man named Garrent spoke.

"You think too continually."

"Dawn is soon," Domallon said.

"Back to the palace," said the other.

Wil heard them rise from the bench. Then their shoes crunched the path's gravel, the sound waning, gone.

"No!" Wil thought. "The Taker did not flee—he found a slither hole!"

"What's a slither hole?" Tobi said.

"It means that when you can't find your way, and it seems there is no way, it may be there, but low down and narrow, and hard to see."

"Oh," Tobi said.

"Sneak," Wil said.

"Sneak," Tobi said.

They glided shadowlike across the palace park. A fountain hid them, then the statue of an armored man astride a rearing horse. They reached an obelisk. Wil couldn't read its inscription in the dark, but he guessed it extolled deeds of their magnificences, the generations of royal Torpans. Ahead, torchlight—the palace's main gate.

From the darkness beyond the torchlight, Wil looked through the gate at the great Imperial Way, running north across the city. It lay dark, except for sporadic pools of yellow light from pole-hung lanterns. Pike-wielding constables guarded the gate. Wil counted twenty.

"Not here," he told Tobi.

They crept on in the darkness. Farther along the wall, they saw ahead another patch of torchlight. It marked a smaller gate. This one, Wil remembered, led to the Street of Glory, a lesser artery. They hid under a Linden tree. For a long time Wil studied the Glory Gate. Here fewer torches burned, creating a smaller circle of illumination. Pike-holding constables guarded this gate, too, standing outside a small guardhouse, backed against the palace wall, but fewer.

"I count seven constables," Wil told Tobi.

No reply. He looked down. Tobi lay sprawled on the ground, asleep. Wil smiled a little, in the dark, and resumed staring at the gate.

Should they move farther along the wall, and at some dark spot climb over? But surely no stretch of wall went unwatched, especially here, facing the city.

Dawn neared. Already the sky imperceptibly brightened. They might hide under this tree until day. Then people would move through the gate. Might they slip away in the throng? But the guards would stop every passerby. They'd demand papers, ask questions, peer at faces, and on the least suspicion make an arrest. Wil doubted he could escape such intense scrutiny.

"What will we do, Tobi?" he asked.

But he asked only to feel less alone. Tobi slept.

Wil thought: "How can you sleep at a time like this?"

But he supposed it must be different for a dog. Tobi, he knew, hardly ever thought beyond right now. Right now, he felt tired. And lying here in the darkness, he felt secure. His friend stood beside him.

In any event, Wil thought, no constables guarded the palace from a dog. No dog needed papers to walk Imperia's streets.

A dog was merely a dog.

"Tobi," he said. "Wake up."

A few minutes later, Wil had crawled—alone—as close to the gate as possible, to the last dark patch. Five steps away stood the guards. But they didn't see him, prone in a shrub's shadow.

He called, in his mind.

201

"Tobi, do it now!"

From the palace park—barking.

Loud. Furious.

Pikes went up. Eyes squinted into the murk.

Wil ran, crouched low, soundless.

Those averted eyes—how long?

He passed, soundless, three steps behind them. Where their guardhouse backed almost against the palace wall, he squeezed in. He stood, staring at the wall's stone blocks, an inch from his nose, awaiting the thrust of pike into his neck.

"Just a dog."

Guards speaking.

"Over that way."

He silently sighed. They hadn't seen him. Just to his left stood the open gate, and beyond it, the Street of Glory.

"A stray."

"Hey, you watch that gate."

Their sergeant's voice, Wil guessed. He could see only the wall's stones. But he heard the guards' boots scuffle on the walkway as they resumed their positions.

"Tobi!" he called, in his mind. "Do it!"

For a moment, silence.

Then, at the guardhouse, sudden snarls.

"Hey, the vermin bit me!"

Shouts.

Barking.

Wil peeked out.

Their backs to him, the guards brandished their pikes toward the darkness. Abruptly, low to the ground, Tobi hurtled toward them, a gold-and-white missile, at the last moment swerving to avoid a pike thrust, hurtling back into the darkness. Constables chased him, but Tobi shot back, into the remaining guards' midst, zigzagging through their legs, eyes sparking.

Wil squeezed out from behind the guardhouse.

He ran.

He sprinted up the Street of Glory, his shoes soundless on the paving stones, until he abruptly slipped into a darkened doorway and looked back through the gate.

Tobi erupted from the park's darkness, leapt up to a startled guard's chest, nipped the man's nose, jumped down, pelted back into the darkness. Three constables ran after him.

In his mind, Wil called: "I'm out, Tobi—run for the gate!"

"Bark!" Tobi said, exultant. "Jump! Bite!"

"It's not a game, Tobi! They'll kill you!"

From a different angle Tobi once more arrowed out of the darkness. Wil could see the dog's tongue out from the exertion, his eyes bright with glee.

Four grim-faced constables went for the dog with lowered pikes.

Wil, with a despairing groan, reached back over his shoulder into his knapsack, and pulled out his sword. If it came to it, he'd fight. So it would end like this.

He saw Tobi glance at the pikes aimed at him, abruptly dodge. Glee still in his eyes, the dog shot forward, through the sergeant's legs. He ran out the gate, then down the Street of Glory.

Two constables chased him, swords clanking in their clapboards.

Wil shouted in his mind: "Up the street into the dark, Tobi!"

"They can't catch me! They can't catch me!"

Silence.

After a few minutes, the sound of trudging boots. Back down street walked the two constables, arguing.

"I'd a had him if you'd stayed out of my way."

"You'd of had your own pike in your own foot."

"'Cause of you, the vermin's got away."

"Oh, it's just a dog."

"They'd of liked to have that one at the palace, wouldn't they? They like the feisty ones."

"Dawn soon—we can get back to the barracks and get breakfast, and forget dogs!"

At the guardhouse, the constables rejoined their fellows. Shouts. Remonstrations. Laughter.

"Tobi, I'm coming!"

He slipped his sword back into his knapsack.

All seven guards, on their side of the gate, argued, traded barbs, laughed. He slipped from the doorway, ran lightly up the dark street. After a block, Tobi darted from an alleyway, still panting from his exercise.

"Did you see, Will! Did you see me fool them!"

"When we get to the apartment, you can make up a ditty about it," Wil said.

Man and dog made their way along the Street of Glory. Here and there, a hanging lantern cast a pool of light on the cobblestones and on the stone blocks of adjacent buildings, but they kept to the shadows. Where the street ended at the city's western wall, they turned right, onto Wall Way.

Ahead, torchlight. The city's Western Gate. From there, The Street of the Heroes of the Stone cut eastward across Imperia. It was this street Wil sought. But they must avoid the Western Gate's guards and torches.

He stood looking inward, studying memorized maps. Then they walked forward a way. Finally, turning right, he led Tobi up a narrow lane, then left into an alley. They emerged on the Street of the Heroes of the Stone. Two blocks to the west, they could see the Western Gate's torchlight.

"We'll just walk eastward a little, then left into Ragpickers' Lane, and we're there," Wil said.

He tried to suppress his exultation, lest it make him careless. But they'd done it! Found a slitherhole. Sneaked into Imperia. Already he'd gleaned vital information—from Domallon himself! Now, just a short walk to the apartment. And there, awaiting them, Mita and Blossom.

Wil walked feeling light as air. Tobi padded beside him frowning, and Wil knew the dog concentrated on composing a ditty about his exploits at the palace gate. He looked forward to hearing it.

They passed shops, shuttered for the night, their signs offering tea for sale, or cloth, or pots, or salted fish. Above these first-floor shops, Wil knew, the proprietors lived with their families. Soon, as the sky brightened, they'd clump downstairs, open shutters. The great city would stir.

"Stop!"

A gloved hand gripped his shoulder, spun him around.

Eyes glared into his own.

Red jerkin, yellow cape.

Tobi growled.

Three constables had come up behind, taken him by surprise. To one side, two more constables. They flanked a smaller person, robed in black, cowled.

"Tobi, stop growling!" Wil said.

"Bite!" Tobi said.

"No," he said. "Slink away—I may have to send you to Blossom and Mita."

"Wandering at night, Filth?"

Both hands now gripped his shoulders, shook him.

They mustn't find his sword, his knife.

"It's almost dawn," Wil said.

Silence from the constable.

"That's curfew lifting," Wil said.

"Bell hasn't tolled yet, Filth—why are you wandering the streets with that knapsack?"

"I look for what's thrown away, and put it in my knapsack, and try to sell it as I can, to eat," Wil said.

"Scavenger, huh?" said the constable. "Out early getting ahead of all the other vermin, eh? Snatch up the best rubbish?"

"Yes," Wil said.

"You stink like your cur."

Another of the constables: "Drag him in?"

"Yeah, and nobody'll drag him out again."

He gripped Wil's arm, the hand like iron, and began marching him down the street.

"Oh, la di la!"

A woman's voice. The cowled figure.

"Yes, Ma'am?"

"I'll speak with this man."

"But, Ma'am, he's just a scavenger...."

"Ah!" A voice like air. "I need your permission, Sergeant? To speak with whom I wish?"

"Ma'am, we're charged with your safety...."

"Oh, la di la!"

Wil could see the cowled woman stare up at the constable, thoughtful.

"Sergeant, could you guard me without your head?"

"No, Ma'am, but...."

"Snick-snick, Sergeant."

He heard the constable sigh in frustration. The man glared down at his boots.

Silence.

"Well, then," said the woman, "let us sit on that bench at the corner, Sergeant, this young man and I, under the lantern...."

"But, Ma'am...."

"…where we will chat, this fascinating young man and I, and you will stand out of my sight, hmm?"

"He's vermin, Ma'am…."

"Snick-snick, Sergeant."

"As you wish, Ma'am."

She led Wil to the bench, the five constables clumping along behind. Tobi had slunk away, as Wil told him to. But he sensed the dog standing nearby in the dark, and he could hear Tobi growling inwardly, thinking "Jump! Bite, bite, bite!"

"No, Tobi" he said. "Let me talk."

Patting the bench beside her, to show Wil where to sit, the woman sat down. She threw back her cowl, and shook black hair, down to her shoulders. Her face, even in the yellow lantern light, looked pale, as if she rarely walked in sunlight. A woman his own age. Long black lashes, unblinking blue eyes, but pale almost to white.

Cat eyes? But she seemed like a moth, too.

Now the woman gazed at the sergeant, who lingered beside the bench, his jaw clenched. She raised her eyebrows. He looked stubborn.

Wil saw the woman silently mouth two words at the sergeant: "Snick-snick!"

With a silent snarl, the sergeant ushered his constables into the darkness beyond the bench. They watched him, Wil knew, his every movement. He sat still, hands in his lap. But he held his legs tensed, ready.

If it came to that, he'd vault from the bench into the darkness, drawing his sword from his knapsack as he ran, and his dagger from his pocket. He'd try to outrun them. If not, he'd seek some narrow dark place where they must come at him one at a time, so he could fight them each in turn.

But even if he killed them all, and escaped, Domallon would know strangeness lurked in the city. And what that strangeness might be, Domallon would guess.

She sat studying him. Finally she spoke, her voice like a child's.

"Where is your little dog?"

"He ran away, Ma'am, frightened," Wil said.

He called her "Ma'am" as the constables had. Clearly she ranked high, this young woman. And he guessed "Ma'am" must be the proper term of address.

"Do you understand animals?" she asked.

Was it a trick question?

"Foresters, I'm told, speak with beasts," she said.

"I'm not a Forester, Ma'am," he said. "I just search the streets for what people throw away, handkerchiefs, food, sometimes I find a lost copper or even a silver…."

"Oh, la di la," the woman said, looking cross. "Foresters they describe as sly spell casters, treacherous and tricky, gnawing at our realm, like rodents, malice in their strange eyes, and so on…. You're merely simple and poor, and you smell badly."

"Yes, Ma'am."

"I asked you about animals."

"I understand them a little," Wil said. "My dog, anyway— he wants food and water and a warm place to live, and he wants friendship perhaps even more, and he likes to sleep in sunny places and to…."

He almost said, "compose ditties about his own exploits." But he stopped himself.

"I've been thinking about animals," she said. "And about heads."

"Yes, Ma'am."

"Do you think, young man who understands animals, that what's in a head could go into another head?"

208

"I don't understand," Wil said.

"Ma'am," she said.

"I don't understand, Ma'am," Wil said.

"Those sounds, from down under, they do a little disturb me...."

She sat silently now, forehead furrowed.

"Do you think animals feel pain?"

"Yes, Ma'am," Wil said.

"Ah, and persons lower down, like you—could you feel pain?"

"Yes, Ma'am."

Now she pursed her lips, looking slyly into the darkness where the constables stood. She raised her voice.

"Let us say the sergeant displeased someone, and the axe chopped off his head—would he feel pain?"

"He would, Ma'am," Wil said.

"That might be nice," the woman said, canting her head to one side and looking into the darkness thoughtfully.

Wil found this conversation confusing. But he believed her talk about head chopping more than playful malice. And he thought, one wrong word....

"If what's in your head went into your dog's head, would your dog be improved and more useful?"

"That's too deep a question for me, Ma'am," Wil said.

"Oh, la di la, you're not helping me at all," she said.

She sat silently, looking cross. Wil fought the urge to abruptly leap up and run as fast as he could, into the darkness. But now it seemed less dark.

A distant bell tolled. Two dongs. Soon other bells tolled, from all parts of the city, some nearby, some far.

Curfew lifted.

"I suppose they'd like to have you," the woman said. "And your dog...."

Wil felt a chill.

She stood. She looked, Wil thought, petulant.

He, too, stood. He waited now, for what would happen.

Now the five constables clumped out of the shadows.

"Are you done with him, Ma'am?" the sergeant asked.

"Hmm," the woman said, looking with her pale eyes from Wil to the sergeant.

Wil made his jaw slack, trying to look stupid, and frightened. He did feel frightened. But he kept himself ready to suddenly heave himself at the constables, hoping to knock them aside in their surprise, and to run past them off into the streets, still dark enough for hiding.

Again the sergeant grabbed Wil's arm in that iron grip.

"We'll take him then, Ma'am," he said, his voice quietly triumphant.

"Did I say that?" the woman demanded.

"It's time this vermin got put into a rat's hole, where it belongs," the sergeant said.

"Ma'am," the woman said.

"Ma'am," the sergeant said.

They looked at each other, those two, the sergeant holding Wil's arm, looking belligerent. The woman looked petulant.

"I'm still having chopping thoughts," she said.

"Ma'am, this scavenger violated the curfew rules," he said, looking implacable.

"Ah," she said. "And would it pleasure you, Sergeant, to bring him in, and put him in a cell, and so on?"

"Yes," the Sergeant said, a sound like a hiss.

"Well," the woman said. "In that case, Sergeant, let him go."

"What?" the Sergeant said.

Wil saw redness rising from the man's neck to his face, muddying it. He saw the woman watching the constable's suppressed rage, too. She pursed her lips.

"Yes, I said let him go, Sergeant—that's what I want."

"But he's street vermin, he's...."

"Snick-snick, Sergeant," she said. "Snick-snick."

Wil felt the grip on his arm tighten. He felt his arm might break. But abruptly the sergeant flung him away. Wil reeled, fell to the paving stones at the feet of the other four constables.

Standing over him, the Sergeant glared. Wil could see the man getting control of his fury.

"I'll be looking just for you," the sergeant said, almost under his breath. "If we ever see you on these streets again, we'll rip off your arms, and then we'll stick a sword up your throat into your head."

He stood, legs spread, staring down at Wil. He spat.

Then the man wheeled, beckoned to his constables to follow, and started down the street. Wil saw the woman's face— impishly amused—before she threw up her cowl and walked behind the sergeant, with the other constables falling in behind her. She didn't look back at him lying on the paving stones.

Wil lay until they were gone. Then he sat up and buried his head in his hands.

After a while, he felt something wet on his cheek, Tobi licking.

"It's all right now, isn't it, Wil?" Tobi said.

"It's all right," Wil said.

He stood.

"Just a little way now, Tobi, to the apartment," he said.

He started up the Street of the Heroes of the Stone, with Tobi padding behind him. They walked together in the dawn's faint gray light, Wil's shoes scuffling on the paving stones and the sound echoing from all the stone buildings that rose up on all sides.

Between a shuttered shop selling butterflies in string cages, and a shop where a stooped old woman stood opening the shutters to reveal displays of scarves and ribbons and handkerchiefs, ran a narrow alley. An askew sign, faded by time and pigeon droppings, said Ragpickers' Lane.

"Down here, Tobi," Wil said.

He felt weary.

At the tenth door on the right, Wil led Tobi up the stairs and inside, a dark corridor smelling of boiled eggs, and then up a rickety interior stairway to the second floor, down a hall.

He knocked at a door. One loud rap, a soft rap, then two more loud raps in succession, as arranged.

After a moment, the door swung open. Silhouetted in the darkness, Wil saw the figure of a huge man.

"Nabob or pauper?" the man asked.

And Wil stood in the dark hallway unsure how to answer.

CHAPTER TEN

"That woman you met, Wil…."

Blossom stared at him.

"Princess Ranyan, that was, Torpan's own daughter—and with head-chopping on her mind!"

He spread his hands, palms up.

"Yet, here's our Taker, still got his head."

Wil lolled on the apartment's tattered divan. He luxuriated in weariness, and in Mita's presence, and Blossom's, and Tobi's. He even listened benignly as Tobi recited his latest ditty. Palace guards confounded! Hurrah for Tobi! Its underlying theme—Tobi saves feckless Wil—usually irritated him. But he felt peaceful beyond vexation. He even translated for Blossom, who lacked the Foresters' inner ear for animal talk.

All three applauded Tobi's verses. They praised his gallantry. Now he slept at Wil's feet.

Dawn. Through the apartment's open window, Wil heard hooves clip-clop. Wooden wheels rumbled on cobblestones. Donkeys brayed. At a nearby bakery's pier, a canal-boat crew thudded down flour sacks.

As the sun rose, venders cried—

"A copper for tea, a silver, a gold, ten-thousand kinds!"

"Fates in burned bones, two coppers!"

"Sugar bears, sugar lions, sweets for the small!"

"Hot water to wash! Be clean!"

"Riddles! Sly riddles! A copper to guess!"

Now the city roared. It drew Wil. As a Fishtown boy, he'd imagined these streets, but he felt too weary, just now, to explore. Besides, they must exchange news.

Wil reported Kobar's leading a battalion into the great forest, hunting High City. Blossom shook his head dubiously.

"I'll tell our agents, send word," he said. "But those constables—weirdlings they'll meet in that forest, enchantments...."

"I traveled through unharmed," Wil said. "First to High City, and now coming out."

"But you had Lal guiding you going in, and coming out, Tobi's help, and Bear's, and Raven scouting," Blossom said. "Besides, you're Forester-born, Wil, you have sorcery in you...."

"I've never worked magic," Wil said.

"It's strong in you," Mita said. "I feel it—stronger now than ever, but why does it strengthen?"

She studied him, brow furrowed.

"At the Horse Skull Tavern, when Pim and I first saw you...."

She peered, as if straining to look inside him.

"Bamba Moke, watching over you—she worried you cared only about ale...and girls, Wil! But you've changed, as if...."

Mita, too, seemed different.

When he first saw her, in the tavern, she tipped trays. Worry made her awkward. Wil sprawled on the divan, looking at her sitting erect in the chair beside him. More than worry perturbed her now. Something in her eyes....

"Are you peaceful, Mita?" he asked.

"I feel the Starstone," she said.

"How does it feel?" he asked.

"Near, and wanting me, Wil."

She put her long, thin fingers to her forehead, then pulled them away. She looked at him, hazel eyes wide.

"I can't explain it," she said. "It's in our world, the Stone, but it's elsewhere, too, and it draws me, demanding…. I don't know what."

They sat silently, all three.

Blossom spoke.

"We might as well tell the truth aloud, that putting the Starstone in Mita's hands, well, probably we'll fail—even finding where they keep it…."

"I know where they keep it," Wil said.

Blossom and Mita both looked at him.

"Lord Domallon told me," Wil said.

He recounted hiding under the tree in the palace park, listening to Domallon and the other nobleman talk.

Nightly, they said, the emperor himself inspects the Stone. Holds it.

"So we know it's within the palace, and surely in the emperor's own quarters," Wil said.

Blossom threw up his hands.

"Once more our Taker astonishes us—to glean this from Domallon, no less!"

"But to get into the palace," Mita said, in a whisper. "To the emperor's own chambers…."

"I'll find a way," he said.

But how, he could not imagine.

Mita suddenly cried out: "Oh, Wil!"

She put her two hands over her mouth, her eyes wide.

He thought, she has the sorceress's prophetic eye.

"I'm the Taker," he said. "I'll do this."

He put his hand on her knee, to reassure her, and also because it touched him, to be cared about. She continued to stare at him, eyes widened with dread. Slowly, she looked down at his hand, as if it mystified her. He took it away.

Nobody spoke. Blossom finally broke the silence.

"Tomorrow's worries are tomorrow's," he said. "Today's worry is lunch, and that'll be fried turnip and good lentil-bean soup, and yesterday's bread with today's butter on it, if you can stand a one-eyed old smuggler's cooking."

After lunch, and a sleep, Wil jostled through the crowd on the Imperial Way, south toward the palace, thoughts careening.

He'd unsettled her, touching her knee.

Had anyone ever reached out? Touched her?

They'd plucked her from home. Then, potions to master. Spells....

"You, our Wielder!"

All on a tot's shoulders.

To reach into others' lives.... How did they dare?

But, the empire....

Bamba Moke, murdered.

Marston ker Veermander, and all his family.

Kobar's father.

Old Tunkle.

And look here....

An old man passed, eyes hollow. On each thin shoulder, a teetering bundle of clothes, to be laundered. No sleeves to the old man's shirt. Iron rings around his wrists. And burned onto his skinny white arm, "C2-875"—his slave number.

Fishtowners, too. What they caught or made, the empire took. Even their thoughts....

Foresters remained free. But the empire plotted their extinction.

So, what choice for Pim and Zadni?

Send the Taker and Wielder.

They must. An obligation, even. Because only Foresters lived free.

But then….

Mita would surely become the Starstone's slave.

So, which mattered most—a people? Or a person?

He shook the thought away.

He must play Pilfer.

These passersby, for one thing. So many hundreds. Their lives twined into a fabric. How might he thread himself into that cloth?

To become invisible….

Nobles passed lolling in enclosed palanquins, borne by slaves, the poles digging into their shoulders. Gold-trimmed carriages rumbled by, too. Red or blue plumes bobbed at the horses' foreheads, their reins silver studded.

Oats, those horses wanted. He overheard their longings. And to run free.

A shop, displaying brocaded gowns on mannequins. Peering in, a wealthy merchant's wife, with two plump daughters. One girl points at a bonnet decorated with dead thrushes and butterflies.

A legless man, listless, holds out a cup.

Wil tosses in a silver.

He presses another into an urchin's outstretched palm.

Scavengers, like his pretended self, shuffle by. Eyes downcast, seeking. What? A dropped copper, perhaps. Or a spoilt child's tossed-away tart, half-eaten.

Up ahead, a pushcart heaped with oranges. One fallen beneath. A ragamuffin eyes it. A customer averts the vender's gaze. Quick, the scavenger drops to his ragged knees. Snakes under an arm. Snatches. Oaths. Heels fly. Melts into the crowd.

So—a Pilfer lesson. Playing in Fishtown, you lie belly down in reeds. Or crouch in a tree. On the Imperial Way, you blend with the swarm.

A shop selling fine threads and yarns, the walls lined with spools—red, saffron, pumpkin-orange, blue. Like a sunny autumn afternoon in Fishtown. And next door, from a smoked-fish stall, that familiar reek. Fishtown mudfish? Its proprietor, looking as smoked as her fish, glares at him.

All Imperia hunts the Taker.

If she suspects....

But what does she see?

Dark hair, not yellow. No mustache. A soot streak—applied by Mita's long finger—smudging one cheek. Brown eyes, not blue. A vacuous expression, perfected at the apartment's cracked mirror. Mouth slack. Gaze dull.

Just another scavenger, in a half-starved stupor.

But the disapproving fishmonger reminded him of Bamba Moke. So he gave her a jaunty grin. A wry wave. He let the crowd carry him away.

Practice.

From a spice shop, a heady redolence of cinnamon and turmeric. Oregano. Peppermint. And sausages roasting on pushcart grills. Ladies' perfumes, lavender and musk. Garlic. Sweat. Trampled manure....

"Coming through!"

Two slaves lurched past, carrying a rolled carpet, suspended by straps from a shouldered pole. They staggered down the street. Nobody looked at these non-men, their naked backs striped by whips, struggling to deliver some grandee's new floor covering.

"Hey, try my fig juice—one copper!"

"Come in, silk gowns, southern, and ebony combs for madam's hair...."

"Watch where you walk, ragpicker!"

He kept alert for red jerkins, yellow capes. In particular, he watched for Princess Ranyan's sergeant. Seize you on sight, the sergeant vowed last night.

"Pilfer," Wil thought.

He might yet hear: "Burglar, robber, thief—I bring you grief!"

Grief indeed.

"But see how far I've come," he told himself.

Ahead, the palace gate.

It stood open now, men and women passing in and out. He pretended to gaze longingly at a shop's stemware, its cream-colored china, its silver spoons and forks. Aslant, he studied the gate. Workmen walked through, toolboxes on their shoulders. Aristocrats, in silks and velvets. A foreign delegation cloaked and hatted in black-striped gray fur, from beasts unknown in this realm.

Constables stopped them all. Gauntlets held out, fingers snapping for papers. Questions. Searching looks.

It would be the same at each palace gate.

Better to scale the wall at night? He and Tobi did it, sneaking into Imperia. But would his luck hold?

If he did dare the gate, he might be a workman toting his toolbox, with forged papers to show. But what projects did the palace have underway? He could not know. And constables surely consulted lists of such projects, each assigned workman named, described.

Still pretending to look into the shop's window, he studied the gate.

Even if he did get in somehow. What then? Every room, corridor, passageway, door—watched. Who belonged inside, they knew. And who did not.

He had come this far....

But his elation faded.

Back at the apartment, while Blossom chopped onions in the apartment's small kitchen, and Tobi slept on an armchair, Wil paced.

"Can you make me invisible, Mita?"

"If I had the Starstone…."

"Until you have it, what can you do?"

"Change your hair, or eye color, cast spells of immobility and forgetting…."

He stopped.

"How widely can you cast such spells?"

"Inside a room, perhaps, but outdoors the spell weakens as it broadens…."

He paced again, slowly.

"If we did it at the palace gate…"

"I could freeze the constables at the gate, and the people standing around the gate, some…."

"But others farther off would keep their memories," Wil said. "And they'd see magic wielded, and they'd know."

"I'm sorry," Mita said.

He threw up his hands. Slumping into a chair, he stared at the floor.

"Where did you spend your childhood?" he asked.

"With Zadni Druen, mostly, and with Pim," Mita said. "I hardly remember my parents—it was in one of the forest villages—because I was so little…."

"Have you had boyfriends, Mita?"

"No."

"Does it anger you, their taking you away?"

She looked confused.

"I worry, that I'll be unable to…."

"Does it frighten you, Mita? To wield the Starstone?"

She looked at her hands resting on her lap.

"Are you frightened, too, Wil?" she asked, not looking up.

"Yes," he said. "And, also, I resent them—putting their hands on my life, before my birth, even...."

"But we must...."

She looked at him, beseechingly.

To wield the Starstone, she must become its slave.

But to bring down the empire, save the Foresters....

It would cost Mita her self.

He held his tongue.

She looked at him, eyes troubled.

"What we must do, Wil....Taker, Wielder.... It's so important...."

She clung to that, he saw. It held her up.

Rightly so, too.

What they must do, they must do.

"When I first saw you, I thought—there's a girl with reddish hair, and I don't care for red hair, and hazel eyes don't match red hair," Wil said.

"That's cruel, Wil," she said.

She looked hurt.

"Now I find you beautiful," he said.

All the next day, Wil scrutinized the palace. He studied its gates. He circled its walls, studying them, inch by inch. That evening, he returned to the apartment gloomy.

"We need the Starstone to get the Starstone," he said.

"Without it, I can only do magic," Mita told him.

Wil stood gazing out the window. Mita sat stiffly on the divan. Blossom had gone to instruct his agents to tell High City of Wil's safe arrival, and of Kobar's battalion, and that they needed more money. Tobi went, too—"I want to smell things!"

And if we had the Starstone?" Wil asked.

"Magic is just cobbling," Mita said. "Spells, incantations, they're just awls, needles, thread, tiny nails. But I could do sorcery with the Starstone..."

Her eyes lost expression.

Her body remained on the divan, but Mita went away.

Should he grip her shoulders, try to bring her back? He felt lonely. But then her eyelids flickered.

"I thought about it...and it drew me," she said.

She shuddered.

"It's so near, so powerful...."

"Did you see it?" he asked.

"I feel it," she said.

Again she shuddered.

"It's not like magic, like making shoes," she whispered. "If I held it, I feel I would see the world—not as it seems—but as it really is...."

She whitened.

"And, seeing, I could reach into it, with my mind...move things."

"Mita," he said. "The closer you get to it, the more you feel it?"

She nodded, unhappily.

Wil flopped onto a chair, staring at the ceiling.

"If we got even nearer to it, Mita, would you be able to use the Starstone, a little?"

She inhaled suddenly.

Stricken, she nodded.

"Or it would use me a little," she said, whispering. "Like what Pim and Zadni argue over...."

Wil remembered, in High City, the tension between the Lord of the War and the High Enchantress.

"Why do they argue?" he asked.

Mita looked at her hands.

222

"I shouldn't be telling…."

"I'm the Taker," he said.

They looked at each other.

Mita sighed.

"Things happened long ago, when the Foresters wielded the Starstone," Mita said. "I don't know what. It's not in the *Codex Mysterium*. Just handed down…."

"And Pim and Zadni argue over it?" Wil said.

"Pim means to use the Starstone to rule, for the good of all, Forest Kings…."

"And what does Zadni say?"

"She wants us to use the Starstone to become sorcerers again, to maintain the realm's peace, and to work at snuffing out the ancient dark spells, and to…heal sickness, help crops grow…."

"But not to rule as kings?" Wil said.

"She thinks the Starstone is too dangerous to use for that," Mita said. "She thinks it's too dangerous to use much at all, except there's no choice…."

And then the door burst open. Blossom strode in, carrying a sack, Tobi at his heels.

"Took me twice as long to get back, because they're all out crowding the streets, at the markets buying up those little candles for the March of Lanterns….

"What's that?" Wil asked, still sprawled in his chair.

"Every year at this time they do it," Blossom said.

"Wil, it's all strange smells out there, and lots of rats," Tobi said brightly. "I found a piece of sausage under a bench…."

Blossom emptied his sack onto the table. Bread. Apples. Butter. A cabbage.

"So where do they march with their lanterns?" Wil asked.

"To the palace," Blossom said, sinking into a chair and unlacing his boots.

Wil sat up.

"To the palace?" he said.

"Oh, it's this one time when ordinary folk get in there, marching down with all their lanterns, those little candles flickering inside, which is quite a sight...."

"Into the palace?" Wil said.

Blossom yawned.

"I'm thinking about tea," Blossom said, looking around the room for a stray cup.

"People go into the palace?" Wil said.

"Well, they go into the grounds, and march around with their lights, and then they go—those that fit, anyway—into the Great Hall, right where you walk into the palace, and the emperor appears, says this or that...."

Blossom suddenly stopped.

Mita and Wil both stared at him. He stared back. They sat in silence.

"I'm ready for biscuits now," Tobi said.

Just at sundown, the day's chill wind died. Above the rooftops, the sky turned silver, with crows cawing across.

Wil carried a tin lantern, paper-thin. It held an unlit candle. He'd bought both from a pushcart vender, who appeared this afternoon where Ragpickers' Lane met the Street of the Heroes of the Stone. Tonight the vender would vanish. So would his brethren, across Imperia. But this one afternoon a year, they did brisk business.

From side streets, tenement dwellers streamed onto the Imperial Way. Shouts. Laughter. Infants bawling. Boys snatching other boys' hats. Pennywhistle toots....

All toted unlit lanterns, purchased earlier today, or last year's, saved. At pushcarts, laggards dickered for what lanterns remained.

"Nine coppers."

"My brother, this afternoon, he paid two."

"Nine."

People crowded the walkways, spilled onto the street. Atop one man's head, a cloth-and-wire crown, painted gold. A woman draped in a tablecloth danced a ludicrous jig, caricaturing a gowned grand dame at a ball, in her hair, dinner forks—a tiara. She gestured imperiously, provoking titters.

An elbow nudged Wil's back.

A woman, hair dyed inky black, face whited with flour, drolly eyed him.

A pretend Princess Ranyan, he guessed.

"Oh, la di la," she said, pitching her voice high and airy. "Lord Domallon?"

Wil felt fear.

Then he remembered his own costume, made with Mita's and Blossom's help out of old clothes from his knapsack. He wore a black jacket and trousers seemingly threaded with gold, although merely paint dabbed, and a cotton shirt dyed silver, to resemble shiny silk. A floppy cap, pulled low, hid his face, should Princess Ranyan's sergeant see him. He meant to simulate any noble. But he supposed the Minister of Justice sufficiently famous for the woman to guess he aped Domallon.

"Perhaps, Ma'am," Wil said, playing the reveler's game.

"Ah," said the fake Ranyan. "Palace plots, Dapik—heads off!"

"Not mine, I hope," Wil said.

Evilly grinning, the woman pretended to study his neck.

"Snick-snick!" she sang, breaking into a dance, spinning away. Her voice faded into the uproar.

"Snickety-snick!"

Roars of laughter. Snatches of song. Sudden curses over a trod-upon foot. Earthenware jugs tilted up for swigs.

Wil milled with the rest. Waiting.

A gong. From the palace, he guessed. Then a bell, higher pitched, from the city's western quarter. A deeper bell tolled in the east. From the north, bells like chimes. Now, all together.

A hush. Then, a clacking, thousands of flints struck. It echoed down the stone street. All along the Imperial Way lanterns flickered yellow. Wil lit his own. With a surge, the march began. Wil moved with the crowd, a sinuous snake of yellow light. A baritone voice sang out, joined by others, then hundreds, a great roaring chorus....

"Duke for a day, am I, am I,
And dame for a night,
Are you...."

Mita waited beside the palace gate, as arranged. Wil exchanged a glance with her. She wore an ordinary dress, but carried a lantern. Thin, she looked. And pale. Brow knitted.

He smiled at her, quickly. Reassurance.

"Why cannot we speak wordlessly, Mita and I, as we do with animals?" he wondered.

He let the crowd carry him through the gate. He glimpsed Mita falling in behind him.

Now the marchers passed between phalanxes of scowling guards. Lit yellow by the marchers' lanterns, the constables looked surly. Every year they must suffer this sanctioned breach of their authority to bully.

From the crowd, muttered imprecations. Who cursed, you could not say. But with each malediction others, too, mustered courage to revile the guards.

Boldly, a shouted jeer—

"Red jerkins,

Yellow capes,
Garb for apes."

Constables glared. But the voice fell back into the din. Whose voice? Impossible to determine. Others took up the refrain, hissing it.

Pretending disdain, the guards looked away.

Titters.

It amazed Wil. They mocked the emperor's men.

But his first night in Imperia, hiding in the palace park, he heard Domallon speak of a commoner on the Imperial Way, defying a constable. Domallon worried: did Foresters already prowl Imperia? And might that alone—the Wielder's mere proximity—start the realm's unbalancing?

Ahead, the palace's bulk, all windows lit. Entrance doors open, light blazing from inside. Upon the steps, head and shoulders above all, Blossom. A momentary shift in the crowd revealed Tobi at his feet. As Wil passed, and then Mita, a few steps behind, Blossom winked his one eye.

"Wil! Here I am!"

Tobi's voice in his mind.

"I saw you, Tobi."

"Bark! Bite!"

"No, Tobi—what we talked about, what we planned."

"All right, Wil."

Wil squeezed with others into the palace's grand entrance hall. Marchers crowding behind pushed him toward the far wall. On either side, black-marble stairways curved upwards. Between the stairways, at the room's end, stretched a podium of white marble. And upon the podium stood a purple-velvet throne, its legs like golden war-horse legs, golden hooved.

Nobody stood upon the podium. Nobody sat upon the throne.

Wil stopped four rows back from the podium, feeling the room fill behind him. In the air a stench of sweat, and jugged rum, and pipe smoke, and ill-cleaned clothes. He smelled misery, too, like rotting lilacs, seeming to seep up from below, as if the palace tainted its supporting earth.

It unsettled him, that scent.

Wil glanced back at Mita, standing two rows behind, and saw she looked pale. He guessed the Starstone powerfully pulled her.

Was it right, asking this of Mita?

She'd been born the Wielder, schooled since childhood in potions and spells. Yet, she seemed more young woman than sorceress. He feared the Stone's nearness might overwhelm her. And if he succeeded, put the Stone into her hands? Then she'd feel its full power. The Stone would wield the Wielder. He caught her eye and smiled to reassure her....

Blackness swirled around him, like bats—angrily, he shook the vision away.

I see with no inner eye!

Foresters spread pox. They colic your baby, blight your corn, sicken your cow, give you bedbugs, rats, lice, ague. Their spells steal mudfish from your nets, and coppers and silvers from your box, and their breath is like swamp muck. At night they sneak from their weird forest, spreading malevolence and woe.

Yet, he'd just seen blackness swirl. He'd seen it with an inner eye, just opening.

He thought: it's the Starstone, so near now. It knows me. It reaches into me.

And I carry the Opal of Living and Dying.

Usually, it rested in a sack, hung from his neck by a thong. Tonight, he meant to leave it safe in the apartment, but did not. Instead, he slipped it into his sock. He clenched it now between two toes, the gem so small and smooth he hardly felt it. Yet, possessing it seemed vital.

What magic he had in him, he supposed, the Opal nurtured. But he shrugged. If tonight's plan failed, would magic ward off that blackness swirling over Mita and him?

"Born for this, we two," he thought grimly. "Bred for this. Fated for this."

Now the pushing behind him stopped, the room finally filled. Somebody started a chorus of "Duke for a day," but only a few voices joined in, then wavered away. So they stood still, Imperia's commoners, on their one privileged evening, awaiting their emperor.

Wil studied the chamber.

Two black-marble staircases curved upwards. He'd memorized the palace's plans in High City, and knew these led into the building's innards, but constables guarded the steps—too many. Even with spells of immobility, and then forgetting....

Magic worried him.

If they cast spells, and anyone saw, Domallon would know—Foresters! He'd scour the city, house by house. Magic might bring them down. Yet, two Foresters, an old smuggler, a short-legged dog...what could they do but cast spells?

At the podium's two ends, doors swung open. From each spear-holding constables marched. They lined up along the back wall, glaring at the crowd with stone faces.

A door now opened at the podium's center, behind the throne. Out filed men in velvet, silk, soft leather. Among them, Lord Domallon. They gathered beside the throne, talking among themselves. Domallon, however, spoke little. Wil saw his thick-lidded eyes scan the room. He looked for a lanky young man, no doubt. Unkempt yellow hair. A ragged yellow mustache. Blue eyes.

After a time Princess Ranyan walked out the door onto the podium, followed by the same sergeant who guarded her the night she waylaid Wil in the street, and asked whether animals felt pain, and if commoners did, and whether one head's contents might go into another head. Wil pulled his floppy hat lower over his face. If the sergeant recognized him....

In the hall's bright torchlight, Princess Ranyan seemed more mothlike than ever, for she wore a white gown of some fabric like spider webs, and her face seemed even whiter. In her black hair, she wore a tiara of white gold, glittering with diamonds.

Her bodyguard snapped his fingers toward the door. Two blue-liveried palace slaves carried out a divan, in purple velvet. They placed it beside the throne and Ranyan sank into it. She lolled. Her pale eyes squinted, as if so much torchlight felt alien, distasteful. Finally she sat up. She leaned forward, elbows on knees, chin resting on fists. She peered at the marchers filling the room, brow furrowed, as if perplexed over what to make of such creatures.

Minutes passed.

In the room's silence Wil heard the nobles on the podium murmur among themselves, although he couldn't make out their words. Nobody in the great crowd spoke, but he heard feet shuffle and children shushed and sighs.

Nothing seemed to happen, except the silence deepened. Princess Ranyan lost interest in the commoners and lolled back on her divan, legs crossed, one gold-slippered foot kicking a little in the air. Now she eyed the nobles beside the throne, looking bored and cross.

Out the center door marched red-liveried slaves. Under their arms, silver horns. They lined up along either side of the door, raised horns. A fanfare. Nothing happened. They tooted again. After an uncomfortable moment, one of the nobles standing beside the empty throne walked through the door. A moment passed. Then he backed out the door, resuming his place with the other aristocrats. With an uplifted index finger, he signaled the trumpeters. Once more they blew their fanfare. A tall man strode out from the door, between their ranks. He stood taller even than Blossom, but so lean his cheekbones jutted out, and Wil saw the bones in his wrists. He wore a purple cloak and on his graying head a golden crown, slightly askew. He stood, hands clasped behind his back, bending forward slightly to stare at the crowd through rimless spectacles.

Torpan the Twenty-Ninth.

A face like an eagle, Wil thought. Through his spectacles, Torpan scanned the crowd with a hunting bird's fierce gaze.

After a moment, he vaguely threw up his hands, as if whatever he sought in the crowd he did not find. Then he sat upon his throne, long legs stretched out before him. From a pocket in his cloak he withdrew a book. He began to read, as if he sat alone in his study.

Wil saw the nobles debate among themselves. They spoke to Domallon, who made dismissive motions with his thick hands. Finally, though, with a resigned shrug, he stepped forward.

"Citizens," he said. "Know this—Foresters skulk among us, perhaps even here!"

Wil heard gasps. Some in the chamber moaned in fear. Eyes darted about the room, as if they might identify invading Foresters by sight. Wil, too, assumed an expression of fear, and pretended to look for Foresters.

He saw Mita, behind him, stricken. To the room's side, Blossom stood above the crowd.

"Tobi?" Wil said, in his mind.

"I'm here by Blossom," Tobi told him, the dog's voice in his mind weakened a little, by distance.

"Tell Mita it's all right," Wil said. "Tell her Domallon doesn't know—he only guesses, and wishes to keep the people on edge."

"I'll tell her, Wil."

It would be better if he could talk with Mita directly. But at least he could speak to her through Tobi. He hoped Tobi conveyed his messages correctly.

"Citizens, what if you spy those wicked sorcerers, Taker and Wielder?"

Domallon fell silent, sweeping his eyes over the crowd. Abruptly, he shouted.

"Rend them!"

At that, a cry went up from the crowd, gathering strength—"Kill the filth."

When the refrain waned, Domallon motioned with his thick hands for silence.

"Imperial soldiers now march through their foul forest, hunt their secret city…."

"Kill the filth!"

"Yes, to exterminate this vermin!"

Again the crowd's cry: "Kill the filth!"

Domallon smiled, held up a hand.

"Yes, vigilance! For these Foresters wield vile magic. But look!"

He turned, slowly spread both arms, palms up, toward the tall, gaunt man on the throne, who continued reading his book.

"His Magnificence, Torpan the Twenty-Ninth!"

Now the crowd roared, crying "Torpan! Torpan! Torpan!"

But the emperor only pointed a long, thin forefinger at his book, to follow a particularly intriguing passage.

Wil saw Domallon turn up his eyes. But instantly the minister of justice stifled that expression of irritation. He resumed addressing the crowd.

"Our Emperor fears no Forester sorcery! Fearless, he stands before you. Fearless, he speaks!"

Now the crowd again took up the cry, repeating the emperor's name, over and over. But the emperor continued frowning over his book, as if the current passage engrossed him, yet perplexed him.

Wil saw Domallon exchange a look with the other nobles, then faintly shrug, eyebrows raised. After a moment, Domallon walked to the throne, bent over and whispered into the emperor's ear.

Torpan jerked up his chin, startled. He turned his fierce eagle eyes on his justice minister, who spoke words Wil couldn't make out.

"What? What?" he heard the emperor say, his voice surprisingly high-pitched, querulous.

Domallon spoke again, deferential, patient. But his face and neck looked more darkly muddy than usual. Wil guessed Domallon suppressed anger.

"Oh, them," the emperor said, taking a final long look at his book and then thrusting it into his pocket. He stood, his long legs seeming to unfold.

Torpan peered fiercely through his spectacles at the crowd. Yet, despite that fierce eye, to Wil, he looked distracted. And when the emperor finally spoke, in that high-pitched voice, it seemed unclear whether he addressed the nobles or the great chamber's crowd of commoners, or nobody in particular.

"March of Lanterns, yes, ancient rite....Give 'em something, eh? Distract 'em, eh? Well....Foresters! Now's their time. Thousand years, and all that. But it's mine! By ancestral right, and so forth. Valiant hard men of the horse took it. Men of

the lance! No magic for them, yes? Just valor, pluck. Still....
Tactics! Strategy! For us, constables. Lots of 'em, too. And the
peonage—addle 'em up. Keep 'em muddled. Good! But the
enemy's got Wizardry! All right. Then wield our own secret
weapons! Yes, our own necromancy. Speak, do they, with beasts?
All right! There's your key! Put your finger on that...."

Abruptly, the emperor stopped speaking. He stared out at
the crowd in the room as if abruptly awakened. He turned to
Domallon, his voice thin, querulous.

"Dapik—this vexes me."

Domallon stood looking at the emperor, his face
inscrutable. Then he whispered something and Torpan folded
himself back onto his throne.

Once more Domallon addressed the crowd.

"You heard your emperor—he spoke of the insidious
Forester threat, and of his determination to protect us all...."

From the crowd a few cries of "Torpan, Torpan," went
up, but weakly. Quickly, they died.

Again the emperor sat oblivious upon his throne,
studying his book.

"Go about your city open eyed, and any strangeness you
see, a sneakiness, perhaps, or some oddity of clothing or speech,
even—report to constables," Domallon said. "But now, citizens
of Imperia, and of the realm, refresh yourselves! On side tables,
through the munificence of His Magnificence, Torpan the
Twenty-Ninth, find food! Find drink!"

With the mention of the food and drink, the crowd
erupted with cries of "Torpan, Torpan," which became a roar.
Wil cried out with the rest.

But he felt increasingly despondent.

Around him, the crowd surged toward the room's sides,
where long tables stood laden with pewter trays of steaming meat
and tureens of punch and plates piled with cakes and tarts. Wil let

the crowd carry him along, noticing from the corner of his eye Mita swept along with him. They must not be seen together. But he saw Mita glance at him, look quickly away, then glance at him again.

He gave her a wink, reassurance.

But he felt grim.

They would fail. So much stood against them. More than he anticipated, back in their apartment, making plans. And those plans so flimsy. Seek an opening into the palace. Wield spells for access. Tobi to bear messages between them. Blossom to watch.

Hope.

That was their plan.

Yet, they had just tonight. Only during the March of Lanterns did commoners enter the palace. He'd found no other way in.

He meant to slip up the stairs. He hoped his aristocrat's costume would avert suspicions, at least from a distance. If a guard blocked him, he'd tell Tobi to warn Mita. Hidden in the crowd, she'd cast a spell to momentarily fog the man's eyes. Blossom, so tall above the crowd, would see guards lurking ahead. He'd tell Tobi, who'd tell Mita and Wil. And so the Taker would make his way up the stairs into the palace.

Pilfer.

But he hadn't anticipated a guard on every third step.

Wil guessed, so near, the Starstone reached out to Mita. He felt it, too. It had opened an inner eye new to him, showing him blackness swirling overhead. But, even with Mita's spells magnified....

Paltry, their spells.

But they had only tonight.

Wil pretended to choose from a plate of sweets. He pretended to relish a tart. But all the while he scanned the room and thought what to do.

A trumpet fanfare hushed the room. All watched the emperor, carrying his book, unfold himself from the throne and walk through the central door behind the podium, followed by his trumpeters. Wil saw Princess Ranyan wander about the podium, peering at the crowd, until Domallon spoke to her. They argued a moment, he thought, but then Ranyan shrugged, beckoned to her bodyguard, and left the podium through the center door, with the sergeant following. Now the nobles, led by Domallon, disappeared through the center door.

Along the podium, only the row of guards now eyed the crowd. At some signal Wil didn't hear, one by one, constables marched off through the two doors at the podium's ends. Finally, only two men guarded each of the podium's three doors, crisscrossing their spears across the opening.

Wil stared at the doors.

He felt weakness in his knees.

But he thought of Bamba Moke, and Marston ker Veermander, and Kobar's father, and peg-legged old Tunkle.

"Tobi," he called, in his mind.

"Blossom gave me some meat from the table, Wil."

"Talk to Mita," Wil said. "Tell her I'm going through one of the doors at the back of the podium...."

"What's a podium, Wil?"

"That long platform," Wil said. "Mita knows. Tell her to watch me, and to judge the right time to send dust into the guards' eyes, so I can slip through the door while they rub their eyes, and then to make them forget."

"That's a lot, Wil."

"Platform, guards, eye dust, forgetting...."

"I'll tell her."

"That's good, Tobi."

"I want to go with you, Wil."

"You help Blossom watch, and tell Mita what I said."

"All right, Wil."

Wil pretended to eat cake, but studied the podium. By now, the punch bowls' tide had ebbed, and the crowd grew raucous. "Duke for a day" choruses welled up, the words slurred. Somewhere in the crowd, fists thudded, a fight, partisans cheering. A commoner climbed onto the podium. Two guards hurled him off. But that incited shouts from the crowd—

"Duke for a day! Duke for a day!"

More men and women scrambled onto the podium, too many for the constables. They retreated to their posts guarding the doors, sullenly eyeing the interlopers.

Wil, too, now climbed onto the podium. He shouted and milled with the others.

A fat woman plopped onto Ranyan's divan. She leered at the crowd.

Applause.

A shout—"There's a sorry princess!"

Now the woman on the royal divan slackened her jaws, glazed her eyes, playing a simpleton.

Hilarity.

A constable ran to pull her off, but three more women squeezed onto the divan beside her. All four women folded their arms and crossed their legs, each kicking her foot a little in the air. They sat that way, staring insolently at the guard. A second constable, enraged by their defiance, ran from his post to help. But now a burly man, wearing a robe of stitched-together rags, dyed purple in berry juice, his crown of wired-together tin cups askew, staggered drunkenly to the emperor's throne and flopped down, to cheers from the crowd. He sang in an off-key baritone—

"Duke for a day, am I, am I,
And dame for a night,

237

Are you...."

Two constables rushed to pull him from the throne.

That left one door—the center door—unguarded.

Through that door the emperor had walked onto the podium, and Ranyan, and the nobles. Through that door they had left.

For this instant, no guard watched it.

"Tobi," Wil called in his mind. "Tell her I'm going through the podium's center door, and to cast no spells."

"All right, Wil."

Tobi's voice sounded faint now. Muted, probably, because so many heads buzzed with punch.

Wil staggered toward the unguarded door. He leaned against the jamb, as if too tipsy to stand, but carefully noting each guard's position, and where each guard looked. All the while he blinked, pretending to peer through a stuporous fog.

"All those nights at the Horse Skull Tavern," he thought. "Useful training!"

Wil slipped through the door.

He put a supporting hand behind him on the door jamb, seeming to nearly swoon from drink, but letting his eyes adjust to the dimness.

A chamber. Along either side, soft stuffed chairs. For dignitaries, no doubt, while they waited to deliver speeches on the podium.

At the chamber's end a shut door. Wil staggered toward it, still pretending drunkenness. Guards might watch this room through peepholes.

He swung open the door.

He groaned.

Before him, in a wide corridor, constables swarmed. And, as he stood in the doorway, all eyes looked at him.

"Hey!"

Hands grabbed him on either side.

He pretended head-spinning intoxication, lurching and clutching, as if unable to stand.

"Where're you going, dressed up like your betters, eh?"

A guard pulled the lantern he still clutched in his hand, dropped it onto the floor, stomped it flat. Another pulled off the hat partially concealing his face and threw it onto the floor. They peered at him, and Wil knew they looked for a blue-eyed youth, with yellow hair.

"Just a street rat."

Wil began to sing "Duke for a day," but a guard's heavy glove smashed across his mouth and silenced him.

"Whip him?"

He felt himself thrown against the wall. He rested his shoulder against the tiles, to keep from falling.

"Ah, it's their one night, isn't it?"

"All right, then, toss him out."

Hands lifted him, so only the balls of his feet touched the floor. They hauled him towards the door.

"They're letting me go," he thought.

Oddly, that thought left him downcast.

"I'll never get back in."

They hustled him through the chamber with the soft chairs, pushed him toward the open door to the podium.

"Let me see that one."

A voice he recognized.

He found himself staring into the face of Ranyan's sergeant.

Slowly, the man's mouth, inches from his eyes, broadened into a grin.

"Well, well, Vermin, we meet again."

For the second time that evening something within Wil showed him blackness. It streamed like swirling bats through the chamber, and was gone.

"Tobi!" Wil called.

And he heard Tobi's voice say, "Wil?"

But it sounded so faint he barely heard it.

"Tobi, tell Mita—they've caught me. But they don't know who I am. Tell her to get away, with Blossom and you, back to the apartment."

"I'll save you, Wil!"

"No, it's not like that—you must all go, all three!"

"What's going to happen, Wil?"

"I'll find a way, Tobi—go!"

"I'll come back, Wil."

"No, Tobi!"

"Yes...."

But the dog's voice faded.

With a sudden blow, the sergeant knocked him from his feet. He sprawled on the floor, his back against the wall.

"Trespassing on royal premises," the sergeant said.

He pulled a book from his jerkin's pocket. Wil supposed it must be regulations.

"Let's see," the sergeant said, leafing through the pages.

He made it plain that he only pretended to consult the regulations, for his own amusement.

"Yes, here it is, and look at that—it says, 'Beheading.'"

Now the guard stared down at him, grinning, triumphant.

Abruptly, he reached down, grabbed Wil's collar and lifted him to his feet. Then he marched him back through the door, into the palace. Down the corridor, the sergeant ushered him, guards scrambling out of the way. Beyond the corridor, a narrower passageway, empty. With a terrible momentum, his hand on Wil's collar, the sergeant dragged him forward.

Slung from the sergeant's belt, a scabbard, his short-sword's hilt protruding.

Wil's arms dangled free.

He thinks I'm drunk, Wil thought. Insignificant.

He envisioned the steps: grab the hilt, pull, swing up the sword's tip. Trust it upwards through the man's throat, into his brain.

What then?

Take his cape and jerkin, quickly. Disguised as a guard, hurry back the way he came, out onto the podium, away.

No!

Go forward. Into the palace. Find the Starstone.

He reached toward the sword's hilt.

But a voice came into his mind.

"Oh, it makes me so sad to see you doing that, Wil."

"Marston?" Wil thought.

But it was not Marston. It was something within him, speaking to him in Marston ker Veermander's drawl. He understood the voice assumed Marston's identity to get his attention, to make him heed this new sensibility, beyond eyes and ears, that now opened inside him.

"Why, if you go with that little old plan, they'll catch you, and you'll die for sure, and you'll never get the Starstone, anyway—wandering around the palace pretending to be a guard!"

True.

Within the palace, faces would be known. And they'd find the dead sergeant. With luck, he might last a half-hour.

"Now you just go along with that nice sergeant, whose taking you right inside the innards of their palace, Wil, and you see what you can do."

"They'll axe off my head!"

From within, he heard only silence.

He wished to act.

His hand yearned for the hilt. But he stayed it.

Born for this, he thought. Bred for this. Fated for this.

He let the sergeant continue to hustle him forward. And his thoughts turned black.

Now they entered a great room, where aristocrats in silks and furs lounged at tables, talking over emptied dinner plates, sipping wine from goblets. Wil noticed Lord Domallon at one of the tables. Beside him sat the emperor, speaking, gesturing. As if making a point of deep significance, the emperor pointed a finger at his own head. Domallon listened respectfully. Green liveried slaves hurried through the room, carrying trays of drinks and sweets, sometimes stopped by an upraised aristocratic arm, a gloved hand reaching for a goblet, but otherwise unnoticed. Everywhere along the walls stood constables.

Now the sergeant hurried Wil along one side of the room, out of the nobles' way. They headed, Wil guessed, toward a cell. Or perhaps directly to the executioner's workplace, with its bloodstained block. Leaning against the block, his bloodstained axe. Thus did the realm eliminate annoyances.

"Oh, Sergeant? Whatever are you doing, so busy and bumptious?"

Princess Ranyan's voice, behind them.

Now the guard stopped. Wil felt the man's irritation.

"Caught a vermin trespassing in your majesty's home," the sergeant said. "Taking him to the executioner—snick-snick, Ma'am."

"Let me see."

Wil felt himself spun around, the sergeant still gripping his collar. Ranyan now gazed into his face.

"Do I know this one?"

"We met the other night on the street, Ma'am," Wil said. "You asked about my dog...."

A jerk of the sergeant's hand on his collar shut him up.

"Oh, well," Ranyan said, waving one white hand languidly. "Snick-snick!"

Again the sergeant spun him around. Once more he felt himself hurried forward.

"Wait."

Ranyan's voice.

"I do remember that one. I remember him interesting to talk to, a little. Better than you sergeant...."

"It's just vermin, Ma'am, off the street...."

"Certainly more interesting than all them!"

Wil couldn't see, because the sergeant kept him facing forward. But he guessed that Ranyan gestured toward the nobles at the tables.

For a while, nobody spoke. Wil sensed the sergeant irritated, Ranyan thinking.

"Snick-snick," the sergeant muttered.

"No," Ranyan said. "Put him in livery."

For a moment, the sergeant didn't reply. Wil felt him grow enraged.

"Any particular livery, Ma'am?"

"Oh, I don't know—let Malaga decide."

"Whatever she decides?"

"What did I just say?"

He sensed her walking away behind him. Then her voice came again, fainter.

"La di la!"

Now the sergeant chuckled.

"We'll send you south, into the swamps, tap trees for turpentine," the sergeant said. "You'll enjoy the heat and the mosquitoes and the snakes and you'll die."

Out of the great chamber where the nobles dined. Down a passageway. Then a narrower passageway. A room.

Three constables lounged on benches, playing cards. When the sergeant barged in dragging Wil, they stood up.

A charred wooden blacksmith's block occupied the middle of the floor. Off to one side, a forge smoldered. Wil felt its heat.

"Do him."

With a sudden push, the sergeant toppled Wil to the floor. For a moment he leered down at him. Then he turned and left.

"Clothes off."

A corporal gave the order, an older man with a graying mustache. He sounded uninterested.

They scissored off Wil's clothes.

"Take off those boots."

Wil sat on the floor and removed his boots, and his socks. Between his right foot's big toe, and the next toe, he clenched the Opal of Living and Dying.

A bucketful of cold water suddenly splashed over him.

One constable threw him a rag.

"Rub yourself clean."

He did as they said.

"Hold out your arms on this."

They indicated the wooden block. He rested his hands on it. Wielding huge pliers, they now bent an iron band around each wrist, until its two ends overlapped, forming a bracelet. From the forge, one man withdrew a poker, heated white. He applied the poker's end to the seam in one of Wil's bracelets, heated it to melting.

Heat seared into Wil's wrist and he screamed.

"Shut up."

They welded the bracelet into a solid band around his wrist.

"Other arm."

Again the searing in his wrist.

"Got one ready?"

"Here."

Now they took another poker from the forge, this one ending in small metal rectangle. Abruptly, one of the constables thrust the white-hot rectangle against Wil's shoulder.

He smelled burning meat.

And then he felt the pain. He yelled with it.

They withdrew the poker.

Wil looked at his seared shoulder, now branded.

"D6—903."

His slave number.

CHAPTER ELEVEN

He sat resting his forearms upon his naked thighs.

Only minutes ago, constables had welded the iron bracelets onto his wrists. His wrists still burned. So did his shoulder's seared-on slave number.

"Stop moving or you'll get it in the neck."

He knew the constable standing behind him held a sword.

So he sat still, in the small room, and waited.

Stone floor, stone walls. Where he sat unclothed upon a crude bench, the stones lay bare. But in the room's back half, tapestries draped the walls, a forest scene of wolves and lions and bears and deer and owls and other creatures in a conclave. They seemed to speak with robed men and women who sat among them, listening. Wil thought the tapestry's people must be Foresters. A thousand years ago, he guessed, the southern invaders took it from the Forest Kings.

On that side of the room, a carpet covered the floor. Its colors—green, brown, gold—evoked a sunny forest afternoon. Wil guessed Foresters loomed the carpet, too.

A chair of woven ash slats, surely Forester made, faced the bench upon which he sat. Beside the chair stood an oaken table, strewn with documents and parchment sheets and writing quills and an inkbottle. He recognized the table's design, simple but sturdy. Forester made.

Behind the chair, a door stood closed.

"Where will they send me?"

"Wherever Malaga decides."

"Who's Malaga?"

"Shut up."

246

So he waited, wrists and shoulder afire.

He felt glimmerings in the room.

Despair still seeped up from below, the same misery he sensed earlier, in the palace's entrance hall.

And he sensed, too, fingers of silvery mist playing about his forehead, chest—Starstone.

He thought: it feels a Forester close, and it desires to be wielded.

Momentarily, those silvery fingers touched the Opal of Living and Dying, still clenched between his toes. He felt the gem swell, as if it inhaled.

Tiny voices chattered. In the walls, in the rafters. He knew he overheard the palace's mice and rats, speaking of dropped morsels and rivalries and sexual urges and concern for their pups.

Still nobody came.

Just to see, Wil relaxed a little his resistance to the Starstone's probing mist. Silvery fingers slid through his skin. Inside him, a turning. Doors, shut all his life, cracked open, stood ajar. Through those doorways he glimpsed a fabric, each thread one life within this palace, and then more lives, spreading outwards. They twined, those strands, untwined, writhed, and he could….

"No!"

"Hey, I told you to shut up!"

A sword hilt whacked the back of his head.

Now the mist fingers evanesced. But he sensed the Starstone waiting. Already he felt changed in some way he did not understand.

It unsettled him.

Nameless Ones forged the Starstone. They forged it from starshine, for Foresters to use. But the Nameless Ones made it. So the Stone's starlight must be alloyed with their darkness.

Between his toes—quiescent now—he held another thing of ancient wizardry. Long before Nameless Ones arrived, to work dark sorcery, the Opal of Living and Dying lay in the earth. How it came to be, no one knew. But he trusted the Opal.

At the back of the room, the door opened and a woman came into the room, walking on shortened legs, a dwarf. She looked sharply at him, naked upon his bench, then away, as if he held no interest. She reached high up behind her to grasp the knob and close the door.

When she climbed into her chair, she looked unexceptional, for she had a normal woman's torso. But her legs, so shortened, stretched straight out in front of her upon the chair's seat, the way a small child's do.

She examined a document she picked up from the table. He recognized his own forged papers.

What was this face?

Ferret, he thought. A triangular face, mouth wide, eyelids lowered to slits. But he thought, too, of a wasp's head, and of its sting.

"Name?"

A small, dead voice. In it, he thought, a bit of snake hiss.

"Deek Ald," he said.

That name they agreed upon in High City. A poor man's name. A common name in Imperia. His scavenger name. The name upon his forged papers.

She held those papers in her hand now. She read them.

"Parents?"

"Dead, when I still toddled."

She looked up from the papers. Unsettling, that sudden stare.

She resumed reading.

Her brown hair, center parted, fell to her shoulders. She wore a blue robe, sashed about her middle. Its voluminous sleeves hid her hands.

"Where do you live?"

"No particular place," he said. "Wherever I may be, there I sleep for the night—under a bench, maybe, or...."

Seemingly, she read his papers as he spoke. But he saw that her eyes slid to the side, and she studied him askance through slitted lids.

"Take care!" he admonished himself.

Now she put down the papers and examined him openly. His nakedness embarrassed him little. He'd been naked before women often enough. But his nakedness reminded him—as his masters intended—of his enslavement, of his negligibility.

"Do you prefer life in a village, or here in Imperia?"

He thought, would it be better if they sent me to some village? Escape then might be easier. But the Stone lay here....

Abruptly, he understood the trap.

"I've only lived here, Ma'am," he said. "I know nothing of villages."

"Don't call me Ma'am," she said. "I'm a slave like you."

She pulled back her sleeves to show the welded-on bracelets. For a moment, she stared at the iron bands around her wrists, her expression inscrutable.

"You no longer have a name," she said, again pulling down her sleeves. "You are a beast of burden. You are D6-903."

He said nothing.

She studied him again.

From the table beside her she picked up a document. She handed it to him and he took it.

"Fourth paragraph, first line—read that to me."

"New slaves shall be sorted by ability and appropriately assigned...."

She held up a hand for him to stop.

Now she gazed, eyes glinting. He felt he'd moved his piece badly.

"Go away, Constable," she said suddenly.

"But, I'm supposed to…."

"Go away—I'll summon you when I want him taken."

Nothing happened behind him. Wil saw the dwarf glare at the constable standing at his back, holding a sword. It lasted only a moment.

"All right, then," he heard the constable mutter.

A moment later the door behind him opened, then slammed shut. Now he sat alone in the small room, with the dwarf Malaga.

"So, an orphan, growing up a street scavenger—how did you learn to read, D6?"

Surely she hunted the Taker. She screened new slaves. And the Taker might be among them.

He had slipped.

"A man befriended me," he said. "A teacher, once, from somewhere up the river…."

"His name?"

He heard the snake's hiss in that small, flat voice.

"I knew him only as Gray-Head, what all the street people called him…."

"He, too, lived upon the streets, a scavenger?"

Wil nodded.

Again she examined papers from her table, but only seemingly. Her eyes slid sideways, to study him askance.

"And how did Gray-Head come to be a street pauper, D6? This teacher of literacy?"

"He said he admonished a magistrate's child in his school, and the child lied about it to her father, said he struck her, so

Gray-Head fled to Imperia, and sneaked in, and had no papers to teach or find work, and must hide, so…."

She put down the papers she held. She leaned back in her chair and studied him.

"What shall we do with you, D6?"

"What do you mean, Ma'am?" he said.

"I told you, scavenger who speaks so well—I'm a slave," she said. "Call me Doctor Gant."

"But if you're a slave, shouldn't you be called only a number?"

"Such a clever boy. I have a number. But I am…a slave of a different sort, with responsibilities, and I retain my name."

"What are your responsibilities, Doctor Gant?"

He thought amusement glinted, just a moment, in those dark eyes studying him from behind their slitted lids. For an instant, that long, thin mouth's ends tilted up.

"I assign incoming slaves," she said. "And I have additional responsibilities. And you have a certain impudence, D6. You may call me Malaga."

He said nothing.

They looked at each other.

He remembered his sessions with Blossom, back in High City, learning to wield a rapier. At a duel's start, often the opponents stand facing, swords lightly flicking, each fighter gauging the other. So this seemed.

"Did you know that Foresters have the magic to change hair color and eye color?"

Fear, like a lightning strike, coursed through him.

"I know little about Foresters," he said.

He added, "Malaga."

"Oh, but you should, D6," she said. "What could be more interesting?"

"Why do you find Foresters interesting, Malaga?"

She sat back in her chair, not concealing her amusement.

"Such a clever scavenger," she said.

She considered a moment. Then he saw her straighten in her chair, minutely, as if she had decided upon a course.

"Once upon a time, Fox—shall I dub you Fox? Sometimes we assign such nicknames to slaves of particular value. Shall I? Yes, certainly. You shall be Fox."

All this said in her small, dead voice. But now, underlying that flat tone, he heard a new note. He thought of a ferret scenting mouse. And something beyond that, too, thoughts too tangled for him to discern.

"Once upon a time, Fox, I also taught, like your benefactor Gray-Beard...."

"Gray-Head," he told her.

She eyed him aslant, her face turned away.

A successful parry, he told himself.

But take care!

"At the Imperial University I held the post of Distinguished Professor of Ancient Lore, and I occupied the Royal Chair of the Enemy."

"Enemy?" he asked.

"Foresters," she said. "I studied the Foresters."

Studying the Foresters, did she despise them? He wondered. A life devoted to learning about Foresters....And a professor, enslaved by the realm....

"How did you become a slave, Malaga?"

"Fox, you are wonderfully impudent. You refresh a weary soul."

Why did she speak to him in so familiar a way? Friendly, even?

Take care!

252

She leaned forward and rested her elbows on her knees and her pointed chin upon her cupped hands and stared into his eyes.

"I had the great honor to be selected by His Magnificence, Torpan the Twenty-Ninth, and her High Eminence, the Empress Lenala, to tutor their only child, the Princess Ranyan, and I did that for many years, while also fulfilling my responsibilities at the university, daily visiting the princess at the palace."

She wished to beguile him, draw him—newly enslaved, alone, frightened—with her seeming warmth. Give him hope. Hope might weaken his brain.

He sensed that in her. But more, too. Intermeshed motivations. Feelings. Thoughts. So complicated a weave….

Take care!

Again he warned himself.

"We studied many things, the Princess and I, and an apt pupil she was, as a small girl and later, too….realm history, we studied, and what fit the invaders—her people—to rule, and the inferiority of the despicable Forest Kings, who ruled by sorcery instead of swords. Filthy magic, they wielded, without honor…."

She spoke looking, seemingly, at the tapestry. But he saw her eyes slid again aside, to study him askance.

A test.

If she vilified Foresters, if he were one, anger might muddy his face. One moment, unguarded, would reveal him.

"Yes, always I've heard that Foresters work evil, and sneak," Wil said.

"Hmm," she said, eyeing him.

"They pox children, I've heard, and steal hens, and snitch people's coins, and…."

"That's Fishtown nonsense," she said.

A bolt of fear shot through him.

"Fishtown?" he said.

"You don't know Fishtown? Breming? Those upriver villages?"

"I've never left Imperia," he said.

"Too bad," she said. "You might learn something, Fox."

Now she sat still, studying his face. Plotting her next thrust, he supposed. Abruptly, she exhaled sharply, and he felt real anger in her.

"Steal hens, snitch coins—that's peasant thinking," she snapped. "Evil is far more subtle, more pervasive, and corrosive....Agree?"

"I don't know," he said. "I never thought of such things."

Nor had he.

But he thought she steered the conversation into waters too deep for him, where he might founder.

"How did you become a slave, Doctor Gant?"

She stared at him now, genuinely angry. But suddenly she laughed, a single snort.

"Well, well, Fox. I am, after all, a teacher. And so I must admire, I suppose, and encourage so ardent an urge to learn."

"I don't mean disrespect," he said. "Malaga."

"Would you like to be my pupil?" she said.

"If I could be as good a pupil as the Princess Ranyan," he said.

She turned her head away and looked at the tapestry. He remained silent. After a time her eyes slid to the side. She looked at him that way.

Abruptly she climbed down from her chair. It shocked him to see her stand, a dwarf. He had forgotten.

In a corner of the room behind her chair, a sash hung. She pulled the sash. Then she stood, waiting.

A minute passed. He sat naked on his bench, silent. She stood behind her chair, silent.

A loud rap on the door.

"Come in, Constable."

When the constable entered, she continued standing. She glanced at the constable, then turned her gaze back to Wil.

"Put him, for now, in green livery," she said.

"Green?" the constable blurted.

"Do as I say."

Two hands gripped his shoulders and lifted him to his feet. Turning him, the constable shoved him toward the door.

As they left the room, Wil heard Malaga's small, dead voice.

"Constable, this one has a palace name—call him Fox."

Another room, smaller. Bolts of cloth leaned against the stone walls.

She sewed, the seamstress, without looking at him, hemming green trousers to fit. He supposed she must spend her days here. And—on the cot in one corner—her nights.

Through the room's one narrow window, high up, a shaft of light fell upon her worktable. Sometimes, as she held the fabric and worked her needle, her wristbands touched and clinked.

A tall, emaciated, gray-haired woman, eyes dead.

Clink.

How long, he asked, have you been a slave?

No answer. Just the needle pushing in, pulling out.

Clink.

All her life, he supposed.

If life it was.

She never glanced at his nakedness.

Clink.

Green thread, green fabric.

Ushering him here, a constable told him the palace's livery colors. Red for the emperor's slaves. Blue for Princess Ranyan's. Ordinary palace slaves wore green.

What of the empress, he had asked? What color do her slaves wear?

He received only a sword hilt's rap on his skull.

Now the seamstress held out for him his garments. He pulled on his new trousers.

Green.

So, no turpentine tapping for him. Or salt mining. Nor would he drive a donkey cart at night, collecting Imperia's trash, or cleaning its cesspools.

He would be a palace slave.

Malaga meant to keep him at hand.

She suspected him, clearly.

He buttoned his green shirt.

His story seemed plausible. And they couldn't trace the paperless Gray-Head, his fictitious tutor. Malaga couldn't prove he lied.

Yet, what scavenger could read?

He remembered his interview with Malaga, word by word. He guessed what pricked up her ears. Early on he said his parents died when he still "toddled," not a natural word for an uneducated street urchin.

He spoke too well.

Now he must live on edge. If he erred, Malaga would sniff him out.

But if she suspected him, why did Malaga not send him for torturing, wrest from him the truth, and the Wielder's whereabouts, before he died? And if he proved truly a street pauper, what did one more slave's killing matter? In a realm like this?

In this room, too, a sash hung down in a corner. A pull from the seamstress. Within a minute the constable returned, licking the remains of some tidbit from his fingers.

Not a word from the constable, just a shove from the room.

Down the corridor.

Coming the other way, a large man in a red jerkin and a yellow cape, and a smaller man in black velvet. Wil recognized Ranyan's sergeant. And the other man he recognized, too—the aristocrat who spoke with Domallon in the palace park the night he and Tobi arrived, and hid under a willow.

To make room in the corridor for the approaching men, the constable guarding Wil shoved him against the wall, and then stood beside him. He heard the men speaking as they approached.

"She still wanders at night?"

"Most nights, Count Dagin."

"And nights when not?"

"Visits the mother."

Now the two men brushed by. Wil heard the count mutter, to himself, "Aah, fascinating conversations those must be."

But something else struck him.

As they passed, the sergeant's gazed slid over him, standing there in his green livery. Wil expected the sergeant to turn, grasp his collar, express anger that he'd not been sent south to labor in mosquito-infested forests, to suffer, and die. But the man's hard eyes passed over him without seeing. And then the two disappeared around the corridor's turning.

Wil thought, to find the Starstone, I wished for invisibility, and now I'm enslaved. Slaves become the unseen.

I am invisible.

Except to Malaga.

One day passed. Then another. No word from Malaga. He began to hope.

He lived in a barracks room, with other male slaves.

Blank eyes.

We could work together, he suggested. Escape.

Blank eyes.

"Meat for supper, I hear."

They spoke of that. And of their menial palace chores. And their spats and feuds. They discussed which female slaves they fancied. For slaves could marry, with the palace's permission, to breed more slaves.

Born into slavery, his barracks mates. Wil learned that. They knew no other life, and feared the world outside. Who'd shelter them out there, clothe them, feed them?

But slaves aged, too frail or sick to labor. Others died from beatings. And often slaves' birthrates fell too low to generate sufficient replacements. Then constables would go out into the city and the realm to seize and enslave likely young men and women. Such freeborn slaves might be more amenable to plotting. So it seemed to Wil.

He met such a man in the laundry, his face scarred from lashings.

"Constables everywhere," the man said.

They spoke in whispers as they worked, without moving their lips. Other slaves also worked over the tubs of steaming water and soiled clothes. They might hear. To gain a morsel of favor, they might tell.

"And suppose you do squirm out—then what? No papers. No food. They'll hunt you down. They'll kill you slow."

With a shrugged, the scarred man resumed washing clothes, and would speak no more.

So Wil carried trays of meats and sweets to rooms where aristocrats met on realm business. And he shined fine shoes. And he swept floors and mopped them. And he walked downstairs to the kitchens, when directed, and sliced potatoes or scrubbed the grease from dishes.

Fox, they called him.

He watched. He considered. He noticed palace ways, He sensed currents.

Always, the Starstone drew him. He found himself wondering what he might do with that power. Such thoughts repelled him. And attracted him. He felt it in his chest, pulling him towards it. But he had no access to the royal quarters.

He polished forks and fetched tea and carried chamber pots. Enslavement tasted acrid in his mouth. Yet, here lay the Starstone. Only here, in the palace, could he find it, take it.

Born for this, he thought. Bred for this. Fated for this.

But here, every day, he walked closer to his death.

Constables guarded every hallway, back stairs, pantry. They hunted the Taker across the realm, but especially in the palace. For here, to the palace—here the Taker must come. And that sideways look from Malaga—she suspected him.

If he sneaked into palace regions closed to him, his slave's invisibility would end. He saw no way around it.

But suppose he did, somehow, grasp the Starstone. That, too, would be his end. For the Presence had marked him. He must return the Stone to its makers. Blossom and Mita would see the Presence draw him. Mita must then cast a death spell.

He might elude the spell. He might return the Stone to the mountain of its forging. Then, too, he would die. His usefulness ended, the Presence would snuff him out. And, he would die gladly, for returning the Stone would ruin the world.

So whatever he did, death.

One morning, as he pulled on his green trousers in the barracks, and buttoned his green shirt, and shrugged into his green jacket, a constable clomped into the room, sword clanking, keys on his chain jingling.

"Who's called Fox?"

"That's him, the lanky one over there."

"You're wanted."

Up stairways the constable ushered him, into sectors where most slaves they passed wore blue or red. They walked along a marble-lined corridor, thrice as broad as downstairs corridors. They trod on marble floors. Upon the walls, golden sconces. And where the ceiling rested upon the walls, golden filigree concealed the joint.

Passing open doors, Wil peeked into parlors, the chairs and sofas upholstered in red satin and brocade. Red carpets, too. And red drapes embroidered in gold. A dining room with a vast table of black marble inlaid with pure gold, and chairs of gold, cushioned in black velvet. On the walls ancient paintings of haughty men and women, purple robed, golden crowned. Depictions, too, of fierce warriors on armored horses lancing men on foot, so many their bodies lay three deep, bleeding, the horses rearing over them.

They came to a door, and the constable knocked.

"Enter."

Malaga's small, dead voice.

"Go away now," she told the constable, not looking up from her desk.

She didn't look at Wil, and he didn't know what to do. So he stood, waiting, while she read from a tome and scratched notes on parchment with a quill.

Bigger, this office, than her slave-interrogation room downstairs, sunlit through three large windows, which overlooked the palace park. In that other room of hers, tapestries and carpeting decorated only the room's rear half, where Malaga sat. Slaves undergoing interrogation stood or sat amidst bare stone. But in this upper office tapestries covered every wall, and a carpet softened the entire floor, all loomed long ago.

One tapestry showed a white-robed woman holding up her left hand, thumb and fourth finger forming a circle, the other three fingers spread, amidst fields of wheat and barley aglow with intensifying fecundity. In another, two men in brown trousers and jackets, and a small girl in a tan tunic, walked through deep forest, a lion and stag walking beside them, all five faces serene.

"Those are ancient tapestries taken from the Forest Kings," Malaga told him. "Did you guess?"

She didn't look up from her tome, didn't seem to be looking at him.

"I don't know of such things," he said.

"This carpet, too," she said, still not looking up. "You'll notice the lightness of its colorings, yellow for sunlight, green for leaves, blue for morning sky and forest lakes—realm carpeting, on the other hand, such as you see about the palace, is darkly heavy, the maroon of imperial battle pennants, for instance, or of congealed blood."

He didn't know what she meant by these comments, or where she hoped to lead him. So he remained silent, watchful.

She continued studying her tome and scratching notes, not looking at him.

Against one wall stood a case of many bound books. More books lay piled on the carpet. Manuscripts, too, and scrolls. Malaga worked at a Forester desk, simple and light and sturdy, of ash, smoothed and varnished, once white, now darkened by centuries to the color of honey.

"Do you like my office?"

He didn't know what to say. If he said he did, would that show partiality to Forester things? Yet, she clearly felt partial to Forester crafts, for she surrounded herself with them.

"I've never seen such work," Wil said. "I wouldn't have thought a lion and a stag, as shown in the tapestry, would walk together many minutes before the lion would eat the stag."

She glanced at him, from behind those slitted lids, then resumed reading.

"Long ago such things were," she said. "Do you like animals?"

"Mostly I've seen only rats and pigeons," Wil said, after a moment's thought.

"Really?" Malaga said. "And yet in his report the sergeant who took you said a dog accompanied you on the streets."

"Yes, a small dog did follow me about, because when I found something to eat, I shared a little with him," Wil said.

Malaga looked up from her book now, still holding her quill. She regarded him.

"Sit down upon that divan, Fox, and we shall talk."

He sat as directed.

"You look foolish in green," she said.

He did not reply.

She resumed studying her book, scratching notes.

"Here, a passage of interest," she said. "Let me read to you—'...and in that time, seers foretell, when the thousand years ends and the dire time comes, the young Taker will not dwell among his own kind, but within the realm, among the unmagical, seeming one of them, and his place of upbringing is foreseen, along the great river, a village....'"

Wil felt chilled.

He now understood.

Malaga served as Domallon's informant. What the justice minister must know of Foresters, the enslaved professor told him. Domallon, stalking the Taker, looked through Malaga's eyes.

This text, Wil guessed, she encountered long ago. So she sent Domallon hunting the Taker up the river, in the villages. But which particular village? She couldn't know. Then they took Kobar slave. They asked him, as they must ask all newly taken villagers, if a Forester lived in their midst. Kobar eagerly told them about his childhood friend, Wil Deft, foster-reared by a fisherman and his laundress wife.

"Forester born, though, I've always thought…."

So he must have told them, his lifelong friend, Kobar.

Then galleys rowed upriver. Then constables scoured Fishtown. Then the forest cat appeared in Wil's window.

She said: "It is time."

"I know nothing of these things," Wil said, keeping the tension out of his voice.

"This text is not from the *Codex Mysterium*," Malaga said, not looking up. "It is from the time just after the Forest Kings fell to the invaders, when disagreement about reasons for their defeat clove the Foresters into schisms, and the rival factions produced manuscripts from their own points of view."

"These things are beyond me," Wil said.

He pretended to study the tapestries, as if with only passing interest.

Pim, he remembered, said it was he who decided to send the infant Wil to Fishtown for rearing. No doubt Pim knew this ancient text, and its prophecy. Probably that shaped his decision.

So, once again he saw it. Others—even seers centuries dead—chose his life's path. His anger flared. But it quickly faded because Malaga, at her Forester desk, put her Forester tome aside. She laid down her quill. She studied him through those slitted lids.

He felt afraid.

"Fox, you shall help me," she said.

That small, dead voice. Just a trace of hiss.

He said nothing.

"Yes, you will be my amanuensis, for I am engaged in important studies, just now, and here's a young slave who speaks so well, and reads so well, and what a help you will be—or would you prefer sawing cedar in southern swamps?"

Yes, send me to the swamps, far from you.

So he thought.

But if he said that, she'd know he feared her. No sane slave would otherwise choose swamps over palace. And she'd know why he feared her.

Also, here lay the Starstone.

He gazed at her, pondering.

She gazed at him, waiting.

"Let me work with you," he said. "Malaga."

"How delightful," she said. "Fox."

She sat back in her chair and regarded him, eyes glinting. She'd set a trap. And it just snapped.

He tried to sense her thoughts. At that art, he grew ever more adept. He supposed the Opal of Living and Dying nurtured it. Once more the Opal hung from his neck in a small sack, his amulet. But he found Malaga opaque. He sensed a roiling within her. But she held that inner storm in tight check. Outwardly, she showed none of it.

He couldn't read her, he guessed, because her emotions and wishes fought, and that inner contention remained unresolved.

Abruptly, his stomach turned, with a realization: he'd never stood so close to death.

Malaga might save him. Probably, though, she'd kill him.

"Go away now," she said, pulling her sash to summon his guard. "When I'm ready, I'll summon you."

He resumed washing clothes and carrying trays.

And he thought: she plays cat to my mouse because she must be sure. If she names me Taker, and they slay me, they'll relax. And if she erred, their relaxation might allow the real Taker to strike.

They'd blame her. So she stalks me, waiting to be sure before she pounces. It's not only I who must take care.

"Malaga wants you."

A constable, filling the doorway of the slave barracks, beckoning for Wil to follow, down a corridor, to a stairway.

"Go up."

With that, the constable walked away. Perplexed, brow furrowed, Wil walked to the stairway and started up, slowly.

To be left unescorted in the palace....

Malaga's orders, he supposed.

Impressive, her sway.

But, her intentions, a puzzle.

She suspected him. She taunted him, even, with her suspicions. Yet, she ordered him upstairs, unescorted. So near the royal quarters.

A trap?

Perhaps they secretly watched him. If he sneaked off, searched for the Starstone, he would reveal himself, the Taker.

But he felt unwatched. Aristocrats passed on the stairway. They gave him not a glance, gossiping—

...and His Magnificence, this morning, snappish, I thought....

....Did you see? At dinner last night? Count So-And-So offering the baron just that condescending smile? But then....

.... so her ship docked yesterday, up from the south, three tons of ebony....

Slaves passed. They carried trays of teacups, or soiled clothes to be laundered. They, too, didn't glance at him. Mostly they looked down, eyes deadened by drudgery, submission.

Just days a slave, he thought. Yet, I cut no potatoes. I serve Malaga Gant....

Take care!

On the upper floors, all slaves hurrying along the corridors wore the emperor's red livery, or Princess Ranyan's blue. His own green trousers and jacket stood out. He supposed Malaga relied on that—if he trespassed in regions prohibited to green livery, he'd be challenged.

Still, letting him walk free—she took a risk.

If he exploited her laxity, sought the Starstone, the blame would be hers, and so he thought: she tests me, but maybe not only me.

He'd sensed her inner contention. By putting herself at risk, she might test herself. It might help her see her true wishes.

A complicated personality....

He slowed almost to a stop, thinking.

This letting me walk the corridors alone. She also sends me a message. A kind of code.

But I can't read it.

He walked a straight path to her office.

"So, you came directly," she said.

He said nothing.

She shrugged, he thought, more with mouth than shoulders. She plucked a parchment from her desk, handed it to him.

"Copy this, Fox."

"Yes, Malaga."

It seemed some ancient document.

"Sit at this small desk, which I had brought in for you."

"Yes, Malaga."

He picked up his quill and read the passage she wished him to copy.

And in those days the Forest Kings' sorcery waxed to its utmost. Over that region they chose to rule, they wielded great powers. They made crops fecund, and deepened river channels for the passage of barges laden with ores and lumber, and healed many sicknesses and injuries. But a faction among them said, we can do more.

They saw how to use the Starstone to reach deep into the essence of what is, and adjust it. They learned to alter the world's underpinnings, and redirect its currents, and thus guide events as they saw fit. They learned even to alter a person's being, so that a criminal might be remade honest. But as they did these things, growing ever more proficient at wielding the Starstone to shape the world, some of them became giddy with it.

In villages along the river, and on farms, and in the mercantile city then growing up at the great river's mouth, the unmagical felt the alterations in their world, even their own inner selves, and not by their own will. Many felt abused. They grumbled in their cottages and their fields and on the streets, and sent delegations to complain to the Forest Kings. But those now ministering the sorcery said only, "We exert our power for the good of all." They reached even deeper with the wizardry, changing lives' courses ever more.

Nor would they listen to their own Forester brethren, who counseled moderation in the Starstone's wielding. These counselors admonished: "We wield the Stone to change the world, but our wielding changes us!"

They spoke to unlistening ears. And the discontent grew....

"What is this I copy?" Wil said, putting down his quill.

"Ah," said Malaga, looking at him sideways from behind her desk. "Does it interest you, Fox?"

"It confuses me," he said.

"I'm sure it does," she said, and he thought she spoke drolly.

He expected her to say, "Do your work as told, Slave, and shut up."

Instead, she at back in her chair, staring at him through those slitted eyes, her short legs straight out before her on the seat.

"You won't read such things in the *Codex Mysterium*...."

"I don't know what that is," he said.

"Ah," she said, amused. "That is the history of themselves the Foresters wrote just after the Forest Kings fell, laying out their plan to gather their strength, to strike back at the new realm."

"Yes, evil plotting," Wil said.

She held up a hand.

"Village prattle—don't bore me Fox, or I'll send you south to saw cedars," she snapped. "Now, history depends on the story's teller—I told you the fallen Foresters divided into factions...."

"And this parchment, one faction wrote," Wil said.

"Do you sense truth in it?" she asked. "For the invaders fell back, their swords weak weapons against the Forest Kings' magic. Therefore, as a new tactic, they incited revolt. And why were the realm's people so willing to rebel?"

Wil said nothing, merely looking at her.

"Think about it, Fox," she said. "Now, do as I told you— make a copy."

She resumed studying her tome. He set to work with his quill.

Only the turning of her pages made a sound in the room. And his quill's scratching.

A bang—the door flung open so aggressively it smacked the wall.

Lord Domallon strode into the room. His heavy features looked muddy.

A thick finger, pointed at Malaga Gant.

"I awoke this morning impatient," Domallon said.

He spoke softly. But in that softness, flashes like lightning.

"Impatient…My lord?"

"Where is the Taker?"

"How could I know?" Malaga said. "I am always in the palace, I see this office, these rooms…."

"Distinguished Professor of Ancient Lore," Domallon said, even more softly. "Occupier of the Royal Chair of the Enemy."

"I directed you to his village," Malaga said, and Wil sensed a smoldering in her voice. "Because of me, you learned his name, and his appearance, and if your constables failed…."

A thick fist slammed onto Malaga's desk. She flinched, Wil saw. But she stifled it.

"I believe we forget ourselves," Domallon said, his voice now so soft he nearly whispered. "I believe we think ourselves still the daughter of a wealthy lumber merchant, and we forget that—for all his gold—papa was a commoner, one of the realm's sheep, and that we are no longer a distinguished professor, and tutor to the princess, but just another of the princess's slaves."

"I forget nothing," Malaga said.

"Do you remember the occasion of your enslavement?"

Malaga looked at him, silent.

"It happened long ago, of course, but as I recall, you sent word to the palace that you ailed, and would spend the day coughing and sneezing in your bed at home, and that upset the princess, and so she sent constables to enslave you, so you would not again disappoint her…."

269

Malaga said nothing. She continued to stare at Domallon, and Wil could not read her eyes.

"Now, here is my point, Malaga—our princess is, shall we say, mercurial? Suppose someone speaks a few words to her one day, and then a few more words another day.... Somehow, our princess becomes convinced her slave, behind her back, mocks her. Might our mercurial princess send that slave away? To the southern swamps, perhaps? To cook for cedar sawyers?"

Malaga said nothing.

"Or even—Remember! Mercurial!—our princess fancies yet another beheading? Or perhaps she sends her erring slave to participate in His Magnificence's fascinating experiments down below? Would you like that, Malaga? I think you should say something."

"I do for you the best I can," she said.

"Do you?" Domallon said. "Yet, at this moment, in the Foresters' infernal thousandth year, I do not know where their Taker hides, except that I see small flashes of...let's say insolence...out on the streets, which leads me to suspect Taker and Wielder both now hide in Imperia, and their nearness to the Starstone already infects the populace—tell me Malaga, what do you think?"

Domallon glared at Malaga. He seemed not to see Wil at his small desk beside Malaga's, with his parchment and quills. Enslaved. Thus, invisible.

Malaga spread her hands, palms up.

"Do your constables not watch the city's perimeters?"

"I've doubled the guards, tripled them, alerted all."

"Then?"

Domallon's face grew muddier.

"Maybe they sneaked by. Could they?"

Malaga considered, studying Domallon sideways, through those slitted lids.

"They bred the Taker, over a thousand years, from Foresters with peculiar magical talents—the ability to hide themselves, and adapt, and fit in, a knack for stealth, and sensitivity to others' thoughts and intentions…."

It seemed to Wil she held back her true thoughts. She spoke a fog of words.

This game she played….

If she led Domallon to the Taker and the Wielder, the Forester threat ended. So did Malaga's usefulness. On a royal whim, she might spend her days washing royal dishes. Or worse. Domallon, having relied upon her, might avenge his reliance.

She, too, must take care.

A thought flashed through Wil's mind. Malaga knew the Foresters could alter hair and eye color. Yet, clearly, she never told Domallon.

What other games did she play?

"Don't blather at me," Domallon said.

"Of course he could sneak into Imperia," Malaga said. "He was bred for it."

"And the Wielder?"

Malaga, he saw, considered.

"That person, whether man or woman, we do not know," she said. "They bred the Wielder for magical prowess, sorcery deep inside, to grasp the Starstone and use it…."

They stared at each other, the thick-bodied aristocrat and the enslaved dwarf.

"And?" Domallon said finally.

"I would guess, with the Taker's help…. and as the Wielder approached Imperia, ever nearer the Starstone, that person's magical power would increase…."

She pondered.

Domallon again slammed his large fist onto her desk, glaring.

She gazed at that fist. What her eyes showed, Wil could not read.

"Yes," she said. "It's possible—Taker and Wielder, both in Imperia."

"Where?" Domallon said, his face pushed close to Malaga's.

"How could I possibly guess?" Malaga said, unflinching.

And at that moment Wil heard a voice in his mind.

"Wil?"

He knew the voice. He loved it. But it chilled him, to hear that voice so close.

"I snuck inside, Wil, but you have to tell me where you are!"

Fear welled within him.

"Tobi!" he said, in his mind. "Terrible danger! Go back to Blossom and Mita!"

"I hear where you are, Wil!"

He groaned, almost aloud.

And then Tobi's voice reappeared in his mind.

"I'm coming!"

CHAPTER TWELVE

"Tobi, don't come here!"

Wil shouted it in his mind.

"I'm coming, Wil!"

"No!"

"I'm sneaking upstairs now!"

"Tobi, please—go home."

No response.

He imagined the dog ascending the marble staircase, frowning in concentration, making not one claw click.

"He's playing," Wil told himself.

Watchers would see merely a dog. Short-legged. No tail. Honey-colored and white. Peculiar, how it climbs the stairs with such exaggerated stealth.

Still, just a dog.

But palace guards surely hunted down stray animals.

Wil stood silently in Malaga's office. Nobody knew he spoke with a dog.

Domallon, who had been staring down at Malaga, sitting at her desk, abruptly grabbed an empty chair by the arm. He dragged it one-handed across the carpet, bumping it against Malaga's chair. Swirling up his cloak, he sat.

"Let us talk."

He rested his velvet-sleeved forearm atop Malaga's desk.

Wil sensed her inwardly flinch. But she rested her own elbow upon the desk, her hand cupping her chin. She leaned toward the minister of justice, as if eagerly anticipating their tete-a-tete.

Not since Domallon entered the room had he looked at Wil. He did not look at him now, but he issued an order.

"You—get tea."

Wil put down his quill. He stood.

I am a slave, he thought. A mop, a broom. Invisible.

He glanced at Malaga, but she gazed fixedly at Domallon. He left the room, closing the door behind him.

"Wil!"

Tobi hurtled from a corridor closet.

Up on his hind legs, he rested his forepaws above Wil's knees. Eyes glittering. Head back to jubilantly bark.

"No," Wil said. "Danger!"

He hurried Tobi back into the closet, closed the door. In the darkness, Tobi leaned against his leg.

"Why don't you come back, Wil?"

Reproach in that voice.

"After I find the Stone," Wil said.

He rested his hand upon Tobi's head, startled by the warmth. He now lived in chill.

"Blossom gets me meat pies, Wil, and they're good."

"Why did you come?"

"To be with you, Wil. Every day I walked around the palace, and I found a hole under the wall, just big enough, and it smells like rabbit, and...."

"Do they know you're here? Mita and Blossom?"

"They said, don't go there, but I did, and when I found the rabbit hole, Blossom did that throwing up his hands thing and he said, if you find Wil, say I'm ready to come with swords and knives, get him out."

And die doing it, Wil thought.

"Bark!" Tobi said enthusiastically. "Bite, bite, bite!"

"No, tell him no," Wil said. "What about Mita?"

He felt the dog's mood darken.

"She wants to get into the palace, too, nearer to the Stone thing, Wil, because maybe she could do something for you, but that Stone scares her, and it makes her sick…."

"Tell them I'll find the Stone, and get it out," Wil said.

"I'm staying here, Wil, with you."

"There's no place to hide here, Tobi, and no food…."

"Meat pies," Tobi said.

"No meat pies," Wil said.

Tobi fell silent.

"I'll come in the day," he said.

Stubbornness.

"At night I'll go back to Blossom and Mita, then come again…."

A compromise. It amused Wil that it included nightly meat pies.

"Do you understand the danger here?"

"I'm a good sneaker, Wil, and I run so fast, this way, that way, under things where they can't go—Hah!"

"It's not a game, Tobi."

"Can't catch me."

"Go home now," Wil said. "Tell Mita and Blossom what I said."

"I don't like it when you're not there, Wil."

"Sneak, Tobi."

He cracked open the closet's door and peeked out.

Nobody in the corridor. He opened the door and stepped out. He watched Tobi sneak toward the stairs, placing each foot with exquisite care. Tobi looked back at him, for approval.

He's playing, Wil thought.

Tobi sneaked around a turn in the corridor and was gone.

Wil hung his head, shut his eyes. After a moment he straightened, then hurried down the corridor, to fetch tea.

"…but I had thought it was your son who…."

"You know that one-eyed smuggler murdered him."

Wil stopped just inside the doorway to Malaga's office, holding the tray with its gold-inlaid cups and saucers and teapot.

Domallon tapped a forefinger atop Malaga's desk, to show him where to put the tray.

"But her own wishes in this matter," Malaga said. "Wouldn't she…."

Domallon put up a hand.

They sat silently. Malaga finally spoke.

"So your protégé…."

"Village boy," Domallon said.

He shrugged.

Wil put down the tray. He poured tea into a cup.

Should this first cup go to Malaga? Or to Domallon.

He placed it in front of Domallon.

As he did so, his hand passed the hilt of Domallon's rapier, in its sheath, belted to his waist.

Malaga, he sensed, saw his hand hesitate.

So easily pulled out, this sword. So easily plunged through Domallon's chest.

One aristocrat would die.

But a thousand more walked these corridors in soft shoes. Their mansions surrounded the palace. They commanded armies of constables. Commoners, those constables, but a peat digger's son, or a fish-market navvy, donning that red jerkin and yellow cape…. Your needs, supplied. License to bully your fellow commoners, granted. Thus, loyalty. So many loyal minions, upholding the realm.

Wil let his hand pass Domallon's rapier hilt.

Malaga, sideways, caught his eye, just a flicker.

He poured tea for her.

With a slight motion of her left index finger, she directed him to sit at his small desk. He picked up his quill, dipped its nib in his inkbottle. He resumed copying the manuscript upon which he'd worked when Domallon barged into the room, but he listened to what Malaga and Domallon said.

He thought: she wants me to listen.

"Kobar...."

Domallon said the name, then fell silent. Finally, he spoke again.

"We toyed with the idea, using him to soothe them, one of their own, and reinvigorate the line, too, with—what shall we say?—blood less refined. But...."

He sat looking at his hands.

"But he's not my son."

Silence again.

"In any event, he led constables into the forest, hunting the Forester city, but no word from him, so undoubtedly...."

Again he shrugged, this time wearily.

"We must reconsider certain plans."

No sound, except Wil's quill scraping on parchment. Domallon spoke again.

"You continue tutoring the princess?"

"Less, considering she's of marriageable age...."

"Careful, slave woman—you might die of sarcasm."

"Yes, I tutor her still, whenever some question troubles her mind, such as a recent inquiry as to whether commoners like myself are truly people, or a form of beast...."

"And what did you tell our princess?"

"That we are people, too, but lesser, conquered, not conquerors."

"How judicious of you."

Silence again.

Wil scratched at his parchment, but listened. Covertly, he watched for an eye's blink, or a brow's furrow, signs to decipher. A gaze might intensify. Fingers flex. Or clench.

Domallon ignored the green-clad slave, scribbling at his little desk, but Wil saw Malaga glancing sideways at him, through those slitted lids. He thought: her game's still undecided, but if she convinces herself I'm really the Taker, all positions on the board change—I become her key token. How would she play her Fox?

"You know Dagin?"

"Of course," Malaga said. "Bor, Count Dagin, minister of protocol...."

"His son is Fladd."

"Hmmm," Malaga said.

Domallon stared at her, widening his eyes and raising his eyebrows, to indicate a question.

"I think another youth courts our princess, Binter, son of Count...."

Domallon raised a silencing hand.

"Hot-headed, stupid, insolent," Domallon said, dismissing Binter with a scowl. "What do you know of Fladd?"

"A dissolute boy. So it is said. Although what could a slave know? Still, talk of taverns, idleness....Hmmm....easily led, I'm told, weak...."

They looked at each other.

"I see," Malaga said.

"Has she spoken of him?"

"You know, the aristocracy lately irritates our princess, and she craves...something. What, even I don't know."

"Ahh, 'even' you," Domallon said. "My point exactly."

"I cannot tell Princess Ranyan when to go to bed, much less whom to marry," Malaga said.

"Tell?" Domallon said. "Certainly not, slave woman. But influence, perhaps. All her life, you've taught her, advised her. So. A thought might be planted."

Malaga looked at him, face blank.

"Let us say time passes," Domallon said. "Let us say our Ranyan marries—for she has no brother. Torpan has no heir. And the throne must pass, must it not? And in time, His Magnificence joins his ancestors, and Prince Fladd, husband of Princess Ranyan, ascends. Changes, now. And for a slave who helped...."

Malaga gazed at him, silent.

"Manumission, shall we say?"

"Our emperor is not so old," Malaga said. "A decade may yet pass, or two."

"Or perhaps not," Domallon said.

Malaga eyed him. When she spoke, her words sounded sharp.

"Why all this?"

Domallon's face muddied. His lips compressed. He sat that way. Wil saw him, after a time, consciously relax his shoulders. When he finally spoke, his words came softly, almost a whisper.

"You press, Malaga, dangerously," he said. "Yet, as you perceive, you do have a dram of power here, for you have utility...."

She looked at him through narrowly slitted lids, her ferret face unexpressive.

"So I will tell you the realm rots, just a bit, and the people mutter, as they behold our current imperial paragons."

He held up a hand to forestall Malaga commenting. With a shake of his head, as if expelling unpleasant thoughts, he continued speaking.

279

"Were the riffraff not distracted, all these centuries, by ragamuffins hiding in trees, with their piddling legerdemain…. Although now, with their thousand years, those ragamuffins do truly threaten…."

"But surely you would not let their Taker even enter the palace, much less steal the Starstone," Malaga said blandly.

Wil saw her eyes slide sideways, momentarily glance at him.

"Surely not," Domallon said. "Especially not with your help, Distinguished Professor of Ancient Lore, occupier of the Royal Chair of the Enemy."

"I tell you what I can," Malaga said, shrugging.

"We'll destroy their Taker, and their Wielder, too, and when the regime changes…."

"Which might be soon," Malaga said.

Domallon turned up his palms and shrugged.

"What changes might we see in our realm?" Malaga asked.

"Perhaps the Starstone should not reside within the imperial chambers," Domallon said.

"But even we, the unmagical, derive some power from its proximity, so—proximate to the emperor—it strengthens the realm," Malaga said.

She sounded thoughtful. Wil thought this question of the Starstone drew her back to her concerns as a scholar, a student of Foresters, and all their ways.

"Yet, proximity seems to affect the minds of the proximate," Domallon said.

"Has it been suggested to his Magnificence that the Stone be moved?" Malaga said. "Away from the royal chambers? For his health?"

"He will not hear of it."

They regarded each other in silence.

"And, if we were to enjoy the rule of His Magnificence, Torpan the Thirtieth, the former Prince Fladd, there would be additional changes?"

"You go beyond yourself," Domallon said. "You were told there might be manumission for the deserving, who serve well, and that is the extent of your concerns in these matters."

"Of course," she said.

They sat looking at each other, speculatively.

Once again that morning the office door abruptly swung open. Princess Ranyan stood in the doorway, glaring from Domallon to Malaga Gant, white-faced, looking like an irate moth. Finally she settled her glare on Domallon.

"Oh, la di la!"

"Your Resplendency," Domallon said, lowering his chin a fraction of an inch, to signify a bow.

Ranyan irritably shook her head, swirling her black hair.

"Why are you here?"

"To consult a moment with Malaga," Domallon said. "A matter of Forester lore."

"You should be somewhere else," Ranyan said.

Domallon regarded her. Wil thought he saw in that gaze contempt. Abruptly, however, the minister of justice rose to his feet and smiled. Wolfishly, it seemed to Wil.

"Exactly as you wish, of course, Your Resplendency."

Domallon glanced at Malaga, sardonic.

Malaga kept her face bland.

Ranyan tapped her silk slipper's toe, impatient, glaring crossly at Domallon.

With a swirl of his cloak, Domallon shouldered past the princess and through the door. His shoes tapped away down the corridor.

"Oh, la di la!" Ranyan said. "Make that green thing sitting there close the door."

Malaga raised an index finger. Wil jumped up and closed the office door.

"A terrible, terrible thing!" Ranyan cried out.

"What is it, Child?" Malaga asked.

"Papa stares at my little Poko!"

Malaga sat silent, gazing at the princess. After a moment, Ranyan cried out again.

"And that odious Binter should be banished!"

Malaga still remained silent, regarding the princess thoughtfully. Wil guessed the enslaved professor walked a cliff's edge. Failing to reply might irritate Ranyan, and the Princess's irritation could prove fatal. Yet, for a slave, so much is forbidden. To speak familiarly of nobles. To connive against them. To merely seem insolent. Transgression meant death.

Malaga finally spoke, a question. "

"Why does His Magnificence look at Poko?"

"To send my Poko below!" the princess said, her mouth contorting, although no tears came. "Where all the others went!"

"His Magnificence said so?" Malaga asked.

"That nasty Duzzle saw Poko fetch my slipper when I asked him to, and he said, 'Your Magnificence, here is a thinking dog, just the sort of beast with which Foresters converse,' and now Papa stares at Poko, and it's hateful!"

Ranyan pressed her long index finger against her forehead. Then she twisted the finger, as if boring it into her skull.

Malaga reached out a consoling hand and touched the princess's shoulder.

"And what of the young Count Binter?" Malaga asked.

"Oh, la di la," Ranyan said, grimacing. "He stomps his boots on the floor when he walks."

She gazed with vexed eyes at Malaga, lips pursed.

282

"And his voice sounds like a sword's edge, and he smells like leather oil, and he has one ugly black eyebrow all across his forehead!"

"I see," Malaga said. "He proposes marriage?"

"I tell him no, but he won't stop."

"Perhaps he loves you," Malaga said.

"What is that to me?" Ranyan said.

"Count Dagin has a son, does he not? Fladd?"

Princess Ranyan stared at Malaga. Then she wrinkled her nose and turned down her lips, as if smelling something vile. After that, she pretended to throw up. Then she sat back and stared at Malaga with angry eyes.

"I see," Malaga said.

"Domallon, and Dagin, all those boring men—Heir! Heir! That's what they're up to. And am I a mare to be pastured with some smelly stallion, to make a colt?"

"You're of marriageable age, Child," Malaga said.

"But not of marriageable mind!" Ranyan said. "I'll run to the forest and live in trees with Foresters, and learn magic."

Malaga, despite herself, faintly smiled.

"I would," Ranyan said. "And take Poko with me, too, and he could tell the Foresters his philosophy."

Malaga looked thoughtful, considering. Ranyan gazed at her fiercely. Finally the princess spoke again.

"I want you to live in our chambers, like you used to, because whom can I talk to now?" she said. "I talk to Mama, but you know….And all Papa thinks about is what Duzzle says about speaking with animals, and Foresters attacking, and how we must battle magic with magic…."

Malaga now seemed to withdraw into her thoughts. Her face remained blank. Yet, behind that mask, Wil sensed she imagined possible moves in some complicated chess game she played, and each move's ramifications.

Abruptly, she exhaled.

Wil felt the world turn a little.

"I have this assistant now," Malaga said, pointing a finger at Wil. "Perhaps he should move with me, into the imperial quarters…."

"Oh, la di la," Ranyan said. "Now everything will get better!"

Wil walked down the corridor past constables, stationed along each wall, until he finally reached the imperial chambers and knocked on the golden door. A footman opened it, a haughty old man in scarlet livery, who disdainfully looked Wil up and down.

I'm put in my place, Wil thought.

Red livery disdained blue. Both red and blue despised green. Thus did the enslaved replicate their masters' mores.

Elite imperial troopers guarded this royal foyer, and Wil saw them memorizing his face. He told himself: I've lost some invisibility, but now I've advanced far along the game board, close to the Starstone. He already felt its ethereal hands swirling about him.

"I serve Malaga," he told the footman. "I am summoned here."

Suddenly the invisible hands slipped into his skull, and he felt wrenched.

Locks, long sealed within him, snapped open. Doors inside swung ajar. Sweat beaded his forehead. Through a mist, he saw the footman before him as a skeleton wearing red gauze. On either side, skeletons in red jerkins, yellow capes regarded him with empty sockets. This foyer's maroon curtains, gilded chairs, carved cornices seemed mere stage props.

He fought, slamming shut each door as it opened. Even as a boy in Fishtown he'd sensed these sealed inner places, and kept the doors locked, not wanting to see inside.

Stinking Foresters. Workers of filthy magic.

He thought: it's nearby, and it seeks the numinous, to express itself.

"You sick, sonny?"

Once, in Fishtown, a stranger came, bearing a royal license, an itinerant horse trainer. All the children, Wil and Kobar included, followed him through the village to a fenced meadow beside the forest, where a farmer kept a colt, now grown into a powerful stallion, which watched the oncoming trainer with fiery eyes.

Horse bucked, kicked, intended murder. Rider clung, grim, intending mastery.

Abruptly, it ended. Horse, man lightly astride, leaped the fence, thundered down the path, man and horse now welded, a partnership.

I'm the horse, Wil thought. This thing would ride me.

No!

But it might guide me, where I never thought to go....

No!

Inwardly he bucked and kicked, until the ethereal hands withdrew from his head. Yet, he felt they hovered about him, waiting.

He was of the magical people, and the Stone meant to ride him. A thought came to him, though, just a glimmer: might I be the rider?

"I felt dizzy a moment," Wil told the old footman in scarlet livery. "It's gone."

Beyond the foyer lay a vast reception hall. Here the royal family granted audiences to highborn visitors, or dined in state at

285

a marble table intricately veined with inlaid gold, under crystal chandeliers. Here nobles whispered together, awaiting audiences with His Magnificence.

Only four imperial guardsmen watched this reception room. They stood unobtrusively, one in each corner. With many constables standing watch in the outer corridor, and guardsmen in the foyer, what enemy could enter here?

Inwardly, he smiled. A bitter smile.

Off the reception room opened three golden doors. One led to the emperor's quarters, one to the empress's, the third to Ranyan's. So said a passing slave in red, carrying a carafe of honey wine. A carved ebony door led to offices for the exchequer and other palace officials. A door of plain oak led to servant's and guards' barracks, and kitchens, and storage rooms.

Within the reception hall, Wil stood aside, in his green livery. He watched.

Officials, in small clusters, stood about the room, leaning in toward one another to speak softly. Others sat in ornate chairs, around low circular tables. Slaves, in blue or red, glided silently through the room carrying trays, and offered the visiting nobles tea or tarts. Others carried baskets of laundered clothes toward the three golden doors.

Every so often, a constabulary captain marched through the room, or a colonel or general. He'd rap on Torpan's golden door, then disappear inside, only to reappear moments later. Wil guessed these officers carried reports to the emperor, and left with orders to issue. Aristocrats' youngest sons, he supposed. While the eldest brother managed the family enterprises, primogeniture forced these younger brothers into the constabulary.

"Miss, please, Princess Ranyan's door?"

She wore blue, this maid, still in her teens. Palace raised, Wil thought.

He rolled his eyes about, widened, gazing at the trappings of the great ones, for the maid's benefit. She noted, he saw, his appreciation of redness or blueness, versus mere greenness. She drew herself up a little, and sniffed. As an urbane sophisticate might address a bumpkin, she warned him to beware the princess's "bitey mood."

Wil looked fearfully toward the golden doors, all three at once, since he didn't know which led to the bitey princess.

"She misses Domallon's son!" the maid told him, voice lowered.

Wil doubted that, but listened wide-eyed anyway.

"He joined the constabulary, you know, and he didn't even need to, being Lord Domallon's only child and only son," the maid confided. "And he volunteered to go on the river!"

She examined Wil's expression to make sure he appreciated her knowledge of the great ones. His gazed at her raptly.

"His father's stern, you know, and the boy meant to prove his courage," she said. "But," she added, her voice sinking to a whisper, "there's more!"

"What?"

Wil asked it breathlessly.

"He was to marry the princess!" the maid whispered. "We all knew it. So the constabulary, you see, that was part of his training, for the throne."

"So young Domallon will be emperor?"

"Dead!"

Wil looked appropriately shocked.

"River pirates killed him," she whispered.

Wil thought, Blossom.

"One year after her son died, to the day, Lady Domallon died—heartbreak!"

Now the maid crossed her arms, a dusting rag hanging from one hand, and regarded Wil knowingly.

"When the princess heard young Domallon died, she acted frolicsome!" she said. "But that was pretend, for show, him being so handsome."

Wil gazed at this fount of information admiringly.

Licking her lips with her tongue tip, she looked furtively from side to side, fearing she might be overheard, gossiping about the masters. Yet, she burned to tell.

"Now it's that young Count Binter—he courts the princess something fierce," she said. "Every day he comes, lots of times, and he adores her, but she treats him bad."

This maid, Wil understood, found the young count dashing. She thought about him as she polished candlesticks.

Sad, it seemed to Wil. Yet, in her drudgery, the maid's preoccupation with the wearers of velvet gave her bright daydreams.

A menial in red shooed the maid back to her dusting. He showed Wil to his cot in the imperial slaves' barracks. Minutes later, when Wil reemerged into the reception hall, he found Malaga awaiting him.

He began his new duties. Slave to a royal slave.

Malaga led him back through the palace to her old office, and then to her old quarters, to collect belongings she wished transferred to her new two-room apartment, within Princess Ranyan's suite. Manuscripts, she wished him to carry, and books, and two trunks.

"We'll mostly be working here now," Malaga said, as he put down her possessions where she instructed. "Will you like it, Fox, working so near the imperial family?"

He sensed her secret inquiry: do you see I've placed you near the Starstone?

"I am glad to serve you, Malaga, wherever that might be," he said.

"Subtle boy," she said.

He could see she frowned, thinking. Her best moves, he guessed, still eluded her.

Just within the princess's golden door lay Ranyan's personal reception room. Here visitors must wait until she deigned to see them. From here, a corridor led to the princess's other rooms. One door off this corridor opened on the two rooms Malaga now occupied. Others opened onto rooms for tea and private dinners. Finally, at the corridor's end lay the princess's private quarters. Here she lived, served by slaves in blue. Aristocratic young women milled about these rooms, too, the princess's official friends. But their prattle about palace intrigues and love affairs and the relative attractiveness of various young nobles seemed to irritate her.

Ranyan gave most of her attention to her small, white dog, Poko. She carried him in her arms. At her command Poko would roll on the carpet or sit up and waggle his forelegs.

Often, as Ranyan spoke with someone who bored her, she'd abruptly say, "Bark, Poko." And Poko would sit up and bark.

"Hello, Poko."

Poko, stunned, stared at Wil.

Never in his three years had anyone spoken to him like this, in his mind.

Malaga and Ranyan sat talking. Wil had brought tea. Now, still in his first day in the royal quarters, he rested.

Toting luggage for Malaga didn't tax him, but it wearied him to feel her, all that day, covertly studying him, for a revealing sign. The Taker? She watched, he knew, to see if increased proximity to the Starstone affected him.

289

And it did.

Its ethereal hands played about him. Allowed in, they'd unlock those doors he'd kept closed since childhood.

Stinking Foresters. Filthy magic.

He shouldered Malaga's trunks and shelved her books blank-faced, but inwardly he fought the Starstone, all the while fearing her sly eyes. Speaking once again to a dog offered some small relief.

"To me, you saying my name?"

Poko sat upon the carpet, looking up at Wil, his black eyes nearly hidden behind white bangs. Malaga and Ranyan sat at a small table, sipping tea and talking. Wil slouched upon a servants' bench in the corner, resting his back against the wall.

Poko's words sounded stilted. Wil guessed the princess's pet never before spoke. Probably he never met another dog. People spoke to him, but only aloud. Of their words, he understood few. Instead, he observed how they held their arms, or the widening of their irises, or the slowness or suddenness of their movements, or their head's tilt. Thus did he gauge mood and intent, but he'd never before spoken in this way. Tobi spoke volubly, for he grew up a free dog, talking with all in High City. Yet, despite Poko's stilted words, it soothed Wil, conversing with an animal, even this spoilt morsel with sullen black eyes.

"You, not liking."

"You dislike me, Poko?"

"Smell strange."

"Why is that?"

"Strong ones, wear furs, heads up, step sure, flower smell, eat special things and smell of that, too."

"What about me, Poko?"

"Weak ones—you wear roughness like them, and you smell like them, sweat, their food…."

"So you think I'm a weak one?"

Poko sat looking up at him through his white bangs.

"Bad one," Poko said. "Weak outside, inside too strong...."

They sat looking at each other, the small white dog on the carpet, the lanky man in green, lolling on a bench with his feet out.

"Change, you smell of," Poko said.

"Is change so bad?" Wil asked.

"Everything now good."

Said fiercely.

"Ranyan sometimes leaving me alone, but...."

Poko reviewed his life, and Wil saw it—dainty morsels in a silver bowl, soft pillows for sleeping, lap sitting, the princess stroking his fur, others petting, cooing, at least when the princess watched.

Wil sent images he'd seen through Tobi's eyes. High City's wooden streets, free for the wandering, friends at every turn, butterflies, sunshine. Then the great forest. Wildness. Scent of fallen pine needles, sun-warmed for lying upon. Burrow smells, feral. Danger's reek. Imperia—avenues of aroma. Roasting sausages and rats' holes and horse manure and wagon-wheel oil and shops displaying smoked mudfish....

"All that, where?"

"Outside," Wil said.

He tried to give Poko a vision of the world beyond the palace's walls. Imperia stretching out. The river. Beyond, the great forest, lakes, mountains.

"I come from there," Wil said.

Poko considered. Glimpsing the outer world, Wil sensed, mesmerized the small dog. But it unsettled him. He liked his pampering.

Abruptly, a shudder from Poko.

No! Want pillows. Laps. Silver bowls.

"Why you here?"

"I've come to find a thing that belongs to me, and to people like me, and to take it away," Wil said.

"Find it, you go, never come back?"

"Yes," Wil said.

Again the dog sat gazing at Wil, considering.

"What thing you want?"

"It's called the Starstone," Wil said. "It's the size of your paw, round, clear with a blue glow."

"Don't know that," Poko said.

Wil sensed the dog's disappointment. Poko hoped he might lead Wil to the thing he wanted, so Wil would go, taking with him the threat of change.

Wil smiled.

"Do you know Ranyan's father, the emperor?"

"Tall, never says, 'Good Poko,' ice eyes…."

"He loves the Starstone and every night he visits it."

Poko sat gazing at him with a new light in his sullen eyes.

"Down, down, down," Poko said.

He gave Wil a glimpse of a marble door set in a marble wall. Carved into the lintel, the imperial crest, studded with rubies and amethysts. Beyond the door, stone stairs circling down into murk.

"Where is that door, Poko?"

In the corridor, boots stomped. A young giant, black mustachioed, lumbered past the doorway, glanced in, halted. He rushed into the room.

"Ranyan!"

She continued talking in low tones with Malaga.

"I've come," he said.

"I'm occupied, Binter," she said, not looking at him.

Wil saw anger flush red up his neck and crimson his face.

"You're just talking to that slave."

"My slave," the princess said. "Who addresses me politely."

"I want you to marry me."

He spoke through clenched teeth.

"Oh, la di la," Ranyan said.

Wil saw the youth's muscular shoulders bunch up. Abruptly he thrust out his arms and grabbed Malaga by both shoulders. Crimson faced, he lifted her into the air, held her like a doll. His eyes—fierce, stupid—looked for a likely spot against which to hurl the dwarf.

Wil jumped to his feet.

Malaga, suspended from Binter's hands, looked directly at Wil. She shook her head.

Ranyan, too, jumped up, glaring at Binter.

"You dare!"

Binter glared back, his thick black eyebrows knitted into one bar across his forehead.

"I dare say marry me," he cried. "I dare that! But you'd rather gossip with this slave."

His darting eyes fixed on a spot along the wall, where he meant to hurl Malaga's tiny body. Wil moved toward the spot, to catch Malaga when he threw her.

"She's mine!" Ranyan said. "Put her down."

"It's not even a person!" Binter cried.

"If you hurt her, it's your head," Ranyan said.

"Is it? Is it?" Binter bellowed. "You think I'm afraid? You think I wouldn't die for you?"

But he dropped Malaga back onto her feet, suddenly. Malaga's legs crumpled and she sat upon the floor.

"You spit on me!" Binter yelled at Ranyan.

Now his darting eyes stopped at Poko. With a squeal, the dog scurried to Ranyan and leaped. She caught him in her arms.

Binter turned his enraged gaze on Wil. And in those eyes, one of them half hidden behind a shock of dark hair falling over Binter's forehead, Wil saw a small boy, spoiled and thwarted.

At that moment, in his mind, he heard a familiar voice.

"I'm back in the palace, Wil."

"Tobi—no!"

"I feel where you are now, Wil—Trouble!—but I'm coming, up the stairs...."

"No!"

With one step Binter reached Wil and caught hold of his green jacket's collar with two huge hands. His breath smelled of meat and garlic.

Wil dangled. He felt Binter's arms thrust powerfully. He found himself flying. And then his back slammed into the wall, the spot intended for Malaga. Oak slats behind him cracked. He slid to the floor and sat, back against the wall.

Inside, he felt inflamed. Hurt, he thought at first. But then he knew that fire.

"Wil, I'm running right through their legs—Hah! And now I'm in where you are."

Wil sat on the floor, staring up at Binter, burning.

What had Blossom told him, so long ago in High City, teaching him to fight?

"If they're bigger than you, Wil, you go inside, see? Because, close in, it's hard for them to stab you, or punch, get their arms around."

So he'd rush Binter, dodge the inevitable blow, grab the bigger man's throat, squeeze until Binter's eyes clouded.

He got onto his feet, crouched. He felt burning anger, and elation.

Malaga, still sitting on the floor where Binter dropped her, saw that fire. She waved her hands at him, to stop.

For a slave to fight a noble—death.

Binter, staring down at Wil, suddenly roared. He stomped the three steps to where Wil crouched. He drew back one huge booted foot. When he kicks, lean sideways, Wil thought. Let the boot pass. He'll be off balance. Go inside!

But before Binter could kick, a growl.

Tobi hurtled through the doorway, leapt, sunk his teeth into Binter's calf.

Binter, startled and hurt, bellowed.

Wil saw ferocious glee in Tobi's eye. And he saw that Tobi wore his backpack.

Binter now stomped his leg, trying to shake Tobi off.

"What that?" Poko asked, from Ranyan's arms.

To see, for the first time, another dog. To smell it.

"Tobi!"

Wil screamed it in his mind.

"Let him go, Tobi. Run!"

"Bite, bite, bite!"

Wil heard boots clattering up the corridor, imperial guards attracted by the growling and bellowing.

Malaga still sat upon the floor. She looked from Tobi to Wil. He saw she took in Tobi's knapsack. Surmise in her eyes. Then certainty.

And what would she do?

A guard looked in the doorway, took in the scene. Wil saw him suppress laughter.

Malaga sat upon the floor, short legs straight out. Wil crouched against the wall. Ranyan held Poko in her arms, and both dog and princess glared at Binter. At the center of it all, Binter jumped up and down, kicking his leg, trying to dislodge Tobi, bellowing.

"Tobi!"

He called so urgently that the dog finally shifted his attention from Binter's bleeding calf.

"Tobi—right now, in the confusion, your only chance."

"What should I do, Wil?"

"Let go that oaf, dash through the guards' legs, and—if you make it out—run faster than you've ever run down the passageway and find something you can hide under, or in a closet...."

Wil saw Tobi's eyes shift and take in the guards now pushing through the doorway. He saw the dog fighting with himself. Tobi wanted to hang on, biting Binter's leg forever. But....

A new game to play.

Tobi let go, with Binter in mid kick. He dropped to floor. Binter, unbalanced by the weight leaving his leg, kicked too hard and toppled onto the seat of his pants with a thud.

Guards rushed to the fallen aristocrat, hardly concealing their laughter.

At that moment, Tobi dashed to the doorway, zigzagged among legs. He sidestepped reaching hands. And then he disappeared up the corridor.

In his mind, Wil heard Tobi laughing to himself.

"Get that dog!" Binter, sitting on the floor, yelled at the guards.

They left the room, clomped down the corridor after Tobi. Wil heard them snicker.

Malaga now stood. She stared at Wil, triumphantly.

A simple slave. Yet, from nowhere, a beast ran to his rescue. A dog wearing a knapsack. Who but a Forester would have such a friend? And she knew which Forester he must be.

Her game token, the Fox—now infinitely valuable and powerful.

Wil wondered, how will she play me?

Domallon walked into the room. Following him, a short man, bald, red-bearded. His blue eyes—pale nearly to white—bulged, darted.

Both men took in Poko shaking in Ranyan's arms. Malaga's blue robe in disarray. Wil crouched by the wall. Binter sitting on the floor.

Binter, snarling to himself, wrapped a handkerchief around the tear in his trousers, through which blood oozed.

"A new game?" Domallon asked blandly. "Something popular among the young?"

Beside him, the red-bearded man's strange eyes darted. Wil sensed him astutely evaluating the situation. Anything here to his advantage? He thought, too, the man's eyes looked like stone-struck glass panes, cracked.

"Dog bit me," Binter snarled, from the floor.

"Ahh," said the little red-bearded man.

His bulging pale eyes turned to stare at Poko, in the princess's arms.

Ranyan, holding the dog, turned her back to the little man, hiding Poko from his gaze.

"Spirited little chap, eh?" said the red-bearded man, in a high-pitched voice.

Domallon, meanwhile, considered Binter, sprawled on the floor.

"Did I interrupt a tea party?" he asked. "Does the princess wish to be uninterrupted in her visit with the young count?"

He glanced at Malaga, eyebrows slightly raised. Wil saw her, almost imperceptibly, shake her head.

"Binter barged in—rude, rude, rude!" Ranyan said, her back still turned. "He's leaving, and he's never to bother me again."

Wil saw Binter's neck flush red, and then his face. He stared at Ranyan's back in stupid fury, and something like pain.

"I'll...."

He never finished his sentence. Instead, he got up. He rushed—limping—from the room, glowering over his shoulder at Ranyan's back. She didn't see that look, but Wil did. A threatening look.

"What do you want?" Ranyan demanded, now turning. She included in her scowl both Domallon and the red-bearded man.

"It happened that Dr. Duzzle and I met in the corridor, Your Resplendency," Domallon said, with a slight bow, which struck Wil as sardonic. "I merely sought Malaga here, on another question of Forester lore, for we do hunt their Taker, who so evilly threatens you and your family, Ma'am."

Malaga glanced at Wil.

"Oh, la di la," Ranyan said, shaking her hands in the air, as if to clear Domallon from her mind.

"And I," said Duzzle, in his high-pitched voice, smiling through his red beard, "have come on orders from His Magnificence, who desires a personal interview with our so-spirited friend Master Poko, biter of counts!"

"Poko never bit anyone!" Ranyan said. "That stray bit him. What a good dog, to bite Binter."

"Oh?" said Duzzle.

"Guards are chasing that dog right now," Ranyan said. "I hope they don't catch him, because Binter deserved a biting."

Domallon smiled to himself.

"Ah, yes," he said. "Strays in the palace, always a problem....Do you know, Your Resplendency, that not long ago I discussed that particular issue with the excellent young Fladd?"

Domallon glanced at Malaga. He didn't see Ranyan turn up her eyes.

"Now there's a boy in whom our people's warrior blood runs bright red," Domallon said. "Fladd said to me, in fact…."

"He's even more disgusting than that odious Binter," Ranyan said, glaring at Domallon.

At no point did Domallon's smile fade. But his lips, Wil saw, flattened against his teeth. Still smiling, Domallon turned to Malaga.

"I must be off, Your Resplendency," he said, still looking at Malaga. "I have an erring slave with whom I must deal— promised a reward for good work, utterly failed, now comes, what? Lashings? Beheading? Slaves who fail their assigned tasks amount to nothing, do they not? Or maybe we'll grant one more small chance to atone."

He withdrew his gaze from Malaga.

Wil saw a look in her eyes he hadn't yet seen: fear, but also fury. He thought the fire in Malaga got lit when the palace demanded she stint her own studies to tutor the emperor's spoiled daughter. Then, on a royal whim, her enslavement. She had—because she must—swallowed it. As a slave, she made what moves she could to better her position.

And what moves would she choose now?

Domallon, with an exaggerated bow to Ranyan, and a glaring glance at Malaga, now left the room. He stopped momentarily in the corridor.

"What's this?" he demanded.

And a voice from beyond the doorway answered, "We caught the dog, your lordship."

Laughter from the corridor.

Domallon shrugged. After all, street dogs often strayed into the palace. Glowering, he disappeared down the corridor.

Guards crowded into the room, carrying Tobi.

"They found me under the bench," Tobi told Wil. "I didn't get far enough under."

299

"Look, the cur's wearing a backpack."

Duzzle leaned over to peer closely at Tobi. One guard held the dog while another unbuttoned the knapsack's flap. From inside he removed a meat pie.

Wil groaned inwardly, thinking: "He brought it for me!"

"What do you make of that?"

"Probably the dog belongs to some street vender, Sergeant, and totes things for him."

"Take it out and kill it."

So it ends here, Wil thought.

He'd rush, grab the sergeant's dagger from his belt, thrust it. Because the room confined the guards and limited their movements, he might kill two, even three before they put a sword through him. Maybe, in the scuffle, Tobi would escape. He hoped so, but he doubted it.

Should he turn his back upon the Foresters, he thought? Trade a realm for this dog?

He tensed, eyes fixed on the dagger's hilt. He sensed Malaga watching him, alarmed, but he no longer played the game.

"I'll take this dog," Duzzle said. "Spirited little biter, eh? Warrior dog! And a backpack carrier—does errands. Brave and smart, eh? Yes, I'll take this dog...."

"But not Poko," the princess said.

"I believe His Magnificence will be quite interested in the qualities of this beast—carry him to the emperor, Sergeant, and then see about a leash and a muzzle, and a cage."

Duzzle now left, followed by the guards, carrying Tobi, and Wil heard Tobi's voice.

"What should we do, Wil?"

He'll live, Wil thought. At least a while.

"Tobi," he said. "I'll find a way."

So he hoped.

CHAPTER THIRTEEN

In the morning, when he arrived at Malaga's office, she handed him a manuscript.

"Find a passage, Fox," she said. "It foretells how the Foresters would wield the regained Starstone—read it to me."

He only pretended to study the parchment. All night, sleepless on his slave-quarters cot, he'd called out to Tobi, and heard no response. Now, in his mind, he called once again. No answer.

Malaga leaned back in her chair, head tilted to one side, studying him, and he guessed her thought: yesterday a knapsack-wearing dog defended him, her final clue. He was the Taker.

He thought: kill her.

Hide her body.

Next, kill a constable. Take his uniform. Hide his body, too. Disguised in the stolen uniform, slip through the gate.

He grimaced.

To kill....

If he didn't, she'd surely reveal him to Domallon. Why not? She'd be the realm's savior. They'd free her.

"Fox." she said, and he looked up.

She still studied him, head tilted aside. Three paces separated their desks.

She said: "My life's work is studying Foresters."

This room's heavy door would muffle sound. Forester tapestries, from Malaga's former office, covered the walls. Her thick Forester carpet covered the floor. No scream or moan would escape. And this office's one other door merely opened into the adjoining room where Malaga lived and slept.

Three paces to where she sat.

"Fox, nobody knows more about them, maybe not even the Foresters themselves," she said.

He thought: if she lives, I die. Then, the Starstone's theirs, and they rule forever, these ice-hearted people. They'll hunt down the Foresters in High City, and in the forest villages, and slaughter them.

He thought: "Forester magic would drain from the world."

He'd never wished to be a Forester. Fishtowners called Forester magic "filthy." Always, growing up, hearing their revulsion, he'd fought against what pulsed within him.

But a world without enchantment....

Yet, not quite without magic—there'd be what the Nameless Ones of Darkness laid down eons ago, like stains. And these descendants of southern conquerors, possessing the Starstone, uncontested, would strengthen. Even the unmagical, unawares, feel magic's touch.

"A lifetime studying them," Malaga said. "Yet, I've never met a Forester."

He stood, pretending to stretch his desk-sore arms.

"Was the dog with the knapsack your pet?" Malaga asked.

"He's my friend," Wil said.

To kill Malaga, easy. To kill a constable, not difficult. To escape from the palace, possible.

But what of Tobi? And the Starstone?

"I weigh you, Fox, against Lord Domallon."

He took a step toward Malaga, still pretending to stretch.

"Should I say how I weigh you?"

He shrugged. He took a second step.

"Domallon is the power of swords, and political sway," she said. "He is arrogant, intelligent, implacable, cruel—to him, we commoners are wheat for scything."

302

"He could advance you," Wil said.

"Yes," Malaga said. "Or kill me."

He took a third step. He rested his hands upon her desk's edge.

"Would you like to know, Fox, what weight I assign you?" she asked.

She looked at his hands upon her desk.

He lifted them, and spread them, palms up. In one swift moment, now, they could grip her neck.

"You are what I've studied all my life, and never known," she said. "You are mystery."

"Even to myself," he said.

He said that because he felt himself pause. Would he murder?

"I think you kind," she said. "I think you, in ways I cannot understand, more powerful than Domallon."

"I'm a slave," he said.

"Yet, an animal adores you, would die for you," she said.

And she said: "I do not think you will strangle me."

He froze.

"To protect yourself, you think of killing me, as would I," Malaga said. "But you will seek another way."

Motionless, he stared at her.

"Foresters shrink from killing," she said. "Even an insect."

He looked down at her where she sat, a rangy man gazing at a dwarf. She looked back, tensed.

He thought: Foresters do shrink from killing. It's because, even in a mere butterfly or beetle, they feel sentience.

He stepped backwards one pace, stood looking down at her. After a moment, he sighed. Then he walked back to his own small desk. He picked up the parchment she'd given him.

Malaga now said: "What they almost were, the Foresters, that fascinates me."

She spoke faster, relieved by his retreat.

"And what they might yet be."

He gazed at the manuscript, but instead of reading its words he let remembered bits of conversation, overheard since he arrived in the palace, dance in his mind, puzzle pieces, now fitting together, showing where Tobi must be.

Torpan and Duzzle sought magic to wield against Foresters. They believed the key lay in Foresters' ability to speak with beasts, and maybe they intended merely to try speaking with Tobi.

No, he thought, grimly. Not so benign.

He remembered Ranyan's horror, fearing they'd take her dog "below," and Poko had showed him a marble door, opening on stone steps winding downward. Poko said those steps led to the Starstone, so their chamber for magical experiments must be down there, too. Proximity to the Stone might lend them power, they'd surely think. But the stairway descended from the emperor's private quarters, and Wil saw no way in.

Malaga still regarded him.

"Foresters overreached with the Starstone," she said. "They began controlling people's thoughts, their innermost being—and the people felt robbed of their selfhood, so they rebelled."

Wil said: "A thousand years…."

But he thought of Pim's fixation on regaining the Foresters' lost power. How would that owlish Lord of the War wield the Starstone? How, though, might Zadni Druen wield it? And Mita? He pictured the Wielder's worried face, and wondered how she fared.

"Sensitive spirit," he thought. "Hard world."

Malaga spoke again, staring intently at him.

"I might say to Lord Domallon—here, the Taker—reward me!"

She stared into Wil's eyes.

"I might get something," she said. "But, with the Taker dead, my usefulness ends—I might get sent to launder clothes, or for my arrogance, deeming myself helpful to my betters, I might earn execution."

On the parchment, Wil saw the passage Malaga sought.

"I am a child of wealth, Fox, become a professor, distinguished, and yet—on a royal whim—enslaved."

Wil put his finger on the passage.

"Do you see?"

He heard Malaga's tone sharpen, and he looked up.

She no longer veiled her ferret face. Looking at that face, now naked, he saw pride in her intellect. And fear. A slave must tiptoe, lest she displease her masters, genuflect. Disgust, he saw, at her debasement, and rage. She smoldered.

"Do you see?" she said.

Wil looked at the parchment's passage his finger marked. He read aloud.

"In that thousandth year, the empire's days will number not even in tens. But now two paths diverge, for both the magical peoples and unmagical. Murk hides those paths. For the path taken remains undecided, until the final moment. Only this do we see: a struggle, not solely in this world, with one alone to decide, and one alone to act, and that one alone to determine the path taken."

"What does it mean, Fox?"

"I don't know," he said.

"What should I choose?" she asked. "Domallon offers me some small chance for reward, and freedom—what do you offer?"

Someone knocked on the door, a blue-smocked maid.

"Her Resplendency summons you to the empress's quarters."

"Tell her I shall arrive quickly," Malaga said, shooing the maid out the door.

She stood, and eyed Wil speculatively.

"Come with me, Fox, for you should see this—it is a Starstone matter, and it tells us something."

Another golden door off the royal reception room. Another walk down a long corridor from which doors opened into rooms for dining and entertaining, but here with sheets shrouding the furniture.

A slave in red passed, carrying an emptied silver teapot and two jade cups upon a silver salver. Two more slaves, in blue, toted by its handles a wicker basket heaped with soiled clothes. Clearly the empress commanded no liveried servants of her own.

At the corridor's end, a second massive golden door, this one studded with pearls.

Malaga knocked.

From inside, Ranyan's voice bid them enter.

Upon a huge bed sat a woman stunningly corpulent. Pillows propped her up. Wil doubted she could stand unsupported, or walk.

Once, he guessed, she stood tall, slender, stately. He could see that in her. But now, under stringy gray hair, her bloated face sagged to a cascade of blubbery chins. Her cheeks drooped into pouches. Her eyelids struggled to stay open under the weight of their fat.

Ranyan sat upon a bedside hassock, elbows on knees, fists pressed against temples. She looked at the floor. Her black hair hid her face. Besides the wrecked woman on the bed, and the princess, only Poko occupied the room, sitting at Ranyan's feet. He glared at Wil through his white bangs.

"What is it, Child?" Malaga said.

"She worsens," Ranyan said, not looking up.

Poko spoke to Wil, words only Wil heard: "Bad one—go away."

"To lose a parent, inch by inch…." Malaga said.

"That I can bear," Ranyan said, still staring at the floor.

"Then what troubles you so?" Malaga asked.

Ranyan straightened and looked at Malaga, eyes wide.

"It infects me," she said. "I'm now cursed, too."

Stirring slightly upon her pillows, the ruined empress spoke, a voice like birdsong.

"Foggy fingers gaily play, so cold," she said. "They seek within what isn't there, poor things."

Malaga glanced at the queen.

Pity in Malaga's eyes, Wil thought.

But what the crazed woman described, he understood. For those misty fingers now danced about him. Whoever neared the Stone, he guessed, it tested. It sought to express itself. For such as this empress, the unmagical, it had no use. Yet, even they, it seemed, too long exposed, felt its force.

Wil gazed at the ruined woman upon the bed, and wondered. If it does this to them, what of us?

For those dancing fingers now explored within him, seeking inner latches to unfasten, knobs to turn. He fought them, his forehead beading, until he pushed them away. Each time, this inner battle taxed him more. One day, he supposed….

Mita!

If she wielded this thing, what fate for her?

Malaga studied him, he saw, that sidewise look. She guessed, no doubt, what he battled.

"We sleepers reel," the empress cheerily sang. "Drunk on dreams."

Ranyan clutched her own head.

"I feel them, too, now...."

She shuddered.

"Dear Child," Malaga said.

She laid a consoling hand upon the princess's cheek, and Wil thought, this girl who enslaved her, she loves. Yet, what Ranyan is, she despises.

Love the girl. Hate the princess.

"I walk out at night, into the city, to get away from that Stone," Ranyan said.

She shuddered again.

"Papa keeps it down there, just under this room—I suppose that's why it's hurt Mama most."

Malaga asked: "Should not your mother move to other quarters then?"

"Papa wants her like this!" Ranyan said, her pale eyes fierce. "He sends Duzzle to write down what Mama says, because they believe she's the Stone's seer, and that it speaks through her, telling them what to do."

Malaga looked at Wil.

"What do you think, Fox?"

It startled him, to be addressed so directly before the princess. Did it show Malaga meant to turn him in?

"I think...."

He stopped, bemused by a thought: even now he struggled against the misty fingers flitting around him. Did his wrestling with those Starstone tendrils strengthen whatever magic he had? Maybe the Stone thus prepared him, as Blossom had prepared him, teaching him to fight. And in a pouch suspended from his neck he wore the Opal of Living and Dying. Maybe, together, Stone and Opal molded him, but into what?

Malaga still stared at him, her question unanswered. He shrugged.

"Everything's confused, unclear," he said. "Its ways are…."

Hearing his voice, Ranyan looked up, peered at him, then away. Abruptly, she turned to Malaga.

"I remember this one!"

She spoke looking at Malaga, and Wil thought, as a toddler this princess learned, never regard a slave directly, even to give an order. Yet, she looks directly at Malaga, and not just because the dwarfed scholar is Ranyan's slave. That wreck on the bed…. Malaga has become Ranyan's mother.

"On a night walk in the city I talked with this one, because of his dog," Ranyan told Malaga, not looking at Wil. "Short legs, no tail. It bit Binter. That same dog! Strange!"

Wil stood silent.

"We spoke of heads that night," Ranyan said. "Of putting things from one head into another, because of Papa and Duzzle, and…."

She pointed an index finger downward, toward the floor. Her gesture suggested ugliness below, unspeakable.

Malaga looked from Ranyan to Wil.

"So tell me, Fox, philosopher of the night, advisor to royalty on dog matters, what do you think of Her Resplendency feeling these misty fingers she describes?"

Wil looked down.

After a moment, he looked up, and met Malaga's gaze.

"One choice leads to upheaval," Wil said. "But for you, and one you love—only turmoil offers hope."

"What hope do you offer me?" Malaga asked. "And this child?"

"A promise," Wil said.

Malaga looked at him, brow knitted, waiting.

309

"To struggle—every fiber—to do right."

"What a strange conversation!" Ranyan said.

She looked at them in exasperation, but neither looked at her. Malaga stared at Wil, brow furrowed. Wil looked back at Malaga, open-eyed.

"Oh, la di la," Ranyan said, waving her hands as if brushing away cobwebs.

A cautious knock on the door, the maid in blue to whom Wil spoke when he first entered the royal quarters. She curtsied.

"Count Binter and Count Fladd sit in your reception room, Ma'am, and they both earnestly entreat you to come!"

This maid's brown eyes sparkled. So much excitement!

"Oh, la di la," Ranyan said, making a face suggesting exposure to a noxious scent.

"What shall I tell them, Ma'am?"

"Say I wish them both buried to their noses in dead rats."

"Please, Ma'am, I couldn't...."

Ranyan pursed her lips. Finally she smiled faintly, in her pale eyes glints of mischief.

"You come with me," she told Malaga. "And bring that."

She pointed her finger at Wil, without looking at him.

"Maybe his dog will escape the chamber and bite Binter again."

With both hands, Ranyan shooed away the maid.

"Poko!" she said, and the tiny dog leaped into her arms.

Then she strode from her mother's room, carrying Poko, looking back to make sure Malaga and Wil followed.

From her bed, the queen called after them.

"Tiny moments turn the world!"

She laughed, a tinkling sound, as if her words brimmed with humor.

In the princess's reception room, Binter sulked in a chair, which seemed too small for him, arms crossed. He scowled at the wall. One scuffed boot rested atop a hassock. He tossed his head to sweep away unkempt black hair covering one eye, and the movement toppled his sheathed rapier, lying askew across his lap. It rattled against the stone floor.

Across the room, the falling sword's clatter startled a ginger-haired youth, also in a chair turned to the wall. He swiveled his head to look back. Seeing the princess enter the room, with Poko in her arms, Malaga and Wil following, he stood. He smiled at Ranyan, showing even white teeth under his narrow mustache.

"Your Resplendency," he said, formally bowing, which hiked up his green-velvet jacket above the seat of his black trousers.

Binter glared over his shoulder at the princess. With a snort, he turned back to the wall.

"Poko and I visited delightfully until Binter and Fladd bothered us," Ranyan said, as if to the ceiling. "What do they want?"

Binter snorted again, still glowering at the wall. Wil saw his neck reddening.

"My dear Ranyan," said Fladd, cocking his head to one side.

He leaned his hip against an armchair and crossed one green-velvet boot over the other.

"We're no longer school children, you and I, running along the corridors," he said. "But we had fine times then, didn't we? Remember your gray kitten, such a winsome thing? Let's see, what happened to that kitten.... Oh yes, I remember—Binter had one of his fits and threw it out the window. You were so upset. Remember? And do you remember how I tried, in my childish way, to soothe you, saying His Magnificence would get you another kitten…."

Binter kicked the hassock. It thudded into the wall.

Fladd glanced toward Binter's back. Turning to Ranyan, he sadly shrugged.

"Well, as it is," Fladd said, "I'm here to formally…."

Binter, back still turned, snarled.

"On my own, I'd never have dared," Fladd said. "Never thought…."

Ranyan sighed. She turned up her pale blue eyes.

"But I've been conferring with my good friend and mentor, Lord Domallon!" Fladd said.

He paused, waiting for Ranyan to express admiration over Fladd's powerful protector. But she merely stooped to put down Poko.

"Yes, well," Fladd said, smiling brightly with his even teeth. "To my astonishment, his lordship feels that, in the matter of your marriage—and he believes it's time, Your Resplendency, even past time!"

Ranyan looked back at Malaga and made a face indicative of nausea. Fladd, not seeing that look, spoke on.

"Well, as it turns out, His Lordship has, for quite a while now, had his eye on me, thinks highly of my potential…."

"Does Lord Domallon, then, frequent Imperia's taverns, and keep his eye on you there?" Ranyan asked sweetly.

Fladd looked chagrined. Then, in his weak blue eyes, Wil saw something approaching canniness. Fladd now grinned brilliantly.

"A royal jest!" he said, as if delighted. "And I do sometimes sport about in the city's taverns, which I'll never deny, and in other places, too, but you see—I go to study the people! Yes, we rule them, and to rule them well one must know them!

And I feel, after speaking with his lordship, that perhaps ruling is my true vocation, far in the future, of course...."

"Emperor of beer and brothels," Ranyan said.

Fladd pretended not to hear. Instead, he looked at Ranyan beatifically, and deeply sighed.

"I've come," he said, extending an arm for dramatic effect, "to formally petition you for the right to ask His Magnificence for permission to seek your hand!"

"Poko?" Ranyan said. "Bark!"

Poko sat up and barked.

Fladd eyed the dog, flustered. But he rallied.

"You don't know how I daydream about you, Ranyan, your beauty and intelligence, and...."

"Manure!" Binter yelled.

He jumped to his feet, quickly for so huge a man. His head seemed to reach near the ceiling.

Fladd, involuntarily, stepped backward.

"You're mine, Ranyan!"

Binter's voice sounded strangled.

"I belong to me," Ranyan said. "And only me."

Binter reached out a hand to grab her shoulder. She stepped out of his reach.

"Oh, go drown in mud, both of you," Ranyan said. "You're repellent, and Domallon, too, and all the rest, strutting in velvet, and plotting in whispers, and extolling our ancestors for murder, and you're cruel...."

She stopped, arms crossed, frowning at her feet. Then she jerked up her chin and glared from one to the other.

"So repellent that I wish to live with Foresters in trees, and study magic!" she said.

Binter glowered down at her. His hands clenched into fists.

"You'd choose this weakling?"

313

Ranyan's pale blue eyes suddenly glittered.

"Let us see," she said. "Here, a donkey who rinses his mouth in lavender water to hide the reek of rum, and there an ox whose brain stopped growing at six months, and I must choose?"

"Choose now," Binter hissed.

Wil saw Binter's hand hover near his rapier's hilt. Alarmed, he glanced at Malaga.

"Perhaps it is time for tea and cakes, Your Resplendency," Malaga said. "And postpone these important deliberations to a quieter moment."

Ranyan set her face.

"Choose?" she said. "I choose to live in the forest in trees, but if I actually wished to choose between the donkey and the ox, I would do it thus...."

She shut her eyes, pointed an index finger, and pirouetted three times. She stopped and opened her eyes. Her finger pointed at Fladd.

"Oh dear," she said, laughing. "Donkey."

Binter's face contorted.

"You choose him?"

Wil saw that Binter stupidly misunderstood Ranyan's teasing. And he saw that Ranyan, amused by her game, failed to see that Binter took her seriously.

Ranyan pretended to look at her pointing finger. Then she looked where her finger pointed, at Fladd.

"Why, so it would seem," she said, laughing. "Donkey."

Binter roared.

He unsheathed his rapier, a sound like slithering.

"What is this?" Fladd said, stepping backwards.

"Draw!" Binter said.

"But this is idiotic," Fladd said, again stepping back.

Binter, snarling, thrust. A thin line of blood appeared on Fladd's forehead.

Fladd reached up to touch the cut. He looked at his blood-smeared fingers.

"Stop it, Binter," Ranyan cried. "I command you."

Binter glared at Fladd, who looked confused.

"Draw," he said. "And if you're too cowardly...."

Again he lashed out his rapier, this time slicing Fladd's shoulder. Blood oozed through the slit velvet.

Malaga now rushed to the doorway.

"Send guards!" she shouted to someone Wil couldn't see. "Before there's murder!"

Malaga beckoned to Ranyan to follow her out, but the princess stood frozen, as Fladd now drew his own rapier. In his face, Wil saw fear.

Binter slashed at his rival. Fladd parried, thrust, lunged. His point passed through Binter's sleeve. Fladd struggled to withdraw the trapped blade. Just as he got it loose, Binter thrust has rapier's point into Fladd's velvet jacket. With both hands now upon the hilt, he shoved.

Fladd's jacket bulged in back. Then the rapier's tip cut through, and a foot of blade—reddened—slid out.

"What's this?" Fladd said, looking down at the blade, where it penetrated his chest.

He dropped his own rapier. It clanged on the stone floor.

Looking stupidly at the dropped sword, Fladd crumpled to his knees. He looked at Ranyan, astonished. Slowly, he toppled sideways. He writhed. Then he lay still.

Binter, face ugly, withdrew his rapier.

"What have you done!" Ranyan cried.

Binter now strode to the doorway, where Malaga stood, desperately beckoning to Ranyan to run with her from the room. With a swipe of his huge hand, Binter knocked the dwarf aside. Then he slammed shut the door.

Face contorted, his back to the wall, he shouted at Ranyan: "They'll execute me, but you go first!"

He raised his rapier, tears running down his face, and stepped toward Ranyan, who backed against the far wall. Binter lurched toward her.

Wil found himself kneeling over the fallen Fladd. He found, in his hand, the dead man's rapier. His feet moved, without him telling them to. He stepped between the princess and Binter, rapier raised, waiting.

"A slave!" Binter screamed.

He lunged, aiming his rapier's point at Wil's heart.

Wil half turned, letting the blade slide by. Binter, bellowing, pulled back his blade. Wil could now strike the off-balance count. Instead, he resumed his position, between Binter and Ranyan.

Wil still thought nothing.

Binter slashed at Wil's face. With a blade flick, Wil parried.

Now the noble stopped, stared at the slave before him. A commoner? Adroit with a sword? He launched a slashing attack.

Wil ducked, letting the blade pass over him. A quick thrust upward would pierce Binter under his chin.

Wil instead slid his own blade along Binter's, to its base, and abruptly jerked his rapier's hilt. Binter's sword flew from his hand and clattered onto the floor.

Binter gaped at his weapon lying at his feet. Wil resumed his position in front of Ranyan, waiting.

Binter scooped up the fallen sword. He charged Wil, lunging. Wil's blade, in parrying, sliced his opponent's forearm. Binter ignored the spurting blood. He swung his massive left fist against Wil's temple, knocking him aside. Wil, stunned, watched Binter now raise his rapier, aim at Ranyan's heart, begin to plunge the point home.

Wil thrust.

His rapier's tip passed through Binter's neck.

Binter gurgled.

"Ranyan...."

Binter, with Wil's weapon through his neck, again raised his rapier to pierce the princess.

But his sword's point sank toward the floor and he slowly toppled, thudding onto the floor. He lay still. Ranyan, backed against the wall, slid down and sat, her face in her hands, sobbing.

Wil heard Malaga's voice, from somewhere.

"Fox, what have you done?"

He stood, befuddled.

What had he done?

His Magnificence, Torpan the Twenty-Ninth, sat upon his golden throne, upholstered in purple velvet, and whistled.

"What is that tune?" he said, vexed.

A duke, standing beside the throne, leaned over and quietly hummed in His Magnificence's ear.

"Yes, that's it," said the emperor, adjusting his rimless spectacles. "The ancient war song of our people, yes, stirring!"

He whistled again, the war song.

When he finished, the room's throng of nobles and constabulary officers and ladies of the court applauded.

"Eh?" said the emperor.

His eagle eyes glared about the room.

Another of the aristocrats standing about the throne leaned over and quietly spoke to the emperor. He pointed, directing Torpan's gaze to Wil, who stood before the throne in his green livery, his wrists and ankles chained.

"Ah, yes, odd case, eh?" Torpan said, peering at Wil.

A constable, in a colonel's uniform, stepped forward. Bowing, he handed Torpan a parchment.

317

Torpan regarded it uncomprehendingly.

"A report, Your Magnificence, if it please you," said the officer. "Of the incident?"

"Yes, yes, odd affair," Torpan said.

He pulled his glasses down to the end of his nose. Holding the report as far as his long, sticklike arms could extend, he peered through his spectacles and read.

"Fladd!" he said. "Murdered?"

He peered at Wil.

"A count! Worthless, certainly. But, still, a count! And this green thing before me...."

Now the constabulary colonel stepped close to the throne and whispered to Torpan. He pointed to a passage in the document Torpan held.

"Hmmm," Torpan said, reading.

His reading of the passage continued, with nods and "hmmms." A rustling swept the room, for the reading seemed interminable.

Finally, the emperor looked up, his raptor eyes combing through those around the throne.

"Duzzle?" he said. "I want Duzzle."

"Here, Your Magnificence!"

A voice from the far back of the room. Wil saw the crowd ripple, and then the little man emerged beside the throne.

Duzzle bowed to Ranyan, who stood beside her father, white face distraught. Beside the princess stood Malaga. She gazed at Wil, stricken.

What had he done?

"Ah, Duzzle, good, good," the emperor said, laying the constabulary report on his lap. "I've had a thought, just now."

Duzzle bowed, and stood listening raptly as Torpan posed a question.

"It's from the head's side we've augered, eh?"

He pointed a bony index finger at his own skull, just above his right ear, and twisted the finger to indicate boring.

"Exactly correct, Your Magnificence," Duzzle said. "You have it just so!"

Torpan eyed Duzzle, considering. Finally his eyebrows lifted.

"And there's been no success?" he said. "No magic?"

"We're closing in, Your Magnificence," Duzzle said, smacking his left hand with his right fist. "Closing in!"

"Still, when we've spooned out the gray matter from one head, and spooned it into the other, they've all died, have they not?"

Duzzle sighed. He shrugged, showing his palms.

"In all experimentation of this type, Your Magnificence, there will be small setbacks, of course, as we explore hitherto untrodden…."

Torpan waved a dismissive hand. Duzzle fell silent.

"Now, this thought just came to me," Torpan said, eyeing Duzzle. "What if we augered in from the top?"

He pointed his index finger at his own graying crown and twisted it.

Duzzle clapped his hands in delight.

"Your Magnificence, brilliant!" he exclaimed.

"Worth a try, eh?" Torpan said.

Wil heard a rustling among the courtiers, and whispers.

Now, from the nobles surrounding the throne, Domallon stepped forward. He lowered his chin, signifying a respectful bow.

"Your Magnificence," he said. "We know how important you find your researches into magic, and how you endeavor to arm us with magic, to fight the enemy's magic with our own magic, and we all applaud your efforts."

Torpan eyed his minister of justice, perplexed.

319

"Vital work, to be sure, Your Magnificence," Domallon said. "But today's tribunal addresses matters of justice and protocol, and requires your close attention."

"Eh?" Torpan said.

His bird-of-prey eyes swept the room, focused on Wil, then returned to Domallon.

"Seems simple enough," Torpan said.

"In a sense, certainly," Domallon said. "However, it also...."

"Don't see why I'm taken from my vital studies, trying to save our realm from armies of enemies—Sly! Powerful!—merely for a slave matter," Torpan said, regarding Domallon with raised eyebrows.

Domallon seemed to study his feet. Wil sensed that he summoned patience. Finally he looked up.

"Nobody wishes to intrude upon our emperor's time, of course," Domallon said evenly. "However, protocol requires that, in such a complicated case as this, only Your Magnificence can...."

"Protocol?" Torpan said. "Well, where's Bor Dagin? He's minister of protocol, isn't he? Why doesn't he settle this?"

"It's his son, Fladd, who lies dead in this incident," Domallon said. "He mourns, and has asked me to carry out my own duties, of justice, but also his duties."

Domallon now bowed his head, politely.

"This becomes annoying," Torpan said.

He clasped his hands and looked down at them, thinking. Silence now filled the room. After a few moments, Torpan looked up.

"I have it," he said.

Domallon and all others in the room waited expectantly.

"Take off his head, eh?"

Ranyan wailed.

Torpan looked at his daughter, standing beside his throne. His brow furrowed in perplexity.

"This slave defended me!" she cried. "We can't behead him for defending me!"

Wil saw Malaga look from the princess to the emperor. She seemed far away. This throne room's proceedings all seemed distant.

"But he stuck a sword through Fladd," Torpan told Ranyan. "And that means…."

Ranyan banged her fists against the arm of Torpan's throne. He looked in bewilderment at her.

"Papa, this slave did not kill Fladd—Binter killed him."

"Eh?" Torpan said.

Again he picked up the constabulary report. He read it. Finally he put it down and frowned, first at Ranyan, then at the room in general.

"Binter kills Fladd—bad thing that!" he said. "Then the slave kills Binter…."

"Protecting me against Binter," Ranyan cried, exasperated. "Binter meant to kill me, too!"

Torpan looked judicious. After a moment, however, his brow furrowed. He bit his lower lip. Finally his mouth turned down.

He scowled at Domallon.

"Well, what do you have to say, Dapik? This grows tiresome."

Domallon stood, considering. Then he held out his left hand.

"It's a two-handed problem, Your Magnificence," he said. "On this left side, our laws say that to protect a member of the royal family, particularly at risk of one's own life, merits high reward, and…."

"Somebody protected the royal family?" Torpan said.

321

After a pause, Domallon proceeded evenly.

"In a dispute over who might seek the princess's hand, Binter challenged Fladd and slew him," Domallon said.

Torpan threw up his hands in exasperation.

"Foresters, thousands upon thousands, a powerful army of spiteful sorcerers, aiming spells against us, and curses...."

Torpan glared at Domallon.

"I'm waging war—Tactics! Strategy! Make our ancestors proud!—and....What were you saying?"

"On this left hand, Your Magnificence, the slave protects Her Resplendency from Binter, who means to kill her because she refused him...."

Torpan waved a hand and nodded.

"Yes, yes, brave and loyal to his mistress, and so on," he said.

"Your Magnificence," Domallon said, executing a formal bow that struck Wil as sardonic.

Now, with his left arm still held out, Domallon extended his right arm.

"On this side, a slave dares touch the weapon of a count, albeit a dead one, and take it, and then dares raise that rapier against another count."

"Terrible!" Torpan said.

He glared at Wil. He shook his head. Then he turned up his eyes toward the ornate ceiling, in revulsion.

Domallon spoke again.

"So you see, for this one act—slaying Binter—our laws call for both reward and beheading."

Torpan now slouched on his throne, his long legs stretched out before him, bony fingers moving in the air before his eyes.

Finally he sat up.

"I have it," he said.

"Your Magnificence?" Domallon said.

"Reward the slave for his service to the princess with an official scroll saying, 'Because of its beneficence, the royal family, in the person of Torpan the Twenty-Ninth, hereby offers its appreciation.'"

"Papa, thank you!" Ranyan cried.

Torpan held up a hand, demanding silence.

"Then, in punishment for his insolence, behead the vermin."

In the silence that now filled the court, Ranyan gazed at her father. It seemed to Wil that gaze held horror, and fury.

Somebody clapped. Another. Now the room filled with applause.

Torpan smiled vaguely at the room, acknowledging their appreciation of his judgment's subtlety. He held up a hand and waved it.

After the applause died away, Domallon once more bowed formally to the throne.

"Wise, discerning," Domallon said.

Torpan nodded, looking pleased with himself.

"But a small question troubles me," Domallon said.

Torpan exchanged a look with Duzzle, exasperated. Ranyan now sat upon the carpet, slumped, her head in her hands.

"I wish to know," Domallon said, "how a slave, a former street scavenger, we're told, learned to wield a sword so adroitly he outfenced a trained nobleman."

Torpan eyed Domallon, considering.

"Hardly seems to matter, since the creature is about to be dead…."

"Your Magnificence, in recent months I have become concerned about a rising number of instances in which commoners stepped beyond their station, showed disdain for the constabulary, and hence insolence to the ruling aristocracy."

"Insolence?" Torpan said. "Stamp 'em out!"

He stamped his foot, twice.

"Yes, of course," Domallon said. "However, I wonder if this rising tide of restlessness among the commoners might indicate Foresters have infiltrated Imperia…."

"What? You're supposed to keep 'em out!" Torpan cried, alarmed.

"And we have, Your Magnificence," Domallon said. "Still, it is wise to follow all suspicious threads, and so—with your permission—I will now direct certain questions to this miscreant."

Torpan looked sullen. He exchanged a look of exasperation with Duzzle.

"Shouldn't be talking directly to these lice," he said. "So how do you propose to do it?"

Domallon looked thoughtful. Wil guessed that, in privacy, Domallon would happily question him directly, using thumbscrews to help the conversation along. However, now Domallon's gaze settled on Malaga.

"I'll put my questions to Malaga Gant, here, who's a slave of a higher order," he said.

Torpan threw up his hands.

Domallon beckoned Malaga forward, to stand facing Wil. Looking at Wil, she imperceptibly shook her head, a gesture of misery.

"Ask him how he learned to handle a rapier," Domallon commanded.

With a sigh, Malaga repeated the question.

Wil's mind raced.

He wished to say, I learned from the same good man who outfought your arrogant son, and slew him, and who is a better man than you, and all your kind.

Why not? His life would end in an hour.

324

Fight, he told himself.

"I learned to handle a rapier as a small boy," Wil said, "from a man I met on the street, a former constable, dismissed for some infraction…."

"Ask him," Domallon told Malaga, "what he and this renegade constable he describes used for swords, in their practice."

Malaga asked.

"Sticks," Wil said.

Domallon considered, eyeing him.

"Perhaps," he said, speaking aloud to himself. "But you are of the correct age, I think….Yet, dark haired, dark eyed…."

"Are you satisfied?" Torpan asked irritably.

Domallon bowed.

"We impose upon Your Magnificence's time," he said. "So, yes, send him along to the axeman but—along the way—perhaps a session on the rack, to see what we might learn…."

Torpan shrugged.

"As you wish," he said.

He began to sweep his purple cloak about him, preparatory to rising.

Malaga abruptly knelt beside the princess, still huddled upon the floor beside the throne, and whispered. Ranyan stood and grabbed her father's sleeve.

"Papa," she said. "Malaga has a thought for you—will you let her speak?"

Wil thought: do you mean, Malaga, to plead for my life?

Torpan looked vexed, but waved a hand in half-hearted approval.

Malaga knelt before the throne. She looked, with her short legs, like a child kneeling before a giant.

"Your Magnificence," she said. "I have a thought regarding your experiments, below."

Torpan, for the first time, looked interested.

"You have recently taken for those purposes a short-legged dog, with no tail?" Malaga said.

"Ah, yes, spirited cur," Torpan said, glancing at Duzzle. "He's in the experimentation chamber now, awaiting an appropriate human subject, for it is Doctor Duzzle's contention, with which I concur, that if we blend the contents of heads, between man and beast, that should enable the two to speak, man and beast, and that—again, so contends Doctor Duzzle, and I concur—should lead to magic!"

Wil saw Domallon gazing thoughtfully at Malaga.

"It is my thought that this slave has shown spirit and courage," Malaga said. "Why waste him on beheading? Would he not, Your Magnificence, be an excellent subject for your experiments with this dog?"

Torpan bestowed upon Malaga a wintry smile.

He snapped his fingers, in appreciation.

"Excellent!" he said.

He beckoned to a squad of constables standing against the wall. Wil heard their boots tramping along the throne room's stone floor.

"If it please, Your Magnificence," Domallon said.

"Enough!" Torpan said.

Domallon stepped back. Again he studied Malaga, frowning.

Wil felt iron hands grab him, march him from the throne room. He tripped on his ankle shackles, so they hoisted him, and carried him from the room, down the corridor, while he thought, she finally chose. It felt bitter in his mind.

They carried him into the emperor's own chambers. He saw gold and marble and royal purple drapes and upholstery and, upon a table, a drinking cup carved from one giant emerald. And he saw the marble door in a marble wall, which Poko had showed him.

Now they carried him down a winding stairway.

Malaga, he thought. What have you done?

Suddenly, he saw it, just what Malaga had done, and her courage in doing it. Even as they carried him down, he laughed.

CHAPTER FOURTEEN

"I've been waiting for you, Wil."

"I'm here now, Tobi."

"I don't like it here, Wil."

"It's a bad place, Tobi."

"What will we do?"

"Wait."

In the dark, Wil slumped against his cage's bars. He heard Tobi, in his adjacent cage, lie down to patiently wait, trusting him to find a way out. But he saw no way out.

When the guards carried him down the stairs, he'd felt elated. The Taker! Brought to the Starstone!

Then they'd shoved him into this cage and their torchlight revealed a windowless chamber with stone walls, stone floor, a stone ceiling. He'd glimpsed side-by-side tables, fitted with shackles for paws and hands. He saw boring instruments, encrusted with dried blood.

When the guards left with their torches, all turned black. Gradually, though, a glow illuminated the chamber, emanating from a marble podium near the far wall—atop a purple cushion lay a crystal disk, its glow steadily intensifying. And the Opal of Living and Dying, in its pouch suspended from his neck, pulsed as if it breathed the Starstone's cold glow, touched with starlight's blue.

"Do you see the Stone's light, Tobi?"

"No, it's dark in here, Wil, and I can't see at all, and I don't like that."

So he knew the Starstone glowed with magical light. To see it, you must be magical.

"I am magical," he thought.

He'd yearned only to be a Fishtowner. Yet, since early childhood, beasts spoke to him, tame and wild. As he grew, those voices clarified. So he'd known what he was.

Loathsome Foresters. Filthy magic.

He'd fought what was in him, but now he'd die soon, for being a Forester. And this dog beside him would die, for befriending him.

"I'm sorry, Tobi," he said.

"I don't understand, Wil," the dog said.

He thought, I could have told Pim, "No."

High City would have expelled him, but he'd heard ancient Forester villages still lingered, scattered deep in the forest. They kept apart, not trading with High City or its associated villages. They lived as their ancestors did thousands of years ago, before Foresters acquired the Starstone and became Forest Kings. Lal, he guessed, might have led him to such a village, seeking refuge. He might have quietly lived his life.

But he'd chosen to be the Taker.

He'd accepted it.

And from that, all ensued.

He thought: so I'll die, and Tobi will die. And, because I've failed, Blossom will die, and Pim, and Zadni Druen, and all the others.

Mita will die.

And we'll never make a life together.

That thought surprised him. He hadn't known he meant to make a life with Mita. Did she wish a life with him?

He smiled, wanly.

"Have you got it yet, Wil?"

"What, Tobi?"

"Your plan, to get back outside, to see Mita and Blossom."

"Not yet, Tobi."

Malaga, too, would die.

In the tribunal, when she suggested to the emperor that he imprison Wil in this chamber, to experiment upon, Domallon eyed her suspiciously, but Malaga had chosen. She chose him.

Knowing what she risked, she'd positioned him here, five paces from the Starstone. It lay before him now, shining upon its purple cushion.

She'd given him this small chance to get free and take the Stone, to bring down this realm, but he saw no way. For now, he could only wait.

"Why are you moaning, Wil."

"I didn't know I moaned, Tobi."

"Are you hurt, Wil?"

"In a way."

He felt the Starstone's force, as if he stood in the great river at the tide's ebb, and currents pulled him toward the sea. Fighting that inexorable pull, he braced his feet against the bottom, but wearied. He ached from his resistance. He need only lift his feet, just a little, to be carried away.

Overhead the ruined empress lay helpless upon her bed. If he surrendered to the Starstone, would it do that to him? Or something different?

He wondered....

Yellow torchlight, descending the stairs.

330

Into the chamber walked Torpan the Twenty-Ninth, wearing a white nightgown and conical nightcap. He looked eager. He set his torch into a stand, where it guttered and flared. It threw the emperor's attenuated shadow upon the walls' stones and made it dance.

He glanced at the Starstone.

Talonlike fingers rubbed together, as if he anticipated the Stone's feel. But, before satisfying his desire, he peered into Wil's cage.

Wil, sitting upon the floor stones, stared back.

"Yes, a bold eye, this one," the emperor muttered to himself. "Those are best."

"Why don't you let me go?" Wil said.

As if an arrow had passed through him, Torpan stared at Wil.

"You speak?"

"Of course, I speak," Wil said. "People speak."

"But a slave…."

"Slave, not a dishrag or broom," Wil said. "Person."

"It dares address me so?"

Wil laughed.

"What will Your Magnificence do to me for addressing you so?" Wil said. "Bore out my brains in a brainless attempt at magic?"

"Eh?"

Torpan regarded him with his eagle's gaze.

"Why don't you let me go?" Wil said.

"Why should I?" Torpan demanded, now giving Wil his full attention.

"To atone," Wil said.

"Atone?"

Torpan drew himself to his full, towering height. In his nightgown and nightcap, he looked like a scarecrow.

"I am the war emperor," he said. "I battle my realm's foes, who attack by stealth, wielding filthy magic instead of fighting like warriors, sword against sword!"

Wil, sitting in his cage, eyed the emperor, thoughtfully.

"Then let me out," he said. "Fight me like a true warrior, sword against sword."

"Eh!"

Torpan frowned at him.

"Or does the war emperor fear a slave's sword?"

Torpan exhaled sharply.

He turned from Wil, strode the few paces to the marble pedestal. He picked up the Starstone from its purple cushion and stared down at it in his hand.

"You're its slave," Wil said.

Slowly, as if partially awakening from a trance, Torpan turned his head to look at Wil.

"It eats your brain," Wil said.

Torpan glared at him, then returned his gaze to the Stone in his hand.

"Gibberish," Torpan said, caressing the Starstone with bony fingers. "We rule."

"No, you're weakened," Wil said. "You hide behind constables, and you rely upon commoners for food, and shelter, and clothes, and to rear your horses and your children."

Torpan held the Stone in his left hand and caressed it with the fingers of his right hand.

"We are high-born," Torpan said. "Your kind is vermin."

Wil laughed.

"You believe the empress speaks for that thing in your hand," Wil said. "Just a while ago, she said this—'We sleepers reel, drunk on dreams.'"

Torpan stood still, stroking the Starstone, brow furrowed.

"I'll get Duzzle to help me translate that message," he muttered.

"I'll translate it for you," Wil said. "One thing it means is that you dream of mastery, while that thing in your hand masters you."

Now the emperor glared at Wil, raptor eyed.

"Lies to confuse me!" he said. "I'll get Duzzle."

"Why don't you let me out?" Wil said.

But the emperor, gently, replaced the Starstone upon on its cushion. He seemed not to hear.

"Fight me like a warrior," Wil said. "Sword against sword."

Grabbing his torch from its holder, Torpan shook his head, as if dispelling Wil's words. He hurried up the stairs, muttering to himself.

Wil slumped back against the bars.

He waited.

"Wil? I really don't like it here."

"I don't like it either, Tobi."

"I want to get back out into the light."

"I do, too."

"What should we do, Wil?"

"Wait."

"….and so he spoke to you in that way….How odd…."

Again torchlight descending the stairs. A clomping of many feet.

Duzzle appeared at the bottom of the stairway, followed by the emperor, still in his nightclothes. After them came four constables.

Duzzle peered into the cage at Wil. Wil returned his stare.

"It is indeed odd, his speaking to you in such a way, Your Magnificence," Duzzle said. "You did well to fetch me—remember, this one slew Count Binter...."

"But he challenged me, Duzzle," Torpan said.

"No, never, Your Magnificence," Duzzle said. "To honor vermin with a duel?"

"Yes, of course," Torpan said. "Still, I am war emperor, and...."

"Also," Duzzle said. "If you slay him, Your Magnificence, as surely you would, then we cannot use him for our experiment, and he seems such an excellent prospect, and the dog, too."

Torpan snapped his fingers, as if remembering.

"He dupes you," Wil told Torpan. "To advance himself."

"You see!" the emperor said. "How he speaks to me?"

Duzzle studied Wil. Abruptly his round face set.

"We should proceed at once, Your Magnificence," he said.

Torpan looked confused.

"Dupes me...."

Duzzle crooked an index finger at the guards, then pointed at Tobi's cage.

"It occurs to me we've never attempted the exchange at just this early hour of the morning, Your Magnificence," Duzzle said. "Let us try it now, hmmm?"

"Yes, perhaps the hour does...."

Torpan looked distracted, as if his thought wandered off.

Duzzle nodded at the sergeant in charge of the constables. Immediately the sergeant produced a key. He unlocked Tobi's cage door.

Tobi growled.

"We'll be together, Tobi," Wil said.

More than that, he could not offer.

"Ouch," a guard said, putting his hand to his mouth.

334

"Fool," the sergeant said. "Did you think he wouldn't bite? Use this."

He handed the man a muzzle. Three men held down the struggling dog and the fourth roughly pulled the muzzle over Tobi's snout.

"Wil!"

"I'm here, Tobi," he said. "We'll be together."

They placed the dog upon the table, on his stomach. They snapped the iron shackles onto his front legs, then his back legs.

Tobi, helpless upon the table, snarled.

"Next that devil," Duzzle said, pointing to Wil.

Another key. Now they unlocked Wil's cage.

He sprang forward, shoved open the cage door, knocked a constable aside. He darted from the cage, reached for a constable's sword hilt, projecting from its sheath. He got hold of it, but the constable twisted away. Hands pinioned his arms.

Abruptly, the two men holding his arms toppled him onto the floor. Instantly the two remaining guards gripped his ankles.

They swung him up, suspended him over the table, thudded him onto his back. Cursing, because he thrashed, they clicked a shackle onto his left wrist. Then his right. Then his ankles.

"Excellent," Duzzle said, regarding with satisfaction his two prisoners, shackled.

Wil felt a throb against his chest, and knew the Opal of Living and Dying sensed imminent death. Now the Starstone struck him, so powerfully he groaned. It buffeted him, probed, insistent on entry. He fought it, brow dripping sweat, face contorted, barely able, now, to resist the Stone's pull.

"Dog first," said Duzzle.

He selected one of the boring tools. He inspected the auger's point. Wil—amidst his silent struggle—saw the little man's eyes glitter.

Duzzle pointed to a spot above Tobi's left ear, indicating to Torpan where he meant to drill.

"No!" Torpan shouted.

"Your Magnificence?"

Eyes wide, the emperor stared at Duzzle, his mouth open. For a long time he stood like that. Finally he found his voice.

"We decided to go in from the top!"

Duzzle let out his breath, as if exasperated with himself.

"Of course," he said. "I became so enthralled with our great work that I forgot."

"Tobi," Wil said. "I'm sorry."

He felt his death rush toward him.

And he thought: then why not?

He wearied of fighting against what lay within him, although Fishtown had taught him to despise it. Now, though, he'd die. Why fight against himself now? Why resist the Starstone?

With a sigh, he let the current carry him away. If he must die, then he'd die as he truly was.

Blue light filled him.

Within, vastness, more than a world. A cosmos.

He thought: I've lived blind. Now I see.

He saw the world to be insubstantial, even these stone walls, all made of swirling thought. And these people—sleep walkers.

He thought: we dream our lives.

Then his vision wavered, like a guttering torch, and the world seemed solid again. He saw Duzzle placing his auger against Tobi's head, ready to drill.

Yet, inside him, all had changed.

"Oh!"

Something wrenched the auger from Duzzle's hand, just as he began to drill. It hovered above his head.

"What...."

It plummeted, pressed against Duzzle's crown. He swatted at the instrument, but couldn't budge it. He gripped it, tried to lift its point from his skull. Failed.

"Duzzle, do you like augering into heads?" Wil asked.

Now the auger flew, smacked against the chamber's far wall, then clattered onto the floor.

"Look!"

A guard, pointing at Tobi.

One of the dog's leg shackles lay open.

Another, seemingly of its own volition, opened. Then the final two. As the guards watched, the leather muzzle they'd pulled over Tobi's snout rotted, its remnant tatters falling away, and Tobi jumped up. He growled at the guards, but only Wil heard the dog's jubilant cry: "Bark. Bite, bite, bite!"

Tobi lunged at the constables, teeth bared, and they backed away, confused. Lying upon his table, Wil laughed, and his own shackles snapped open.

He stood, rubbing his wrists. Torpan and Duzzle, and the four constables, stared at him. He regarded them with amusement.

"Who rules?" he asked Torpan.

Duzzle recovered his wits first.

"Constables, grab him!"

Wil blandly eyed the constables who now rushed toward him

Abruptly, the legs of the sergeant leading them wobbled. He fell. Each constable in turn toppled to the floor, as if his legs lacked bones.

Torpan knelt, pulled from its sheath the sergeant's sword.

He glared at Wil with raptor eyes. He stood that way, in his nightgown and his nightcap, looking from Wil to the sword in his hand. Then, face fierce, he aimed the blade at Wil's chest and lunged toward him, a scarecrow possessed. Wil merely gazed at the oncoming sword.

Tobi barked, leapt, caught Torpan's sleeve in his teeth, but the sword's blade had vanished. In his hand, the emperor clenched only a bladeless hilt.

"Eh?" he said.

"Enough," Wil said.

From the floor, loud snores, for the guards now slept. Duzzle, too, sank to the floor and lay upon his side, his head pillowed upon his hands. He, too, slept.

"As for you…."

Torpan froze, a living statue. But then, as if upon second thought, Wil unfroze his head. Now the emperor couldn't move, but saw all, and could speak.

"You must witness," Wil told him.

He walked to the marble podium and gazed down upon the Starstone, glittering upon its purple cushion.

"You're the Taker," said the frozen emperor.

"Yes," Wil said. "And I'm taking."

He reached out a hand for the Starstone, but stopped. He ached to hold it.

It had whetted him, sharpened him. It had changed him from a villager to a magician. Now it must complete its work. He must hold it. He must let its power flow through him. His eyes must fully open. It wished him to become a sorcerer. It wished, through him, to express itself.

"You fear it," the emperor said.

"I do," Wil said.

Remembered words hissed in his mind.

"You will seek it," the Presence had said. "For that you were bred and born. You will think the seeking is for your own people. Perhaps you will die. But if you finally put your hand on it, what remains of it, this mountain will know. You shall be summoned. You will try to bring it to your kin, but you cannot resist the summons. You are marked. You will bring it here. And then the world, as it was of old, will begin anew."

"Weakling," the emperor sneered.

Wil sank to the floor before the marble podium. He sat, elbows upon his knees, chin upon his hands. He looked up at the glow rising from the thing on the purple cushion.

"Look! You sweat with fear!" the emperor cried, delighted.

Wil did fear.

If he touched the Stone, he must bear it back to the Presence's mountain, but even more he feared himself, for now he felt famished for the Stone. He ached to grasp it, hold it. Then his eyes would fully clear. Power! What could he not do then?

"I am not the Wielder," he said aloud.

"Creep in the dark, Forester!" the emperor sneered. "Spread your filth."

Wil sat thinking. A minute passed. Then another.

"Tobi?"

"Wil, I'm still angry and I want to bite."

"Tobi, will you do something important for me?"

"Bite that tall man in white?"

"No, come here beside me, Tobi."

"All right, Wil, but I really want to bite."

Tobi now sat upon the floor beside him. Wil unbuckled the straps holding on the dog's knapsack and pulled it off. He felt silent growls rippling through Tobi.

"No more need to fight, Tobi," he said.

He laid the knapsack upon the floor.

"Tobi, do you see that Stone on top of the marble pedestal?"

"I can't see up there, Wil, because it's too high."

"Yes, but I want you to take it for me, in your teeth."

"It's too high, Wil," the dog said. "I can't reach."

Wil stood. Gently, he gripped Tobi just behind his forelegs and carefully lifted him, until he hung level with the pedestal's top.

"I see it now, Wil—that little round thing."

"Yes," Wil said. "Take it in your mouth, Tobi."

Tobi stretched out his neck and carefully clenched the Stone in his teeth.

Wil lowered the dog and released him.

"Now see if you can put it in here," he said, holding open the flap of Tobi's knapsack, as it lay upon the floor stones.

Tobi reached his snout into the knapsack and dropped the Stone. Then he withdrew his head and looked brightly at Wil.

"Good, Tobi."

Wil now closed the knapsack's flap and buttoned it. He strapped the knapsack back on Tobi.

He heard the frozen emperor groan.

"You give it to a beast?"

"Who better?" Wil said.

"I have held it, and loved it," the emperor said.

"Better if you'd loved your wife," Wil said. "And your lost daughter."

"Eh?"

Wil now stood, regarding the frozen emperor.

"You won't escape," Torpan said. "You're still our slave—Domallon will get you."

Wil looked at the slave bracelets upon his wrist. They vanished.

"Look at your own wrists," he told the emperor.

340

Torpan looked down at his frozen arms. On each of his wrists, a slave bracelet.

"We all are slaves," Wil said.

He unbuttoned his green livery jacket and threw it upon the floor. Then he loosened his green shirt and pulled it down over his left shoulder. He looked at the number seared there.

D6—903.

His slave number.

"As for this…."

But he paused. Then he shook his head.

"No, I won't give you this," he told Torpan. "It's mine, and I've earned it, and I'll keep it a while."

"Wil?"

"Yes. Tobi?"

"I really want to bite."

Wil smiled.

"Do you see that little round-headed man sleeping on the floor?"

"Yes, Wil."

"Give him a nip."

Joyfully, the dog ran to the sleeping Duzzle. He considered, eyes glinting, and then bit the sleeping man's arm. Duzzle's snoring remained unchanged.

"Do you feel better, Tobi?"

"Yes."

"Then follow me up the stairs, Tobi, and no barking."

He knocked on Malaga's office door.

"Come in."

Malaga's voice, toneless.

When he entered, followed by Tobi, he found her sitting upon a chair. Ranyan knelt by the dwarf's side, with her head in Malaga's lap. Malaga stroked the princess's hair.

"Fox!"

"My true name is Wil Deft," he said. "And this is my friend, Tobi."

"How...."

"His Magnificence now stands in his stone chamber, frozen a while," Wil said. "Duzzle sleeps, also for a while, along with four constables."

"And you have...."

"The Taker has taken."

"Is it over then?"

"No," he said. "It is for the Wielder to complete the changing—I must get the Starstone to her."

Malaga sighed.

"This morning's tribunal piqued Domallon—he's got constables thronging through the palace, and he's got the palace surrounded by brigades, because he suspects you're the Taker, and might escape."

Ranyan sat up. She looked at Wil with reddened eyes.

"Domallon told Malaga he would order her execution!" she said. "I said, 'No, I command you,' and he just ignored me!"

Ranyan addressed him directly. He still wore his green livery trousers and shirt. Yet, she looked him in the face.

So already changes began.

"I've come to ask what you wish," Wil said.

Malaga looked at him, thinking.

"Will the regime go down in havoc and murder?" she asked.

"I don't know," Wil said.

Malaga shrugged.

"I would wish to resume my professorship, and my studies," she said, glancing worriedly at Ranyan.

Wil said: "And you, Your Resplendency?"

He saw that Ranyan wept.

342

"When they riot, let them kill me," she said.

"Child!"

Malaga again stroked her hair.

Ranyan now hid her head in Malaga's lap. Her voice sounded muffled.

"I cut off two heads!" she said.

"You did not know," Malaga said.

"I did know!" Ranyan wailed. "I saw a cat fall off the Bridge of Swords into the great river, and a barge bore down on it, and I told a constable to jump off the bridge and save the cat, and he said he would surely die, which made me angry, because he was only a commoner, defying me, so I had him executed."

"You didn't know what you did," Malaga said, stroking her hair.

Ranyan looked up now at Wil, eyes red and tears running down.

"A man in the street hurried by in a donkey cart, when I shopped at a stall," she wailed. "And the donkey stamped in a puddle and splattered my best dress, and I was vexed because I could not find the silk gloves in the exact shade of rose I wanted, and I saw the man smile to himself at my ruined dress, so I told my constables to cut off his head right then, and they did."

"Child," Malaga said. "Those were terrible things, it is true—but since infancy they taught you commoners were not people, did not feel as people did, so you did not know."

"But they screamed," Ranyan said. "And ever since I've heard those screams in my head, and the screams from Papa's horrible chamber, and I go out at night to get away from that awful Starstone he keeps down there, and to try to escape that screaming I hear, and I can't!"

Malaga stroked Ranyan's hair and looked at Wil.

Wil stood, arms crossed, looking down upon the princess, pondering.

"If you die, you escape what you did," he said. "Then you cannot atone."

Neither woman spoke. Malaga continued to sit in her chair, Ranyan's face hidden in her lap, stroking the princess's hair.

Wil regarded them.

"You should come with me, to a safe place," he said. "And afterwards...."

Ranyan looked up at him.

"Poko?" she said.

"Poko, too," Wil said. "Although he despises me for what is now happening, which he foresaw."

They made their way through the palace corridors, the princess leading, a small white dog in her arms. A dwarf followed her. Then a short-legged dog with no tail, honey-colored and white, wearing a backpack. Last in the procession walked a lanky bald man, red bearded, dressed in a minor merchant's brown trousers and tan shirt and yellow vest. From his vest's pocket poked a scrolled parchment order form.

At a corridor's turning, a constable.

"Halt!"

"Oh, la di la," Ranyan said airily.

"Your Resplendency!" the guard said, bowing as he suddenly recognized the emperor's daughter. "My apologies, please...."

Ranyan swept past without deigning to look at him. Her entourage followed.

Malaga looked back over her shoulder at the disguised Wil.

"What you just did," she said. "All my life I've wished to see such things."

"Make myself bald, and red-bearded? Alter my clothes?" Wil said. "It's because the Starstone is near—yesterday I couldn't do even such simple magic."

"Incantations?" Malaga said.

"No, how I do it is strange, beyond me," Wil said. "But the Stone reveals all is woven from thought, and thought can be changed."

"Oh, la di la," Ranyan said.

Another turning, another constable bowing to Ranyan. Upon the great stairway, a guard at every fifth step. Now, ahead, the palace's main portal. Sunshine slanted through.

"If they see me outside the palace, they'll stop me and ask questions," Ranyan said.

Wil pointed them to a shadowed nook, under the great stairway, and ushered them in. There he looked at them, considering.

Abruptly, the princess's satin gown became a hooded brown cloak, as any modest Imperia housewife might wear. Poko's fur turned black, lest some constable recognize the royal pet. Malaga's blue livery robe became a child's cloak. She looked like Ranyan's little girl, walking behind her. Wil left himself unchanged, the little family's red-bearded daddy, returning from a palace visit to peddle a bolt of satin to some duchess, or a just-in load of yams to a cook. Tobi, too, he left unaltered, for no constables would be hunting a dog.

They walked in procession toward the palace door. Guards at the doorway scowled, but merely perfunctorily. They walked out of the palace into the sunshine. It seemed to Wil a long time since he last stood in the open air, under the sun.

Ahead, constables lined the path to the palace gate. Through the gate, Wil glimpsed the Imperial Way. And there, too, he saw milling constables. A high-stepping black horse pranced past the gate, a noble astride. It seemed to Wil to be Lord Domallon.

"I'll go first," Wil said. "Tobi, walk beside me, so the Starstone is close."

"All right, Wil," Tobi said, although only Wil heard.

Under his breath, Tobi growled.

"No," Wil said. "Let me do what I must."

Tobi made no answer. But Wil heard the dog mutter to himself: "Bark! Bite, bite, bite!"

He led the little procession along the pathway. Each guard they passed eyed them stonily, but then looked away, contemptuous. Only at the gate itself did a constable step into their path and block their way. Wil recognized the sergeant who guarded Ranyan on her nighttime treks through the city.

He looked them over carefully, each in turn. Suddenly his eyes flicked back to Tobi's backpack.

Wil thought: he remembers what he heard about the dog that attacked Binter.

He cursed himself for failing to disguise Tobi.

"What's this?"

Now the sergeant eyed Ranyan suspiciously, brow furrowed. Something in the way she held herself, no doubt, or the way she walked.

"You, with the red beard, let's see papers," the sergeant demanded.

He held out a big palm toward Wil. Impatiently, he snapped his fingers.

Wil hung his head, subservient. He put a hand into one of his vest pockets and pretended to fish about for papers. But he had no papers.

He moved a step closer to Tobi, so that his leg brushed against Tobi's knapsack. He stood, brow furrowed, as if searching for his papers.

Abruptly, he raised his head and gazed at the sergeant.

As if pricked, the sergeant slightly flinched. His eyes, sharply studying Wil, turned vague.

"I thought…. But, no, just a merchant and his family. Yes, I see. Well, get along then. Why do you waste my time?"

Wil nodded respectfully and walked on, with Tobi at his side. Ranyan and Malaga followed.

"How long before he comes to his senses, I don't know," Wil said, shrugging. "I'm new to magic, so we better hurry."

He walked faster now, along the Imperial Way.

Ahead, he saw, a line of constables, arrayed to encircle the palace wall. Anyone leaving the palace must pass through that line of guards.

Once again Wil saw the noble on the prancing black horse, riding along the line. As he suspected, Lord Domallon.

Wil now spoke to Ranyan and Malaga.

"My doing magic, it's only because the Starstone is so near," he said. "If too much happens at once, quickly…. It'll overwhelm me."

"I don't want to go back to the palace," Ranyan said.

"No, not back," Wil said. "I must get the Starstone to the Wielder."

He stopped, thinking of Mita.

If he did this….

He'd felt just a little of the Starstone's power. If that gentle girl held the Stone, what would it do to her?

But she must wield it. For that she was born and bred.

"Whatever I tell you to do, instantly do it," he told Ranyan and Malaga.

"What will you tell us?" Malaga asked.

"I don't know," Wil said.

Nobody heard him speak to Tobi.

"You especially," he said. "Do exactly what I tell you, Tobi, instantly."

"Bite!" Tobi muttered.

"Will you do whatever I ask?"

"There's a bad feeling here, Wil."

"I'm depending on you, Tobi."

"All right, I promise."

They walked ahead. Nearing the line of constables, Wil saw them stopping whoever approached them, even crones and toddlers. So they'd be stopped. He tried to formulate what he'd do.

"You lot, stop right here!"

"Yes, corporal?" Wil asked, as if bewildered by so many constables arrayed for no reason he could fathom.

He stuck his hand into his trouser pocket. He shut his eyes, frowning.

"What's wrong with you?" the constable said. "Let's see your papers."

Wil continued to stand before the guard, eyes shut, hand in his pocket.

"Hey, hurry up, or...."

Wil opened his eyes. He withdrew his hand from his pocket.

He held a document, which he handed to the constable. He watched the man scrutinize the paper, then peer at Wil.

"Well, we're not looking for a bald huckster with a red beard and a family...."

Abruptly, the constable handed back the document, still staring at Wil, then at each member of the party. Wil stuffed the paper back into his pocket.

"Oh, move on, then," the constable said.

They moved on. Wil led. Tobi walked beside him. Malaga walked next, seemingly a child in a cloak, hooded. Ranyan, also hooded, followed, the newly black Poko in her arms.

They walked up the Imperial Way. One block. Another. Not much farther, Wil thought. We near the Street of the Heroes of the Stone.

From behind, a rumble.

He looked back. Constables, hundreds of them, ran up the Imperial Way, led by a man on a black horse, and he had no doubt: they ran toward him.

He guessed the sergeant at the gate had come to his senses, realized a spell dulled him. He'd rushed to tell Domallon. Now an army chased them.

"I can't enchant so many," Wil thought, feeling himself just a child in magic, still learning to walk.

Across the street, Wil saw Blossom, staring, and realized he recognized only Tobi. Mita must have sensed all this, Wil thought, and sent the huge old fighting man. He pointed at his own face, to signal he was disguised.

Blossom opened his cloak, revealing two swords sewn into the lining, and multiple daggers. Wil shook his head. Two against so many?

Now the attacking army neared, just a block away. In front galloped Domallon.

Tobi and I might run faster, he thought. We might sneak away, but they'd catch Magala and Ranyan, and Domallon would kill them both. He'd say Malaga killed Ranyan, and so he executed her, but killing Ranyan would open the line of succession. Then, whomever Domallon thought to place on the throne....

Perhaps Domallon himself.

"Tobi?"

"Yes, Wil?"

"Do you remember the way to the apartment where Mita is waiting?"

"Yes."

"Good—run there, and give Mita your knapsack, and tell her where we are."

"I want to stay with you, Wil, because all those bad men are coming...."

"No, you must do this for me, Tobi—and I want you to lead Ranyan and Malaga to Mita."

"Wil...."

"Do it for me, Tobi."

Tobi looked sullen. But then he brightened.

"I'll do it, Wil, and then I'll run right back!"

Wil sighed.

"Follow Tobi," he told Malaga and Ranyan. "He'll bring you to a safe place."

"What about you?" Malaga said.

"I'm going to lead them astray, because it's me they're after," he said. "They don't know Tobi carries the Starstone."

He and Malaga looked at each other, saying nothing.

"Tobi, go!"

Tobi ran. It reassured Wil to see the dog look back, making sure Ranyan and Malaga followed.

Now he looked down the Imperial Way, toward the palace. Constables ran toward him, a horde, led by Domallon on his prancing black horse. He felt one small pulse of magic remaining to him.

Abruptly, the charging constables halted, staring, because the bald, red-bearded man suddenly grew hair, long and shaggy, the color of corn. His red beard vanished. In its place appeared a ragged yellow mustache. His eyes became blue.

"Want the Starstone?" Wil shouted. "Then catch me."

He turned and ran.

350

After a moment, he heard a thousand footsteps running after him, and horse hooves.

He veered into a narrow lane, into shadows, then down a side passageway, even narrower, but a wall stopped him, the passageway's end. No door.

Footsteps clattered after him. He turned to fight, but it was Blossom.

"Whew, haven't run so fast in years," the old man said, wheezing.

"You shouldn't have come," Wil said.

"Brought this for you," Blossom said.

He opened his cloak and extracted a sword. He handed to Wil. Then a dagger.

"There's a thousand constables," Wil said. "What's two swords and a few daggers?"

"Enough to nick them some," Blossom said, pulling out his own sword and sticking two daggers into his belt.

Blossom threw off his cloak now. He swiped his sword in the air, getting its balance. Wil stuck his own dagger into his belt. He swung his sword, too, feeling its heft.

"Tobi's got the Starstone in his knapsack, taking it to Mita," Wil said.

"Good," Blossom said. "That'll be the realm's end, curse it."

They stood silently.

At the lane's opposite end, they heard voices.

"They're going to this lane's opposite end," Wil said.

"Yes, and when they find we're not there, they'll come down here," Blossom said. "Meanwhile, they'll leave a contingent at the crossroads, so we can't sneak out."

Again they stood silent, listening to the constables' muffled shouts.

"We'll die," Wil said.

"Are you afraid?" Blossom asked.

"Yes," Wil said.

"Well, I'm an old man, and I'm tired, and I've lived mainly to see them brought down, and if I can take a few with me, I'm satisfied," Blossom said. "But you're young."

"I'm twenty-six, but I feel old, too," Wil said. "And now the Taker's sent the Starstone to the Wielder."

"So," Blossom said. "Nabob or pauper?"

Wil thought.

"I don't know," he said.

He smiled, wanly, hearing that old question one more time.

"A pauper has nothing in him, except maybe money," Blossom said. "A nabob might be penniless, but he's rich inside, full of his life in this world, and trying to do right, and trying to understand."

"I'm a nabob, I think," Wil said.

Shouts. They knew the constables had returned empty handed from the opposite turning. Now they'd come this way.

"My father had a farm, not so far from Fishtown, good land it was," Blossom said. "A duke from Imperia came by in his pleasure boat, and saw it, and wanted it for himself, to get away from the city in the summer heat, I suppose...."

"So he bought out your father?" Wil said. "Some paltry price?"

"No, too much bother—he put my father to the sword, and my mother, and took the land," Blossom said. "My brother and I ran off, and found haven with river pirates, preying on imperial pleasure barges, and later we turned smuggler, for that was all we could do."

They stood silent, listening to the approaching constables, their running footsteps echoing off the lane's stone walls.

"If I take some with me, I'm satisfied," Blossom said.

Now the oncoming constables were nearly upon them.

"This lane's narrow," Blossom said. "They can come at us only eight or ten at a time, so you stand there, and I'll stand here."

"All right," Wil said, taking his position.

"Blossom?"

"Yes?"

"You've been the father I didn't have."

Blossom stood in silence. Finally he spoke.

"I never married, had children, and you, and Mita…."

They both stood silently now, waiting.

Wil felt sad, but less afraid. Better this, he thought, than the Presence.

Two constables appeared ahead in the lane. They stopped and pointed.

"There they are!"

Wil and Blossom raised their swords.

More constables filled the passageway, then stepped aside as Lord Domallon cantered up on his black horse and rode to the front. His minions closed in behind him, filling the passageway, as the minister of justice stared at Wil's yellow hair and mustache, at his blue eyes, and at the huge bald man beside him, one eye patched.

"You!"

"Your Lordship," Blossom said, and bowed, sarcastically.

From its holster at his horse's flank, Domallon pulled a lance.

"I'll have that one," he said, pointing the weapon at Blossom.

Blossom eyed him.

"You murdered my son!"

Blossom continued to regard the man on the horse without expression.

Domallon's mouth abruptly grimaced, in hurt and rage. It seemed the smile of a skull. He spurred his horse. The animal reared, then lurched forward, and Domallon aimed his lance at Blossom's chest, spurring his horse to charge.

Blossom pivoted, grabbed the passing lance's shaft, yanked.

Momentarily, both men seemed frozen, Domallon twisted back on his rearing horse, Blossom pulling mightily on the lance, until Domallon thudded onto the paving stones. His breath knocked out by the fall, supine, he glared up at Blossom.

Two constables behind Domallon now charged, meaning to protect the fallen aristocrat.

Wil sidestepped a blade, thrust, felt his rapier slide into the man's chest. He pulled it out, reddened. He hardly noticed the man fall at his feet, for he watched Blossom parry the other man's blade. Without even looking at the constable, Blossom pierced him, keeping his eye on the fallen Domallon, now sitting up.

"Would you like a fair fight, aristocrat?" Blossom asked.

"With vermin?" Domallon snarled.

"I could just skewer you, sitting there on your noble rear," Blossom said.

Domallon got to his feet. He drew his own rapier.

Two constables now left the mass of men behind Domallon and charged at Wil. He ducked one man's slashing blade, thrust his own rapier into the man's heart, then spun, slashed the other man across the neck.

"They're commoners I kill," Wil thought, sickened, watching the man fall. "They're corrupted, turned against their own."

But now the constables charged, as many as could fit across the narrow passageway. Wil parried, thrust, thrust again.

He glanced aside, saw Blossom and Domallon dueling, but more swords came at him, and more behind them.

Domallon suddenly lay upon the paving stones, blood flowing from his chest. Blossom stood over him, looking down, expressionless.

Wil felt a change in the air and stepped back, just in time to avoid a blade slashing at his head.

Ranyan's guardian sergeant confronted him.

"Why do you fight your own people?" Wil asked.

"Shut up, Forester," the sergeant sneered.

Again he slashed. Wil sidestepped.

"You've got a sword, Forester," the sergeant said. "Fight like a man."

Wil shook his head. He no longer had a stomach for killing.

Another swipe of the blade.

Wil ducked. As he did, he glanced aside, and felt something die within him.

Blossom lay upon the paving stones beside Domallon, surrounded by dead constables, lying in heaps. Five men stood over him.

Wil saw that Domallon lay dead. And so did Blossom.

Out of his eye's corner, he saw the sergeant's blade slashing toward him. He thrust up his sword and caught the oncoming blade near his own rapier's hilt, the strongest part. Blossom had taught him that. He riposted, felt his point slide through the sergeant's jerkin, saw surprise in the man's eyes.

"Filthy Forester, I'll…."

But then the sergeant thudded onto the pavement, already dead.

Now a grim mass of red jerkins and yellow capes advanced upon him. He backed away until stopped by the lane's final wall. From here, no place to go.

Wil let his point drop. He watched the phalanx of constables advance, and he waited.

He would die. No matter how many of them he killed, he'd still die. And he wished to kill no more deluded souls.

"He's alone…."

"Get him…."

"I've got him on the right and…. What's happening?"

Wil, too, stood watching, no less aghast than his attackers.

Blossom's body ascended from the pavement. It floated, above their heads. Blossom lay on his back in the air, arms folded across his chest.

Higher the body rose, then higher still, above the lane's adjoining rooftops. Abruptly, the body flared, pure yellow light, shot with red.

Then it winked out. Not one ash drifted down upon the men below, looking upwards.

Mita.

Wil felt a surge of love.

Before all else she gave Blossom a fitting end.

"You wield the Starstone," he thought.

Around him the air crackled. He felt enormous energy.

"So much power so soon?" he thought.

But then he understood: Mita didn't wield the Starstone alone. All the Foresters, far off, sensed she grasped it. And all the Foresters, their powers husbanded all these years, now worked with her, amplifying her hold upon the Stone.

And the energy coursed through Wil.

He stood, stunned, watching three constables suddenly recover themselves, raise their swords, rush toward him.

But then one man halted.

"Hey, that sergeant's dead, and high-and-mighty Domallon's dead, so what are we doing?"

"What they tell us to do."

"Well, I'm not—I've got a wife to home, and two daughters, and what did Foresters ever do to me?"

He threw down his sword.

Wil saw the other two men look at their comrade. And he knew the Wielder worked upon them, changing their thoughts.

One man shrugged. He, too, threw down his sword. As it clanged on the paving stones, he turned. Then the third man dropped his sword. They walked away from Wil, pushing through the constables massed behind them. He saw one man stripping of his red jerkin and yellow cape as he walked.

Wil thought: Mita did this.

Now the constables milled, uncertainly. More jerkins came off.

Wil stood backed against the lane's terminating wall, in wonder, as the entire mass of men wheeled about and walked away from him. At the corner, they turned toward the Imperial Way and were gone, leaving the street littered with discarded red jerkins and yellow capes.

Wil started down the lane, alone. After a while, though, a small dog, colored like honey and cream, ran toward him on short legs, and then the man and dog walked together.

CHAPTER FIFTEEN

Children trooped along Ragpickers' Lane.

A round-headed boy led them, pounding a ladle upon a pot. They wore red jerkins and yellow capes, so oversized the capes dragged behind them. As they marched, they sang—

"Duke for a day, am I, am I,
And dame for a night,
Are you...."

Wil watched from the apartment's window, knowing this was Mita's work.

Last night, Zadni Druen and Pim had knocked on the door.

"We just strolled into the city!" Pim exulted. "Bonfires in the streets! Not a constable to stop us!"

This morning, Wil went out to gauge the changes. Everywhere he saw children like these, parading in constables' discarded jerkins and capes. He no longer bothered disguising himself. Nobody hunted the Taker now. And no nobles rode haughtily by in slave-borne palanquins. He supposed the aristocrats huddled in their mansions, fearing what might come next.

"...and when Mita finishes the changes, we'll announce Forester rule, which will..."

"Pim, this needs thought."

Zadni's voice.

Silence after that. Wil saw the High Enchantress studying Pim, white eyebrows raised, while the Lord of the War glared at the wall. This argument had simmered for decades.

Wil thought: "And what of Mita?"

He forced himself to look.

She sat erect, cupping the Starstone in her palms. She stared, head bowed, into its bluish-white light. Five days ago, when he returned to the apartment after the battle in the lane, she sat like this, but she'd looked at him then, and spoke. Never since.

"Wil?"

Tobi sat at his feet, looking up earnestly.

"I just made this up, Wil."

"Jerkins, capes! Block the lane!

Three to fight 'em,

Smite 'em,

Bite 'em,

Three heroes brave!"

"That's a good start, Tobi."

Only two "heroes brave" fought the battle, not three, but he didn't mention the inaccuracy. Blossom's gone, he thought. Maybe that's the sadness I feel.

"I don't know how it should end, Wil."

"Neither do I," he said. "Keep working on it, Tobi."

Eyes bright with the encouragement, Tobi padded to his favorite corner and lay down, brow furrowed in thought.

Malaga Gant sat at the kitchen table, drinking tea with Pim and Zadni. He saw she noted their every word, gesture, expression. She'd studied Foresters all her life, but never met one. Now she lived among four.

359

"...provisional, of course, until we fully get back our powers, in a year, let's say...."

Behind his spectacles' lenses, Pim's eyes glinted, exultant, and Wil wondered, now who'll sit on Torpan's throne? Grimacing, he looked away.

Ranyan sat on a low stool, Poko beside her, his back turned to Tobi, whom he despised. Tobi, working on his verses, pretended Poko did not exist.

Ranyan, elbows on knees, resting her chin on her cupped palms, gazed at Mita. She often studied Mita this way. Wil didn't know why, but he knew Ranyan, being unmagical, couldn't see that Mita now glowed white, faintly, and her eyes glowed blue.

When they returned the Starstone to High City, he guessed, that light would gradually pervade them all. Year by year, their magic would strengthen, until Foresters again became sorcerers.

And Forest Kings? Once more to overreach, and mold people's very thoughts?

Mita's lips moved. Sometimes she spoke like this, silently. Perhaps she spoke to the Stone.

He remembered Blossom's tavern, that new serving girl. Eyes startled, she'd tipped her tray, bumped tables, spilled ale.

"Life startles us," he now told himself. "And in an unsure world, to move unsurely...."

Blossom's absence hurt. So did this, Mita's sinking into the Starstone.

Five days ago, when he returned here, she'd looked up from the glowing crystal, hazel eyes wide, and asked him: "Is this the world, truly?"

Since then she sat gazing into the Starstone like this, receding.

Silently, he cursed. He didn't know whom he cursed. Himself, perhaps, for feeling lost, and helpless. Once the Taker takes, what is he? And his hands ached to grasp the Starstone. Mere proximity let him glimpse what Mita saw, but if he could hold the Stone, gaze into it….

What then? Help Mita? Lead her back to this world?

No.

Fear shot up his spine.

If the touched the Starstone, he must bear it back to the Presence's mountain, to that Nameless One of Darkness, for he'd been marked.

Now he cursed aloud.

He strode to the door, yanked it open, and rushed down the tenement's creaking stairs.

Walking toward the palace, he turned up his jacket's collar. Late-autumn frost now whitened the bark of the Imperial Way's sycamores, but everywhere he saw signs of warming, Mita's work.

Strangers, passing, grinned at him. Somewhere in the crowd, a bass voice sang out: "An earl met a countess, oh!" A ribald old tune. Others joined the singing: "In the palace garden, oh!"

Wil stopped at one of the stalls thrown up overnight, each marked by a crudely drawn rasp. Here eight customers waited in line, and he spoke to the last one, a short redheaded man, who uncontrollably grinned.

"Slave, I was," he told Wil. "Got snatched by constables, filling their quota, then eleven years polishing a duke's boots, and mucking his stalls, him fancying the whip—now I'm getting these rasped off!"

He held up his wrists to show his iron slave rings. Many former slaves preceded him in line, and his wait would be long.

"I'll take my turn, and glad to do it," he said. "Get 'em off!"

Wil impulsively removed his jacket. He unbuttoned his shirt. He pulled it down over his shoulder to show the man his own seared-in slave number.

D6-903.

"Palace," he said.

"A few's stayed slaves, them's was born to it," the man told him. "But that's their choosing—whenever they want, they can walk away."

Wil grinned.

"And dare freedom," he said.

"I'll take that dare," the red-headed man said.

And he, too, grinned.

Wil walked on, listening to the Imperial Way's roar of voices. People spoke louder now, and laughed more. Venders, as always, hawked potatoes and woolen caps and mudfish, smoked or pickled. But they called out to passersby with new gusto.

From a fruit vender, he bought a pear. "No more making ten coppers and paying nine to them there," the man said, jerking his chin toward the palace, as he took Wil's two coppers. "Upriver people, too—talked to farmers at the market, just in on a skiff, said no more getting just coppers for their carrots and corn, with the silvers and golds going to the great ones."

"Fishermen, too?" Wil asked. "And peat diggers?"

"Them, too, and people's now started rowing free along the river, trading town-to-town."

As he walked down the Imperial Way, he talked with other walkers and venders. He asked, circumspectly, about Foresters. Mostly, he received indifferent shrugs.

"Them forest people was called frightful, being magical," one sidewalk hawker of knitted scarves told him. "But lots been saying—'They plotted against the realm? Good! Maybe they'll help us ordinary folk now, cast some white spells our way, you know?'"

Yet....

At the palace's north-wall gate, youths milled, shouting, laughing. Some brandished constables' discarded swords, pretending to duel. No guards blocked the gate. Whenever they wished, these young men could saunter onto the palace grounds, but for now, Wil guessed, old fears kept them out.

"Where're you going?"

A stocky youth, blocking his way. Wil saw him glance at his friends, making sure they supported his belligerence.

"I'm going into the palace," Wil said.

"You one of them dukes?"

"No," Wil said. "I was a slave here, and now I want to see how things are."

"Because we've got it in for highborns."

More glances for approval.

"I'm not a noble," Wil said.

"My uncle, he got kicked by some high-and-mighty's horse, so he said, 'Hey!' And they cut off his head for that 'Hey!'"

"I'm not a noble," Wil said.

Now a voice from the crowd of sword-swinging boys.

"Maybe we'll chop some heads, too, hey? Highborn heads, hey?"

"Then you'd be like them," Wil said.

"Oh? Maybe we'll bust into those grand houses, take what's rightfully ours!"

From the crowd, murmured approval.

Now the boy swished his sword past Wil's nose.

"What do you think of that?"

"Revenge is dark," Wil said.

"I don't like the way you talk, Mister."

With a jerk of his arm, the boy raised his sword over Wil's head. Its sharp edge threatened his neck.

Wil felt fear, but not of this youth's rapier. Blossom trained him. He could easily disarm the boy, or grab another's sword. They held weapons clumsily. Probably none ever before gripped a hilt. He could kill a few, and the others would run, but of killing he wished no more.

He didn't fear these youths. He feared their anger, and the hate smoldering inside them, because such embers could leap from head to head.

Constables? Or murdering mobs? Which was worse?

"Maybe I'll stick you, hey?"

Laughter from the crowd.

"Who's to stop me, hey?"

In this youth's eyes Will saw burgeoning darkness swirl, and it revolted him.

"Ow!"

The boy flung down his sword. He gaped at his hand. Blisters appeared on the palm.

"You made it burn!"

"Your own fire, inside you, burned your hand," Wil said.

Even here, he thought, so far from the Starstone, magic now hums inside me, and he felt the old disgust. "Filthy Forester magic." Then, inwardly, he shrugged.

"Step aside, now."

Wide-eyed, the boy stared at Wil, then at his blistered hand, holding it with his good hand. He stepped from Wil's path. His friends also made way. Wil walked among them.

As he passed the hurt boy, Wil stared at his hand and its blisters shrank away. The boy looked stupidly at his healed palm.

Behind him, he heard a whisper: "Forester!"

Wil passed through the gate. He walked up the stone path toward the great entrance door, and it stood open before him.

He'd left this palace only five days ago. It seemed five decades.

His footsteps echoed in empty halls and rooms. He passed only a few liveried servants, and they scurried away.

Five days before, in these corridors, wearers of velvets and silks whispered, conspiring. They sat at grand tables, set with tureens and goblets, slighting inferiors, flattering their betters. Now they hid in their empty mansions. No constables protected the great ones now.

And who would feed them?

As if in answer, a maid passed before him in the corridor, carrying a tray. Upon the tray, a bowl of pea soup.

They depended, he thought, these descendants of conquerors, upon the conquered. So they'd made themselves children.

On a whim, he turned his mind to heating the soup in the maid's bowl. She halted and stared in wonder at the bowl's sudden steaming. Then she hurried on, carrying to some hiding earl a bowl of magic soup.

Magic.

They despise it, Wil thought. Yet, they live spellbound, for eons go the Nameless Ones laid down enchantments, darkening this people's souls. Now they sleepwalk, obeying ancient sorcery.

A familiar corridor. A golden door, studded with pearls.

He knocked.

From within, a voice.

"Eh?"

As before, the empress rested upon her bed. Pillows supported her. By her side, upon a chair, sat the emperor. He wore his ermine-trimmed purple mantle. His crown slipped down over his forehead nearly to his spectacle's rims. Upon his knees rested a rapier.

He jumped up, raising his sword. He glared at Wil, in the doorway, that eagle stare.

"I mean you no harm," Wil said.

"Harm?" Torpan said. "I'm the war emperor!"

"Yes, but the war ended," Wil said.

Torpan looked confused.

"Who're you? Robber? Rioter?"

"I'm the Taker," Wil said.

Torpan stared.

"Your hair…"

"You saw me disguised," Wil said. "I look like this."

Torpan giggled. He laid his sword upon his chair and held up his arms. His sleeves slid away, revealing slave bracelets.

"Yours."

"No, yours now," Wil said. "A memento."

They stared at each other, silent.

From her bed, the empress spoke, a voice like birdsong: "A thousand years of blame! A thousand to come?"

She spoke to the ornate ceiling.

"You cowered behind your filthy magic," the emperor said.

He picked up his laid-aside weapon. Aiming its point at Wil's chest, he clenched its hilt, hefting it.

Wil sighed.

"Yes," he said. "You taught us that magic is filthy, and it did shame me…."

He shrugged, spreading his hands, palms up.

"Eh?"

Torpan stared at the rapier in his hand.

Gently, the hilt twisted from his grip. Just beyond his fingers, the sword momentarily hung in the air, then sailed across the room. A window opened for it and the sword glided out to hover, just outside, moving its tip in mimicry of a duel's thrust and parry. It vanished.

Wil and Torpan both gazed through the window, at the spot where the sword no longer hung.

"What moves the world, I feel it flow through me," Wil said. "It flows through you, too, but I reach inside, turn it, just a little—magic."

Now the emperor dropped back into his chair. He slouched, arms folded, long legs sprawled.

"What do you want?" he said.

Wil stood, silent.

What did he want?

"You meant to bore out my brains, and my friend Tobi's brains," he said. "You've gouged out so many brains, and tortured and killed and spread misery beyond knowing…."

He stared at the emperor. What, he wondered, did he seek?

"I want understanding," he said.

Torpan stood, drew himself to his full height. He glared down at Wil.

"I did my duty," the emperor said. "I was bred for that, born for that."

They stood looking at each other, Torpan eagle-eyed, imperious, Wil perplexed. And again the bird's voice from the bed.

"We swim the river, drink it, breathe it," she sang. "It shapes us, pulls us, and who leaves the water?"

Her eyes remained distant and crazed, but in the chamber below, the Starstone's marble podium now stood empty. Wil wondered if the empress would regain herself.

Mita! Would she ever be Mita again? It hurt, to think of Mita.

"Bred to rule," Torpan repeated. "Born for it."

Now the empress gazed directly at Wil.

"Do you resist the current?" she said.

Wil walked to the doorway and stopped there, head down. Finally he looked up.

"I don't know," he said.

Then he left the palace forever.

Night in the apartment.

Mita sat erect in her chair. She gazed down into the Starstone's glow. Wil sat upon the couch, leaning toward her, elbows resting upon his knees. All the others slept.

"Mita?"

No answer. She continued gazing into the blue-white light.

He reached out, held her shoulders.

"Mita?"

He thought she looked at him, but from a distance. From the world's edge.

Knee to knee they sat. This close, he felt the Starstone might sweep him away, and he didn't even hold it. Mita did.

A memory: Fishtown's ancient mill, replaced by a new mill, upstream. Its wheel no longer turned the millstone, grinding wheat and oats. Yet, the ruin retained a sort of life.

Summer, a sultry evening. Nighthawks dart overhead. Boys clamber up the old mill's walls. Stone by stone they climb, three stories. They balance—just their toes—upon a narrow ledge. They reach up, grip the flat roof's overhang. They gather strength.

One boy vaults upward, swings his legs over. Now he rests upon the roof's tar, still warm from the afternoon sun.

Another boy pulls himself over. Then another. All stand. Laughter. Shouts. Then all line up along the roof's edge. Silent

368

now, each within himself, they look down upon the river's black water, far below. A broken-off oar blade speeds by—the current shoots it southward, like an arrow from a crossbow.

One boy yells. He plummets. Splashes. Another leaps. Another.

Wil, as a boy on such summer evenings, vied with Kobar to splash first into the river. As he plunged into the water, immediately the current lurched him southward. Fight that current and it tired you in a few strokes. It pulled you under, drowned you. He learned to let the current take him, but to swim slantwise, angling across its pull toward shore. A quarter-mile below the mill, his feet finally touched bottom. He'd crawl onto the bank and lie on his back, gasping.

"Mita!"

He tightened his grip on her shoulders. He willed her to hear.

"Let it take you, but go aslant!"

Deep in her eyes' blue glow, he saw a flicker. It seemed so.

"Angle back to us," he said. "To me."

He meant to tell her about the mill....

"Stop!"

Pim.

He stood in the parlor's doorway, in nightclothes, one arm upraised. He fumbled his spectacles onto his nose. His gaze sharpened.

"You dare meddle?"

"She must be saved."

"Saved?" Pim said, and his face reddened.

He stood still, the little man. When he finally spoke, he hissed.

"She was born for this, and trained," he said. "And this she chose."

Wil let go of Mita's shoulders and stood.

"She's not a broom, for beating out a fire," he said. "Not to be burned, left blackened."

They stood taking each other's measure.

"Mita knew," Pim said.

"Knew?" Wil said.

"That it would change her," Pim said.

Wil stared at him.

"To change a world, you must change," Pim said.

"What about you—what cost to you?" Wil said.

"My every minute," Pim said, teeth clenched.

Mita continued staring into the Starstone. Even now, Wil supposed, she reached into the world. She beheld thoughts, events. She traced their intertwining. She made adjustments. Someone's intended step leftward became a step to the right. Somebody's fury mellowed into a shrug. Thus, strand by strand, she changed the weave of what is.

And this breathing statue of Mita, upon the chair, holding the glowing Stone? He supposed it remained part of her. But when she first touched the Starstone, her awareness broadened and deepened, beyond her body. She stayed, yet she traveled away, ever farther. And, as she journeyed, she plucked at the world's fabric, pulled threads. She rewove them, changed the pattern. Just enough to undo the realm. To begin a new age.

And that new age—what might it be?

"You gladly let it take her," Wil said.

Pim, irritably, looked at the wall.

Yes, look away from me, Wil thought. Look away from guilt.

Acrid words came into his mouth, and he spat them out.

"King Pim."

Pim looked at him, eyes like stones behind those spectacles.

"I want her back," Wil said.

Pim exhaled, a sound of disgust. He spoke in a whisper.

"You're not one of us."

"No," Wil said. "And who banished a baby, to make a better thief?"

Pim sneered.

"What does a village boy know?"

"I am the Taker," Wil said. "I took."

Pim sighed.

"Yes, you did your part," he said. "High City grants you a house, a stipend for life, whatever you want…."

"I want Mita," Wil said.

"Can you not understand?"

Pim said it, then threw up his hands.

"She's not one of your giggling village girls—she's the Wielder!"

"She's Mita," Wil said.

In the room's darkness, the Starstone in Mita's hands glowed. Pim and Wil stood silent in its blue-white light, glaring at each other.

Wil stepped toward Mita. He reached a hand toward the Starstone.

"No!"

Pim extended his left fist, little finger extended. He made a gesture upwards.

From the ceiling, a giant's hand reached down. It clenched Wil's arm, held it.

"No more husbanding magic," Pim told him. "No need—our war is won."

Wil looked at the giant's hand holding him, with scorn.

Hummingbirds filled the room. They shot to the hand. A thousand pecks. Slowly, the huge hand dimmed, vanished. One by one, the hummingbirds puffed into smoke, drifted away.

"So!" Pim said.

"Yes," Wil said. "So."

Once again they took each other's measure. Pim finally shook his head.

"You used no gestures for that, no spells."

"I have no need," Wil said.

Again they eyed each other, measuring. Pim's face finally twisted with anger, disgust.

"Whatever you've become, we know you're marked."

Wil said nothing.

"If you touch it...."

"Yes," Wil said. "Mita...."

Pim finished his thought: "Death spell."

Again they stood silent. Finally, ardently, Wil spoke.

"You take it from her, Pim—redeem yourself."

Pim frowned.

"No," he said. "She must finish, a thousand years...."

A new voice spoke.

"And it's too late."

Zadni Druen now stood in the room.

"You two shout the house awake," she said, shaking her head, swirling her white hair.

"Too late?" Wil said.

Zadni sighed.

"She's held it too long for going back," she said. "When it lay upon a dais, in High City, in ancient times, none touched it."

"But its closeness gave us ever-growing power," Pim said.

Wil turned his back. He strode to the window, looked at the night.

"She becomes what she must become," Zadni said behind him. "She accepted...."

"What is she becoming?" Wil said, his voice flat.

He guessed.

372

He remembered a winter afternoon in Kobar's parlor, with his slate. Peat smoked in the hearth, while Kobar's father taught them their lessons.

Forester lore. Forbidden, hence thrilling. Kobar's father taught what the realm banned. He taught true history, gleaned from ancient books he hid in his attic. Today they learned the Foresters' hierarchy of spell casting.

"Lowest are magicians…."

They fool the eye, Kobar's father said. Tricks of levitation, small alterations. Next, enchanters. They foresee. And they can lay down lasting spells. Higher still, wizards. They glimpse the world's underpinnings, but only a little. Sorcerers above that—their eyes penetrate, seeing deep and wide, and they can move the world.

"Beyond sorcerers," said Kobar's father, "the ancient texts hint…."

Little Wil and little Kobar sat upon the floor, openmouthed. For they sensed their gentle-faced teacher led them beyond understanding.

"Sorcerers see deep into reality, and they can reach into it, change it, but there are some even above sorcerers…."

Kobar's father stood silently reading his text. Finally he looked up, spoke again.

"Boys, listen to this sentence—'Our eyes see only a dream we dream.'"

"What does it mean?" little Wil asked.

Kobar's father looked at him. So kind. Now murdered by a realm shot through with darkness. By a son corrupted.

"I don't know," Kobar's father said, that winter afternoon. "I cannot know."

Now, in the apartment on Ragpickers' Lane, Wil looked out the window into the night. Behind him, Zadni spoke.

"It had to be," she said. "This realm…."

He held up a hand.

"She's all but done her work," he said, not turning. "For her sake, take away the Stone now!"

"She mustn't stop before she's done," Zadni said. "Because what she's done might unravel, go ill."

"And if she continues?" Wil said.

"In the end, she becomes…."

Wil slowly turned to stare at Zadni, eyes wide. She stared back. And in her eyes he saw hurt, for she, too, loved Mita. What he'd guessed he now whispered.

"You've made her a Nameless One!"

Zadni said nothing.

"You've made her dark!" Wil said.

Zadni shook her head.

"Wil, no, not a Nameless One of Darkness—if Mita's training holds…."

He moaned.

"What have you done?" he said.

"To bring down the realm!" Pim shouted at him. "To make a better world!"

Wil cried out her name, and strode the two paces to where Mita sat. He looked down at her, shaking, then thrust out his right hand toward her cupped palms.

"No!"

He ignored Pim's shout.

Wil took the Starstone.

Fire in his hand. Ice. Minutes danced upon his hand, years. He held height, length, breadth. Threads of awareness, he saw, twining, untwining, retwining, this world's fabric. People's thoughts did the weaving, but voles' thoughts, too, and the knowing of wolves and trees. He could reach in, adjust….

He knew he couldn't though, for now he must take the Starstone to the mountain. As he must breathe, he must take it, and he couldn't long resist.

He resisted for now, though, because he saw Mita, although far off.

She didn't truly stand, for her body remained in this room, sitting in its chair. Yet, she stood looking back at him from far away, and he heard her distant voice.

"Look!"

He looked.

He saw Pim's bones, and Zadni's. He saw their hearts beat. Their lungs draw air, expel it. He saw their muscles stretch, contract, their blood pulse, their brains like gray mushrooms within their skulls. Permeating all, a glow. Their being. He saw them to be more than stood in this room. He knew them to be more than they could know.

"Now you see," Mita told him, across the distance.

"Yes," he said. "Now I start to see."

They spoke without tongues.

"Come back to us," he said.

He felt her regard him.

"I am what I am," she said.

"I hoped we could make a life together," he said.

"As did I," she said. "Perhaps we shall, in another time, for I see that time is broad, with room for more lives than one."

He knew Pim and Zadni saw him standing immobile, staring. He saw their horror, and Pim's thought to leap upon him, wrest away the Starstone, never let him bear it to the dark one. He saw Pim would willingly die to keep the Starstone from the Nameless Ones of Darkness. But so much power now coursed through him that none could take the Stone from his hand, even if he wished them to, because the power didn't come from him.

So he must swim with this current, let it take him where he must go. He couldn't resist its force.

But to swim aslant....

Wil spoke again to Mita.

"Can the Presence's marking of me be broken?"

"No."

She sent him understanding. Too deep a spell, this marking, drawn from the foundation of what is. Such a spell bound even the Nameless Ones of Darkness, when they visited this world. It imprisoned them in their mountain.

"Then cast a death spell against me," he said.

Silence.

He spoke again.

"I don't want to take the Starstone to that mountain."

Far off, she stood, at his ken's border. He sensed she spoke.

"It is fated," he heard. "For the new age must begin."

"What will that age be?" he asked.

"You will decide."

She stood looking back, from the border of his ken. She turned. She stepped across. She was gone, beyond his knowing.

Wil returned to the apartment. He returned as a deep diver kicks upward, back to the sunlit surface. He saw the apartment as before, built of solid wood and plaster. Now, though, he held the Starstone, and saw he dreamed the apartment, as did they all.

He must bear the Starstone to the mountain.

"Put it down," Pim commanded. "Death spell!"

Wil looked at him, seeing the little man's fury, bone deep, at his people's long-ago loss. He'd truly devoted his life, each of its minutes, to restoring the Foresters, and so he'd become fanatic. Forest Kings once more. It ruled his mind. And who better to lead his people? King Pim. Wil pitied him, as he pitied

Torpan the Twenty-ninth. For each swam in the river of cause and effect, and each breathed its water, and knew nothing else. And neither could outswim that powerful current pulling him down to the sea.

"No," Zadni said. "No death spell."

Wil realized the High Enchantress gripped his arm, stood with her eyes closed. She opened her eyes.

"I saw this in High City," she said. "Nothing has changed—he must go."

Pim's face contorted, twisted, then went slack. Abruptly he slumped onto the sofa, listless. He spoke to the High Enchantress without looking at her, his voice dead.

"What then, Zadni? What happens?"

"Undecided," Zadni said. "What becomes of the world, he decides."

Pim looked at Wil, with weary contempt.

"So the fate of all rests in the hands of a village boy," he said.

"No," Zadni said.

She gripped Wil's two hands. She lifted them up.

"These are sorcerer hands."

Wil shrugged on his knapsack, given him so long ago by Marston ker Veermander's wife, now murdered. It contained food, made by Malaga and Ranyan. Inside, too, the Starstone. He'd touched it once, so now whether he held it or not didn't matter.

Pim slouched on the sofa, staring at the wall.

Zadni regarded Wil grimly. Beside her, Malaga looked at him with open concern. She'd asked, and she understood what he faced.

Ranyan, holding Poko, looked from Wil to Mita, confused. Mita sat in her chair gazing far off, never speaking.

Wil regarded them all. Since childhood he'd sensed people's inner being, faintly, as he'd heard the thoughts of beasts. Now his perceptions had sharpened. He supposed the Opal of Living and Dying strengthened him, but since touching the Starstone he could look into a soul, as he now looked into Ranyan's.

She'd said, once, she wished to live in High City, out of disgust for her kind, and herself, chopper of heads. Now, he saw, she had a new wish: to serve Mita. If she hadn't been palace bred, but forest born, she might now be a young woman like Mita, with no blood on her hands. Mita's absence baffled her.

"Ranyan," Wil said. "She focuses elsewhere, where we can't go, but she'll revisit us, sometimes, and speak to us, and this physical part of Mita must be attended to."

"Well," Ranyan said. "La di la!"

Wil smiled at her. His smiles now looked grim, beneath that ragged yellow mustache.

Tobi padded into the room, wearing his knapsack.

"I'm ready, Wil."

"Who put on your knapsack?" Wil asked.

"Zadni did," Tobi said.

"What's in it?" Wil asked.

"Food, Wil, for our journey."

Wil looked at Zadni, eyebrows raised.

"I've put my hands on him, and looked ahead," she said. "Your friend must stand by you once more."

Wil thought to refuse, but didn't.

"What will happen, Zadni?"

"It's undecided, to the last," she said. "Except that—in the end—the decision will be yours."

He looked at the toes of his shoes.

"We'll help you, if we can, the Foresters," Zadni said. "If you need it...."

378

"All I've done, I've done alone," Wil said.

"No," Zadni said, and he saw it was true, because he remembered Marston ker Veermander's drawl. And he saw Bamba Moke's disapproving scowl. Kobar's father. Even old peg-legged Tunkle....

"Wil?"

Tobi's voice.

"I'm ready to go now."

Wil looked down, smiled.

"Three heroes brave," he told the dog. "Two remain."

He walked to the door and out, without looking back. Tobi walked with him.

Fishtown.

They arrived at dusk. Frosty, but the western sky pink, presaging spring.

They camped within Wil's former hut. Empty now. Cobwebs across the window. Once, through that window, a cat had jumped, a forest cat.

"Come," she'd bade him.

And she'd said: "It is time."

Remembering, he lay upon his cot's mattress, mildewed and mouse chewed. He slept. On the floor beside him slept his friend, a dog.

Dawn.

Pale light illuminated the window. He sat up, stretched.

"No need to hurry," he told himself.

From Imperia, he might have struck out westward, through the forest, straight to the mountain, but he'd paid three silvers for passage upriver on an emptied sailing scow, bound back after unloading its baled wool and knitted sweaters in Imperia. It beat north against the current, riding floodtides to its homeport, one village south of Fishtown. Wil and Tobi hiked the remaining seven miles.

"No need to hurry," he repeated.

Tobi breakfasted. Wil ate a slice of bread from his knapsack, although he felt no hunger.

"Why did we come here?" Tobi asked.

"I don't know," Wil said.

They walked the stone streets.

Bamba Moke's house, empty.

Kobar's father's house, also vacant, but unused swords stood stuck upright in the yard, like iron corn. Unused backpacks lay heaped upon the stoop.

"Wil Deft?"

A thatcher whom he'd sometimes helped, to earn ale money.

"Wil, you look different," the man said, peering at him.

"Much is different," he said.

"Yes," the man said.

He waved an arm to indicate the swords stuck in the yard, and the backpacks.

"Kobar set out from here with his army, into the forest," said the thatcher, and shrugged. "Nobody's dared touch these leavings, but now…."

"And it goes well?" Wil asked.

"Nobody fears slave ships," the man said. "And we've set up a council already, to decide village things—I'm on that myself, and we've got a ferry now, to Breming."

Wil and Tobi walked to the river. They boarded the ferry.

It swerved, to round Horse Skull Island's south point. Once, windows in Blossom's tavern shone here, welcoming on dark nights. Wil glimpsed charred ruins.

Breming.

So long forbidden, for the emperor forbade travel. He and Kobar had ventured here as boys, on a dare. They'd landed their skiff with hearts pounding. Breming now seemed to Wil, as he walked its stone streets, much like Fishtown.

He asked where the peat bogs might be. Then he and Tobi walked a path from town, worn by the wheels of laden carts, to where men dug with picks and spades, and sliced the exposed peat into blocks.

Wil walked among the men until he found whom he sought. They were the two brutes who'd accosted him in the Horse Skull Tavern. They'd said, then, that Foresters spirited away their peat, for spite. Now, despite the air's chill, they labored shirtless. Sweat glistened on their backs and arms, and dripped from their brows.

They didn't know him. In the tavern that night, Mita laid upon them a spell of forgetting.

"How goes it?" Wil asked.

One man put down his pick and spread his hands.

"No highborns taking our coins now," he said. "But the peat's near gone, and we work harder and get less, and after it's all gone, what?"

Wil looked at the dug-away pit. All around lay emptied pits, dug long ago. As far as he could see, emptied pits.

He looked into the earth. His awareness coursed eastward, following granite seams, and quartz, and basalt. But he saw only rock and soil and roots. So he looked northward. He followed subterranean water flowing through bedrock cracks. He saw where the soil lay deep, and where it shallowed. Twenty-two miles northward, a mile east of the river, where no town ever was, he found uncut peat. A vast bed.

"It goes to waste," he thought. "If it were here…."

His brow furrowed, as if he strained at heavy work. Then it smoothed.

381

He opened his eyes.

They stared at him, the two diggers. No doubt he looked strange, this lanky man with corn-colored hair, and a ragged mustache. Young, yet no longer looking young. He regarded them calmly.

"Look," he said.

They looked.

Silence.

All through the peat pit, workers stood silent, looking at what now lay beneath their feet. Finally, the bigger of the two diggers before him found his voice.

"But how...."

"I brought this peat here to you," Wil said. "I sent your dug-away bed to replace it, where it was."

"But how...."

"Magic," Wil said.

They gawked at him.

"I am a Forester," he told them.

And he knew he came here to say those words.

They hiked westward beneath the great forest's hemlocks and oaks. Each day, the mountain's pull strengthened. Thousands of years it waited, but now what it sought neared.

Wil skirted Forester villages. Not knowing, they'd greet him as the Taker, restorer of the Starstone. And he couldn't bear it.

Camped one night, in a clearing, he tried to explain to Tobi all that happened, and what he now faced, but his telling bogged in complexity, and he fell silent.

"Wil?"

"Yes, Tobi?"

Their campfire smoldered. Sometimes a pine branch's pitch bubbled and burst, sending up sparks.

"Do you remember my poem about the battle in the lane?"

"Yes, I do."

"Wil, I said three heroes fought there, but I know only two fought."

"I know, Tobi, but it doesn't matter—we're going to a battle fiercer than any ever fought, and more important."

"Wil, I want to show you what a good warrior I am."

Hearing that, Wil felt dread.

Midnight, their journey's third day. They lay drowsing by the campfire. Thuds. Nearer. Tobi snarled, glared into the darkness.

At the clearing's edge, something huge loomed. Fangs. Yellow eyes. A foul smell of menace. Abruptly, it roared, thudded toward them. Tobi stood his ground, barking. Wil glanced at it, sighed. It turned to moths, and the moths fluttered away.

"It's gone, Wil," Tobi said. "I scared it."

Wil smiled.

How had he gained these powers? Surely holding the Starstone hastened it. But he suspected, too, the Opal of Living and Dying, in its pouch suspended from his neck by a thong—it helps you become what you are.

"What have I become?" he asked Tobi.

"You're Wil," the dog said, perplexed. "You're my friend."

And so they walked on through the forest, ever westward, toward the mountain. With each step, Wil felt heavier.

They found a sword flung down, broken. Farther along, heaped knapsacks, shredded and bloodstained. More lost swords.

A clearing. Nodding in the sunshine, huge green flowers, twice his own height.

Wil stopped, and motioned for Tobi to stop.

"Flowers that eat you," he thought, and he remembered Lal.

"Go around," she'd counseled.

But that was a different time.

"Stay exactly beside me," he told Tobi.

He set out through the flowers. As they passed each flower, it reared back, as if to strike. Wil glanced at it, and it wilted. After they passed, it sprang back up.

Among the stems, as thick as his waist, Wil saw footprints. He saw bloodied jerkins flung down. And capes. Skeletons, he saw, and scattered bones.

When they reached the clearing's edge, he saw only one set of footprints remaining, and those made by a man who staggered and reeled. No doubt he didn't live long, this last of Kobar's army.

"Kobar," Wil thought, and sighed.

Now the ground slightly tilted upward. He stood under a maple, looking ahead through the trees. They seemed to thin before him, and shrink, so he knew they neared the place—of all places—where he feared to go.

"Raven's here," Tobi said.

Wil looked up. On a maple branch above them, Raven perched, looking down.

"Spiders on the slopes," Raven told them.

Wil shrugged.

"Raven," he said. "Will you fly north and ask Bear to come? And will you find Lal, wherever she might be in the forest, and ask her to come?"

"Huge, this forest," Raven said, sounding sulky. "Heavy flying."

Wil opened his knapsack and found a slab of cheese. He tossed it up. Raven caught it in his bill.

"Strength for flying," Raven said, sounding cheered. "Shall I try?"

"Yes," Wil said. "Try."

With a thrust of its broad wings, the black bird lifted from the tree and flapped away, zigzagging through the trunks. It was gone, and they walked on.

Afternoon. Ahead, through the thinning trees, Wil saw where the mountain began its rise. He remembered it well. Near here, an invisible line marked the edge of the Presence's realm of cliffs and caverns and spiders. They walked to that invisible line.

Just across, on a large stone, sat a man. He wore tattered black velvet, and from his belt hung a rapier.

As if he awaited them, he smiled, just one side of his mouth.

Wil spoke first.

"Kobar," he said.

CHAPTER SIXTEEN

"You've become its creature," Wil said.

From across the invisible line, Kobar smiled again, just on one side. He wore black-velvet rags, smeared with dried mud, but his eyes seemed most changed. They looked dead.

As if abashed, Kobar looked at his feet, shaking his head.

"Ah, Wil," he said, looking up. "Remember playing Pilfer? And jumping into the river? Remember when we chased village girls?"

"Remember when you murdered your father?" Wil said.

Those dead eyes stared.

"My men all died in the forest, but I went on alone, and I found this mountain…."

Wil said nothing.

"Here, Wil! Power—beyond imagining!"

Wil stared back, silent.

"Those great ones I admired," Kobar said. "They're just twittering wrens."

Kobar held out his palm.

"It is time," he said.

"No," Wil said.

Kobar shook his head, as if sad.

"Wil," he said. "You must give it up."

Tobi growled.

"Master demands it," Kobar said.

They stood looking at one another. Again the dog growled.

Wil shrugged off his backpack. He took out the Starstone, cold fire in his hand. He set it on the ground, between him and Tobi. Then he sat.

Kobar snickered.

"You have to bring it over the line."

He knew he must. He could resist, for a while, but to do what? He'd sent Raven to bring Bear and Lal, an impulse that came to him, but he had no plan. And what were three animals against such a being as this?

He thought: when I fight the Presence, I'll die. So why not cast my own death spell?

He couldn't conjure away the Starstone. His marking surely prohibited such counter magic. Nor could he keep it here much longer. He must—compelled by his curse—bring the Starstone into the Presence's realm. Already he felt himself dragged toward the line, as if by powerful hands.

"But if I'm dead...."

Then it would lie beside his body, here on the boundary's nether side. Starstone-wielding Foresters laid down that line, made of the forces underlying all that is, and even a Nameless One couldn't break its spell. So the Presence couldn't send its eight-leggers across, or Kobar.

Wil sagged, suddenly realizing any passing chipmunk or squirrel could be induced to fetch it across. Here, little fellow, an acorn.

"It's time, Wil," Kobar said.

His dead eyes almost glittered.

"Tobi?" Wil said. "Would you take this Stone away for me?"

"I don't care about that Stone thing, Wil—I want to fight them for you."

"But they'd kill you, Tobi."

"I don't care."

And he understood. Tobi truly didn't care.

"Tobi? If I wanted more than anything for you to bring this Starstone to Zadni Gruen, would you do that for me?"

"I don't want to," Tobi said. "Unless we both go."

"I can't leave here," Wil said.

"Bite!" Tobi muttered.

"Would you do it for me?"

Tobi radiated unhappiness. Wil unbuttoned the flap of the dog's knapsack and slid in the Starstone.

Kobar watched with interest. Wil rebuttoned the knapsack's flap. Kobar stood.

"Here, doggie," Kobar said. "Here, boy—bring it here."

Tobi growled. He showed Kobar his teeth.

"Bad dog," Kobar said.

He sat back down on his rock. He resumed watching Wil with dead eyes.

"Go now, Tobi," Wil said.

For a moment, Tobi gazed up at him, defiant.

"Please," Wil said. "It's what I wish."

Tobi hung his head, in resignation. He turned, took a step. Another. But he stopped.

"Wil?"

"Yes, Tobi?"

"I can't move."

Wil sighed.

So the spell tethers it here, he thought. Until I deliver it to the Presence, here it stays.

He thought: "I must fight the Presence."

Dread filled him.

He wielded magic. Since leaving Fishtown, all he'd experienced strengthened his magic. And taking the Starstone from Mita, that especially released something locked within him.

Zadni Druen said he now had sorcerer's hands. He could summon forces he still only dimly understood, and wield them, but that was puny against a Nameless One.

From Tobi's knapsack he took the Starstone. It felt fiery in his hand, yet cold. He didn't know what he might do with it, but just holding it he felt augmented.

He heard laughter, but Kobar sat on his rock, as dead-eyed as before.

"I fear death," Wil thought.

He'd pay that price, to keep the Starstone from the Presence. Any price.

A voice.

"Indeed?"

It chilled him, that voice.

He looked up the mountainside. Phalanxes of eight-leggers now stood upon the slope, staring down at him, ruby eyed. Floating above them, a blue globe.

He heard the Presence mock him—"You took, Taker, and now you must deliver!"

Down the slope it floated, that glowing globe, and hovered above Kobar's head. Once again Wil confronted the blue eyeball. It gazed down upon him, unblinking.

"Wil Deft, you return enhanced."

He recoiled from that voice. Tobi, beside him, stared up at the eyeball and snarled, baring his teeth.

"I didn't fight in the lane, Wil," the dog said. "But now I'll fight!"

Wil said nothing

"What a stout-hearted little dog."

That hated voice.

Again: "So, Wil Deft, to keep the Starstone from returning to this mountain of its making, you'd pay any price?"

Laughter.

He felt the voice amused itself, playing with him.

"You cannot keep the Starstone from its maker."

I can fight, Wil thought. That I can do.

"You left here a village boy, Forester born, and you return a sorcerer, although untempered...."

He felt the eyeball scrutinizing him.

"But what is a sorcerer to us? And you stand alone, Wil Deft. Even your Mita Sooth.... Yes—now one of us!"

"No!"

Wil cried it aloud.

"Yes, a Nameless One."

Wil knew it to be true, and to himself he moaned her name.

"Mita."

"She is a Nameless One," the Presence repeated.

And again: "Yes, a Nameless One."

Wil thought: What use?

"I won't take it across until I must," he decided. "That much I can do."

And so he stood on his side of the line. Tobi, standing beside him, growled. They both stared at Kobar upon his rock, and at the eight-leggers arrayed as if for battle, farther up the slope. And they stared at the blue eyeball, floating in the air.

Wil felt the Presence considering. He saw Kobar stir.

What now, he thought?

Kobar, as if jerked, leaped to his feet. Face blank, he raised his rapier. He sighted along its blade to Wil's chest.

"What's this?" Wil wondered.

Kobar aimed the rapier's point at Wil's heart. He thrust.

With a snarl, Tobi lunged forward, teeth bared.

"No, Tobi!" Wil yelled. "He can't cross."

But Tobi ran, snarling, across the invisible line. He leapt, sinking his teeth into Kobar's sword arm.

"Tobi! It's a trick!" Wil yelled. "Come back."

Kobar abruptly crumpled, like a puppet with its strings cut. He sat upon the ground, dead eyed. Tobi released his grip upon Kobar's arm and tumbled onto the ground. He lay motionless.

"Wil?"

"Yes, Tobi?"

"I can't move."

And the voice in his head said: "Starstone, for the dog."

An hour passed. Another. Night fell. In the darkness, high up the slope, Wil saw a thousand red fireflies, the eight-leggers' eyes.

He sat upon the ground, beside the invisible line. No moon shone. He supposed the Starstone showed him a different light, because he saw the dog lying on his side, frozen. Tobi, uncomplaining, awaited his aid. And still he sat thinking.

Beside the dog, Kobar sprawled. His animation withdrawn, he looked like a straw man, discarded. Wil guessed his childhood friend barely existed. Most of himself, Kobar gave to the great ones. What remained, the Presence commandeered. And now the Presence's emanation, the blue eyeball, floated above Kobar, contemplating Wil. Finally, the Presence spoke.

"Thousands of years, waiting," the voice said. "What are minutes more?"

Wil reached for the Starstone, grasped its cold fire.

"Yes," the voice said. "It amplifies your powers—but, even so, how paltry those powers."

Wil said nothing.

From the forest behind him, a whir of great wings. Wil didn't look back as it flew over him, across the line, a winged horse, its forelegs ending in hands. It descended, grasped Tobi, lifted him.

Laughter.

Blue lightning flashed. It struck the horse. Tobi fell back to the ground. Horse became smoke. A breeze dispersed the smoke. It blew nickering away.

"Fool," the Presence said.

Wil sighed. He tried to think of another stratagem.

"You fail to amuse," the Presence said. "Now this will end."

Kobar jerked to his feet, a puppet pulled by its strings. Once more he raised his rapier. He aimed it at Tobi.

"No!" Wil cried, jumping up.

"No?" said the Presence. "Then what in exchange for this animal's life? Hmm?"

Wil stood as if paralyzed.

A dog for a world?

Kobar lurched toward the frozen Tobi. He pulled back his rapier, for the thrust.

A world for a feckless dog, who made up ditties about himself? Who wanted to be Wil Deft's friend, and nothing more?

Yes, he thought. For this dog!

Wil crossed the invisible line.

Blue flames danced around him, and he knew it was the Presence's exultation. Time stopped—Kobar aiming his rapier, Tobi inert on the ground, Wil hurrying toward Kobar, one foot in the air.

He heard the Presence sneer.

"Weakling!"

"You don't have it yet," Wil said.

"Do you plan to keep it, Dust Mote?"

Laughter.

He still clenched the Starstone. It seared his hand, that cold burning. And the Opal of Living and Dying, in its pouch suspended from his neck, now throbbed like a live thing.

Why did the Presence not kill him, take the Stone?

He heard its voice.

"It ripens, our Speck."

A pause.

"Yes, it ripens, each moment, so…. Hmm."

Kobar thrust his rapier into Tobi's side.

A scream. Tobi's or his, Wil didn't know.

He thrust out his arm, index finger pointing at Kobar. From that finger white light streamed. It struck Kobar's forehead, and his flesh smoked away. A skeleton held the rapier. Then bones turned to dust, and the rapier fell.

"Wil, it hurts!"

"I know, Tobi, and I'll…."

"Goodbye, Wil."

He saw the dog's eyes close. And he knew his friend left that body.

"Go after him, Speck! Your friend! And while you are gone…."

Wil understood. If he went after Tobi, his physical self would stand here defenseless.

He went.

Darkness unfolded before him, rushing by, until far ahead he saw a spark. He flew faster. Just ahead now, a white light, small, but bright.

"Tobi," he said to the light.

"I fought for you, Wil—did you see?"

"I saw, Tobi."

"I was brave, Wil! Bark! Bite, bite, bite!"

"Tobi, come back."

"I fought, Wil, but now it hurts too much."

"Tobi, I promise to stop the hurt."

He sensed the dog thinking, as they sped through the darkness.

"Please, do it for me."

And then the white light veered, speeding back the way they had come. He followed.

As they flew through darkness, Wil reached into the world they'd left and touched Tobi's inert body, preparing it for painless sleep. He looked inside the body, and saw ruinous damage. To heal it—if he truly could heal it—would take many weeks. But he had no time. Rushing back through the darkness, he saw his own body standing upon the mountainside, as if enchanted. And he saw the Presence reach toward the Starstone in his hand.

Nearing the world, he saw Bear loping up the trail to the mountain. He sent Bear a thought: hurry.

Wil stood once more upon the mountainside, within his body. Beside him Tobi lay, unconscious. Tobi breathed, but raggedly.

And in all that going and returning, no time had passed.

Wil now saw the Presence. It had no body, and it had dispensed with its emanation, the blue eyeball. Wil saw a towering blue flame. It burned brightly, but radiated chill. Wil saw the flame reaching toward him, to take the Starstone, and before it he stood a dwarf.

Malaga.

Memories of her appeared in his mind.

Highborns had towered over Malaga, cruel, ruthless. So she'd studied them sideways, out her eyes' corners. She'd sidled through their palace. In the end, her sidling placed the Taker beside the Starstone. So the great ones fell, and the dwarf survived.

Wil stepped aside from the Presence's grasp.

Laughter.

"Where will you run, frightened mouse?"

"I could fly," Wil thought. "Up and over."

If he flew fast enough....

A dog lay before him upon the ground, mortally wounded. He'd put Tobi into a deep sleep, to numb his wound's pain, but he had no time for healing. In an eyeblink, the Presence would wrench the Starstone from his hand.

"Why not give it up, hmm?"

Wil wondered: why don't you just take it?

"Give it up, and perhaps you shall not die writhing in agony, hmm?"

Again Wil stepped to one side.

From the darkness, beyond the invisible line, Bear now peered toward him, smelling him and Tobi. What that nose scented of the Presence, or the thousand eight-leggers arrayed on the slope, Wil didn't know.

He sent an image to Bear, of the invisible line just beyond his forepaws. And he said, "Don't cross."

From the darkness, a sound like a cough, so Bear heard him.

"What is this, Speck, a little friend in the dark?"

Laughter.

"And do you believe this friend might save you?"

No, Wil thought. Not me.

Yet, he didn't know what to do, because Bear had no hands to hold Tobi. And if he laid Tobi on Bear's back, the sleeping dog would fall.

"What do you care about this world?" Wil asked the Presence.

Another step aside, to gain time.

"Why not just leave it?" Wil said.

He thought, I'll die, but I'll do it saving this dog.

"You trouble yourself much over this little world," Wil said.

This time he heard the Presence speak.

"It is ours."

An edge, now, in that voice. Wil thought, what have I touched?

"We shaped it, in its infancy, and they shall not...."

Now the voice stopped. Wil felt the Presence considering him. In that consideration, he sensed a new note.

His knapsack, he saw, lay at Bear's feet. Tobi would fit inside. But its straps could never stretch around Bear, to anchor Tobi upon his back.

"You are clever, Speck," said the voice. "What do you plot to save yourself?"

"I do not expect to save myself," Wil said.

"Hmm," said the voice.

Wil knew the Presence perceived he spoke truly.

Tobi, asleep, still wore his knapsack.

"You shaped this world, you said, but fear its taking— who might they be, those takers?" Wil said.

Another step aside. For time. He needed to be quick.

Tobi disappeared. He reappeared across the invisible line, beside Bear. Now, as if by itself, Tobi's knapsack unstrapped from him. Its fabric raveled. Also, the straps of Wil's knapsack raveled. Those ravelings joined. They reknitted themselves to Wil's knapsack, as long straps.

"You expend time on that dying animal!"

"I do," Wil said.

Tobi's sleeping body slid into Wil's knapsack. Now the knapsack floated upwards to rest upon Bear's back. Its newly lengthened straps wrapped themselves around Bear's belly, and fastened.

All in one beat of a fly's wing.

"Take him to Zadni Druen, for healing," Wil said. "Hurry."

He saw Bear turn, lope away into the forest.

Wil turned to confront the towering blue flame. He was ready to fight now, and then die. He thought he saw a flicker.

"It hesitates," he thought.

That the Nameless One hesitated astonished him.

Blue flame abruptly became a viper. It looked down at Wil far below, this giant serpent, its hood extended, each fang the size of a man, its glare icy blue. It reared back to strike.

Wil ran from it, up the mountain, but before him the slope blinked with ruby fireflies, eight-leggers' eyes. They descended towards him. He turned to run aside, but that mass of giant spiders curled around his flanks. So the viper and its minions encircled him.

He raised his arm, pointed at the serpent. From his index finger's tip flashed a white beam. It caught the huge snake in its open mouth. and the viper exploded into blue dust.

Wil stood transfixed.

Upon the ground, in the serpent's blue dust, something fluttered. Only a tiny bat, Wil saw, beating its delicate wings against the earth.

"Have I slain the Presence?" Wil wondered.

Laughter.

Abruptly, the bat grew to a horse's size. Again it grew. Now it loomed over Wil, wings spread, as large as a house. Then even larger. It glared down upon him, blue eyes flashing.

It flapped its leather wings, rose above him, and stared malevolently down. Behind him, and around him, ruby fireflies surged.

He felt alone, and his knees gave way.

Yet...

Why didn't it kill me long ago? Why didn't it just take the Starstone? For he still held it in his hand, felt its icy burning. And the Opal of Living and Dying pulsed.

"It seeks to weaken me with fear," he thought. "But why weaken me? I have no strength. And why does it hesitate?"

These thoughts confused him. And terror overwhelmed him.

All around the massed eight-leggers now pressed in. He smelled their fangs' venom. He looked up to find the serpent gone, and again the blue flame towered over him. Its burning chilled him.

He huddled on the ground, hiding his head in his hands. And he felt the Presence's exultation.

"Give up the Starstone, and be granted life, as our servant."

Relief ran through him, like warmth.

Why not?

His mind filled with images. Fishtowners, he saw, whispering "Forester spawn." Pim, mistrusting him. He saw all he'd faced, since leaving Fishtown. All he'd risked. And for whom? Sneering Fishtowners? Scorning Pim? And it came to nothing. Now the Presence would seize the Starstone, and darkness would reclaim this world.

"Do you see?"

Wil hesitated, another step aside.

"Fool."

What might be, the Presence showed him. He saw himself the Nameless Ones' satrap upon this world, wielding enormous power. Tobi might now be wounded beyond healing, but if he surrendered, with his new powers he'd save Tobi. And he might speak with Mita, as she was now. He'd see other worlds, wonders unimaginable. And he'd no longer walk this world alone.

Those thoughts the Presence gave him. And they drew him.

But other thoughts came, too, although dimly.

He saw Kobar's father teach little Wil, just as he taught his own son. For tutoring a Forester foundling, Kobar's father attracted certain villagers' spite. Kobar's father guessed they'd one day turn him in. Yet, what he did he thought right. Now Wil saw Blossom and Bamba Moke, secretly watching over him, at great risk. He saw Marston ker Veermander's wife. Facing death, and the murder of everyone she loved, instead of fleeing, she took time to prepare him a knapsack filled with food. Even old Tunkle stood by him, and died for it.

Yet, he might be satrap for the Nameless Ones of Darkness, wielder of immense power.

To do their will.

"No," he said.

"What is this?" said the voice.

He answered: "I'll die."

He stood. He held tight to the Starstone and looked up into blue flames, and waited.

Darkness now shot through the towering blue flame. He saw the Presence draw back to smite him. He shut his eyes. He awaited the deathblow.

"Come!"

Not the Presence's voice.

He went.

Where he went he didn't know. All around him glowed white. Ahead, amidst that white glow, a brighter glow.

"Mita," he said.

"Yes, I was Mita."

"Is Mita gone?"

"No, she is part of what I am now, and she loves you now, as she loved you then."

"Am I dead?"

"Not yet."

"I've failed, Mita."

"Not yet."

"I'm too weak to fight the Presence—it'll kill me and take the Starstone, and even you've become a Nameless One of Darkness."

"No."

He felt her smile. A warmth.

She showed him her long training, with Zadni Druen. He saw that training guided her, as she wielded the Starstone. Wielding carried her ever farther from the self he knew. Magician, she began. Enchantress, she became. Then wizardess. Near her wielding's end she became sorceress. One step remained, out of this world's confines. She'd stepped.

"Into darkness?" Wil asked.

She might, at that last step, he saw, turn left into darkness. It drew powerfully, but her training held. She'd stepped to the right, into light.

So he beheld a white light. No color muted that light, except a touch of sunshine.

"I am a Nameless One," he heard. "But not a Nameless One of Darkness."

More she showed him.

Nameless Ones of Darkness, since before time, vying with Nameless Ones of Light. They wrestled for worlds. So many worlds. For them to clash directly would release infinite power, destroy all things. So they vied indirectly. But their battling generated the energy driving all.

"Who'll win?" Wil asked.

"There's only eternal vying, dark against light," this magnified Mita told him. "And out of that battle comes what is."

"I've lost my battle," Wil said bleakly.

He felt smiled upon.

"Jump from the old mill into the river," he heard. "Let the current take you, but swim aslant."

So he'd once told her, hoping to save her. Now she spoke his words to him.

"Go back."

Her voice faded as he sped away. As he journeyed, even fainter, he heard: "Become what you are."

Again he stood in his body, before the towering blue flame. He'd gone and returned, and once more no time had passed. Still in his hand, the Starstone coldly burned. At his chest the Opal of Living and Dying still throbbed.

Again the Presence stayed its hand.

"So you visited the enemy," it said.

Wil thought: why, long ago, didn't this dark being slay me and take the Starstone? It hesitates. Is that weakness? Or do I offer it some value I don't know?

It saw his befuddlement. He felt it gloating. Now it drew back, finally to strike in earnest, while confusion clouded his mind.

"Then I'll become what I must!"

Wil shouted that at the blue flame, even as it reared back to smite him.

He opened his mind, at last fully, to the Starstone's force, and it surged through him. He let it carry him away, doors inside him opening. He knew it stained him, because when the Nameless Ones made the Stone, out of the energy underlying all, some of their darkness went into it, too. Mita, trained, escaped staining, but he'd had no training. He'd always feared the Starstone, sensing its taint, but now he accepted it. And, even as the Presence smote him, he swam aslant.

Blue fire seared into his flesh and his mind, dropping him to his knees. His flesh smoked, starting to burn away, so he encased himself in ice, knowing it would soon melt, assailed by this power vastly mightier than his own. Then he felt the Presence stopping his thoughts, darkening his mind, and he sought some countervailing strength. Into his mind, though, flew only one small name.

"Tobi."

Blue fire melted his shielding ice, ready to burn away his flesh. In his mind, he stepped aside from the Presence's force, just enough to remember what Tobi said.

"I don't care about that Stone thing, Wil—I want to fight them for you."

He'd said, they'll kill you, Tobi.

And the dog replied: "I don't care."

Each of those words seemed a spark.

Wil struggled up from his knees, and they stood like that a moment, the blue flame confronting the man it dwarfed. They took each other's measure.

"You progress."

That hated voice.

"Yet, you remain mortal still."

Behind him, a rumbling. He turned. Down the mountainside, a thousand eight-leggers charged.

"No," he told the Presence. "You must kill me yourself."

And he smiled.

From the night sky fell a white spark. Another. Now a torrent rained upon the eight-leggers.

Wil laughed.

He caught one falling spark upon his hand. In his palm stood a tiny Tobi. He let it go, to join the other sparks falling upon the eight-leggers.

A sound of barking. A sound of snapping teeth.

One by one, the giant eight-leggers vanished.

Wil looked down. Past his feet marched thousands of spiders, each no bigger than an apple seed. They paraded down the slope. They disappeared into the forest, from whence their ancestors came, when the Nameless Ones transformed them into monstrous servants.

High overhead, rising, Wil heard tiny triumphant barks.

Now blue flame and man stood alone upon the mountainside. And the Presence spoke.

"Well done."

Then it sneered.

"But do you think this mountain stands upon eight-leggers?"

Blue strands, like cobwebs, engulfed him, so cold they burned. Strands held down his arms, bound his legs, wrapped his face. He fell.

Once more the Presence reached down to wrest the Starstone from his inert hand.

He called: "Mita!"

He heard no answer.

"Now my life ends," he told himself. "And what have I ever done?"

Blue cobwebs tightened around him, suffocated him, and he felt a powerful grip wrenching away the Starstone. He clenched it tight, meaning to fight to the end.

"I tried to save Tobi, at least," he thought.

He awaited the searing, when his flesh would smoke and burn away.

Instead, he felt the Presence in his mind. It showed him the palace in Imperia, as it was tonight, at this moment.

He saw a mob storming it. He saw the empress's suite. Within, she lay upon the bed, staring at the door, now flung open. Torpan the Twenty-Ninth stood at his full height, between the empress's bed and the door, through which the mob now pushed. Torpan held a rapier, his face grim.

And the Presence spoke: "Justice, hmm?"

It showed him the past. He saw Torpan with Duzzle, gouging out the brains of men and dogs. He saw the murder of innocents, the taking of commoners' earnings and land and pride. He saw arrogance, cruelty, greed, torture.

"At your life's end I grant you Wielder powers—exact justice!"

Wil thought: "You don't grant me powers—they're mine!"

And he'd wield them.

Torpan! Bedeviler of his people. Bamba Moke, for one. Murdered. Marston ker Veermander, and all his family. Kobar's father. Old Tunkle....

Slay the slayers!

He savored his rage. It tasted sharp, and sweet, touched with smoke. And he wondered at all the anger in him. He hadn't known.

Then he wielded.

To the mob, he sent shame. His own shame. He saw them slink away.

From this mountain, he looked about the realm. He saw a man standing upon a crate along the Imperial Way. Red-faced, he harangued a crowd.

"They killed my son!" he yelled. "They took my daughter a slave!"

Answering yells from the crowd: my father! My aunt!

Wil looked into himself, below his own anger and hurt, deeper down, to a vein of benevolence. He placed it in the haranguer's mind. And the man stopped yelling. Upon his crate, he looked thoughtful.

"Yet, kill 'em and what? I suppose them highborns got little ones, too. So, I'm saying, maybe...."

In a ballroom in the palace, a meeting. Upriver villagers here, and people from Imperia's neighborhoods, come to

404

organize councils to govern in the highborns' stead. An argument, heated—

"...so we got to get the shipping going again, and the factories to make cups and plates, and..."

"Well, who's gonna run 'em? You know how to do it?"

Wil implanted a thought in a woman's head.

"Seems to me the ones as knows all such things is the highborns, what run 'em before, so what if we hire them on, pay 'em something out of the earnings to...."

Wil now returned to the palace. Torpan, he saw, slouched in his chair beside his wife's bed, his sword flung down on the floor. His chin rested upon his chest. No mob now, but in the days ahead no servants would bring food.

Into the ousted emperor's mind Wil placed a notion: an Imperial Inn. Here one-time aristocrats, back in Imperia on business, might stay, and traveling merchants, too. Their innkeeper might regale them with tales.

"When I was the last emperor, a mob attacked, and I alone, the war emperor, raised my rapier and...."

We swim in the river, Wil thought. So the empress once said. All that preceded us fills that river, and all that befalls us. We breathe its waters. Its current shapes us. How many of us leap into the air, to shake off our shaping? And what do we make of our fellow failed leapers?

"Done," he thought.

He'd wielded, now death. Yet, cobwebs no longer bound him.

I swam aslant, he thought.

From its towering height, the Presence regarded him, considering. He stared up into that blue flame.

Still he held the Starstone.

"Am I too strong for it?"

He heard its voice.

"No."

He felt it considering him.

"You remain Wil Deft," said the voice. "But with each bout you do step closer...."

He knew the Presence considered. And, while he waited, he wondered.

Closer?

He cringed. He felt the Presence gird itself, gathering all its strength for a finishing stroke. And against that power he felt himself an insect.

Beneath him the earth opened.

He plummeted, down through darkness. Above him, as he fell, the rock closed over. Still he plummeted, and still the rock closed over him. At last, deep within the earth, his falling ceased. In perfect darkness he stood upon rock. And when he reached out his arms, all around he felt rock. When he reached overhead, there, too, he felt rock.

A deep rumble. Around him, the rock moved inward, an inch. So he would die slowly crushed, buried deep.

And when I'm dead, he thought, the Presence will again open the rock. It'll draw up my body, lay it on the ground. And take the Starstone.

He tried to push back the rock, using his sorcerer's hands, but couldn't.

"It's will is too strong for me," he thought. "It is a Nameless One."

All around, the rock rumbled another inch closer. He felt it press against his shoulders, and upon the hair of his head.

He despaired. Against what assailed him now, the Presence's full effort, his powers couldn't stand. So he waited to die.

He thought of Tobi. Even now Bear carried him toward High City. He hoped Tobi would live, for that would be something.

Mita, too. He'd feared she'd lose herself, but she no longer frowned with worry and walked awkwardly, bumping into tables. She'd left this world. She'd become her true self, a greater self. And that was something.

Another inward rumble of the rock. It pressed down on his head, buckling his knees. But his knees, in bending, bumped against the rock pressing in from the chamber's sides.

"What have I done in my life?" he thought.

He'd taken the Starstone. Now the Presence would take it back. This world would be lost. He'd tried, though, risked himself, succeeded a little. That was something. He'd found the Opal of Living and Dying, and it throbbed now, against his chest.

He thought: this shall be my last effort in the world.

He bent his elbow, squeezed up his left arm, almost pinioned by the rock, and reached inside his shirt. He fingered the pouch, slung so long from his neck. Between his index finger and thumb, he extracted the Opal of Living and Dying. In his other hand he held the Starstone. In a moment, he'd die holding them, crushed.

He had that moment, though. So, squeezing against the rock, he brought his two hands together. He fingered the Starstone until he found the indentation, where the Opal of Living and Dying fitted, long ago.

It's pointless, he thought, restoring it, but a pointless act is at least an act.

So, barely able to move against the pinioning rock, he fitted the Opal of Living and Dying into its indentation.

He felt it hold.

Then the rock moved inward again, pressing against him, cold and rough. He couldn't move.

407

In his hand, the Starstone moved.

"What's this?" he thought.

White light, touched with blue, now filled his prison. It flowed into him, and through him. He breathed it. It flowed through his arteries and veins, and through his thoughts.

Deep beneath the earth, he felt the rock walls move inward again, to finally crush him. And he laughed.

He rose up through the solid rock. He stood upon the ground, under the night sky. And now the towering blue flame confronted a flame nearly as tall as itself, but of white light. However, shot through the white light, a stain of blue.

They regarded each other, these two flames. They took each other's measure.

"Because of what you were, you resisted, and in vying you ripened," said the Presence. "A thought came, as we vied, a hand-staying thought, that you might become one of us, of the dark, and so you were offered anger, a nudge...."

"But from that anger I stepped aside," what had been Wil said. "I did not partake of it."

Once more they faced each other, thoughtful. Then the other spoke again.

"No longer can we fight for the Starstone."

"Not without destroying all there is," answered the white flame.

"But you do not completely win," said the Presence. "You bear its stain."

"I do," said what had been Wil. "But you will not regain the Starstone, and the spell holds, and on this world you remain confined."

He felt the other regard him. And it was as if the other nodded.

"Yet, we shall visit here from time to time," said the Presence. "And of other worlds there are many."

"Many," said the Presence's opponent.

And the Presence left.

What had been Wil Deft stood upon the mountainside in the darkness. It considered its stain, that blue taint within its white light.

Then it turned its attention downward.

Upon the ground before it, looking up without fear, sat a cat.

A black cat, white whiskered. She looked up with faintly malevolent blue eyes.

"Lal," said the flame. "What is to be done?"

"What smells right," said the cat.

She licked a paw.

Now the flame laughed. It felt its laughter spread out through the world, and into the sky.

Before it now a shaft opened into the earth. Up from the shaft the Nameless One of Light lifted the body that had been Wil Deft. It was now crushed, every bone, but the white flame touched the body, and it mended. It lay upon the ground, a living body again, but empty of being.

"Should I relinquish what I have become?"

It asked this of itself, but perhaps the cat heard.

"When I hunt in the forest, sometimes I catch an animal that sprays me, and I smell," the cat said. "I do not like myself when I smell, so I roll in the dirt and in the leaves, and I wade into a stream, day after day, and in time the stench fades, and one day it is gone."

From that towering flame, a kind of smile.

Then the flame shrank. But as it diminished, it grew brighter. It shrank to the size of the body lying upon the ground. Then it streamed into the body and was gone.

Wil Deft sat up.

"So I must spend my life rolling in the dirt and leaves, and wading in streams," he told the cat.

But the cat said nothing. She merely licked a different paw.

For the remainder of that night, and most of the next day, cat and man walked through the forest toward High City. As they walked, the man looked increasingly grim.

Finally, in a clearing, he stopped. He stood, head down, looking at the Starstone still clenched in his hand, with the Opal of Living and Dying attached.

"What will Pim do with this?" the man asked.

He posed that question to himself, and the cat didn't respond.

He sat upon the ground, beside the Starstone. He gazed at it until the sun's light slanted through the trees from the west. Then he nodded, as if finally deciding.

"Lal," he said. "Would you do a thing for me?"

She sat looking at him, blue eyed, lashing her tail.

"Will it be bearable?" he asked himself. "When I'm despised?"

He thought of Kobar's father, who taught him, even though some reviled him for taking in a Forester boy.

Wil sighed.

He picked up the Starstone.

"Lal, will you take this and hide it where nobody can ever find it, and never tell anyone where you hid it?"

She looked at him, tail lashing.

"Hide it one day's walking from High City," he said.

He started to hand the Starstone to Lal, but then he thought again, frowning at it. With his fingers, he plucked off the Opal of Living and Dying from its indentation. That he placed once again in the pouch slung from his neck.

He handed the Starstone to Lal. She took it in her mouth. Without looking back at him, she walked off into the forest.

For a long time he sat alone. Then he stood and walked in the darkening evening toward High City. As he walked, he listened to the trees chant among themselves, about tomorrow's sun, and owls in their foliage, and about their roots deep underground, tasting water.

CHAPTER SEVENTEEN

"Council," Pim told him, barely suppressing his rage.

Wil thought: I've just returned, and here's my welcome.

"Where's Tobi?" he said.

"I'm calling a council in the square, right now," Pim said. "All those who trusted you, and hoped...."

"Tobi," Wil said.

Pim threw up a hand.

"At Zadni's," he said. "We expect you to explain...."

But even as the former Lord of the War spoke, Wil turned from him and strode along the wooden street past the square, then down a wooden side street, lined with wooden houses. At the third house he knocked.

Malaga Gant opened the door, and stared up at him, wide eyed.

"What's happened to you?" she asked.

"Where's Tobi?" he said.

She led him to a room with a cot, where Tobi lay on his side. Eyes shut, the dog breathed raggedly.

Zadni walked into the room.

"Wil...."

She stopped, and she, too, stared at him. Wil spoke first.

"What's been done for him?"

"Herbs, healing spells," Zadni said, and sighed. "He lives, but nothing more."

Wil rested his hand on the unconscious dog's head. Then, carefully, he touched Tobi's wounded side.

With his mind, he followed the wound into the body, studying what he saw. Then, grim faced, he seared away decayed

412

tissues. In their place, he started healthy flesh growing. He mended a torn lung. In the dog's blood, he saw infection. He fashioned in his mind an image, a tiny Lal, and sent her into Tobi's arteries and veins, to stalk the infecting vermin and kill them. He smiled, thinking Tobi would abhor a little Lal within him, if he knew. Then he grimaced, for he saw the sword's point had punctured Tobi's heart. Here he worked with particular care.

Malaga and Zadni saw only a man with his two hands upon the body of a dog near death. Of the two, only Zadni understood what he did.

At last he took away his hands and sighed.

"That's all I can do," he said.

"What have you become?" Zadni said.

He said nothing.

Malaga blurted out: "Your face...."

He regarded her blankly, and she hurried from the room. In a moment she returned, carrying a handheld mirror. She gave it to him, and he looked.

Gray now streaked his yellow hair. His eyes, in the mirror, looked like smoke. Down his face's left side ran a seared scar, colored blue.

He shrugged, handing the mirror back to Malaga.

"Council," he said, and Zadni looked at him, distraught.

Wil again put his hands upon Tobi. He held them there a time, then he turned and walked from the house. He knew Zadni and Malaga followed, but he didn't look back.

"...and we trusted you, and believed in you, and...."

Wil, standing upon the podium in the square, beside Pim, regarded without expression the woman who spoke. So many angry faces glared at him, and disappointed faces, and saddened faces. A thousand years they'd awaited the Taker and the Wielder, placing in them all their hopes. This should be their triumphant

413

moment, but on the dais in the adjoining Council Chamber, where the Starstone should lie, it never would.

"…and we want your explanation!"

Fury in Pim's eyes. Wil gazed at him, then at the crowd before him. Finally he spoke.

"What I thought best for Foresters, and the world—that's what I did," he said.

He saw they awaited more, but he said nothing.

"Don't you understand what you've done?"

Wil didn't respond, so the owlish little man spoke on, glaring at Wil, then at the throng, repeatedly pushing up his spectacles with his index finger.

"You've taken our sorcery! You've taken our kingship!"

Murmurs from the crowd, and nods.

Wil regarded them in silence.

"Even now we'd be assuming the rule…."

Pim stopped because Zadni Gruen stepped forward, holding up a hand.

"We held the Starstone before, and what did we do?" she said. "We seized minds, we altered people's deepest selves to suit us, thinking it was for the good, yes, but…."

A thousand years ago," Pim said.

Murmurs of approval from the crowd.

Zadni spoke over them: "We should be Wise Advisers, not kings, and we should mend wrongs, ease difficulties and…."

Pim waved a hand, dismissive.

"Yet, we should be sorcerers again, " Zadni said, looking at Wil, stricken. "To wield the Starstone for the realm's good…."

Wil regarded her, thinking how to answer.

He removed his jacket. All hushed now, watching. He slid down his shirt over his shoulder. Then he turned to the side, to exhibit the number branded there: D6-903.

In whispers, the number passed backward through the throng, to those too far back to see, and someone cried out: "His slave number!"

Wil rebuttoned his shirt. Now the Foresters regarded him in confusion.

"Nameless Ones of Darkness made the Starstone," he said. "They tainted it."

Pim glared at him, and the Lord of the War demanded: "What of it?"

Wil eye him calmly.

"That taint is enslavement," he said.

Then he turned his side to the crowd, to show his face's blue scar, the Starstone's stain, burned into him. Gasps, but none understood his gesture. Angry murmuring, and then a voice spoke out.

"The Taker took our heritage!"

Other voices now joined, a chant.

"Taker took! Taker took!"

Wil listened as more shouted the chant. Abruptly he raised his arms, turning his palms to the throng, hushing them, and into that quiet, from the sky, fell a wordless song.

Its somber tones expressed sadness and loneliness, a journey across a vast plain under lightning flashes. Fear howled. Anger snarled. With suffering, the music swelled. Then it muted and dulled, as if trudging onwards, hurt. It sweetened, finally, into rueful peace. With a hopeful tinkling of tiny bells, it faded away.

Wil had only that to say to his people.

Before him, the crowd stood still, uncomfortable.

"Oh, la di la!"

From a side street, Ranyan strode onto the square, her gown's white silk swirling. Upon her dark hair she wore a white-silk tiara. Behind her Poko scampered.

"Our princess has appointed herself Priestess of the Wielder," Zadni Druen told Wil.

Ranyan held up her hands imperiously, demanding silence. Wil thought: priestess, perhaps, but ever a princess.

"Our Wielder comes!" Ranyan announced, excitement in her voice. "She has returned."

Around the corner walked Mita. Silent now, the crowd watched her mount the podium. She stood between Pim and Wil, gazing at the Foresters, who regarded her in awed silence.

You're more than Mita, Wil thought. She looked at him, and in those hazel eyes he saw unimaginable distances. Then she turned to the crowd in the square.

"I've come back to live in High City," she said.

Wil knew only a small part of Mita returned.

"Nearby the Starstone lies, never to be found," Mita said. "That is well, for the Taker spoke truly—it bears a dark taint. Yet, its closeness will strengthen your magic, and over the years this people will again ascend to sorcery."

A murmur passed through the crowd. When the hush returned, Mita resumed speaking.

"Your wisdom must strengthen in step, or once more you will do harm," she said. "But you are a good-willed people, and you need only become whom you are."

Now she looked at Wil, and smiled. For a moment, he faced the old Mita, with startled eyes, who bumped tables, but then her gaze receded, far away.

"Your Taker has a gift for you," she said.

Then she turned and walked back toward her house. Ranyan followed, looking officious. Poko ran behind.

Wil guessed what the gift must be.

From his shirt he drew a pouch, which hung from his neck by a thong. Between thumb and index finger, he drew out a gem and held it up.

Pim stared at it, startled.

"It's the Opal of Living and Dying," he announced to the crowd. "Returned!"

Wil carried the Opal into the Council Chamber, followed by Pim and Zadni, with the rest of the Foresters of High City crowding behind, and he laid it upon the Starstone's dais, in the Starstone's stead.

"It's shaped me," Wil told Pim and Zadni. "And it'll help this people become who they really are."

Then he walked away from them. He walked down the street to the house where Mita once lived, and now lived again.

"How long will you remain among the Foresters?" Wil asked.

"As needed," she said.

They sat upon facing chairs in the house's parlor, teacups beside them, brought by Ranyan, who now sat nearby upon a hassock, watching them.

"You're in many places now," Wil said.

"Yes," Mita said.

He regarded her wistfully, because she looked as she did when he first saw her, serving ale in Blossom's tavern, but he knew it was only a twist of light. He sighed.

"Do I have a useful thing left to do?" he asked.

Looking in Mita's hazel eyes, he felt he looked past the moon, into vastness.

"We war by proxy," she said.

That Wil knew. A direct battle between Nameless Ones of Light and Nameless Ones of Darkness would destroy all that is.

"Our struggling shapes all that is," Mita said.

Those eyes regarded him.

"Everyone fights, for one side or the other, with each day's words and acts," she said. "But for the greater confrontations...."

She looked at him.

"I'm tainted," Wil said.

"What better way to dispel that taint?" Mita said.

"How long must I serve?" he asked.

"A lifetime," she said.

Now the winter had passed. Sunshine warmed the treetop city, shining through leaves still in their springtime green.

Wil stood at a street's end, leaning against the railing. He stared off into the branches, brow furrowed.

Beside him sat Tobi.

They'd just seen Malaga off to Imperia, with a delegation of Foresters, to resume her professorship. With her she took a trunk filled with scribbled notes, page after page of Forester observations and Forester lore. As a gift, Wil made the trunk slightly lighter than air, so that it floated along with her party, held by a leash.

As he looked off into the treetops, Wil thought: no more need, Malaga, to examine the world sidewise.

Pim led the delegation with which Malaga traveled. He'd be the Foresters' emissary to the Council of Councils, now governing the realm. That he still smoldered over the Starstone's loss made Wil grimace. He thought: isn't it enough that you'll advise the realm's councilors? And you'll dispatch Foresters to work magic—finding ores or underground water, repairing dams, making crops fecund. Isn't that enough? And you'll send Foresters to heal those dangerously sick. Not enough?

"Wil?"

At his feet, the dog looked up earnestly.

"Yes, Tobi?"

"Poko is annoying, isn't he?"

"I see how you might think that, Tobi."

Ranyan now marched throughout the city, Priestess of the Wielder, highhandedly issuing orders and directives. Poko ran at her heels, barking at High City's other dogs, whom he considered lowborn.

"Wil? He told me I needed a bath!"

"I see why that annoyed you," Wil said.

Most of High City's dogs ignored Poko. And mostly the Foresters ignored Ranyan, except when they judged she truly spoke the Wielder's wish, not just her own whim.

Wil faintly smiled.

Butterflies brightened the branches upon which High City rested. They fluttered around Wil as he leaned on the railing, colored copper and scarlet and violet and sulphur. Thrushes and orioles sang.

Wil sighed.

Tobi moved closer. He sat leaning his weight against Wil's leg. Both felt the springtime sun's warmth, and both looked off into the branches.

"I'm restless, Tobi."

"Will you go into the forest again?" the dog asked.

"Yes."

"Then I'll go with you."

At dawn the next morning, in their apartment, Wil placed upon the floor the knapsack in which Bear had carried the injured Tobi from the mountain to High City. Wil had made it from his own knapsack and Tobi's knapsack, magically weaving them together. Now, under his hands, the new knapsack divided back into the two from which it came, one for him, one for Tobi. Into each, he placed food for their journey's start. As they left the apartment, Tobi spoke.

"Where will we go, Wil?"

"I don't know, " he said.

Nobody saw them off. He'd told nobody they were leaving. No need to tell Mita, for she'd know, and she'd tell Zadni, still his friend. Mostly, the Foresters treated him civilly, but without warmth, resenting his decision to keep the Starstone from them, and many resented even the sorcery now in him, so far beyond their own magic.

He shrugged, thinking of it, as he and Tobi stood at the square's edge. He fastened Tobi's knapsack upon him. He pulled on the straps of his own, feeling its weight upon his back.

Without looking back, he turned both Tobi and himself into twists in the morning's light. They shimmered down through the branches, to the ground so far below. There they rematerialized as the scarred man and the short-legged dog, tailless, honey-colored and white.

They started off through the trees, but then Wil stopped, listening.

Out from the forest stepped a cat, black and white whiskered. Her blue eyes looked faintly malevolent.

"Where do you go?" she asked.

"That way," Wil said, pointing at random.

"Good hunting that way?" she asked.

"It may be," Wil said.

"I'll go along then, for a while, and taste it," she said.

And so the three walked into the forest, first the man, then the dog and cat. They walked northward, toward regions where no one from that realm had yet gone.

They went to see what they might see.

THE END

64571654R00258

Made in the USA
Lexington, KY
13 June 2017